JACKED

THE TRENT BROTHERS

TINA REBER

Hope I jack your heart! ♥

Tina Reber

Jacked
Copyright © 2014 Tina Reber

Cover design by Sarah Hansen, OKAY Creations

Edited by Marion Archer, Marion Making Manuscripts

Interior Design by Angela McLaurin, Fictional Formats

ISBN-13: 978-1505332001
ISBN-10: 1505332001

ALSO BY TINA REBER

The Love Series:
Love Unscripted
Love Unrehearsed

We all have skeletons in our closets.

Doctor Erin Novak was only sixteen when she was accused of a crime she didn't commit. Since that moment, she has made it her life goal to pursue emergency medicine, pouring her heart and soul into assuring another innocent life isn't lost to the hands of the wicked.

We all have secrets we've never shared.

Detective Adam Trent has lost control of everything, starting with losing his partner to a punk with a gun and then everything else to the crushing guilt. Now a member of the elite Auto Theft Task Force in Philadelphia, it's his job to be one step ahead of the criminals stealing expensive cars in the city. Too bad the television cameras keep getting in the way of his investigation.

We all have pasts that we can never escape.

A stolen car, a tragic chase, and a traffic stop crosses the fates of these two, tying them together in ways that are unimaginable. As their love and trust grows, so do the enemies that threaten their survival, testing the strength of their commitment. Can true love endure half-truths, past pains, and secrets never meant to be shared?

Some things are just out of our control.

JACKED

THE TRENT BROTHERS

This book is dedicated to all of the first responders around the globe who, despite how dire the situation, how hopeless the outlook, always make their presence known and give their all. Whether you are a professional or volunteer, you are our first line of defense, performing your duties without second thought or personal regard, serving and protecting others in their time of need. We are all forever in your debt.

A portion of the proceeds from the sale of this novel will be granted to the following:

The Sweeney Alliance, a non-profit, Texas-based organization, provides training programs and educational material relating to grief, post-traumatic stress, and suicide prevention for the emergency response community and their families in North America. We promote a mentally healthy work environment through cooperation with local, state, and national fire service and law enforcement agencies and organizations. We make available local grief support groups and electronic newsletters and bereavement resources globally for the public in general.

For more information, please check out their support blog website: http://grievingbehindthebadgeblog.net/

CHAPTER 1
Erin

MY HANDS TREMBLED under the hot water as I rinsed the blood off Cal's wedding band. A few hours ago his ring was pristine, unmarred by the ugliness of life. Now it was blemished with deep scratches scored into the gold, preserving their horrific moment for all eternity.

My colleague, Doctor Bayshore, had to surgically remove it as the lower portion of Cal's arm had been crushed beyond repair.

I watched the red swirl at the bottom of the stainless steel wash sink while trying not to envision what they had gone through—the terror, the crash, the agonizing pain—how in an instant lives are changed forever.

Anita, one of our ER respiratory therapists, gave my shoulder a quick squeeze as she hurried past. I took the gesture for what it was—a silent "hang in there" between friends that broke the ghastly images plaguing my mind.

I didn't know it was Cal at first when the Life Flight paramedics gave us their ETA. All I knew was that my trauma team was prepped and ready to receive the fifty-eight-year-old male coming in via helicopter at ten minutes to midnight from a multi-vehicle crash on the Schuylkill Expressway. University was the closest hospital with a Level One trauma center, so it was commonplace for us to receive the critical accident victims that resulted from the congested traffic conditions around Philadelphia.

I saw the packing where part of the patient's left arm had been unceremoniously amputated, overheard the Life Flight paramedic inform the nursing staff of the patient's name and vitals, looked up at his bloodied face under the oxygen mask, and froze.

Soon after that, my ex-boyfriend and fellow med school graduate, Doctor Randy Mason, locked his arms around me and physically carried me out of the trauma bay.

I think I yelled, but for some reason, I can't remember.

I'd tended to thousands of patients during my residency and had assisted in about every type of trauma one could imagine. I had seen things and dealt with things made from the depths of people's worst nightmares, but this was the first time I'd lost my hold.

I'd managed to pull myself together enough to call my parents, though keeping my voice steady and clear had been damn near impossible. I glanced up at the large clock on the wall again. I'd made that call forty-two minutes ago. Cal's golden hour of survival had been up well over an hour ago. I was praying he'd make it out of surgery though the odds were stacked against him.

Sherry peeked around the doorframe and pocketed her stethoscope. "You okay?"

I tossed my soiled gloves into the biohazard bin. "No."

"Oh honey, I'm so sorry."

I buried myself into her welcoming arms.

Sherry rubbed my back. "Reception just took your parents to the private waiting room."

I wiped my cheek. "Okay, thanks."

She gripped my upper arms. "I know this is tough but you're tougher. You know that, right?"

I nodded, though not fully convinced.

"Your mom isn't handling things well. She insisted on seeing them and then demanded to see you. She probably could use a sedative but I think they've got her calmed down for now. Do you want me to go with you? You don't need to do this on your own."

I took a deep breath, willing myself to find the courage and professional detachment to get through this. "Thanks, but I think I'll be okay."

"I'll walk with you." She grabbed a box of tissues from one of the supply drawers and then draped her arm over my shoulder. My chest tightened with every step.

Doctor Jen Wyatt trotted around the far corner, clad in her favorite dark blue scrubs and the new sneakers we'd just shopped for a few days ago. As soon as she saw us she started to run. She nearly sideswiped my ex, Randy, as he came past the nurses' station; both of them repelling away from each other like two magnetic opposites. He also noticed the dark look she shot him, giving her one in return.

Despite my current mental state of upheaval, her little reaction brought joy to my heart. So did her rushing to my side in the midst of a crisis.

"Oh my God, Erin," Jen said, ignoring my former lover as he followed her. She pulled me into a crushing hug. "I am so sorry. Are you okay?"

I closed my eyes and hugged her back, hoping that when I opened them again I wouldn't be staring at Randy's sexy new glasses through Jen's long, shimmery black ponytail.

I hadn't had a chance to tell her I'd noticed her new hair color, either. It went well with her complexion.

"Erin?"

Oh no.

I knew that voice well. I used to jump through hoops to hear him utter my name, but now it was like verbal daggers straight into the heart. I squeezed my eyes shut, willing him to go away. "Not now. I just can't," I groaned into Jen's shoulder.

"*Erin,*" Randy called again.

"Oh good grief," Jen said. She spun around to face him, holding her hand up in warning. "Now is not the time, *Doctor* Mason."

Randy ignored her and tugged my arm. "Are you all right?"

What a moronic question. I hadn't been "all right" for quite a while, mostly due to the trauma he had caused on my heart, but that was irrelevant at this point. I'd been managing. I pulled my elbow away. I didn't need him adding to my emotional defeat.

Jen glared at him. "Of course she isn't *all right.*"

He scowled back at her and pointed at me. "I'm not talking to you, okay? I'm talking to her. Erin. Hon…"

"Oh God." The words in my head slipped out of my mouth, constricting my ability to swallow in their wake.

Jen glanced at me, came to some conclusion, and then turned back on the man I thought I'd once loved in some delusional moment of my past.

"Now is *not* the time. So do us all a favor, save your words and leave

3

her be. We've got this."

His mouth dropped open to argue, his body poised to adamantly disagree. I didn't have any fight left in me.

Jen shushed him with her hand. "I said we've got this. Now go on."

I wanted to kiss her and her southern-bred sass for being so awesome.

"I'll check in with you later, Erin," he grumbled, taking a retreating step.

I couldn't keep from watching his sexy ass as he stormed off.

"He's a jerk," Jen said. "You do not need that man in your head clogging your brain anymore. Now you just forget about him and let's take care of you."

I was glad she was being my shield as I was in no position to defend myself or my failing willpower.

Sherry nodded. "I agree. I was taking her down to the family room. Her mom and dad are waiting." She pointed down the hallway.

"Okay." Jen put her hand on my shoulder, steering me. "We'll go with you."

We stopped a few feet from the waiting room door and Sherry handed the box of tissues to me. "Here, take them just in case. You ready to do this?"

NO, I was most definitely NOT ready to do this.

I nodded anyway.

Jen rubbed my arm. "You want one of us to go in there with you? I don't care about protocol."

Actually I didn't want *anyone* to have to go in there and see my parents cry. I wanted to reverse the wicked hands of time and eradicate this entire nightmare from my life. "Thanks, but…" I stared at the ominous door. "I'll be okay. I have to be, right?"

Jen hugged me again. "We'll be right here if you need us."

I took a deep breath and forced myself to open the door.

My mother startled when she saw me. Her eyes were red and puffy and she was sniffling into a wad of tissues. My dad looked tired and disheveled, as if new worry lines had crinkled his forehead and weary bags had formed underneath his eyes. I could tell he'd dressed quickly; his shirt, which was always tucked neatly into his pants in a staunch, business-like fashion, was wrinkled and hanging out.

I should have waited for Doctor Sechler to update them but this was *my* family, not some random group of strangers. I sat down next to my mom, taking her chilled, trembling hands in mine, trying to will her to stop begging Jesus to give her another answer with my steady gaze.

"Mom, listen. Uncle Cal is alive, but… He's in… He's in critical condition." The urge to cry was imminent, but I had to be strong. I couldn't leave the delivery of this information to anyone else.

My mother sniffed. "How…? How bad is he?"

I held my breath for a moment and collected my words—words that were failing me because I knew no matter how I said them they would have devastating effects.

"The truth, Erin," she bit out.

"His left arm was completely severed near his… his elbow, Mom. There was nothing we could do."

The way her eyebrows crinkled, I knew she was confused that such trauma could come from an automobile accident. I tried not to speak in complicated medical terms.

"What does that mean?"

I squeezed her hand in mine. "If he pulls through this, he'll need to wear a prosthetic arm. There was no way… They can't reattach it."

She sucked in a gasp.

Losing part of a limb wasn't the worst of his injuries. "What concerns us the most right now is his head injury. He was unconscious when he came in."

She wiped her nose while her tears made rivulets down her cheeks. "Oh my God. Is he? Is he going to make it?"

I was proud of her for trying to be brave. *Should I lie? Fill her with false hope? Does she even need to know that he went into cardiac arrest during air transport?*

"I don't know, Mom." In his current condition, it was a miracle he still had a pulse. I gave her the standard benign answer that we all recited from rote. "We'll know more as we assess the test results."

She nodded while her pale lips trembled.

"He has the best team looking out for him right now, Mom. Our chief orthopedic surgeon, Doctor Sechler, is working on him. He and Doctor Giffords are experts in their fields." I squeezed her hand. "Just pray for him, okay?"

My mother's gaze grew distant. I knew she was in shock. "Can I see him?"

"Not right now. He's in surgery." I adjusted my hospital pager as a way to divert my telling eyes. "I'll go get another status update in a little bit."

"Okay. And Karen? How is she?"

I took her momentary distraction discarding tissues to peg my father with a knowing stare, our silent communication that we'd perfected over the years when we wanted to keep her from overreacting. When his shoulders slumped and the sob erupted, I knew he understood.

Anguish tore through me with renewed force. I'd seen my father go through the gamut of emotions over the thirty years of my life but this was one of the few times I witnessed him shed tears.

The last time he'd cried openly was when the police had led me away in handcuffs when I was sixteen.

My eyes blurred and I wanted to leap into my dad's arms to hug his pain away, but like that day, I felt shackled. Helpless. My Uncle Cal and Aunt Karen were their best friends. Cal was my mother's twin and her *only* brother. The four of them did everything together—vacations, weekly dinners, shows, you name it. I knew this was killing them. It had to be as it was killing me.

I held back my sob while the spot above my breastplate started to burn, ripping fire up into my throat. "She, ah…"

My mom's focus narrowed, questioning me.

"Their car flipped and rolled, Mom. She's gone."

"No. No. They were on their way home from Nate's. We were there for Noah's third birthday party. No. What do you mean, *she's gone*? What are you saying? Oh, no. Please, no."

Nothing. I was saying nothing. The flight nurse had informed me that my aunt had been partially ejected and then crushed under the vehicle. All I could manage was an unspoken no. As soon as my mom comprehended, her body started to convulse. Thankfully my father pulled her into his chest when she succumbed to the realization. Seeing my mother go through this level of anguish was my undoing.

I covered my mouth, trying to hold back my sputtering, but it was no use; my professional façade lay in a heap in my lap.

My cousin Chris came rushing into the private waiting room, stopping abruptly when he found us.

"What happened to my parents?" Chris frantically demanded, looking directly at me for answers. "Where are they?"

His brother, Nate, was a few steps behind and white as the snowflakes dusting the shoulders of his heavy winter coat. His wife, Andrea, was clutching his hand, looking just as sickly and scared. "What the hell is going on?" Nate asked.

The Chaplain came in behind them, gently urging them farther into the waiting room with sympathetic smiles and soft-toned instructions.

After the Chaplain and I told them what they needed to know, I placed their father's simple gold wedding ring into Nate's hand.

"DAD, TAKE MOM home. It's late. There's nothing more you can do here. He'll be in surgery for a few hours." I held my dad's arm, encouraging him along. "Go and get some rest, okay? I'll call the second I have an update."

He nodded stiffly, unable to fully converse with me.

I held his vacant stare, hoping he'd listen. "He's not in good shape, Dad. You understand what I'm saying?"

He ran a hand back through his peppered hair. His voice hitched when he softly muttered, "Yeah."

"Are you going to be able to drive home? I could drive you."

My father shook his head. "No, no, I'll be all right, sweetheart."

I glanced over at my mother. She was holding Chris, consoling him. They both still had hope Uncle Cal would pull through, sharing their thoughts of his rehabilitation already. I, however, knew better. Part of me felt obligated to stay at work so a family member would be present when the Chaplain administered last rites. I'd seen too many traumas to know the difference, and my uncle was dangling on a very fine precipice.

Nate started crying again, breaking my thoughts. I could tell he was trying to hold it in, but it was too much. Seeing such a formidable young man brought down to his knees was unbearable to watch.

Tears of my own were stinging my eyes again. I wiped my cheeks. "Okay, then I'm going to go home. I've been here for almost fifteen hours now, Dad. I need to get some sleep."

My mother sobbed again, tearing another hole into my heart.

My father frowned at first and then shook off a bit of his stupor, gently rubbing my upper arm. "Okay, sweetheart. Let me gather your mother."

We walked outside to the open parking lot. Dad brushed his hand over my back. "Erin, are *you* going to be all right to drive?"

I pulled my purse up onto my shoulder; the frigid February winter wind sent an icy chill though my body. "Yeah, Dad. I'm okay." I hit the button on the key fob. My car lights flashed, illuminating the darkness as my doors unlocked.

I'd never been one to believe in ghosts but the tall, dark figure that seemed to pop out of shadows from nowhere, slinking and ducking in between the cars in the lot, spooked me a little. I squinted, trying to make out some discernible features on the darting figure, noting it was definitely the shape of a man. After a few steps, the stranger stopped walking. All I could see was his darkened silhouette. Shortly thereafter, he became dimly lit by the glow of a cell phone. I hated that uneasy feeling that swept over me, making me question my safety in the city.

Dad pulled my coat hood up as if I were still a child, tucking my long hair in away from my face. "Okay. Call us if you need anything. Please be careful going home."

I wrapped my arms around his waist and hugged him tightly, realizing how often I take his constant presence and affection for granted. My cousins had their entire world destroyed tonight. Had fate tipped her hand my way, this tragedy could have very well been mine to bear.

My dad kissed my forehead softly, making me hug him even harder. He'd been kissing me and my sister, Kate, that way ever since I could remember and it was just what I needed right now.

Dad released me and I hugged and kissed my mom, wishing with every fiber of my soul that I could have given her different news. There were no tears, no prayers, no medical skills that could bring Aunt Karen back. I wiped another tear from her soft cheek, willing her with the little bit of strength I had left. "Have faith, Mom. He's in good hands."

She nodded. "I know, sweetheart. Call us when you get home so I know you're okay."

I fought the desire to roll my eyes. Any other time I would have internally balked at the idea of calling them to "check in" but now was not the time to be indifferent or discourteous.

I climbed into my frigid car and started it, selecting the button for the seat warmer. I needed a hot shower, a warm bed, and some much needed sleep.

Well, that was my plan. After a twelve-hour shift, three additional hours looking over Uncle Cal's X-Rays and CT scans, consulting with his surgical team, and staving off the crushing feelings of utter devastation, I wished for nothing more than to pass out from exhaustion.

I pulled the strings on my coat hood and cranked the heat up. My dashboard showed it was a brisk twenty-eight degrees outside.

The clock on the square navigation panel indicated it was now 5:12 a.m., but I knew it was an hour fast. At least the traffic in the city at this time was light; I'd be home before the Philly commuter traffic started. Maybe I'd distract my fraught mind with learning how to program the onboard system. Eight years of college, a year of internship rotations, three years of residency in the ER, and I still for the life of me couldn't figure out how to change the clock display. Feeling inept in my brand new shiny car was unnerving.

The bright lights blinding me in my rearview mirror were also quite unnerving. The large black SUV behind me with the foreboding steel plate attached to the front of it had been on my tail for the last six blocks and two turns.

Being followed was making me nervous and edgy.

Just to test the theory and for some peace of mind, I turned one block sooner, knowing that any of the next few lefts would get me home.

As soon as I turned the wheel, my heart rate spiked and extreme fright pricked my nerves. The SUV continued to follow me. This was not the best part of Philadelphia to be driving around in, especially in the wee hours of the morning. All sorts of worst-case scenarios rushed through my mind.

Well, not tonight. I'd already endured enough; I was not going to become a victim on top of it.

I stepped on the gas pedal, trying to make it through the next traffic light before it turned, dangerously catching the tail end of the yellow light as it changed to red above me.

I checked my mirrors; the SUV paused at the intersection then accelerated and ran the red light. Before I could form a rational thought to explain it, red and blue lights flashed behind me.

Oh shit. Shit, shit, shit. Not now.

That pressure you feel when you've done something wrong and been caught hit my chest, shocked my nerves, and surged up into my throat. I let off the gas and looked for somewhere to pull over; after all I should have known better than to run a red light in the city. My attention veered from the demanding flashing lights; there were no open spaces to pull over to the curb.

I gasped as another truck and then another very large SUV with red and blue lights blazing headed straight toward me.

I slammed on the brakes, fully bracing for an impact that fortunately didn't happen. Two more trucks came to a screeching halt along side of me.

What the…?

Holy shit. I was completely boxed in.

"Oh my God. Oh my God," I started to babble as visions of being kidnapped came to mind.

My normally *cool under pressure* heart was working at a frantic pace, overwhelming me with the urge to run.

Bright strobe lights surrounded me, flashing violently and blinding me from all angles. I felt the need to shield my eyes as red and blue police lights bounced off the reflective, wet streets.

No, this isn't happening. This isn't happening.

I froze when I saw guns pointed at me from numerous open truck windows.

"Let me see your hands! Hands! Keep them up!" a man yelled.

My body jerked with fright, overriding my brain's order to do as it was told.

"Hands up on the roof! On the roof! Do it! Do it now!"

A gun was pointed right at my head on the other side of my driver's window. "Get out of the car, nice and slow," a deep voice ordered. "Keep your hands where I can see them."

I was shaking so hard I could barely move let alone follow orders. Bright lights blinded me at every angle. Men were shouting all around me. Several pistols were aimed at me when my car door opened.

A very strong hand grabbed my wrist and hauled me out of my seat. He twisted it behind my back, instantly immobilizing my arm, and pressed me face first into the trunk of my brand new car.

Vivid canary yellow lettering, announcing POLICE and AUTO THEFT TASK FORCE, stood stark against the all-black outfits that surrounded me.

"Ow," I cried out, feeling my tired muscles strain as both of my arms were pulled behind my back. Cold metal handcuffs cinched around my wrists. *Oh God! Not again!* "Stop! Wait! I didn't do anything! Why are you doing this?"

Someone very strong leaned into me; his thigh kept my leg pinned, although I could tell that whoever was cuffing me was reserving his strength.

As if I could ever be a threat to any of them. If I weren't on the verge of tears and a full-blown panic attack, I would have laughed.

"Calm down, miss," an enormously large, dark figure standing to my left said, trying to cajole me. I looked over and then way up into the face of one massive and very intimidating black police officer. "Romeo Seven to control," he said into his radio. "We're ten-fifteen. One in custody."

Custody? What the hell?

Absolute terror clenched my chest, causing me to hyperventilate. My heart was pounding erratically. Everything around me was hazy, blurry, as if I was adrift in some nightmare and unable to wake.

"It was… yel… yellow," I sputtered, my cheek stinging from making contact with the frosted metal. I didn't realize that running a red light was such an offense, nor was it cause for so many cops to converge. Whatever this was, it was far from a typical traffic stop. I was in deep shit.

Cops were shining flashlights into my car, opening doors, inspecting everything. Once I was cuffed, the officer pinning me stood me up, turned me, and tugged my hood off my head.

His strong jaw, shaded by a low growth of stubble, was clenched, and dark eyes were glaring with angered intensity. Short, blunt-cut brown hair rimmed the edge of his black ball cap, turned backwards on his head to show the word "POLICE" in small yellow letters.

Another bright light was shone right on me. I squinted and winced, noting the source of the blinding light was connected to a camera hefted on top of someone's shoulder. Another guy, a few inches shorter, was standing next to the cameraman. He was wearing headphones and a ball cap with the word *Pantera* written on it, staring at some sort of hand-held monitor that reflected colored images back onto his glasses.

Oh please, God, NO! Philly news was here to record the demise of my career.

Just as I was about to question why one, two, three separate cameras were filming me, the officer addressed me again.

"Eyes on me, Miss," he growled.

My head snapped up at his direct order.

"What's your name?" he asked with that foreboding cop authority.

"Erin. Erin Novak," I breathed, fighting the urge to pass out.

"All right, Erin Novak, you want to tell me why you ran that red light back there and why I was doing almost sixty to keep up with you?"

I glanced down the street at the red light in question, my mind drawing a complete blank. "I thought… it was mostly yellow. I don't know. Every time I turned, you turned. I was… I was scared being followed like that. It's late and I just…" I took a deep breath, trying to calm myself. "I just wanted to get home without getting kidnapped or killed."

His eyebrows rose, causing me to focus in on his alluring brown eyes. "You knew we were following you?"

Why the humor in his tone? "Yes. Well, no. I suspected."

The large black officer snickered. "So much for undetected."

Apparently I was missing some part of the joke.

"We tagged you right after you peeled onto Broad Street," my incarcerator said somewhat proudly.

Well, good for you. Tagged me for what, I had no idea.

He looked at my silver car. "Ford Taurus SHO. Nice choice. Expensive ride."

I may have a mound of med school debt, but expensive cars were reasonably priced when your father owned two Ford dealerships.

His eyes rolled up and down my body, from my puffy ski jacket down to my sneakers and back again. *Oh God.* That's when I realized I was still wearing my scrub pants. His flashlight stayed lit on my pants leg and then illuminated a spot on the top of my sneaker.

"You want to explain to me why you've got blood on your pants?"

I looked down to see what he was referring to, already chastising myself for not changing before I fled the hospital. Damn it, I didn't know it was my uncle until we started working on him. There was a lot of blood.

"I'm a doctor. I, ah, I work in the trauma unit at University Hospital. I swear. I just left work." I didn't know why I was pleading with him but I was freezing and my knees felt like they were going to give out. "My ID—"

"Wait, you're a *doctor?*" he asked.

Flashes, like torn pictures from a nightmare, barraged my every thought. Accusations and handcuffs, a hand pushing down on my head, a steel cage separating the front seat from the back.

"I'm... a doctor." My vision fragmented, as though everything was reflected on broken shards of glass. *So bright.*

"Whoa, easy," he said, gripping my waist and arm.

I fell into his chest, feeling strength I knew I didn't have on my own at the moment. He moved me closer to the front fender. "Here, lean back. Easy. That's it."

The world started to spin in new directions as the paranoia rolled throughout my body. I knew I was in deep trouble all over again. "Please," I whispered out, fighting the lightheadedness muddling my thoughts. I wished this nightmare could all just be over.

Part of me started to wonder if someone at the hospital, namely my ex's new bitchy girlfriend, Mandy Haston, framed me by putting a dead body in the trunk of my car. It would be difficult, but not impossible.

Black combat boots and very long, muscular thighs clad in black cargo pants broke my view. A black leather-gloved hand brushed under my chin as he tipped my face up.

"Look at me," he ordered, softening his touch.

It was difficult to do as he instructed being in this state of extreme mortification. I wanted to focus on the police badge hanging from around his neck instead of making eye contact with a handsome face and gorgeous brown eyes that were assessing me as if I were a common criminal. And was that a tiny microphone attached to his coat?

"Please," I said again, remembering what I was asking for. Thoughts of the hospital administration having a valid excuse to squash my employment, and therefore killing my fellowship, made me shake. "Make them turn the cameras off. I can't... My career... I've worked *so* hard. Please. Please. I'm begging you. Don't destroy it."

"Easy, all right? Don't worry about them. You have any drugs or weapons on you?"

"What?" I was stressed and confused, still his question was insulting.

I felt his hands slide over my hips, my thighs, down to my ankles, even at the back of my pants and over my ass. What could have been sensual felt like a huge violation.

"No," I said as his hands sought confirmation. "I'm not some lowlife criminal."

He quickly patted the sides of my coat, unzipping it far enough to peek inside with his flashlight. I was grateful that he zipped me back up. My teeth were chattering.

"How about in the car?"

I shook my head. "No."

"Tell me how you got blood on ya," he asked again, kinder this time. I wanted to scream at him that it was my Uncle's, but what good would that do?

"I, um… I had seven trauma patients tonight. Last one was from a three-car accident on the Schuylkill."

He instantly scowled at me as his grip on my coat tightened. "The rollover?"

I nodded, trying like hell not to cry or throw up from the stress. "We received the Life Flight."

That seemed to agitate him further. He cursed under his breath a few times, eying the ginormous black officer at his side with some unspoken message, rocking me on my unstable feet in the process.

"Jesus Christ," the huge black officer growled low, doing his own bristle of disbelief.

I turned my attention to the red splotches of dried blood on my sneaker, willing them to disappear. Along with running a red light and being handcuffed, I walked out of work with blood traces on me. "I didn't see… I had booties on. I—I didn't change my scrubs before I left."

Another police officer—this one older, very tall and solid with a slightly grayed moustache—stepped next to me. "Miss, try to calm down. We're going to tell you what's going on. We received a nine-one-one call that this car was stolen at gunpoint and you have a fictitious plate on the back."

The severe dizziness worsened by me shaking my head so adamantly. Vertigo was full-on.

"Fic? What? No. Can't be. I bought it last month on my birthday. January seventh. It's mine."

Those dark eyes squinted at me. "Then explain why your plate is coming back as a stolen Toyota Corolla."

Damn, you're arrogant. "I have no idea. But that's my car," I bit out, incensed by his contradiction.

"Got any proof of that?"

I motioned with my chin. "The paperwork is all in the glove

compartment. I never moved it. If you let me go I can show you."

He put his hand on my shoulder. "Hang tight. You have any identification?"

"My license is in my purse."

"Then you give us permission to search your vehicle?"

I was handcuffed and he was intimidating; my options were limited. I gave him a quick nod.

I watched another cop retrieve my purse and place it on the front hood right next to me while two others searched through my car. Officer Hottie's eyes narrowed as he opened the zipper and held a flashlight to it. "It in here?"

I wanted him to get out of my purse before he found my tampon stash and those feminine wipe sample things I'd gotten in the mail. "Yes. It's in the black leather wallet."

He searched the entire contents while some emotion I read as disappointment flashed over his face. "Why is someone like you tangled up in this?" he muttered to himself, fumbling to open my wallet. His eyes narrowed on my license.

I felt as though my world was collapsing. Regardless of my innocence, I was definitely going to prison tonight, just like last time. Guilty before being proven innocent. The images that erupted from that horrid moment fourteen years ago made me tremble all over again as new fear and utter desperation clutched at my chest. "I'm not. Please. Please, believe me, sir. Please, sir."

His gaze whipped back to mine, as if I'd just insulted him. His body stiffened and his jaw clenched and flexed, though his dark eyes and heated stare said something altogether different.

"Trent, we found a Bill of Sale in the glove box," another officer announced, waving the papers in his hand.

Ah, so his name is Trent, my mind repeated while he glared at me.

The forty-something cop with the goatee strolled over with my sales documents in hand. "Seems just license plate is different."

Officer Trent stopped burning holes through me when they compared the information against my registration card.

"Did you put a different plate on your car?" Officer Trent asked me while scrutinizing my driver's license.

This night kept on getting progressively worse. "Why would I do that?"

He frowned and then illuminated my windshield with his flashlight. "Patrick, check the VIN."

The officer with the goatee and dark hair called out each letter and number from the little plate mounted on the dash.

"All right, it matches this," Trent said, holding up my paperwork. "Mrs. Novak—" he started.

"Miss," I corrected.

A wisp of a smile flashed on his face and then quickly morphed into focused intent. "Where was your car parked earlier?"

"In the lot… The lot off of Eighteenth across from the hospital. It's where I park every night."

"How long was it there?"

I had to recalculate. "Fif… almost sixteen hours."

"*Sixteen?*" He drew in a hard breath through his nose and wrote it down. "Okay, let's clear up the blood issue, just so I'm sure."

I nodded, noting he was wearing a bulletproof vest under his black coat. It was a revolting thought to imagine people shooting at him. "My, um, hospital ID…" I glanced at the long zipper of my coat, wondering how to open it while wearing handcuffs. There was no way I was going to reach it unless I used my teeth to lower the zipper. *Maybe I could push it down with my chin?* The steel handcuffs bit into my wrists, reminding me that I was still in big trouble.

The tips of his black boots came into view. "Can I help you with something?"

His gruff tone had completely changed; his words brushed me with something resembling compassion. *Oh officer, you get me out of this mess and I'd be forever grateful.* More of my hair came undone from my hair tie, covering my eye. *Could this night suck any worse? My luck, there's going to be a dead body in my trunk, I just know it.*

"Hey, eyes on me," Officer Trent ordered softly. His thumb swept under my bangs, giving me an unobstructed view of his slight smile. For a moment, I thought he actually cared.

"There are those gorgeous blue eyes," he whispered and then froze, as if the words in his private thoughts weren't meant to slip out from his appealing mouth.

Regardless of his attempt to cover up his gaffe, I still heard him, astonished that he said something like that.

Another camera operator crouched down with his rig on his shoulder near us, apparently getting another angle of my horrific experience. I tried to hide my face by tucking my chin into my jacket, but cameras surrounded me on both sides.

"My hospital identification is inside my coat. Can you please… can you please tell them to stop filming me?"

I saw him stiffen again, and then, as if something else were driving him, he reached out for my zipper.

"Where? In here?"

I nodded, wishing he'd remove the cold metal cuffs instead of undressing me. Something told me he preferred me restrained for the moment. "Officer, please," I whispered my plea, trying to block the cameraman from getting me on film.

"May I?" His hands hesitated near my chin.

I acquiesced, though he didn't ask for permission the first time he opened my coat.

His eyes locked on mine as he painstakingly lowered the zipper, almost as if he were savoring the act while two other cops looked on.

My laminated identification card dangled from where I had it clipped to my scrub top. I realized at that moment in my haste to go home, I'd pretty much clipped it over top of my right breast.

"You look too young to be a doctor." With just the faintest touch of his leather-gloved fingertip, he angled my ID, shining his flashlight once more. "How long you been over at University?"

"Four years. Just finished my residency. So much for that. It's all ruined now." Thoughts of all of my sacrifices, the lack of a social life, working myself ragged while putting in sixty plus hours a week, the fact that I hadn't been touched properly by a man in a very long time or had a meaningful relationship since, spending all of my time focusing on my goal instead—of all of that being for fucking *nothing*—to be wiped away by twenty minutes of false accusations and local news cameras, made me want to scream. The weight of my traumatic evening came crashing down in full force. Visions of my aunt's mutilated corpse, my uncle's severed arm, my family in utter distress; I couldn't stop the tears that welled in my eyes.

He reached up, wiping one away with his thumb. "Hey. Hey. No crying," he whispered as if he were trying to console a child.

I turned my face away from his touch. "Thanks to you and your false arrest, my career is *over*. Once whatever channel broadcasts this I'll have my medical license revoked. You might as well keep the fucking car too since I won't be able to make the payments." I glared at him. "Pray you never get shot, Officer, because there's one less doctor who can save you now."

I heard him growl, but *whatever*. I was beyond caring about his opinions.

"Ritchie," Trent ordered, barking his words over his shoulder but never taking his dark eyes off of me. "Kill it."

Apparently Ritchie or whoever was filming me didn't take direct orders. The camera's light continued to shine right on us.

Officer Trent stormed right up to the camera and reached out as if he were going to grab it. I could see the anger wafting off him. "Jesus Christ, Ritchie, this is done here. I said kill the fucking feed—*now*." He pointed a finger at the other guy. "Scott, call your boss. Tell him this footage never sees the light of day or I will hunt him down. You got me?"

The guy named Scott took a few steps back and I was relieved to see both camera operators shut their equipment down. Considering how intimidating Officer Trent was, I'd say it was a good call to listen.

The entire scene was perplexing. *Why the hell do the police have cameras filming them now?* My mind veered to recall the first officer I'd lost to a gunshot wound. It happened during my residency. Maybe this was another safety precaution?

Trent took his ball cap off and ran his hand over his head. His dark hair was cut short on the sides and spiky on top with that *just fucked* finger-combed hairstyle. I imagined he crawled out of bed every morning looking just as gorgeous.

The hulking black officer strolled over, towering over me by at least an extra foot and a half in height, making his presence even more frightening as he eyed me one last time. "No priors. She's clean."

Trent nodded. "Cap, she needs to be released. The false plate has been removed but her paperwork matches the VIN and her ID."

"Yeah, we've got nothing here," the older man they called "Cap" agreed.

My lungs expelled the breath they were holding. Another cop nudged me to turn around, finally giving my arms relief. I heard the metal cuffs clank together when they were off.

"Mine," Trent said curtly, holding out his hand for them, still glaring down at me.

I rubbed my aching wrists, feeling a phantom twinge of the cold metal as if they were still binding me. He clipped the cuffs back to some loop on his utility belt. Screw him; I glared back.

Damn, the whole package was sexy as hell with those full lips surrounded by a full shadow of stubble and that manly presence, but I'd had enough. As soon as they let me leave, admiring anything about Officer Trent would be done and over with.

I noticed that the cameras never left him. They'd been pointed wherever he was, capturing him at every angle, despite what the other dozen or so officers milling about were doing. *Odd.*

Officer Trent stepped in front of me again, getting even closer than before. "You see anyone around your car tonight or notice anything out of the ordinary?"

It was hard to think straight with the mounting stress and activity going on. "I was... I was inside the hospital all night. Wait, I did see someone... in the parking lot. I don't know. It could have been anyone. It was too dark and he was too far away for me to get a good look at him."

His eyes narrowed, almost scolding me. "Were you alone?"

I didn't care for his assumption. "No. I wasn't."

"Good. You recall if he was white? Black? Hispanic?"

"Didn't get that good of a look. He was definitely male."

He nodded. "Sounds like you probably got there right before he attempted to steal your car. Surprised he swapped the plate." That realization seemed to confound him further. He flashed his light toward the rear of my car and then down the driver side door and up the seals around the door windows. "Not a seasoned pro, taking that much time." He leaned past me, shining his flashlight on the dash. "This has a pushbutton start. Huh. Why the false call to dispatch?"

I followed the path of the flashlight as he scanned the inside of my car again, trying not to allow my imagination to roam too far from his extreme closeness or his alluring scent. "What do you mean?"

"You have a theft tracking system in this car?"

I wished I knew what that meant exactly. *Did I?* I recalled hearing words like "anti-theft" during the sales pitch I got from Dan at my dad's dealership, but did it have a tracking *system*? I had no idea. Having a decent paying job meant that I could finally afford a new car lease and not drive around in the trade-in clunkers my dad affectionately referred to as "life lessons." Being stumped by the dash clock was as far as I'd gotten.

Car headlights swept around the end of the street, flashing a bright beam of light across Officer Trent's back.

The SUV locked its brakes, screeched to a halt, and then gunned it in reverse. The explosion happened an instant after that. I ducked down and cringed from the earsplitting noise, catching only the blur of a large delivery truck before it plowed into another car, and then another.

"What the fuck?" one of the cops shouted.

Oh God!

Metal flew through the air and littered the intersection, creating more sounds I'd never want to hear again, followed by the constant blare of one of the vehicle's horns.

CHAPTER 2

Adam

I DIDN'T REALIZE what she was doing at first when she took off running down the street without me. I ran after her, my legs pumping on pure instinct and unfettered adrenaline.

I needed to stop her before she got too close to any of the vehicles, shield her from impending danger and what was surely going to be an unsightly scene with fatalities. She didn't need to see that level of brutality trapped within the confines of crushed metal. *No one* did.

She pulled out of my grip when I caught up to her.

"Let go," she shouted at me, no longer a shackled, trembling mess. No, now she was all business, demanding that I follow her through the mangled debris and broken glass scattered all over the road.

The pungent scents of battery acid and radiator fluid wafted through the air, assaulting my nose, as we wove through the wreckage. The familiar smells of spilled gasoline and diesel fuel twisted my gut into a sickening knot.

I pushed through it, making a conscious effort not to let it drag me down. I already had too many years of horrendous memories plaguing my mind, and now this? More unnecessary death wrapped up in crushed metal to add to the pile, creating an endless loop of fucked-up shit rattling around in my already fucked-up skull.

I'd been down this dead-end road before. It was why I jumped at the chance to join the ATTF when it came up, to get off regular patrol and being first on the scene.

Most people didn't understand this special hell. They had no clue what emergency responders went through on a daily basis, seeing the unthinkable ways people were injured or the gruesome ways people died.

No, most people went to work every day in their happy, oblivious little bubbles, never knowing what horrors transpire thousands of times a day, how unavoidable and merciless death can be, or the crushing stress placed on those whose job it is to clean up the mess.

The pressure started to build in my chest. I swore I could still smell the burning flesh of that seventeen-year-old girl we'd lost four years ago.

I used to be invincible.

Not anymore.

I'd already seen my fair share of death for one lifetime.

I needed Erin to stop before it was too late.

My throat felt tight again and damn near choked me seeing her long blonde hair floating in her wake.

She didn't need to see this.

No, this was my cross to bear, not hers. I may never get free of the nightmares but I didn't want her memories to become as tainted and bloody as mine were.

Anything she would see now crushed in the mangled wreckage could never be unseen. Even the smell from pumping her own gas might trigger the shakes.

I shouted her name but she ignored me. The anger that manifested from her blatant disregard came on like a tidal wave of heat through my veins.

I grabbed her arm and yanked. "Stop! I need to get you out of here before you get hurt."

Her eyes narrowed on my hand then flashed back to stare me down. "I'm a trauma doctor. I can help. We need to help them."

Somewhere in the carnage, a man's anguished wails and moans cut through the air, pulling her farther away from me, further out of my control. "This is not your turf. You follow my lead out here."

She nodded and grabbed my arm as we rounded the first car.

"My name is Doctor Erin Novak," she said to the man behind the wheel of the small four-door sedan. It used to be a green Mazda.

I yanked on the dented passenger door repeatedly until I finally pried it open and climbed onto the empty passenger seat. A leather briefcase was smashed apart on the floor. Back seat was empty. The interior smelled like fresh coffee and the coppery stench of blood.

"I need you to stay calm, all right?" she said. "What's your name?"

I looked around, trying to find some shred of fabric to use as a temporary bandage for the gash on his forehead.

"Officer, you have latex gloves?" she asked, in between getting the victim's current condition and trying to keep him from struggling and fighting her.

"Easy, buddy," I said to him, trying to keep him from attempting to get out of the car. He was not being cooperative and listening to her instructions. I pulled the only pair of gloves I had on me out of the large pocket on my cargos and handed them to her, keeping him steady with my free hand.

The fact she was an ER doctor wasn't lost on me watching her stay calm and collected while she worked. After doing a quick assessment and instructing several of my team how to attend to this one, she ordered me to follow her, snagging the sleeve of my coat and dragging me along with her like a damned puppy.

We hurried over to what was left of the maroon SUV, finding a young male lying in the road near the opened driver-side door. He was pretty torn up and his foot was pointing in the wrong direction.

Instead of freaking out, she was like a fucking machine, dropping down onto her knees on the icy wet street, ignoring the cameras that followed us.

Fellow ATTF Officer Glenn Martucci trotted up behind us, pushed Ritchie and his camera out of the way, and froze. He pulled an extra pair of latex gloves from his pants pocket, handed them to her, mumbled something about God and vomit, and then quickly backed away. I heard the distinct sound of Ritchie gagging, too. It didn't take long for us to lose the light of his camera.

I watched her tear off her soiled gloves and pull the new ones on over her delicate hands, trussing back up as if she were in the O.R. Somewhere along the way her white ski jacket had gotten big red smears of blood all over it and now part of me was wondering if she was hurt, too. That dry burn started again in my throat, aching for oblivion.

"Officer Trent," she called out again, pulling my attention back to her determined face.

Man, she was pretty: creamy flawless skin with the pink blush of a natural beauty. An angel sent to heal my broken soul.

Heal all of us.

Her cheeks… God, I just wanted to touch them, see if they felt as soft as they looked.

How does she do it?

How does she stay so beautiful amidst this ugliness?

I wanted to know her secrets, soak in her magic.

Surely she had some mystical armor keeping her insulated from the fucked-up carnage.

Everything seemed to blur until I refocused on the vic laying in the street. Young guy, white, late teens or early twenties at most, was in bad, bad shape. I had to pull my shit together.

Adrenaline surged, forcing my years of training to the surface. Still, I was so damn glad she was here. First aid… hell. He was so cut up and gasping; I wouldn't even know where to start with this one. "Tell me what you need me to do."

"You," she yelled up at Ritchie, "shine that light here. Quit shaking." After a quick assessment and telling the patient who she was and that we were here to help, she moved my hands for me, placing them on the guy's thigh. She told me where to apply pressure and why, but this whole scene made me numb. Blood was just everywhere, spilling out of this poor SOB like a punctured waterbed, scorching my mind with more heinous visions that I'd never be able to forget.

"Officer," she said, leveling her eyes on mine. "It's just you and me. I need you to stay calm and listen, and trust me."

I liked her much better when she was wearing my handcuffs, helplessly glancing up at me with those sexy blue eyes. If she only had a clue as to the other shit that she stirred in me when I had her restrained, she'd probably snag my Glock and put a bullet in me right here, right now.

Those blue eyes flashed to me again as she was feeling for the kid's pulse, dragging me back to the unsightly trauma. "No, no, no, shit. He's stopped breathing. You have a bag mask on you?"

I knew what she was asking for but I had nothing to give her. "Sorry, Doc."

She frowned. "I can't find a pulse, either. I need you to keep steady pressure to keep him from bleeding out on us. Squeeze as tight as you can. Okay?"

All I could do was nod, waiting on her next instruction. I wanted to help her give him CPR; I'd been recertified recently, but I knew the second I let go of this kid's leg the blood would flow.

Such a tiny thing and yet she was pumping his chest with renewed strength. I found that I was keeping count with her, but nothing was happening.

We were wasting our time trying to change his fate. Out here on the streets, not breathing and no pulse only meant one thing.

"Doc, I think he's dead."

She never stopped pumping. "No, he's not. Not yet."

I felt useless just doing nothing but clamping his leg. I didn't want to admit that the smell of his blood was getting to me. "Do you want me to do that? You hold his leg?" I switched to breathing out of my mouth.

Her dirty blonde hair bounced off her shoulders with each compression. "No. Your hands are stronger. Keep him clamped tight. You have an AED in your rig?"

Regret and anger poured over me, knowing we should be better equipped but weren't. "No. None of the ATTF units do."

"Shit," she growled out, pressing down on him harder. "Bagger? Oxygen?"

I squeezed the kid's thigh with all my might, not wanting any of her efforts to be in vain. "No. Regular patrol does. We don't carry that stuff. Like you said, it's just you and me, Doc." The moment she looked over at me again with those gorgeous blue eyes, I felt it. It was as if an invisible wavelength tethered us together in this shitty situation somehow. It almost took my breath away. It was that strong. I saw her next question clearly manifest on her face, as if I could read her mind like her thoughts were my own. She didn't need to ask. I scanned the area, yelling over to one of my team members, making sure she'd get whatever she needed as soon as a squad car pulled up.

"Thanks," she muttered, still compressing his chest.

Hearing the added sirens from arriving fire trucks and ambulances was nothing short of a relief, but it seemed to take forever for them to get on scene. I'd been a first responder on numerous occasions, but never had much of a stomach for the sight of torn human flesh.

"Officer, you can let go now," some paramedic said to me as he tried to shoulder me out of the way. I reluctantly rolled back off of my knees, very aware how much they hurt from kneeling on the wet, icy cold road. I didn't want to leave her; we were working well as a team. We'd gotten the kid's heart to beat again, and I felt like I was abandoning her to deal with the mayhem all on her own.

My captain stepped to my side and snagged my arm, attempting to tug me away, but I stood firm. I wasn't going anywhere, not without her, that is. "Come on, Adam. There's nothing else you can do here. Let's go get you cleaned up."

I rolled him off my shoulder, ready to push him away if I had to. She was up to her elbows in trying to save this guy's life. How she managed to keep so calm and in control was awe inspiring. I wanted to drop back to my knees next to her, soak in some of her power. "No, I'm staying here. She may need me."

"Adam."

I contemplated slugging him. "I said I'm good."

He pulled harder, deliberately knocking me off balance. "Come on, Adam. The EMTs got this. Local PD is here. It's their show now. We're just in the way."

"I don't give a fuck," I growled low.

Cap got right in my face, staring me down. "I'm not asking, I'm telling." He gave my chest a shove.

Respect for the man kept me from doing something rash and stupid, like laying him out right in the street.

"You've got blood all over you," he pointed out. "Try not to touch anything. Come on."

Touch anything? My hands felt numb; icy cold to the bone. That's when I noticed my leather gloves were soaked with the kid's blood, causing that chill to roll throughout my body.

Cap walked me back to my rig while my constant shadow, Ritchie, followed us like a faithful dog—still filming my every move.

"Shit, Adam," Cap said, shaking his head in disbelief. He pulled on a pair of latex gloves so he could peel my leather ones off. "Turn your face away until I get these off."

I looked back at the scene; that adorable doctor was still at it, working with the paramedics and the fire department to secure the victims.

"She sure is something," I breathed out, feeling extremely proud of her for some reason. She met extreme adversity head on, making me admire the hell out of her. Not too many women would have the guts or the tenacity to roll from one shitty situation to another.

Ritchie's camera light illuminated the wet street around my feet. Regret for putting her through all of that earlier hit me like a fist to the face, driving my need to right another wrong.

I leaned in closer to my commander, hoping that my words wouldn't get recorded. "Cap, the footage from tonight, it can never be aired. That shit will ruin her." I looked back at her; she was still giving orders, maintaining control of the situation as if she'd done it a thousand times. She was assessing the vics in the other car, pointing, telling people what she needed them to do, without even realizing she was being filmed by a major television network.

A third ambulance rolled up, along with another fire engine, taking care of the truck driver and the fluids spilled on the road. I wanted to run back to the scene and pull her out of there, carry her over my shoulder if I had to.

Cap sighed, eyeing Ritchie warily. "I know, but I'm worried about the shit they're recording right now. You know as well as I do that any shots of your heroics gives 'em serious hard-ons."

I bit back a curse, knowing the deal with the network and how their focus had secretly shifted, making me their primary target. Why we ever agreed to be filmed for reality TV was beyond me, although the amount of money they tossed at us was ridiculous and hard to say no to. At least it helped get the word out that the Auto Theft Task Force was out in full force, cracking down on crime.

Still, I felt like a sellout at times, especially since there were plenty of other hardworking cops on the streets who weren't pulling in an extra five figures to do their jobs.

Several patrol units were on the scene now, managing traffic. None of them were getting a cut of the action being on reality TV, but each of them were putting their lives at risk every time they wore their badge.

"All right," Cap said, dumping my bloody gloves in a plastic bag. "You need to get out of here and get cleaned up."

I held the plastic bag open while he removed his own soiled gloves. After a healthy dose of hand sanitizer for both of us, he used his com unit.

"Attention all ATTF officers, local PD is on scene. It's almost five forty-five. Time to clear out."

I checked my watch and hustled over to her car, assuring myself that her belongings were secured. Her sweet ride was at least forty-five grand to start and it was brand new. There was no way I was going to let her *or* her car sit in this neighborhood.

I didn't need to inform Cap what I intended to do. After being under his command for the last few years, one glance from me was all it took to know I needed to see this to the end. He gave me a nod of understanding.

I turned my glare on Ritchie, pegging him with a pointed finger. "Don't you fucking follow me. Understood?"

I was glad he didn't need me to repeat myself since I was at the very end of my rope. I jogged back to the accident scene alone, knowing I wasn't leaving until she was safe and secure. It was beyond too late to keep her off camera or from her seeing the injured. I found myself shouldering up to her, fighting an urge to wrap my arms around her.

She was standing there, misting the cold air with her labored breath. How many hours did she say she'd worked when we stopped her? Sixteen? And she'd just worked her ass off for another half hour doing field triage. Holy hell, that was admirable. Thoughts of my little brother Jason doing the same exact shit in some war-torn place of hell on Earth blasted into my mind, rippling pain and worry into my chest. Damn, I hoped he was doing all right—that he was safe.

The second ambulance pulled away, lights and sirens blaring.

"Told you he wasn't dead," she muttered, more to herself than me, I supposed.

"I thought for sure he wasn't going to make it." She was a fucking miracle worker. "You did real good, Doc. *Real* good." I rolled her name around my brain one more time, soaking it in so I wouldn't forget.

Erin.

Just standing next to her seemed to calm me, as if she were coated in some sort of magical aura that made me feel as though I wasn't so lost and alone in the ugliness of life.

The urge to haul her up into my arms and protect her from seeing any more misery was strong. "It's time to clear out, Doc." I held out her keys, needing to get her far away from this place, knowing I wouldn't be able to rest until I saw her home. Lights twinkled off the rhinestones that were embedded in the metal letter "E" that dangled from the keychain between my fingers.

She snagged them from the air, practically ripping her key fob from my hand. "Yes sir, Officer. At least I got to do one more good deed before you assholes turned my life to shit."

Wait… What? What the fuck did that mean? I distinctly recalled trying to stop her before her life turned to shit.

She turned on her heels so damn fast and started marching her pretty little ass down the street, I barely had a comeback.

She wasn't going to get off that easy. "Hey. Hold up. Doc. Stop right there."

Did she just flip me off? *Oh hell no.*

I got right into her personal space, holding my position at her car door as she stepped up to me.

"What? What do you want, Officer? Have some puppies you need to run over yet tonight?"

God, she was being such a bitch. Ballsy little thing, I'd give her that. Intriguing as all hell, too. *You aren't going anywhere until you explain that attitude you're dishing out. Try getting in your car with me holding the fucking door closed. I dare ya.*

She stared me down. "You just going to glare at me or do you have something else you need to say? Why don't you run and get your little ticket pad thing. I'm sure I can handle a final kick with a nice hefty ticket on top of it. What's a red light cost these days? Two hundred and three points on my record?"

Damn, she had a mouth on her. "What's your problem?"

She looked at me like I was cracked. "My *problem*? Oh, I'm sorry. Where should I start? The fact that I was already having one of the worst nights of my life *before* you and your posse aimed your guns at my head, or how the last twelve years of my life were just eviscerated when I was filmed wearing handcuffs? Once this hits the media, my career is *over.* Do you understand? Everything I've worked for is gone. Everything! So *sorry* if I'm a little bitter about that. And on top of all of that, four more people were just severely injured, causing even more misery to my horrendously shitty night. So if you haven't any further need for me, I'd like to go home and wash the blood off me that I got *on my pants* from keeping someone else from dying tonight, in case you need to *clear that up.*"

I never wanted to gag a woman so badly in all my life. I wanted to tie this little spitfire up and give her what she really needed—a good, thorough fucking—my way.

Whoa. Where the hell did that come from?

I was holding my jaw so tight my molars were starting to hurt. What did she expect? Her car was reported stolen at gunpoint. It was a justified stop. "If you're waiting for me to apologize for doing my job, it ain't gonna happen."

She tugged on the door handle again but it barely jostled me. Her shoulders slumped with exhaustion. I could tell she was running out of steam. Not only did we scare the shit out of her earlier, she just saved the life of complete strangers in the middle of the damn street. She'd run the gamut of emotions and the stress was making her lash out.

I could totally relate to being an asshole like that.

Those sexy-as-hell eyes turned up and leveled me again, silently pleading, sucking the wind right out of my lungs. I felt the urge to touch her, wondering like a prepubescent school boy what it would be like to kiss the girl. I rested my hand on my revolver instead, especially since I spotted a small crew of the Crips moseying down the sidewalk. Fucking delinquents. I needed to get her safely out of this neighborhood—*now.*

"Just let me go home."

I glared a warning in their direction, surprised that the gangbangers hadn't scattered like cockroaches with so many cops present. "I can't let you do that."

"Why?" she squealed, pulling with renewed force, but still nowhere near getting me to budge. "Grrahhh."

"Not done with you, Doc."

"Am I under arrest for chucking you the finger, because believe me, if that's the case I'll do it again just to make sure you got the message." She pulled on the door again.

The fact that she was so desperate to get away from me was aggravating. "Keep yanking. I got all morning, sweetheart."

Her hands finally slapped down in defeat. *That a girl; listen and surrender to me. I'll be more than happy to keep at this until I wear you down.*

"What if I kick you in the shins?"

Holy shit. Was she serious? "Gets you back in my handcuffs for assaulting an officer. You want back in my handcuffs?"

Her eyes flashed but something told me we had two *very* different versions of that scenario running through our minds. I sure as hell liked my visual of that—her tied and bound, bending to my will. I felt my dick twitch, agreeing with me.

Her chin jutted up. "Then I better aim for your balls instead. C'mon. Just. Let. Me. Go. Home."

Her reply unnerved me a bit. She was a fighter, and a dirty one at that. Surprising. Challenging too, which was also a pleasant surprise. *Bring it, baby, right after we take care of business.* I stared her down. "You going to calm down first and listen to me?"

Damn, she was infuriating and so goddamned sexy all flushed with anger. I just about lost all my breath when she finally relented. Those pink lips, that sexy mouth… Shit, she already had me by the balls.

"Look, we've both just been through a lot. And you don't have a plate on your car. If you give me a damn minute, I'm going to follow you in my rig to make sure you get home safely. I can't do shit for you if you drive away from here and local PD pull you over for driving without a plate. You copy?"

"Copy what?"

My patience was all used up. "Do you understand me?"

Erin finally nodded. The looming shadows and possible vendettas were making me edgy.

"Do not turn around but there are about twelve members of a local gang eyeing this situation from down the block and you've got that kid's blood all over your coat. I need you to listen and trust me. I'm going to get a bag for your jacket so you don't get that shit on your skin or all over your car seat. I've got an extra sweatshirt in my rig for you to wear home. Okay?"

"Okay. Copy." She saluted.

I still didn't trust that defiant look in her gorgeous eyes. "Do not move. You attempt to drive away from here without me tailing you I will haul your little ass in personally. We clear, Doc?"

That knocked some of the starch out of her. It was a relief to know she'd give in when I put my foot down. Good thing she had no clue I was bluffing.

"What are you doing, man?" my partner, Marcus, asked when I passed him leaning on our rig.

I opened the back hatch of our Expedition. "I have no fucking clue," I grumbled, grabbing my black ATTF sweatshirt out of my duffle bag, grateful that Ritchie wasn't on my ass for once. Unfortunately, he and Scott were hovering around her with their standard appearance release in hand. I should have warned her not to sign it.

Shit.

"She sure is a sweet slice of woman," Marcus muttered.

I had to agree. Shame we were fucking up her life like this. "Feisty as shit, too."

"Background check came back squeaky clean. One parking ticket and an old speeding violation dated about six years back. Oh, and no last name changes—ever, in case you're wondering."

I nodded. "You gonna give me shit if we tail her back to Drexel Hill Heights? I'm not going to put her through having her car towed tonight on top of all of that."

Marcus's eyebrows rose up his massive forehead. Then he huffed, surely holding back the desire to jack me up. I could see it in his eyes. Instead, he flashed those big white teeth at me. "I guess I don't have much of a choice. But you'd better hurry if you want dibs on that sweet piece 'cause Ramirez and Hill are sniffing all around your shit over there."

I tossed my bag back into our rig and slammed the hatch, rattling the glass.

What the fuck were those two assholes doing? Ramirez I could understand looking to upgrade women, but Hill? He'd better be playing wingman to his partner 'cause the prick was married with kids.

I stepped into Ritchie's line of sight. "This is done. Shut it down before I bust that camera." Didn't take long for Hill and Ramirez to get my glare either. *That's right. All you pricks just back the fuck up.*

I shook the bag, holding it open for her. "Coat. Bag. Now." I ignored her womanly defiance and the annoying film crew that hovered, assuring myself that my team members were moving the fuck along like good boys.

"You always such a bastard?" she asked, peeling her coat off. She stuffed it into the bag, trying to keep her hands on the clean parts.

"Only when I'm pissed off."

She scoffed and then shivered. "Join the club."

I tied the top of the bag into a knot and tossed it to the ground. She only had a short-sleeved scrub top on over a thin dark blue thermal and it was starting to snow again.

I fixed the neck opening and pulled the hoodie over her head, taking care not to accidentally tug her hair. The sleeves were a few inches too long and it came halfway down her thighs, but something about seeing her in my clothes caused a warm rush to flood my body.

At least she let me roll up the sleeves for her until just the tips of her pretty little fingers were peeking out. Damn, she was a beautiful sight.

I couldn't help but smooth a long piece of her bangs out of her eyes and slip it back inside the hood. She flinched back a bit, looking up at me as if I'd done something wrong. Maybe she was still keyed up from working the accident? Whatever it was, it didn't matter anymore; something in me needed to touch her.

I just about lost it when she tucked her tiny nose inside my hoodie and let out a soft whimper. A brush of pride swelled into my chest.

That's it, baby, remember that. That's all me. "You ready?"

Those big blue eyes stared up at me, clenching my gut.

"I am."

Me too, sweetheart. Me too.

CHAPTER 3
Erin

OFFICER TRENT WALKED me all the way to my front door, making me feel slightly uncomfortable having such a gorgeous man dressed in his tactical police gear this close to me. For the life of me I couldn't remember the last time a guy walked me to my front door, and that was not from a lack of trying. But this wasn't the first time in my life I'd had a police escort, and that recollection alone touching the fringes of my thoughts was extremely unnerving.

He held the glass storm door open while I worked my key into the lock, hoping none of my neighbors were watching. The old ladies on this street just loved to gossip, and seeing a cop at my door would give them plenty to chatter about.

I pushed the door open slightly and glanced up at him. Instead of saying his goodbyes, he was frowning down at me again.

"You have a security system?"

The way he said it made me feel as though I should. Unfortunately, if it didn't come with the little red brick salt-box house I was renting, I didn't have it. Still… "Is that any of your business?"

The muscle along his jaw twitched. "It's a yes or no question, Doc."

Gah, he was insufferable. "No."

His frown turned into more of a scowl.

"You should."

I'll move that to the top of my list, right after I reinvent a new career. "I'll take that under advisement." I set my purse and keys on the small oak table next to the door and started to roll off his hoodie.

He followed me inside. "What are you doing?"

Certainly not stripping for you. "Giving back your sweatshirt."

He shook his head. "Keep it."

Part of me hesitated, hating to give up the warm, wonderful smelling reminder of him, but the other, saner part of me ordered the rest of my body to shed off all reminders of this hellacious night. I handed it back to him. "I don't want it."

He actually looked wounded, scowling down at the jersey twisted in his hand. I was about to ask him if we were done here so I could slam my front door and then go cry myself to sleep, but those amazing chocolate eyes—filled with hints of hurtful regret—speared me, riveting me to the ground.

Officer Trent cleared his throat, fumbling with the fabric. That muscle in his jaw ticked and flexed. "I'm going to fix this. I don't want you to worry."

Okay, fine. Whatever. The damage was already done. I nodded once just to acknowledge him. "Okay, well, um, thanks for seeing me home safely, Officer."

"Adam," he said.

I met his gaze; those deep eyes wrapped in long lashes called to me on some primal level, tugging at my body to respond. I shoved my involuntary reaction back. "Adam?"

He nodded. "Name's Adam, Doc. Adam Trent."

Why is he telling me this? Like I'm supposed to believe I'm going to get a date or something out of this after that humiliating display and almost arrest? Get real. The fact that he was apparently trying to assuage his own guilt irritated me further. I held the door open, casting a glance toward the street.

"All right then," he muttered under his breath. "One more thing," he said, his jaw tightening. "No driving your car until you get a new plate on it. You'll need to come down to the station and get a copy of the police report. You'll need that to get a new plate."

Wonderful. One more thing on the to-do list.

"Got it?"

I fought rolling my eyes at his gruff tone. "Got it."

His gaze softened but still measured me. He gripped the knob on the storm door, keeping half of his body in the doorframe. "You have someone who can drive you?"

If I didn't know better, I'd have sworn he actually cared. Problem was I didn't know why. "I'll figure something out."

"You sure? I can take—"

I held up my hand to stop him. "I'm sure. Really. But thanks." That seemed to stifle him and his misguided pity.

"Okay." He tipped the brim of his baseball hat slightly and then stepped off my front landing. "Thanks for saving a few more lives tonight. It was inspiring to watch you work. Have a good day, Doc."

I watched his incredibly nice ass and gorgeous build all clad in badass black stroll down my walkway and climb back into his SUV, easing his body behind the steering wheel with effortless command. There was no final wave goodbye, no final look in my direction, no nothing. He spun away from my curb without so much as a backward glance.

I slammed my front door, ending the crushing insanity for one day. Suppressed anguish burned up my throat like acid on fire. It was hard to breathe, hard to think, suffocating under the tidal wave of emotions. I couldn't stop my tears from falling. Calling my parents would have to wait a few more minutes.

IT WAS ALREADY dark outside when I climbed into Sarah's car, which was graciously waiting for me in my frosty driveway.

"Hey." I stuffed my backpack between my feet and reached for the seatbelt. "Thanks for giving me a ride. I appreciate it."

"No problem," Sarah said. "How are you holding up?"

Barely?

"I'm okay." A chill rippled over me. "I'll be better once I warm up."

Sarah frowned and nudged me. "You know what I mean."

After four years, I did. "I know."

She turned the radio down. "Any news?"

I was wondering why we weren't moving when I realized she was waiting for me to give her an answer. A flash of seeing my uncle being wheeled in by the flight medics invaded my thoughts. "He made it through the initial surgery but he's still in critical condition."

She gave my forearm a gentle squeeze with her mitten-covered hand.

"He's still with us."

Was he? A medically induced coma with a breathing tube shoved down his throat was far from being *with anyone*.

I recalled the words Doctor Wilson had said to me when I'd lost my first patient, *"You can't save everyone, Erin. You have to realize that everything we do here, every patient we care for and treat, is doing nothing but stalling the inevitable."*

"I can't believe someone stole the plate off your car."

I figured the less Sarah knew the better so I went with the bare minimum disclosure when I had called her for a ride to work. "Me either."

She put her car in reverse, backing out of my drive. "Why the hell would somebody do that? People are so messed up. Oh this irritates me to no end. It's freaking cold outside. What on earth would they need your license plate for?"

After the whirlwind from my traumatic traffic stop this morning, I'd have to guess committing all sorts of heinous crimes would be on the top of their list. "I don't know. I've stopped trying to figure out why people do half the crazy things they do. I'm just glad they didn't steal my new car. I just have to get another plate."

Sarah shivered and turned the heater up. "You should have called me earlier. I could have taken you for one. I was awake."

She was such a good friend. I appreciated her offer but my conscience wouldn't allow it, especially since she was sitting so close to the steering wheel, her growing belly was almost touching. I banished the horrible image that flashed from thinking about what would happen if we were in an accident. "You should have been sleeping."

She gave me a quick scan before turning back to the road. "No offense, but you sort of look like you could use some extra sleep, too."

I shrugged it off, having accepted long ago my constant state of perpetual exhaustion. "Yes, but you have a baby belly to care for. You don't need to be running around unnecessarily. I'm just grateful you're here now."

Sarah scoffed. "Yeah. That's exactly what I need—more sitting on my ass. Perfect for growing these lovely cankles. My ankles are so swollen, I'm starting to look like my grandma. Would have been nice if someone would have warned me about this shit." Her little rant turned into a private smile. "I felt the baby kick yesterday."

"Really?" I couldn't imagine what that might feel like, nor would I ever, but her excitement about it told me it was one of the best feelings in the world.

Sarah rubbed her stomach. "Yep. Little Brett Junior is getting quite active in there."

The notion of her actually growing a human being inside her body made me feel a sliver of envy. Our bodies were truly miracles of science. But also knowing firsthand how childbirth could make a completely sane woman do unspeakable things made the envious desire flee with its ass on fire. I swallowed the terrible memories of my youth, barely hiding the crack in my voice. "Is that what you've finally decided to name him? I thought Brett hated that idea."

Sarah shrugged, making a right hand turn at the stoplight. "He does but until he comes up with a better suggestion, I'm calling him Junior. It really pisses him off when I call him Doctor Junior. He says our boy should be his own unique person and not be forced to follow in his father's footsteps, not that he didn't follow his own father into dentistry."

For some reason I thought about Officer Trent, *Adam*, wondering if his children were following in their father's footsteps, playing cops and robbers all over the house.

Did Officer Hottie have a wedding ring on? Surely by now some prissy Barbie doll model has gotten her hooks into someone as gorgeous as him. Did he? I can't remember. Wait, he was wearing gloves. That's right, black leather gloves. Leather gloves that would probably feel like sinful heaven gliding over my skin. Was he wearing them when he followed me home? Shit, why can't I remember? Oh yeah, I was mad. Pissed off, actually.

I knew I should really be paying attention to Sarah's ramblings about her husband's child-rearing philosophies, but the neglected horny girl who lives in my head and hadn't been laid in a very long time was fighting me for topics to concentrate on.

I wondered how Adam's wife would feel about him lending his sweatshirt to some random woman he almost arrested.

If he were my husband, I'd probably be jealous about that. I should have kept it. It smelled wonderful—like man and manly body wash and several other flavors I'd like to roll my tongue over. But thoughts of having his integrity relentlessly questioned by an irate woman made me accept the fact that I made the right decision to give it back. He didn't deserve that.

As we waited for the light to change, a police car with the telltale blue and yellow-gold stripes of Philly's finest pulled up next to us, preparing to turn right.

Just being this close to a cop made me squirm down in my seat. Visions of being handcuffed, tossed in some god-forsaken hellhole to do time with other hardened criminals, half of which passed through our ER on their way to purgatory, sent shivers through me.

I should have gone earlier to get a new license plate. I could have called a taxi. I knew Jen was working twelve to midnight from her text this morning and Sarah, she was on the go so much at the hospital I hated taking away from the time she needed to rest. I could only imagine how much being pregnant takes out of you.

No. I made the right decision. She needed to rest and I needed to spend the late afternoon scouring the local news websites on my computer to see if my almost arrest made print rather than sleeping.

Even now, being driven to work with the remote chance that my career could be in the balance was making me beyond anxious. So far none of the local channels had listed my name or the circumstances of them pulling me over but that really didn't mean anything. The traffic accident made the local section of the news, but fortunately I didn't see any mention of my name. Regardless, there were three camera crews filming everything so the likelihood of me getting seen, recognized, and then subsequently fired was pretty good.

If Sarah and the girls caught wind of it, gossip would fly at Mach 5 throughout every corner of the hospital from the commotion they'd make.

I wanted to be completely prepared for all of the possible scenarios that could hit me when I walked back into work. I knew that the grapevine was already sharing my family tragedy from last night because I had twenty unanswered texts and several voicemails on my phone when I woke up.

My aunt and uncle's accident was at the top of the broadcast news reports. *Triple fatality on the Schuylkill.* The guy who started it was apparently driving a stolen car. Twenty-four-year-old with a seventeen-year-old passenger—both killed at the scene. Senseless; the tragedies that snowballed from some guy's bad decision.

Sarah glanced over and tapped me on the arm. "Hey, you okay, Erin?"

My body jerked. I'd completely missed part of her monologue. "Huh? Yeah, why?"

"I asked you if you were able to get any sleep."

I took a deep breath, trying to master my emotions. "Some." Not nearly enough, though. "My parents have been at the hospital all day. I called the ICU before I took my shower. The CT scans showed subdural hematomas. It's only a matter of time now before he goes into organ failure." I held back the burn rolling back up my throat. "My parents are going to be devastated."

"Oh man," Sarah groaned.

"My dad was going to pick me up on their way in but I had something I needed to do first." I looked at my cell still clutched in my hand in case I got *the call*. "The, ah, priest from their church came by to see the family."

I felt her hand slide over mine, comforting me. "You need *anything*, you let me know."

I nodded, knowing she truly meant it. Little did she know that just being in the same car with her was what I needed. Sarah was a true friend through and through.

The moment we walked into the ER the familiar scents of the hospital hit me, making the pit of my stomach twist. The plethora of smells of antiseptic, bodily fluids, even down to the chemicals used to scrub the floors, blended into the blur of rushing bodies, rhythmic tones of medical monitors, and hurried orders being called out between colleagues.

I felt as if I were a silent witness, viewing the everyday pulse of the ER as if I wasn't really there. Things seemed to happen around me without need for my intervention.

Two uniformed EMTs pushing an empty stretcher passed by me. One of our RNs rushed into Room Seven. Death happening to the left; miracles of resuscitation happening to the right.

"Erin."

I blinked from the severity of the tone.

"Earth to Doctor Novak."

A large hand clasped around my shoulder, surprising me back into reality. I looked up at the handsome face that'd been the bane of my existence for at least three of the last four years.

Doctor Randy Mason.

Tall, lean, wind-blown light brown hair, short-cropped goatee, studious wire-rimmed glasses, and the owner of the most incredible ass to grace our halls in a pair of scrub pants. He shocked me with one of his killer smiles that, unfortunately, quickly dissipated.

His deep hazel eyes narrowed, assessing me as if I were nothing more than a patient. To think that I once thought I saw my entire future in those eyes when he was between my thighs making love to me.

"You okay? Mandy told me your uncle made it through the first twelve hours. Were you up in ICU?"

Hearing that name leave his lips was like a harsh slap to the face and a knife in the back at the same time, instantly knocking me out of my stupor. Being reminded of how my last love had gutted me so effectively with that tramp from Radiology was the last thing I needed while privately suffering through my family tragedy.

Randy and Mandy—what a joke.

An icy chill ran through my bones recalling that final fight, the seething anger and agonizing disappointment, the way I dumped dresser drawers and threw his clothing out of my bedroom and out of my life.

What he ever saw in her, I'd never know. Perhaps if she had some redeeming qualities I might understand the attraction and why he chose to cheat on me with her, but she wasn't even a nice person. She was the term *bitch* personified, always snipping at everyone like an overindulged spoiled brat and committing my number one pet peeve by talking about people behind their backs incessantly.

I nodded my answer and wrapped my stethoscope around my neck, confused by his close proximity and the gentle rubbing he was doing on my arm. To think how much I used to crave that touch or any semblance of emotional nurturing from him.

"Yeah, thanks. It's been… rough." I pulled my arm away from him before my body caved into the attention. It had taken me months and lots of tears to resolve that the love I thought I had felt for him was totally one-sided and definitely unrequited.

Randy hesitantly reached for me again but I moved farther away. He lost the privilege of touching me a long time ago. "So I, um, I have to get to work, but thanks."

"I'm worried about you. Despite what you might think, I still care. If you need anything, you know, well—"

My hand shot out. "Save it. Just save it." Self-preservation had me darting away from him as quickly as my feet would carry me. The last thing I needed was his pity. I headed toward our automated white-board to check our caseload instead, replaying the subtle nuances of our one-minute interlude, hating the part of me that still craved him. My mind was barraged with fragmented memories: his smile, his kiss, the feel of his hands roaming my body. How I tried so hard and failed so miserably. How the little he *did* give me just wasn't enough.

I fought the urge to turn back, to glance his way just one more time to see if he'd had some magical change of heart and I was the one he truly wanted, but the emptiness I carried told me he may have been what I had wanted, but he was definitely not what I needed.

After all this time, after all the tears I shed for him from how he'd broken my heart into tiny fragments, he still affected me. No, the quicker I could get away from him the better. My self-worth was more valuable.

Falling for him was such a huge mistake…

I heard another deep voice call out my name, this time making me flinch with nervous worry. *Shit. Shit, shit, shit.*

On command, I followed our Chief Resident Director, Doctor Sam Wilson, into his office. The fear of being in trouble quickly replaced lingering thoughts of broken promises.

"Have a seat," he instructed in his no bullshit tone. Being under his direct tutelage for my entire residency, I was well-versed in his moods but still slightly intimidated by him.

"I'm surprised to see you on shift," he started, giving me a lukewarm smile.

That made two of us, surprised, that was, by his line of questioning. If he mentions my almost arrest I was going to lose it. "Why wouldn't I be here?"

He frowned at me. "Your family had a major setback last night, Erin. I consulted with Doctor Sechler."

I'd seen plenty of people fired over the years for their poor work ethics so I felt I needed to justify—immediately. "I know and I'm sorry. I'm actually glad we're meeting now. I had fully intended to discuss my behavior with you. I want you to know that it won't happen again. I should not have frozen up like that receiving a patient. It was very unprofessional of me to let my team down like that and to allow personal familiarity to detract from my attention to the patient's care—"

His hand flew up. "Whoa, Erin, stop. Everyone understands. This was a relative of yours, not some stranger. You're not impervious, for God's sake. No one is blaming you or thinking anything less of you."

"But—"

"But nothing. It could happen to any one of us seeing a family member come in as a trauma patient, and considering the circumstances, you held yourself together better than most."

I nodded even though I wholeheartedly disagreed, feeling the cold shock of tattered nerves seep into my fingertips. He eyed me as I wrung my hands.

"In my eighteen years in this position I have only had a handful of residents who have worked as hard as you do. In all honesty, I felt like a proud father when you completed your residency, but you're too hard on yourself. No one is questioning your leadership and dedication, especially not me, but you have to realize that you're no good to anyone while you have a loved one two floors up in critical care." With that, he crossed his legs, his telltale sign of getting down to business. "Have you checked in with Doctor Giffords yet?"

Shit. Chief neurosurgeon. Not good. "No, sir. I just got here."

He gave me a superficial smile. I knew exactly what it meant. "I know this is a difficult time for you. I hope you can also use this experience and learn from it and expand your growing knowledge of TBIs."

My nerves took another jump. If he only knew just how much experience I'd already had dealing with traumatic brain injuries after my sister's accident, he'd be astounded. But that was another area of my personal history I kept tightly under wraps. After all, it was my fault it happened in the first place. If I hadn't been so self-absorbed in my own problems, Kate would have never suffered.

"Don't let your family's loss be in vain."

I gasped, unable to swallow. "Has he—?"

Again with the fatherly smile. "No, but things are not looking promising. Unless he makes an upswing in the next twenty-four to forty-eight hours, you and your family should probably prepare. Take some time off. I'm giving you permission to deal with the human side of medicine, Doctor."

I shook my head vehemently. "I don't need time off, sir. I have my interview with the Fellowship committee in three weeks and I need to be prepared. I *need* that fellowship, Sam. It's all I've ever wanted."

Doctor Wilson held up his hand again, halting me. "I've known that for years. It's not new news. I've already sent in my letter of recommendation. Doctor Gaudet and Doctor Chanpreet have submitted theirs as well. Everyone knows how badly you want your medical toxicology residency, although I have to again say that I feel you're making a big career mistake. You've never been too keen on sitting on your butt in the lab, Erin." He drew in a leveling breath. "I know you have some personal goal here but I think you're going to be miserable and I really wish you'd reconsider. The Assistant Director position we discussed is still on the table as an option, should you want to reconsider it. Continue to study toxicology on the side if it's still your passion. It will only add to your value in emergency medicine. But honestly, I've watched you grow and thrive and I truly believe *here* is where your true calling is."

I shook my head, though after all this time, it had become somewhat automatic. "My goal has always been singular."

"It means a huge pay cut too. Keep that in mind."

He studied me. "I wish you could see in yourself what I see in you. Well, think about it. No final decisions need to be made, but for now, for today and tomorrow, I think you should take some time to regroup."

I could see his point but being dismissed because of my own emotional weakness was not something I could stomach either. "Sam, I'm fine, really. I'll go check in on things up in ICU and then I'll be back on the floor. I just need maybe an hour—"

His hand slapped down on the desk. "Damn it, Erin. No."

I cringed slightly, caught off guard by his angry retort. I had heard him yell plenty of times over the years, but I loathed myself every time it was directed toward me. "I can do this. I'm not going to let my team down because of it. We're already short staffed tonight."

His reprimanding glare was slightly intimidating, like when your father expressed his disappointment. "I thought you of all people realize that when you go in there without your head in the game, that's when critical mistakes are made. Just because it's *you*, don't think you're immune. I'm not going to let you risk it, even if you're too damn stubborn to realize that for yourself. We'll manage. You go home."

Stubborn? As if I'd never heard that one before. Usually there were other adjectives to go along with that one but now was probably not the best time to be defiant, especially since I'd schooled other residents on the importance of focus.

I knew if I went home, I'd wallow in my thoughts. "I didn't drive."

"Can someone pick you up?"

"No, I need to keep busy. I'll just..." I didn't know what I'd just do.

"Go see your family. Go rest in the on-call room. Just no patients tonight."

As if I'd be able to rest. After I'd been dismissed with my marching orders, I pressed the button for the elevator, knowing he'd follow through with his threat to have me physically removed from the ER if he saw me in there anywhere tonight. I chose being smart over being foolish—for now.

I checked my pager, wondering if Doctor Sechler was available for consult.

No sooner did I make it through the security doors of the ICU, I spotted my mom sitting stoically by my Uncle Cal's side, her cheeks pale and worn with emotional exhaustion, rubbing his non-responsive hand.

CHAPTER 4

Adam

THESE BASTARDS ARE going to nail me to the cross today. I just fucking know it.

Marcus had warned me earlier at the gun range that the guys were going to be relentless tonight, but what was I supposed to do? Not show up for work?

Screw that. I had shit to do.

I headed down the florescent-lit hallway and its dingy walls to our main briefing room, flicked on the lights, not surprised that I was the first one in. And tonight, I was an extra hour early, but not by choice. I grabbed a copy of the hot sheet and got comfortable in my ratty-ass tan desk chair, knowing I had some time to kill. It creaked in protest as I leaned back, like a crotchety old man too weathered by years of hard living to move.

Something sharp dug into my elbow and I wondered for a moment if the chair had grown teeth, hungry to take a bite out of me too. The armrest was all but gone, held together with my repeated attempts to repair it with duct tape. Despite its sad condition, good, bad, or otherwise we were partners, and right then and there I made the decision to wheel him home after shift, see if I could replace the faithful arms propping me up.

I straightened the page and perused the list, hoping I'd find something that would distract me from thinking about not just one but two major traffic accidents that happened on our watch and the blood and gore that coated both of them.

I rubbed my neck. Restful sleep had eluded me again. The nightmare had me sitting straight up in bed this time, gasping. The gunshot, the vacant look on my partner's face after the bullet penetrated his skull, all followed by the silver charm bracelet dangling on the charred remains of another ghastly memory. I rubbed my eyes.

The only thing keeping me from falling into another downward spiral was visualizing that gorgeous doctor we pulled over this morning. Every time the anger, frustration, and haunting images started to swell I'd force my thoughts back to her, finding the memory of her bright enough to break through the darkness.

Her long, dirty-blonde hair had just enough wave in it to make me fantasize what it might feel like threaded through my fingers. Those killer blue eyes and soft cheeks naturally blushed with the cold hit me every time I blinked. Recalling how she fought through an extremely shitty situation to rally in the end with her extraordinary heroics tangled up with images of her sexy mouth and plump lips.

I felt tight in my skin and my chest ached, as if this random female had managed to turn me inside out somehow. I couldn't concentrate on anything else for more than a few seconds before returning to visions of her. My imagination was having a field day with its vivid depictions.

I rubbed a thumb over my breastbone. Funny, thinking of her had gotten me through that burning urge to dull the pain in other ways. *Huh. I wonder if it would be harmful to my health to be addicted to a hot doctor instead.*

Hot sheet. Concentrate on the hot sheet.

I tried to look at the paper in my hand but the print distorted; its allure paled in comparison. I finally managed to note the makes and models of a few high-end vehicles reported stolen this morning, which immediately took over my attention. I sat forward in my chair, circling several on the list with my pen.

The hot sheet was long and I was still slightly distracted by an alluring blonde, so I went over the list twice. Most of the vehicles reported were typical; they were older makes and models, easy to steal with a brick and a screwdriver. But the ones I'd highlighted were anything but. Son of a... While we were screwing around and getting innocent people killed, four new cars vanished off of a dealership's lot.

"Trent, it's time," Cap said from the doorway, jerking his head. "Suits from the network are here."

Fuck. I dropped my pen on the table and followed him out into the hallway. With all that had gone on in the last twenty-four hours I had refrained from thinking about this meeting. This was the television network's answer to me refusing their repeated requests to take another private meeting at their office in Manhattan. This time the mountain came to me at my convenient hour.

A new throb immediately started in my skull. No way was I going into Cap's office unprepared. "And?"

"They want to talk to you."

"I gathered that. Christ, Cap."

"I know."

"Do you? I just had three girls camped out on my goddamned lawn take cell pictures of me when I left my house. I mean, how the hell do they find out where I live? Fans have even started calling up my mom. My *mother*, Cap. She doesn't need this shit and I sure as hell don't either. She's got her hands full taking care of my pop; she doesn't need to add nonsense on top of it." I took a deep breath. "I didn't sign on for all of this."

Cap sighed hard. "Yeah, well, unfortunately you did. We all did."

I glared at the ominous office door down the hall. "If I would have known it would turn out like this I would have said no."

"Just hear them out. A few more months and our contract will be up and we can all get out of this clusterfuck."

I wanted to punch the wall. "We fucked up—*majorly*—last night. This lack of focus is stacking the shit pile higher. I need to know that every one of them has their head in the game and has my back and I gotta tell ya, Cap, I'm not feeling it."

My captain's eyes slid back and forth down the hallway, obviously worried that we might be overheard. I knew we had to be careful; so much was on the line.

When he glared at me in silence, I felt like he needed a wake-up call. Insubordination be damned. "Three bodies on the highway, Cap. Three. And one hanging on by a thread. Bad intel on the Taurus SHO, pulling over that doc last night, then that multi-car wreck. Jesus… We're lucky no one else died."

"Hey, you know damn well that every man on this team takes their job very seriously. You making this personal?" Cap questioned.

He's lucky I didn't turn around and take a walk after that remark. "Yeah, I am. I got blood on my hands and I'm not liking that one bit. We should have stopped that Nissan before it got out on the Schuylkill. But instead of figuring out where we all went wrong tonight, our *team* is going to be distracted by fucking fan mail. We need to sort this shit before someone else gets hurt, or worse—one of *us* gets killed."

Cap growled at me but I didn't give a shit. It was the truth and he knew it.

"Listen to me, son. I get your anger. I do. But like I told you before, sometimes it's out of our power to prevent bad things from happening. We can only do our best, that's it. I'll put foot to ass for the fuck ups. Mark my words."

I tried to take another calming breath. "The call on the doc's car was a complete diversion. I just reviewed the reports. *Four* high-end vehicles were boosted at the same time we were chasing bogies. That's no coincidence."

The entire thing made my skin itch, and that was not a good sign. I had a gut feeling why it played out like it did, and that made me feel even more uneasy. More often than not my gut instincts turned out to be accurate, and if they were on the mark now, the criminals just played us at our own game. "We were set up like chumps, and we fell for it."

Cap heaved a heavy sigh and nodded. "That's not lost on me either, Adam. I got a report back on the driver on the stolen Nissan. They ID'd him as one Harrell Manley."

My brain seized. "*Manley?*"

I instantly recognized the name since I'd busted him a few years ago. He was young but a seasoned car thief, repeat offender, gang member, and I knew for a fact that he had connections with chop shops, using their illegal activities to support their other illegal habits. I also knew who he'd been working for these days.

"Yep. Had his younger brother Dwight in the car with him, too. Both DOA at the scene."

I rubbed my hand down my face as the news sunk in. I'd also busted Dwight back when he was only thirteen. He was a good kid at heart but fell victim to his shitty environment. Mom was on welfare with a heroin habit; dad was unknown and definitely not in the picture. He followed his brother right into the gang life.

I tried to scare him straight when I had him, even put Dwight in contact with free counseling services that worked with at-risk kids. His brother was too far embedded in his ways to turn away and make something out of himself, but I really tried to make a difference with the younger Manley kid. Tried, but obviously failed. Now he was dead and gone and there would be no future for him. No redemption. Just another kid I couldn't save. Before I could stop it, my disappointment turned into physical burn. What a waste of a life.

"That confirms it was a diversion. Both calls were."

Cap sort of agreed, though not as confident as I was. The Manley brothers were in it for the money and had been stripping and selling car parts for years, but lately word on the street said they were boosting cars for one specific client. "Both were armed but there were no drugs on the bodies or in the vehicle."

We'd called off the chase when things got too dangerous. "The Nissan is the only piece that doesn't quite fit. Maybe he was off the clock and working his own deal."

He shrugged. "Maybe. But he's too dead to ask now."

That he was.

"I just briefed Commissioner Quinlan and he agrees that we want you to lead the investigation since you're already working the Mancuso case. See what you can dig up. Hopefully you can tie something back to them."

A guy in a dark suit popped his head out of Cap's office at the end of the hall and waved, demanding our attention.

Cap's exasperated sigh reflected my own. "We'll discuss this later. Let's go get this shit over with."

I reluctantly followed him into his office, noting the small space was already occupied by three bodies, one of whom instantly set me on guard. It was an automatic reaction to being sized up as if I were her next meal.

Long chestnut hair, expensive stilettos, a killer body clad in a dress meant for anything other than talking business—her motives for making this trip couldn't have been any more obvious. Fuck, I hated surprises. Last time I saw her, she was trailing behind her father's shadow, pouting and bored.

Apparently she was taking her father's recent death in good stride.

"There's our star! Mr. Trent! So good to see you," the one suit gushed.

Harry, Herby something.

He was the one who originally lured us into this mess, promising all sorts of things along the way. I sure as hell didn't want to shake the asshole's hand but to avoid doing so would be rude. Instead, I gave the outstretched hand a squeeze until the condescending smile turned into a slight register of pain.

"Yes, of course," his voice rose in pitch. I enjoyed watching him shake out his fingers at his side. "You remember Melissa Werner," he said. "Please, sit." He nudged the other suit I didn't recognize to vacate the chair.

That would put me right next to a pair of long legs attached to nothing but high maintenance trouble.

I avoided looking at her.

"No, thanks. Say what you came to say and then I need to get back to work." I crossed my arms over my chest. There was no way I'd let them talk me into something again this time. Didn't matter how much money they wanted to throw at me. They had turned my life into a small circus and our unit into a joke amongst the rest of the force. That was enough damage as far as I was concerned.

Asshole was smirking like a shady used-car salesman, thinking he already had a chump on the hook. "We'd like to discuss opportunity and your future."

And there it was. This was the same bullshit they spieled before, only this time I wasn't buying it. "That's nice. Not interested."

That answer got the queen up out of her chair.

She stepped over the other suit as if he were nothing more than a pawn. "It's good to see you again, Adam."

Normally I would view a gorgeous, self-assured woman as a challenge—see if I could get her to give up all the power and heed my commands, but this one was nothing more than a spoiled socialite looking for a play toy. Melissa Werner was the kind of pleasure I did not want to mix with business.

I gave her a nod. "Ms. Werner."

"So formal," she chided. "I'm here to make you an offer, Officer Trent. I hope you hear me out before making any hasty decisions."

An offer? Before I could give her my firm "no" she handed a bunch of spreadsheets to me. They might as well have been written in Greek. "What's all this?"

"Those are our ratings for the last nine weeks. As you know, the pilot for the show was highly successful. We had guaranteed a six-month season, renegotiating that for a year. Landing the new air time has had very surprising results. We need to reevaluate how we spend it."

I tried to hand the paperwork back to her. "Honestly, Ms. Werner—"

"Melissa," she corrected.

Yeah, whatever. "Honestly I can give a rat's ass how you decide to spend your time. My job is to catch car thieves and criminals. If you want to film me while I do that, then you get what I signed on for."

She slipped the papers out of my hand. "Do you see this number?"

I had to squint. Fucking printed numbers were small. Thirty-two years old and I probably needed glasses.

She pointed to another set of numbers. "The first number represents our ratings prior to October eleventh. This number, the *bigger* number, is our ratings after we aired the episode where you engaged in the hand-to-hand combat with Mr. Ortiz."

Mr. Ortiz. Yeah, I remembered that night vividly, ending with a trip to the hospital to patch up a two-inch slice in my gut. Asshole caught me with a knife right under my Kevlar when I tagged the back of his jacket.

I was pumped on adrenaline and he was wasted on crack. Ortiz had ditched the Pontiac he boosted on Basin Street but I had him on the ground before he got to the end of the block. Cap made me strip off my vest and bloodied T-shirt while we waited for the ambulance to arrive. Ritchie never took the camera off me. I was surprised that he was able to catch up to me. Kid was fucking fast with that camera.

It was also after that particular episode aired—where they showed me reuniting the baby girl that had been in the back seat of the stolen car with her hysterical mother—when all the ridiculous *fandamonium* started. I didn't know what the big deal was. I was just doing my job, for Christ's sake.

"So?" I still didn't know what she was getting at.

"We rebroadcasted the episode after we garnered the new nine p.m. time slot. In the last few weeks our viewership has jumped *significantly.* The excerpt of you jumping over the hood of the car has been viewed over four million times. You were a global trending topic, Adam. Needless to say, I'm very pleased. Not only have we locked in with a major network, as of last week we currently rank tenth on the overall ratings with an increase of over seven million new viewers."

She beamed at me, and for a moment I was captivated by her excited enthusiasm. Add that to the fact she was a young, gorgeous woman who smelled fantastic, it was almost a lethal combination.

It would be very easy to hike up her short skirt and fuck her over the desk. She'd probably get off on it.

"Seven," she mouthed.

My visions evaporated. "Seven million people watched the show?"

She took the papers from my hand again. "No. Twelve million eight hundred and seventy-five thousand did. The seven million is *new* viewers." She gave me a patronizing smile. "I don't expect you to understand the complexities of ranks and ratings, so don't worry that handsome face of yours trying to comprehend it all."

And right then her presence enraged me. Her tone was brimming with condescension, masked by the seductive way she accentuated certain words. Did she really think I was that oblivious and simpleminded?

"Fox has now given us a new mandate to maintain viewership, so what we need to discuss is how we leverage our assets to make that happen."

I felt her heated gaze singe my cock; her double meaning so blatant even the two other suits in the room squirmed.

"I've decided that we're going to rebrand the show," Melissa continued, lifting her attention back to my face. "Our new marketing goals are to feature you as the primary focus of each episode. It would mean an increase of your on-air time, which we need to amend in your contract."

She snapped her fingers, barely casting a glance back at her underlings. "Harry…"

He fumbled, passing papers in a hurry.

"You'll see we've amended paragraphs seven and nine." She flipped a page. "You'll also be requested to do a few new photoshoots as we will be doing extensive promotion, both in print ads and on social media. Fox will also run promotions on their website. That's all noted here."

The quiet suit cleared his throat. "PR…"

"Oh yes," Melissa continued. "We'll provide you with a public relations manager to assist you with your own social media as well as give you media training for when you conduct interviews." She flicked her fingers at Harry again. "Do you have the preliminary agenda for his personal appearances?"

This shit was hurting my brain. "My what?"

Harry fumbled through his briefcase while she sneered at him with the patience of a demanding child.

"Personal appearances, Adam."

Again? That was twice she'd hit me with the patronizing tone. "Yeah, I heard you the first time." I tried to find the loophole in the contract she'd shoved in my hand. "Doesn't mean I'm going to comply with all of your demands, or any of them, for that matter."

"Demands?" She sighed heavily, obviously displeased. "This is a once in a lifetime opportunity for you. Our requests are not excessive. You'll introduce each episode, which will require some additional voiceovers and B-roll footage. We'd like to splice in some additional footage of you working on your physique and perhaps shooting your gun." She bit into her lip, gazing up at me the way women sometimes do. "You know; sex it up a bit for the viewers."

I was willing to bet she was imagining me fucking her over the desk right now.

"Seventy-eight percent of the new viewership is female because of you," the quiet suit said.

Melissa glared daggers at him for speaking out of turn.

Like Jekyll and Hyde, she turned her pacifying smile back to me. "Yes, *you* are the reason the ratings have increased. We'll arrange for you to do some one-on-one interviews on the major morning shows, get some additional exposure. Who knows? Maybe you'll love the spotlight so much it will lead to a movie career for you. You don't want to be a cop for the rest of your life, do you?"

I sure as hell wasn't the attention-seeking type, but when she questioned my career choice as if I'd settled until something better came along, my decision was instant. "Yeah, we're done here."

"But you—"

I pushed away from the wall, having heard enough. "Save it. I'm not interested."

"Stop," Melissa bellowed.

Whatever she had to say, she had exactly five seconds to say it.

"Twenty thousand," she blurted. "We're prepared to pay you an additional five figures for the next twelve episodes to finish out your contract, contingent upon you signing on for an additional three seasons."

My eyes slipped shut as I let that number roll around. *Tempting. Oh so fucking tempting.* That would put a decent sized dent in some bills after I paid the income taxes.

But visions of Marcus holding his baby girl while he *wasn't* getting the same offer made my teeth clench, not to mention their desire to make me some pin-up jackass was just ludicrous.

"Apparently you don't get it. I'm a cop, for Christ's sake. That's what I am, not some whatever the fuck you want me to be. And those men out there, we're a team. The show is all of them, not just me."

"What if we give everyone a little adjustment?" the quiet suit added, his head bobbing like a curious turkey.

Harry/Herby—whatever the fuck his name was—sputtered and choked as if he'd just had his nut sac grazed with sandpaper.

Stupid curiosity had me waiting for her to toss more numbers. When she didn't go on, I felt compelled to call her on it.

Melissa Werner held her hand out to her associate, shutting him down immediately. She straightened, looking back at me. "I'd like you to consider our position. Your teammates are actually having their on-air time decrease. They've already been compensated for their appearances. It wouldn't be a prudent business decision to adjust their contracts at this time. This new direction only affects you."

I hated being underestimated. "That's where you're wrong, because your tactics divide the team, so it affects them too."

Melissa flit her eyes. I felt my blood pressure spike.

"This, all of this, is nothing but a distraction. It causes the men to lose focus, which puts us all in danger. This isn't child's play, Ms. Werner. We go out there every day knowing that it may be our last, and you and your business goals aren't worth losing a life over."

"Thirty," she tossed without regard.

My knuckles cracked. "Ten thousand more, just like that? What is that? Extra hush money or what you think my life is worth?"

She sighed impassively. "This is a contract renegotiation, Adam, not a life valuation. I'm not prepared to entertain renegotiations for the entire crew and, frankly, it's not warranted."

"Then I guess we're done here."

Melissa handed the pack of papers back to me. "Take the contract. Look it over. Who knows, maybe you'll have second thoughts."

"I doubt it." I took the papers anyway.

"Never say never, Adam."

Funny how quickly an extremely attractive woman could turn into a coldhearted bitch in the blink of an eye.

I pegged Harry with a glare, nodding at him. Cutting through all their bullshit, there was only one thing on my mind that I wanted to accomplish while they were here being a pain in my ass. Well, one woman, actually. I couldn't rest until I righted the wrong we'd done to her. My conscience wouldn't allow it. "Need to talk to you a minute."

Harry eagerly followed me across the hall into the break room.

I shut the door behind me. "This morning we pulled over a doctor, a woman."

Harry's newly formed grin told me we were on the same page. His irritating eyebrow raises confirmed it. "That was some incredible footage. We scanned through it before we left the hotel."

I had to play this one smart. "That was a bad stop that should have never happened. I don't care if your boys got her to sign one of your waivers; something like that airs and it can bring a lot of heat down on the unit. It needs to disappear before I.A. gets involved. You got me?"

"I.A.?"

My mouth was running faster than my brain. "Internal Affairs. They start poking their nose around and it could get messy. Could compromise the staff and your show." I was lying through my teeth but he didn't know that. I needed some sort of leverage to get that footage canned and didn't have a leg to stand on. I had made her a promise.

Harry pushed his glasses up on his stubby nose. "I don't know, Adam. That was a sensational piece. The way you two took care of that accident scene... Viewers love that shit."

Not at her expense, they won't. I got right in his breathing space, holding back the burning urge to demonstrate how serious I was. I was never good at playing games. "Apparently I haven't made myself clear enough. It would be in your best interest to make sure it never sees the light of day."

Harry's smile faltered as he adjusted his necktie, taking a step back. "Are you... are you threatening me?"

Yes. "No, I'm making you a promise. I can be a real asshole on camera if I need to be. You got me?"

"But it's in your contract to comply with the requirements of your appearance."

I ran my hand back through my hair, making the motion to keep myself from putting Harry into the wall. "When I go out there and tell my team that you refuse to adjust their cuts, you think you'll get compliance then? We can play this out and see how good your ratings do. Don't matter to me."

He straightened. "We have a team of lawyers, Adam. Don't know if you want to play that card. That would be a breach of contract for sixteen men."

Damn it, he was grinding on my last nerve. I sure as hell didn't want to get sued. I was all out of plays, but I couldn't let my actions take another innocent person down. I held my breath a moment before committing my next huge mistake. "You shelve that footage and I'll consider meeting her additional demands."

"You'll consider?" he said with an air of annoyed arrogance. "I'll need more assurance than that."

I considered wringing his fat neck. I think he sensed it too, taking another half step backwards. Why I even gave a shit about some random girl plaguing my thoughts was enough to piss me off. Still, that random girl with killer blue eyes, sexy mouth, and fire in her veins that was roaming around in my head was enough to keep me from making other mistakes— ones that would be far more detrimental to my health. Maybe I owed her one. I made my final decision right then. "You meet my demands and I'll meet yours."

"You will?"

I nodded, hating this predicament. "But my team... You see about giving that extra cash to all of them instead of me and you'll get my compliance. But *all* of the footage of the blonde doctor has to disappear— completely."

Harry's eyes narrowed. "One hundred percent compliance? No arguments or making things... difficult?"

I nodded again, feeling as though I was making a deal with the devil.

Harry seemed to mull that over before finally giving in with a nod and an extended hand to shake. "Okay, fine. Fine. I'll see what I can do."

"'I'll see what I can do is not enough." Not for Erin. *Shit.* "Not one hair of hers gets aired." I didn't want him to get any shady ideas. I didn't trust him at all, but my options were limited. "I want that in writing."

Harry nodded, which was enough for me. I was halfway down the hall when my captain barked out my name. I waited, reluctantly.

Cap just eyed me for a few seconds, nodded his chin with that fatherly silence, and gave me a meaningful pat on the shoulder. Enough said.

I heard Brian Sidell's big mouth echoing down the hall, already making plans to win tonight's betting pool, which instantly ticked me off again. He used to be one hell of a great friend before we started this nonsense with the production company filming us. Then things changed, and not for the better.

As soon as he came through the door, grinning like a choirboy who just got his first peek up a girl's skirt, I wanted to shoot him. He was carrying not one but two United States Postal Service mail bins.

Unfuckingbelievable.

Hill, too? And Ramirez?

Two, four, nine, ten, eleven. No way. No fucking way.

I watched each of the men that made up the Philadelphia Auto Theft Task Force carry in mail bin after mail bin filled with fan mail. Why the hell women all over the country were writing to us was beyond rational comprehension.

Sidell dropped his bins on the long table by the wall. "Clear the tables, ladies. Trent's got a monumental haul today."

I took a deep breath to control my anger.

Sidell waggled his eyebrows and gave me a few hard slaps on the shoulder. "Cheer up, Trent. Don't look so glum. You don't want to wrinkle that pretty face of yours. Your legions of fans would cry."

I growled, reining in my desire to beat the shit out of him. Instead of spending his time trying to figure out how he fucked up the stop last night allowing that Nissan to slip out onto the Schuylkill Expressway, he was strutting around without a care in the world, letting petty shit fill the void.

Sidell's rig was right there, in position. He should have rammed the vehicle and stopped it. We were all within range and ready to intercept, but instead we all watched as the car slid right on by.

Another mail bin was dropped onto a desk. This was the beginning of a half-hour's worth of complete torture, with me as the star whipping boy. I might as well climb up on the cross now and take it like a man for what they would dish out on me. And adding to that annoyance was Brian Sidell's cheerful demeanor. I was just about ready to explode.

"Marcus has one more," Captain Paul "Cap" Woods said, slugging another bin on the table.

Not you too, Marcus. His six-foot-eight-inch frame dwarfed the mail bin in his hands, making me feel short at six one. My best friend looked like the black man's version of the Grim Reaper, with a wide jaw and a death stare spooky enough to scare the piss out of most felons. His hands alone were like catcher's mitts, capable of palming a suspect's head like a basketball but also able to hold his ten-month-old baby daughter as if she were a tiny, precious jewel. One of those mitts snagged my copy of the hot sheet.

"Here we go," Marcus muttered as he slid into the chair next to me, seeming just as tired of the game as I was.

Brian wasn't wasting any time. He dove into the bin that contained several boxes and larger manila envelopes, fishing around as if he were mixing them up. He grabbed one and sniffed it. "This one smells like gash stink. Must be more wet panties for Trent." His exaggerated facial expressions were beyond irritating.

It was all a joke—being on television every Sunday night, the false notoriety, the unwanted attention, the lack of focus—everything.

"Cap, boys need something better to do with their time. This has to stop," I groaned, feigning a stretch. At first it was fun. We all got a kick out of opening up the few packages and letters that were addressed to me and the rest of the task force, seeing the slutty array of bras, underwear, and the group's favorite—naked pictures of all sorts of fangirls. But now the shit was getting old.

"Oooh, I wonder what's in this one, Trent," Brian Sidell teased, squeezing a manila padded envelope. "Got your fucking name on it too, just like the rest. You don't mind me opening it? Chick even drew hearts on it. Must be fucking love."

If Sidell only knew how accurately I had fired today at the range, making every shot a center mass kill shot, maybe he'd shut his big, fat yap. I hoped our captain was smart enough to realize this shit was creating animosity within the team that was getting close to becoming irreparable.

An hour ago, I was calm, content even despite finding a few fans waiting outside my house. Since restful sleep was disrupted by the usual nightmares, I'd gone to the gym and had a good workout, even managing to bench press twenty pounds over my last weight. That alone made my day. Forty-five minutes running on the treadmill, an hour at the gun range, and ten minutes listening to my mom rejoicing about her long-distance phone call from my brother Jason, life was normal.

Sidell grabbed another large mailer with a noticeable bulge in the middle, holding it up for all to see. "Okay boys, here's our 'what did Trent get in the mail this time?' entry."

Bastard sniffed both sides of it like a damn bloodhound. "Victoria's Secret. One of those sexy demi-bra things where their luscious nippies peek out the top. Lace. Black. Size thirty-six C. Write that down, Westfield. That's my guess. Here's my ten bucks." He kissed the package. "Don't let me down, babe. My kid needs dental work soon."

Officer Nate Westfield chuckled and then wrote Sidell's answer on the dry erase board—the very same board where we should be discussing tactical maneuvers for blocking the stolen vehicles we chased every night instead of this nonsense.

The muscle along my jaw tightened as the urge to reach for my gun and end this misery made the palm of my hand itch. This constant needling from certain members of my team had surpassed annoying weeks ago. Now it was getting unbearable with no ending in sight. Fuckers were ripping into packages like it was Christmas.

Jesse Ramirez was on me as soon as he walked into our bullpen, grabbing the empty chair next to me and flipping it around to straddle it. "Hey Adam, don't mean to be a pain in your ass, but Ellie wants to know if you're coming or not. We need to give the caterer a final head count."

I didn't know how to tell him I avoided weddings like the plague, especially when the bride-to-be hated my guts now that I'd ended my relationship with Nikki. Still, Jesse and I'd been friends for years.

"You're the only one in the unit who hasn't sent back their thing," Jesse continued.

That's because the frilly invite was still sitting on my kitchen table, reminding me of my failures. I squinted up at him. "Next month, right?"

Guy looked partially gut-punched with anticipation. "Yep. Saturday, two o'clock. You can't miss my wedding, bro. I need to know you're coming."

For a moment, I sort of envied him. He was part of the crew for a long time, a friend from day one, and I respected the hell out of him. "Yeah, man, of course I'll be there. Wouldn't miss it."

Jesse looked relieved. "Cool. One or two?"

"What?" I know I just heard him say it was at two o'clock.

Ramirez used his fingers to count. "One or two? You bringing somebody or you coming alone, 'cause you know Ellie's friends with Nikki and, well, she's invited."

Marcus groaned and glared over at him. "Damn fool. Now why you had to go bringing that sore shit up? Huh?"

Ramirez put his hands up. "Hey, just providing intel, that's all. You could always hook up with Ellie's friend Joanna. She's one of the bridesmaids. You met her at the picnic, remember? Long brown hair... The one with the huge—"

I stopped him before he finished that thought. "Two." I'd end up coming alone and leaving right after the dinner but there was no need to have anyone's expectations brewing for the next few weeks. I'd just pad his envelope with extra cash for the wasted meal.

Ramirez raised a surprised brow. "You thinking about getting back with Nikki then or...?"

Was he out of his fucking mind?

He backed down like a smart son of a bitch. "Okay, two it is."

Marcus met my gaze for a second before shaking his head and chuckling. Even in silence, I knew he had my back.

I just hoped Marcus didn't tell his wife about my little fib because Cherise would grill me for answers, seeing as I didn't do the dating thing much anymore. Bringing a date to a wedding was inviting trouble. But Marcus and I had no secrets. His wife and I, even less. I trusted them both with my life.

"Bets? Bets? You in?" Sidell was going around the room, making sure everyone got their ante in. He knew better than to ask me.

Ballsy asshole stopped in front of us anyway. "Marcus, you in?"

I gave Marcus a little chin nod when I caught his glance out of the corner of my eye—my silent approval for him to do his thing. He'd won two of them already, adding a few hundred to my goddaughter's savings account, but he respected me enough to make sure I was in decent headspace before joining the pool. Despite my loathing of this weekly ritual, I'd even go so far as loaning him ten bucks if it meant more might follow it into Sadie's college fund.

Marcus appeared torn—partially disgusted and partially desiring to stuff another wad of cash in his pocket. "Let me see the package first."

You could tell by the shape of the envelope that it contained a bra with those preformed cups. Fucking deceiving devices meant for men to fall victim from false tit sizes, they were.

"It's a bra," I muttered.

Marcus pegged me with a "thanks Captain Obvious" glare. He palmed it like he was squeezing a boob.

"C?" he questioned privately, apparently wanting confirmation.

With a quick flick of my fingers, he handed it over. I gave it a quick feel, measuring how it filled my hand. "D. Thirty-six."

"Color?"

I shrugged, noting it was February thirteenth today. "Red."

MARCUS MOTIONED FOR the keys to our rig—the black Suburban. It had great heated leather seats that cut the cold right out of the February chill. "I'm driving."

I tossed the set and smiled to myself, knowing how much he hated working the onboard computer system. I slid into the passenger seat. "You know, it's okay to admit you need reading glasses, old man."

Marcus gave me his death glare. "Watch your mouth, Trent. I only got you by three years."

I clicked my seatbelt, smiling while ignoring his exaggerated annoyance. "Yeah, but you're still closer to forty."

"Boy, are you looking to upset me? We just took a hundred and thirty off them assholes, so let me enjoy my moment. And I was going to buy you dinner, too."

Fucking guy made me laugh. "That's mighty kind of you."

"Just call me Mister Generosity. So tell me… how the fuck you know it was red?"

I shrugged. "It's a gift."

"Fucking-A right, it's a gift. You need to play the damn Lotto is what you need to do with how much tit you've palmed."

I grinned to myself, briefly, before the other dirt clogged my thoughts. Getting a willing woman underneath me was never a problem, but the last few months I'd been on a self-induced hiatus. I needed to get my shit together, as getting drunk and trying to fuck the last one out of my system wasn't working. And ever since we started filming, enamored girls making a goal to fuck the cop from TV turned from easy pickings to a huge turn-off.

Somewhere over the course of the rolling seasons what used to be cute and attractive became extremely annoying. *Everything* had become extremely annoying. "You gonna turn the heat up, or do I need to freeze my nuts off over here?"

He leered at me. "Damn, boy. You are worse than my wife."

I buckled my seatbelt. "Speaking of which, you'd better stop by the store for a gift for Cherise before you take your mangy ass home tonight."

I turned on our equipment, getting myself situated while Ritchie, my cameraman shadow, climbed into the back seat with his gear.

"Hey guys," Ritchie mumbled, rubbing his cold hands together. "Damn, it's a cold one tonight."

Scott climbed in on the other side, grumbling at Ritchie to move his shit.

Marcus glared over at me, ignoring them like we usually do, and drove out of the back lot. "What the fuck I need a gift for?"

"Tomorrow's Valentine's Day, butthead." I jerked forward when he crushed the brake.

"No shit?"

I started typing in the plate of the car that just passed by, driving a bit too fast. "And this is why your wife's legs are closed for business."

Marcus grit his teeth at me, motioning with his eyes for me to shut it while Ritchie was filming from the back seat. We even had extra mini cameras mounted in the front by the doors to catch every moment.

"Ritchie…" I snapped.

I heard him sigh. "I know, I know. If that airs, you will skin me alive and piss on my carcass. I got it."

Marcus and I both said "yep" in unison.

After twenty minutes of driving and scanning random license plates, Marcus broke the silence, muttering, "See your feisty little doc lately?"

I knew he was just jacking me up about following her home this morning. Still, I was thankful that I had a fresh image of her face to think about rather than the repercussions of our monumental fuck-up losing that stolen Nissan. I shook my head once, trying not to think about it.

Marcus raised a skeptical eyebrow at me, calling me out on my shit.

"Car was still in the driveway," I muttered, conceding only so far. Okay, so I drove past her place on my way to work tonight. It wasn't really out of my way, considering she lives in the same town. But admitting I went in a big loop to get to the station was all he was going to get out of me.

Smug prick blinded me with his big, white teeth, grinning because he knew me so well. It was in my nature to check up on things; I couldn't help it. I wasn't some sick stalker, not like the chick who tagged my windshield wiper with a semi-naked photo of herself and a phone number the other day.

"Robin in the hood," he drawled, jacking me up again. "Defending the helpless maidens. Well, it's a step. 'Bout time you quit lickin' your wounds and get back on your damn horse."

And that was Marcus's version of a pep talk. Something told me that that little doc was the opposite of helpless, but it was that *something*, that unknown pull that had me driving down her street, making me itch to know if she was at home, if she was safe.

Whatever that something was also had me palming myself in the shower earlier, too. Every time I thought about her I got hard. Out of sheer pain and a desire for some restful sleep, I couldn't take it anymore. I had to relieve myself.

The dash unit chimed, alerting us to a call, which thankfully caused the blood flow that was headed to my crotch again to revert back to my brain. Dispatch informed us we had a carjacking where a male suspect took the car at knifepoint. After coordinating with the other units, it was time to do my bit for the annoying camera behind me.

The rush of adrenaline kicked in when Marcus punched the gas pedal. This was the best part—the hunt—that secret thrill when the predators outwit the prey. We tracked them like a pack of hungry wolves, sneaking down different paths in the city to head off our intended mark.

I was manning the com unit while narrating our actions for the camera. "Okay, what we're going to do is spread out a bit. Since this is a felony vehicle, we want to close in on it as quickly as possible. Our rules of engagement are changed whenever there is a gun or another weapon involved. Safety for civilians and for the team is our priority." I scanned the streets while Marcus maneuvered us through town.

"We've got to be right on top of him," Marcus muttered, eyeing cross traffic.

"Black Beemer, where are you?" Just like that, the car passed in front of us.

"Go, go." I grabbed my com. "Romeo Seven to control. We have suspect vehicle northbound on Twentieth. Looks like two onboard, repeat, two heads onboard." We followed, staying undetected by our mark while getting coordinated with the current positions of the rest of our team. My heart was strumming. A regular patrol unit crossed at the next intersection, causing our suspects to panic. The BMW took off, driving into a more residential section where the rundown units and tightly packed row homes made one hell of a maze.

The driver gunned it down the street, headed for an open spot on the sidewalk, and both driver and passenger were out of the car while it was still rolling.

"Bail out, bail out!" Marcus called out to the team. I was out of the truck, running before he'd fully stopped.

Two other units and local PD were on one of the suspects while I foot pursued the driver. My heart was hammering; fucker was fast. Young black kid disappeared into the shadows of the night between the houses. He vaulted over a chain-link fence and I followed, getting tangled up in someone's backyard shit pile.

Kid hefted over another fence, only ahead of me by maybe thirty feet. I climbed up over the fence and landed hard on something sharp, slick, and very unforgiving. White-hot searing pain sliced into my left palm, like a paper cut amplified with acid coated razorblades. I bit back a curse and tried to recover as quickly as possible, calling in my location while still pursuing the kid. No way in hell I was gonna let him get away. I could see Sidell running parallel; we had the little shit cornered.

The kid running slipped and faltered over some junk in the next yard, giving me a chance to get up on him. I snagged his jacket and tackled him, ignoring that my other hand had a pulse of its own.

Within seconds, I had him flush to the ground. I blew out a few gusts, trying to catch my breath while Officer Nate Westfield pinned him with a knee. Sidell holstered his weapon and relieved me to cuff the kid.

Ritchie caught up to us while the other two camera guys, Raj and another guy we nicknamed Squirrel, filmed the scene. My hand was wet and burning. Once Ritchie pointed his camera at it, that's when I saw how deep it was. Fuck it hurt. The blood gushing out of it made it look even worse.

"What the hell happened to you?" Marcus asked, blocking the camera's view.

A few of the guys crowded around, shining their flashlights on me.

"Good question."

"Damn, Adam. That shit looks bad," Marcus said. "What did you get tagged on?"

I pointed my flashlight in the direction I'd just come from, trying to figure that out. "Think I put my hand through an old window. I heard glass break."

Marcus walked with me while I backtracked, sweeping my flashlight to see just what the hell it was that I'd landed on while silently cursing myself for not wearing gloves. Getting injured in the field was not good. It meant that I'd have a boatload of paperwork to fill out, not to mention playing *twenty questions* with my superiors.

"Ambulance is on the way," Westfield said as he stopped to inspect my bloody hand again.

"Ambulance? You're kidding me."

"You know the rules. Blood like that gets spilled, you don't sit in the waiting room waiting."

I tried to walk it off, but no matter where I went, Ritchie and his damn camera followed me.

CHAPTER 5

Erin

IT WAS ABOUT eleven thirty p.m. when Sarah met up with me in the small break room outside of the ER. I had been sitting in there by myself for all of three minutes, staring at the sterile white walls, feeling as though the small, square room was closing in on me, when Sarah's cute pregnant lady waddle broke the solitude.

It had been the first time I'd sat down in five hours, having been on my feet and on the run since my boss went home.

I watched her retrieve her lunch from the refrigerator, grumbling about the disgusting contents inside, thankful for the mental reprieve her presence provided.

I pulled a shiny green apple out of my lunch bag and stared at it, trying to will myself to be interested.

I was hungry, well, at least my grumbling empty stomach was trying to tell me I was, but after spending a half hour up in ICU watching the life support equipment breathe for my Uncle Cal while my mother sobbed, nothing sounded appealing. My mind was still reeling—flashing between emotional overload and detached medical scrutiny—while years of medical terminology and clinical training bombarded the in-between.

I had tried to take a nap in our resident on-call room while I waited out Doctor Wilson leaving for the night, but images of the ER being swamped and me not being in there to do my part made sleep seem like a guilty pleasure.

Every time I closed my eyes, violent snippets of red and blue lights from this morning's traumatic scene swirled around the mental snapshot of my critically injured uncle. Visions of Officer Trent also fought for mental space.

Despite the fact that he had me in handcuffs at one point, he and his entire sexy package were stuck in my mind in vivid color.

Sarah scraped the chair across the tiled floor before settling in, appearing quite excited about something. "Hey, guess what?"

I twisted the stem on my untouched apple, waiting—knowing Sarah would keep talking whether I answered her or not.

She tugged her scrub top down over her baby belly and unzipped her lunch bag. "Vicky just told me that she overheard Randy and the evil troll fighting outside the X-ray room and apparently it was pretty heated." She bit into her sandwich. "Maybe he's finally realizing what a huge mistake he made."

And just like that, the man who had dominated most of my spare mental space came tap-dancing back through my thoughts. Was that an inkling of hope that just fluttered through me? *Damn it. Why do I do this shit to myself?* I opted for bland indifference, knowing exactly why he dumped me. "I don't think so."

"What? That's it? I thought you'd be thrilled." She actually looked surprised.

Oh God, I so didn't want to get into this conversation but I knew she was doing her best to give me something else to think about. "Come on, Sarah. Randy and I… Look, it's *over*. It's *been* over for a very long time. You know that. I'm over it. Please, let it drop."

Sarah rolled her eyes. "You're so full of shit."

I felt my shoulders slump and the beginnings of another headache forming. "What do you want me to say? Please don't do this to me right now."

"I'm sorry," she muttered contritely. "I shouldn't have brought it up."

I thought Sarah had resigned the topic until she tossed out, "Shame. He's got such a nice ass. Too bad he is one."

Great. Now I'm forced to think about my ex's ass. It was a very fine ass, indeed— especially bare and cupped in my hands when he ground his hips into me. Not stellar like Officer Trent's spectacular black cargo pants ass, but still not a bad ass. Bad ass. I snorted at my own joke. Randy and the good-looking detective were on opposite ends of the bad-ass spectrum, that was for sure.

"What's so funny?" she asked, even though she was smiling, too.

I decided to keep that one to myself.

Sarah bit into her sandwich again, and chewed while eyeing me over. She gave my shoulder a quick rub. "Sweetie, you look so wiped. Are you sure you want to stay here all night?"

I nodded. The trauma here would be far better than the trauma from me being left with free time to dwell on things.

"I thought you would have headed out with your parents, or are they still up in ICU?"

I shook my head, stifled a yawn, and picked at my untouched chicken salad. "No, they left an hour ago. I can't sit and watch my mom cry anymore and I'm sure that's all she's doing right now. She's taking my Aunt Karen's death very hard. If she loses her brother, well, I don't know if she'll be able to deal."

Sarah wiped her mouth then gave me a sympathetic smile. "Why don't you just go home and get some sleep? Maybe we can get someone from Security to drive you home. You won't get any rest curling up on that crappy bed in the on-call room."

I had thought about going home several times, but having the distraction of being at the hospital was a much better option. "Nah, that's okay. I'm good. Besides, Doctor Wilson left and there's no way I'd leave trauma short a doctor tonight, despite his orders. It's been a non-stop madhouse with no signs of slowing down."

Sarah stared at me while she continued to chew. "Ballsy. He's going to be pissed; you know that."

Whatever. "Better to ask for forgiveness than approval? Who knows, maybe we'll get a kid with a toy crammed in his ear tonight and then my services will be totally justified."

Sarah laughed. "One can only hope, but it's pretty late for kids to be cramming stuff in their ears. I can't believe they reduced overnight pediatric trauma coverage. Whoever made that decision needs their head examined. As if we aren't understaffed as it is."

Thankfully life in the adult ER never stood still. I kept a low profile just in case video footage of my debacle snuck out into the world without me knowing. I didn't sign their stupid waiver, but no sense drawing extra attention. I was mastering the art of blending into the scenery while taking care of patients.

That was until Randy came out of exam room four, nearly running me over in the hallway. He sideswiped my arm. "Whoa, sorry."

I stepped around him, giving him a wide berth. Secretly pining for him as the "one that got away" was a waste of time.

"Hey, Erin?"

I skidded to a stop, squeaking the floor with my sneakers. "Yeah?" Hope actually surged its way in for a moment. I beat it down before it had a chance to get ridiculous.

He took a few steps until he was close enough to gently stroke my shoulder, sending all sorts of mixed messages into my befuddled brain. "Listen, I know things have been rough between us but I'm serious. If there's anything you need, don't be afraid to ask, okay? I can cover a few shifts for you, whatever. Whatever you need."

What? He chose *this* moment to be nice? After I spent all that time wishing, crying, hoping he'd just show an ounce of care for me when we were dating, he decides *now* to play the thoughtful card? *Yeah, you know what I need? How about you spontaneously combust or get run over by a beer truck for breaking my heart? Or how about you break up with your evil troll girlfriend, plead at my feet, telling me what a stupid asshole you've been, and then beg me to take you back? Or simply be the kind of man I could wake up next to who would just hold me and let me cry it out instead of being a spineless, chickenshit bastard?*

Instead, I just nodded, trying not to break down in tears and/or throat punch him. I didn't go to medical school and endure four years of grueling residency to cry over death or heartbreaking co-workers with nice asses. I had more important reasons.

"Thanks," I muttered, taking a step backwards, my silent statement that his hands were no longer free to roam over any part of my body.

His concern seemed awfully touchy-feely. "If you need to take a few days, do it. Your family needs you. Forget about this place and go relax, okay?"

I felt my words stick like a wad of gum in my throat, knowing Randy was not only my tormenting heartache, he was also my competition. "You and I both know that's impossible."

Randy scowled at me. "That's your problem. You always make things more difficult than they need to be, Erin."

I knew my mouth was agape when I watched him walk backwards

while giving me the "that's the way it is" look.

You son of a...

Of course it was *me* that was the difficult, confused one in this equation. Silly me for thinking that months and months of sex and sleepovers and leaving his stuff all over my apartment constituted a relationship when the entire time I was nothing more than a casual fuck buddy to him.

God, he was so aggravating. The urge to clock him with an IV pole was powerful. I balled my hands into fists instead, holding back my daily desire to scream and throw a mini tantrum every time our paths crossed. It would do me no good to lose it. I'd spent enough time sobbing in my pillow, being angry, feeling inadequate, and overanalyzing every moment we had spent together trying to figure out where I went wrong. Where *we* went wrong. He wasn't worth it.

Familiar tones chimed through the air, pulling me from my inner turmoil to focus back on an incoming ambulance.

"We've got an injured police officer en route," Todd, one of our male nurses, announced after fielding the emergency call.

"Male, age thirty-two, single laceration to the left palm, BP one thirty over eighty, ETA seven minutes," he continued, feeding the information to Sarah to input into our computer system.

My heart sank hearing that we had another injured cop coming in. That would be four total in the last five weeks and one of them we lost on the table from a gunshot wound.

Damn, not another one of the good guys.

Somewhere over the years of my residency in the trauma unit I unconsciously started placing patients into two mental categories: those who deserved a trip to the ER and those who most certainly did not.

Junkies, drunk drivers, gang-bangers—when they passed through those double doors, a victim of their own stupidity, I had a hard time feeling sorry for them, even though it was my job to save their lives. Car accidents, injured cops, and most everyone else got placed in the victim of circumstance box.

And now another one of Philly's finest was joining the good-guy box. Apparently our incoming police officer got the shitty end of something tonight.

"Erin, take the trauma consult," Doctor Miriam Vonore droned at me, her maroon-framed reading glasses hanging off the edge of her narrow nose as always. I knew she didn't like me; that much was obvious ever since I started my residency and Randy and I started flirting. She was always too busy wantonly smiling at her little pet Randy and scowling at me to be a decent mentor. I was a cheap little trollop in her eyes—something she made sure to punctuate whenever she could.

She was shorter than I was, with thinning dirty-blonde hair cut in a bob. As if a slightly rounded fifty-two-year-old divorcee had a chance with a young hottie like Randy.

The second Miriam was out of earshot, Sarah was up to no good. "Erin, take the trauma consult," she parroted, mimicking Miriam's nasally tones flawlessly.

I couldn't help but snicker, feeling internally grateful for a moment of humor. "One of these days she's going to catch you doing that," I chastised her quietly, making sure not to be overheard.

Sarah grinned madly at me and swiped a loose lock of her dark brown hair over her ear. "Ah, who cares? Your incoming goes in exam room six."

Todd handed over a file as he hurried by. "Your incoming?"

I nodded, putting all the bullshit behind me once again.

"Patient is alert and stable. Bleeding is controlled with pressure dressing and ice," Todd continued.

I took my pen out, stifled another yawn, and noted the time in the file: 11:47 p.m.

Sarah peered up from her computer. "Lab results on your patient in nine are up."

Finally. My current patient, a sixty-eight-year-old woman who came in complaining of hip pain after sustaining an in-home fall, was getting antsy. I entered my password into one of the terminals along the main corridor and checked the status of an open bed upstairs, avoiding the flickering lights from the arriving ambulance.

Just as the two EMTs wheeled the patient through the double doors and down the main chute, shouts and obscenities started flying. It was so loud I couldn't tell who was shouting at whom. I peered down the hall, instantly infuriated that a damn camera crew had stormed in right behind them.

Either something monumentally horrendous had happened in the outside world or the local news channels were sinking to a new low:

chasing ambulances. It was bad enough they were all over me when I got pulled over this morning, but now this?

One of the EMTs tried to stop the cameraman from entering through the restricted entrance but the news crew was already upon the patient, invading his rights. Carl Tanners, one of our onsite security officers, came running so I followed him.

I turned to one of the interns loitering nearby. "Call for additional security. Now."

I pinned the shorter blond male accompanying the cameraman with my angriest glare. Strange, they both looked familiar—especially the short one in the ball cap. And then the shock registered, casting that nervous warmth throughout my skin.

As soon as I saw the face of the patient on the cot, everything dimmed. Firm lips, gorgeous face, incredible eyes staring back at me...

Officer Trent, I think I breathed, though my mouth surely moved.

"You," he said, just as breathily. He appeared just as surprised by our unexpected reunion as I was.

"Turn that camera off right now! You cannot be in here," Carl yelled, trying to bring chaos to order. "Shut it down."

The fact that Adam had been injured snapped me back into the urgency of the moment. His left hand was bandaged like a catcher's mitt.

He tried to move but was strapped down to the transport cot. "Christ, Ritchie. We're in a hospital. Give me a break."

As soon as we locked gazes again, something inexplicable came over me. It was instant and alarming—a potent mix of protectiveness and familiar ownership.

The blond guy removed one headphone from his ear. "Sorry, Adam. We're instructed to keep filming. You know it's in your contract."

These men were irritating. He'd been hurt and I needed to get his care underway. "He goes into exam room six." I pointed, needing the EMTs to wheel him away.

Two men dressed identical to Adam joined in the fray with our hospital security, but the camera crew kept on insisting they had the right to keep filming.

I was astonished and angered by their blatant disregard for hospital policy. "You two—what TV station are you with?" I blocked their view of Adam when they ignored my question. "I cannot believe you would have the audacity to film an injured police officer or any patient for that matter in my hospital."

The cameraman that answered to the name Ritchie took a step back, then returned to squinting his eye in the viewer of his camera. He looked to be in his mid twenties, lanky as hell, unkempt brown hair, wearing skinny jeans and an olive green winter parka.

His partner, the shorter blond guy, moved his headset away from one ear. "We have full clearance to keep filming him, *wherever* he goes."

"Hey!" Ritchie pulled his face away from the camera. "You're that woman that we—"

"Ritchie!" Adam bellowed from down the hall, pegging him with an "I'll kill you if you finish that sentence" glare while being wheeled away.

"Henry says we're supposed to keep rolling," the short blond guy said.

"I don't think so." The hall was filling with onlookers. I reached for the camera to push it away. "You are violating patient rights."

I felt his presence right before I felt his hand cross my stomach. One very pissed off cop slid me out of the way.

"Turn that fucking thing off, *now*," Adam commanded.

Behind them, a huge wall of intimidating black man dressed head to toe in black police attire strolled in. I instantly recognized him too.

"You two assholes are done here." He palmed both of the camera crew by their shoulders and spun them, hauling them toward the ambulance bay doors.

I stepped up to Adam's side, knowing I had to calm him down and get him back into his room. Stress was making things worse. "Officer—"

"Detective," he corrected, pinning me with those fierce eyes again.

"Detective," I repeated, hoping he'd concentrate on me instead of the craziness. My years of dealing with the anxiety that accompanies medical emergencies kicked in. "Let's get you squared away." I hoped the quiver in my throat didn't come out with my words, as it was hard to hide my nervousness.

Adam sat onto the hospital bed. "Sorry, Doc."

I doubted Detective Hottie, with his spiky, short brown hair, perfectly aligned jaw, and wide shoulders ever allowed a moment of weakness show through. Still, I had to reassure him. "It's okay. Let's see what we're working with."

Sarah, who, after getting an eyeful of my current patient, volunteered to be my triage nurse. She nudged Sherry out of the way and commandeered her portable computer.

I pulled on a fresh pair of gloves.

"I told them I was fine. It's just a cut. I don't need all of this. Some gauze and a few Band-Aids will fix it."

I snipped through the pressure packing on his hand to reveal one hell of a deep gash. "You're going to need stitches, Detective. A simple Band-Aid isn't going to fix this."

He stared me down for what felt like an eternity. Damn those dark eyes were gorgeous. "That bad, huh?"

"Unfortunately, yes."

He tried to stifle his curse. "Do what you need to do then, Doc." He rested back on the bed with a bit of defeat. "Sorry, I didn't mean to grab you like that out there."

"It's okay." I hated that Sarah was monitoring our word exchange as if she were taking notes. "Thanks for making the camera guys go away."

His eyes fixed on mine. "I owed you that. Look, I'm really sorry about last ni—"

I shook my head for him to stop and almost lunged to cover his mouth. Fortunately, he halted mid sentence.

"Excuse me, sir. We need to get you logged in. Name?" Sarah interrupted, her voice dripping with sweetness. Had I not known she was already married, I would have said she was attempting to flirt with him.

"Adam…" He cleared his throat. When I looked up at his face, he was watching me intently. "Adam Trent."

Sarah tapped a few keys. "Date of birth?"

My mind registered him saying, "July twenty-fourth." The year caused me to do quick math.

Damn… thirty-two-years-old. Perfect age where he might consider settling down with one woman, if he wasn't already.

I tossed some of his bloodied wrapping into the biohazard bin. *Why can't I ever meet guys like this?* There were a few single males floating around the building but the selection of good-looking ones that didn't have girlfriends *or* boyfriends was very slim. Todd, one of our male nurses, was cute but he was also very gay, and the newest selection of interns—well, let's just say that butterflies failed to fly in their presence. Trying to fish in the hospital pond was a lost cause.

I notice he had a formidable two-inch scar on his forearm. By the looks of it, this wasn't his first tangle with a sharp object.

"Mr. Trent, it appears you're a repeat customer," Sarah stated, confirming my suspicions.

Our eyes locked again as I lifted his wounded left hand, cradling it between my body and arm to reposition him.

He sucked in a quick breath and I immediately readjusted, worried that I'd hurt him somehow.

"Sorry, but I need to see how deep it is." I tried to be gentle. "I know it hurts."

Adam shook his head and flexed his fingers, almost brushing over my breast. "Burns a little. It's like a hell of a paper slice."

Typical man, trying to be tough. "Yeah, I can see that. How'd this happen?"

"Was chasing a runner. Followed him up over a fence and landed on a pile of old junk. Put my hand right through an old window and down over a piece of corrugated sheet metal. Happened so quick."

I hoped my prodding didn't hurt. "This is deep but nothing that a few sutures won't fix. Are you cut or injured anywhere else?"

His hand was caked with dried blood, but I couldn't help myself. I did a quick assessment of his fingers, searching for the telltale gold band or indentation that alerts all women to keep their distance.

No ring, thank God. Maybe there's hope for some single woman after all. Doesn't look like he wears a ring, either. The skin on his finger is smooth, unblemished, but that's not proof he's single. Surely he has a wife or at the very least, a steady girlfriend.

He probably has a kid with some girl that lets him visit every other weekend. Some long-legged bimbo he used to date. Yep. A man this fine—someone's surely claimed their rights to him by now. I bet his ex-wife and current girlfriend fight over him. I could probably beat a few of them if I had a stick. No, a baseball bat. God, listen to me. I'm ready to start beating down other women for this one. What the hell is wrong with me?

He let out a small growl. "No. Only my hand."

I had to recall my last question. *Oh, any other injuries…*

"And your current address?" Sarah's glance locked on mine briefly, confirming my guess that she was doing more than entering him into the hospital's system.

I was shocked to hear him say, "Drexel Hill."

"Doctor Novak, don't you live in Drexel Hill, too?" Sarah asked, but the sneaky bitch knew exactly where I lived. So did the wounded Adam Trent.

"Detective Trent," I started to say.

"Adam," he corrected me, tilting his head to silently say, "come on—we've already met once."

"Sir, has your family been notified that you've been injured?" I asked. As soon as the words left my mouth, I felt like a foolish ass. Sarah smirked while taking his blood pressure.

Is he staring at my chest?

"There's no one to notify," he said when he met my eyes again.

I nodded once, feeling extremely relieved for some reason.

I glanced outside his exam room, wondering where the other officers had wandered off to. "I presume you'll have someone to drive you home."

A little smirk warmed his face. "Not sure." His chin jutted up—so confident, almost challenging me. "You offering to give me a ride?"

Sarah's mouth fell open. So did mine but for different reasons. He knew I couldn't drive my car and he knew exactly why that was.

"No... I..." *Shit.*

"You what?"

Was he amused, riling me like this? His smile faltered. "Sorry. That was, ah. I suppose your boyfriend wouldn't approve of you getting teased like that."

I stood there, completely dumbfounded.

"Oh no, she's single," Sarah quickly clarified, tossing a big, fat elephant into the room with a simple flutter of her hand.

Is he grinning at that now? Great. As much as I'd like to lay someone this gorgeous out on a hospital bed and have the kind of spontaneous, wildly passionate sex you only see in smut movies, even casual flirting like this was breaching patient/doctor ethical code.

I had the overwhelming desire to flee. "I'll be right back so we can get to stitching you up."

A warm, meaty hand with very long fingers clasped firmly onto my wrist, halting me from taking another step. "Sorry, Doc. I was just joking, trying to lighten the mood. It's been a long night. One of my team members is waiting on me." Damn, those eyes were so repentant, like a young boy caught being naughty. I imagined they worked well on his mother. He waited until he received my unspoken acknowledgement before releasing his hold on me.

I grabbed Sarah's elbow when we got to the nurse's station. "What was that?"

"What was what? What are you so mad about?"

I pointed down the hall toward his room. "That, back there. Telling him where I live." She didn't know he already knew where I lived but regardless, I didn't want my busybody friends telling strangers my personal information.

"You're kidding, right? Have you not noticed the way he's been staring at you? He's been eyeballing you like a hungry lion since you got in his line of sight."

A split second evaluation of her observation led me to believe she was cracked in the head. "He has not."

She laughed at me. "He sure as hell has. You may not have noticed but I sure did. Hungry. Lion. He licked his lips every time he looked at you." She growled for emphasis. "I think he likes you."

"Shh. He does not. And stop smiling at me like that. Do you know how much trouble I can get into here, Sarah? Do you?"

She shrugged, peering past me toward his exam room. "He looks worth the trouble, Erin. Did you see those biceps? And those tribal tattoos? Damn. That extra large cuff barely fit around him."

His build was hard to miss. Intricate black ink tattoos, which resembled bands of braided rope, peeked out underneath the sleeves of his T-shirt. They wrapped around the thickest part of both of his arms, stopping at points at his elbows, adding to the whole sexy package.

"Yes, I noticed, all right? I'm not blind. Shoot." This was so dangerous, breaking so many ethical protocols.

"Why are you so upset? And what was up with that camera crew? That was weird. Why the heck were they filming him?"

I finished my notation in his chart and curled a stray hair back over my ear, knowing he was being filmed earlier in the day when we met, too. "I have no idea. Maybe cops are tired of getting sued or something."

My dear friend, Jen, rushed over to us, all flushed with excitement. "Oh my God! Did you see the gorgeous cop in room six? He looks so familiar."

My friends were incorrigible. "You ran all the way up here from the pharmacy to look at a patient?"

"He's Erin's," Sarah said, mirroring Jen's enthusiasm.

Jen fanned herself with some paperwork, tugging at the neckline of her scrub top. "I was called on a code. Dayum. You are so lucky. Is he single?"

Sarah draped her stethoscope around her neck. "He isn't wearing a ring."

Jen glanced back toward his room, her long black ponytail swished over her shoulder. "Oh, if I wasn't already married I'd be all over that. Wonder if Josh would let me date?"

Sarah nudged her elbow into Jen and then rubbed her baby belly. "I'm thinking the same thing, although he might not go for an instant family."

So much for professionalism. They were salivating over an injured patient. "Geez. Do you two even hear yourselves?"

Sherry bounced in between us, springing around just like Tigger. "Heard you have the gorgeous cop patient in six. I just walked past there to check him out. Did you see his arms? Man he's built. I bet he has a twelve pack going on." She ran her hand around her own stomach. "You need to cut his shirt off. I want to do a tequila shot off those abs."

Jen laughed. "And what? Break your tequila shot virginity?"

Sherry mockingly gaped at her. "For your information I am no longer a tequila shot virgin. Took care of that in Orlando just this past summer, don't you remember? Besides, guys who look like that are the very reason body shots were invented."

Sarah nodded profusely. "He's got these awesome tribal tattoos that wrap all the way around. Makes me wonder what else he's got tattooed, ya know?"

Sherry shrugged. "Get him to change into a gown and make him turn and cough." She flipped her multi-hued bangs back out of her eyes. "Or you can push some Versed in him and we can take turns cathing his penis. That sounds like fun. Jen quick. Run and get some."

Unbelievable! I glared at all of them. Had this been anyone else but the cop who almost arrested me I would have probably been privately laughing right along with them, but joking about sedating and groping him was not funny.

"What? He's freaking hot. You know we're just kidding. Go. Tend to his wounds," Sherry teased, shushing me away with her hand.

Unfortunately, I had to agree with her on that part.

When I reentered his exam room, I had a hypodermic needle loaded with Lidocaine on the small tray in my hand and my nerves wound extra tight, trying not to imagine his penis. "You ready?"

I heard the rustle of the hospital bed behind me, presuming he was looking forward to receiving stitches as much as he would be getting a tooth pulled. "I'm as ready as I'll ever be, Doc."

I wished I could say the same, though his words seemed to be a double entendre. I fumbled with the prep tray, stalling.

"Erin, look at me." His voice brooked no other choice.

As soon as I did, he smiled gently and said, "How've you been? Everything okay?"

I glanced over my shoulder to ensure we were alone. Everything was not okay, but I didn't know him well enough to discuss it. I'd been emotionally twisted over everything that had happened in the last twenty-four hours and was barely hanging by a thread.

Instead, I nodded and shrugged, doing my best to appear convincing and professionally detached. "Just surprised to see you again."

"Me too." A small dimple appeared on his cheek. "I thought maybe you were still mad at me."

Yeah, no… maybe. I hoped no one was within earshot. "I just don't want to have to explain anything to them," I whispered. "But I don't think anyone here knows what happened… how we, um, met. I looked all over the local news sites earlier, but I didn't see anything."

"And you won't," he stressed.

I wished I could believe that.

"Hey, you have to trust me. I made you a promise, okay? Nothing is going to come back on you. Your job is safe here."

"I've worked so hard…" Adam's sincerity tugged at my heart. "Are you sure?"

He sighed. "Come here."

I twitched at his request and melted a bit under his commanding gaze. When I hesitated, he held out his hand. Instant attraction pulled me right to him.

Adam placed his good hand over mine, sending his warmth right through my chilled skin.

"Cold hands," he murmured.

I gulped. "Warm heart, though." I felt a million tiny impulses when he slipped his fingers around mine, as if he had every right to take possession of me. And man, did my body want him to take possession. His simple gesture seemed so natural and completely foreign and totally comforting all at the same time, making me feel dizzy and incredibly lonely.

He pegged me with those amazing eyes. "I never go back on my word. *Ever.* If I tell you that you're good, you're good. Okay?"

My spine stiffened just a bit at his direct order not to doubt him. A small "okay" came out of me, feeling it in my gut that even though I didn't know him I could trust him.

"Okay," he breathed.

"I need... I need to examine you now."

Adam glanced at our entwined hands, brushing his thumb over my skin before relinquishing his hold. A hint of a smile appeared.

The cut had fragments of dirt and debris within. "This looks like it hurt."

He grunted a little at that. "It did."

That deep rumble in his chest was sexy as hell. "I need to give you a local. I'll numb this up, we'll irrigate it, and then I'll stitch you up, okay?"

"Am I going to live?" Again with the sexy smirk and innocent eyes.

"Probably. But the medical bill afterward might kill you. This might burn a little at first."

I wondered how many panties he'd separated from women with that wicked grin. "Then do what you have to, Doc."

Adam's fingers toyed with my hospital identification badge hanging off my breast pocket. "Doctor Erin Novak," he said with husky exhaustion, ignoring the needle. "Good stick, by the way."

"Thanks. I'm trying to be gentle."

"You did real good."

"I actually stuck you more than once."

His nose wrinkled a little. "I know. I felt it. Thanks for not jabbing me."

Before I could stop it from happening, I winked at him. "You're welcome. We'll give that a few minutes to numb you. Your tetanus shot is still current, so you'll only get one needle stuck in you tonight."

"Lucky me," he grumbled.

One of our new interns slid her perky ass into his room. Megan was still fresh; she hadn't been at this long enough to have the spark squashed out of her enthusiasm. "Doctor Novak, do you need help?"

Megan would have been more convincing if she'd actually been looking at *me* when she asked that question. I was just about to tell her "no" to make her just go away when she said, "Doctor Vonore told me I'm to assist with the suturing."

Of course Miriam would remind this one to come bug me; she always paired me up with the lazy ones. This Megan girl had no desire to be in emergency medicine, letting it be known to all who would listen she'll be happy once this rotation was over with. I sighed; after all, it was part of my job to mentor the new interns no matter how long we had them.

"Okay," I said, resigning to having no other choice but to turn my cop over to the new girl.

My cop.

Some sort of possessiveness was taking over. I really didn't want anyone else touching him, especially this single, fresh-faced, barely-out-of-med-school twit. Part of me wanted to grab her lab coat and shove her out of the room, knowing that her lack of basic skills would end up leaving a scar on him, but I couldn't. We were a teaching hospital. "Well, I was just going to irrigate the wound but I suppose you can do that."

Adam seemed to be irritated again.

"Detective Trent, I need you to come over to the sink here. Can you… here, let me help." I held his wounded hand steady while he easily folded his incredible body off the bed, getting to him before Megan did. "I… I mean *we* need to irrigate the wound, clean out any debris."

I tried to concentrate on his injury but his incredible eyes drew me in again, gazing down at me with some unspoken emotion that was so raw it took away my ability to breathe. Damn, he was built. Long legs, too. Had to be over six feet tall given that he passed my five-foot-six height by another head.

"Sorry about all of that bullshit," he said privately, glancing down at my lips for a second, or maybe it was ten. I'd lost count. "And the thing… earlier."

I was distracted by his tone, leading me to believe that he was being completely sincere and genuinely seeking my forgiveness. "It's okay. But, thank you."

He frowned, dipping his head even lower. "No, it's not. It was uncalled for."

I shrugged. "My first priority is you. The rest I can deal with."

He seemed to be taken aback by that, but I didn't care. It was the truth.

JACKED

I really wanted to ask him about the cameraman and the guy with the headphones, but not while someone else was in the room with us. Everything about it seemed to be a source of agitation for him though. The nurses would surely berate me later for not getting the dirty details, but they'd just have to get over it. He'd already been through enough shit for one night from what I could tell and I certainly wasn't going to add to it.

I decided to go a different route while cleaning his wound. Even his long fingers were deliciously seductive. "So, Detective, did you get him?"

"Who?" he asked.

I nodded my chin, feeling a bit braver. "The guy that did this to you. I presume he was a bad guy?"

Adam laughed lightly. It was the sexiest sound I'd ever heard—deep and alluring. "He was just a kid but yeah, I got him. Had to chase him a few blocks, too. Ran like hell. I hate the rabbits."

I blotted off his hand and wrapped him up in a towel. "Rabbits?"

He chuckled again, taking a few steps backwards to the bed. "That's what we call car thieves who ditch and run." He sat back down, curling one knee up on the bed to sit sideways. "The car was still rolling when the kid jumped out of it. You know? Like a jack rabbit? It's just a nickname."

"Interesting." I scooted my little rolling stool closer to his bedside and gently poked at his gash to see if he was numb. "Do you feel that?"

"Nope. Go for it."

"Would you like to lie down?"

His eyes narrowed a bit. "You want me to?"

His words rolled through me like an electric wave, causing me to stutter. "If you want to. I mean, I want you to be comfortable and relaxed. It would be best if you didn't move so…"

I saw the hint of a smirk curl his lip as he pulled his legs up on the bed and crossed his large black boots at the ankles.

As soon as he was settled, I resumed my examination, bothered by more than the fact he'd been injured on the job. "Well, the good news is that it's superficial enough that you won't need to see an orthopedic surgeon."

Adam's brow rose. "Is there bad news?"

I smiled a bit. "Yeah. You're going to have stitches in your hand."

Megan was standing there with a drape, waiting for me to move out of her way. I stood, allowing her to take my place.

"Hold up," Adam said, pulling his hand back. "I thought *you* were going to do this."

I felt bad. I hoped he could sense I didn't have much of a choice here. "Megan is one of our interns. I'll be supervising."

"Supervising? Yeah, no… not today." He rolled his incensed gaze to Megan. "No offense, sweetheart, but the only person putting stitches in me tonight is her." He nodded his head my way. "I'd appreciate it if you could go find something else to do. Erin, Doctor Novak is all I need."

Megan's face fell. "But—"

She didn't get another word out. He unleashed his intimidating cop glare, silently daring her to question the authority wafting off him. He glanced at the doorway, indicating for her to get going. Like *now*.

I stood there, sort of dumbfounded.

Megan was wide-eyed, waiting for me to intervene.

"It's okay, Megan. I'll take care of this. Perhaps you can ask Doctor Mason if he needs assistance."

That apparently was not what she wanted to hear. She ripped her latex gloves off and tossed them in the trash.

"Now then," Adam said, sliding back on the cot, "where were we?"

His authoritative demeanor subsided quickly.

I sat back down on the stool and rolled in closer. "I think you scared her."

Adam put his other hand behind his head, cupping the pillow. "Good. I want this done right." He gave me his cut hand.

He was assuming a lot. Still, I found it amusing. I covered his hand with the medical drape, exposing just his wound. "What makes you so sure I'll do any better?"

He tilted his head. "I trust you. Well, at least until you give me a reason not to."

God, he had a great laugh. I pulled the first suture through and stopped. "We good?"

He smiled and rested his head back. "Keep stitching, Doc."

Damn, if he didn't own one of the sexiest smiles I'd ever seen. While I was throwing my first knot, I was fantasizing about taking him home and locking him in my bedroom. I needed something else to think about beyond stripping him bare. "So, may I ask what the ATTF letters stand for?"

He pressed his chin to his chest, reading his own T-shirt. "Acronym for auto theft task force. It's a special division within the police department."

"Ah, that's right. I remember now. That's why you pulled me over."

He looked so damn remorseful. "I pulled my gun on you." His eyes searched around the ceiling before landing back on my face. "I know you're worried. You have nothing to worry about, okay? That stuff we got will never be seen on TV. I don't want you to worry about your job or anything."

I pulled another suture through. "I appreciate that. I've been feeling quite paranoid all day, worrying that I'd wind up on the six o'clock news. It was quite a traumatic experience. I'm surprised I'm not still shaking."

"Erin, look at me."

His authoritative yet gentle voice made goose bumps rise on my arms. I met his gaze.

"It will never happen. Trust me."

There was so much sincerity in his eyes, I found myself wanting to believe in him so damn bad. "You swear?"

"You have my word. I'd never let anything bad happen to you."

I swallowed hard, finding myself in uncharted territory. I'd never had a guy seem to care as much about me as this man I barely knew appeared to do. But then again, I was never one to allow myself to be vulnerable. The desire to give him a hug was quite powerful. "Okay, thank you. This career means everything to me."

"I know. A blind man could see that."

His insightfulness took me by surprise. "So, is that what you do then? Deal with carjackings?"

He nodded. "That and other things. We mainly chase down stolen vehicles. Most felonies involve a stolen car. You know, like robberies, homicides." He scratched his brow. "The bad guys usually don't want to use their own cars. Go figure."

Again, he got me to laugh, but considering some perpetrator caused him to get injured tonight, his job didn't sound like a pleasure cruise. "Sounds like dangerous work."

He was silent for so long I had to look at him.

"It can be," he said, almost regretfully. "But I guess the good part is there are people like you to piece us back together."

I shrugged, feeling his words like a comforting affirmation, especially since I had just accused him a day ago of ruining my career when he was just doing his job. Things could have been worse; I could have wound up back in jail. "Well, fortunately for me, you didn't require a lot of piecing together tonight. I get it, though. I've often said that cops don't get paid enough to do what you do."

Adam drew in a tight breath. "Did you become a doctor for the money?"

I could tell by the way he asked, he wasn't being purposely hurtful or looking to be judgmental. He was trying to make a point. I tied another stitch off before answering. "No. I didn't. Ever since I was a little girl I wanted to heal the sick. I was forever putting bandages on my dolls and stuffed animals." It wasn't a lie, but it was also my standard canned answer whenever anyone asked that question. It always generated a smile and it was much simpler than the full truth.

"Ah, the caretaker gene. Very noble. My brother Jason was born that gene, too."

I pulled another stitch through his palm. "Is he a doctor?"

Adam scratched his chest with his free hand, appearing a wee bit proud. "Not quite. He's a flight medic in the Army. He's in Bosnia right now, actually. Wish he wasn't but… there's nothing I can do to change it."

I felt a twinge of sickness. "Another group that put their lives on the line to keep us safe."

His face softened in agreement.

"What about you? Always known you wanted to be a police officer?"

His lips twisted up. "Yeah, for as long as I can remember. Although that pipe dream of wanting to be a cowboy doesn't seem so bad right now."

"Never too late to switch," I teased. "But most of the cowboys I remember seeing in the movies always chased bank robbers. Not sure a horse would appreciate the wind chill outside."

The smile washed from his face. "You watch a lot of TV, Doc?"

"Um, no. Not really."

"Why is that?"

Because my nose is usually in a medical textbook until I pass out? "I don't know."

"So you don't watch TV at all?"

I couldn't figure out why he was asking. It was perplexing. "Well, I watch a little, but I'm not a big fan of court TV or paternity tests so I usually don't bother. I watch movies sometimes and stuff on Amazon. Does that count?"

His eyes looked tired and solemn and somewhat relieved, as if he was just about done for the evening. He nodded and a faint smile lifted his lips. "Yeah, it does."

"What about you? You a TV junkie?" The extreme physical shape of his body was enough to confirm he didn't spend too much time on the couch with a remote in his hand. Still… "I'm guessing you're a Flyers or Eagles fan."

"Yeah, something like that." He glanced out toward the hall and then leaned toward me. "Actually, can you keep a secret?"

I nodded, wishing he'd tell me all of his secrets. Desire to know what his throaty moans sounded like was one of them.

"I can't stand the Eagles. I'm a Steelers fan. Don't tell anybody that, okay?"

I stopped suturing and crossed my heart with my forceps, snickering at his admission. "I swear your secret is safe with me. Hate to see you get tossed out of Philly for your insolence."

It felt good to have a hearty laugh. Life had been so serious for so long, feeling a shred of genuine attraction toward someone helped leach some of the loneliness from my bones.

I studied his fingers while I sewed up his left hand. Long, thick fingers. Ideal for touching, pleasuring. No ring indentions whatsoever. "Are you right-handed, Detective?"

"Adam."

I sighed. "Are you right-handed, Adam?"

He smirked. "Yep. With everything."

My imagination went wild with the innuendo that wrapped around his words. "Well, then you won't be too inconvenienced. You'll probably be tender and swollen for a day or two. Keep it bandaged to minimize infection. Ice it if it hurts. All right. You're just about done. Let me get you wrapped up and I think we can get you discharged out of here. Now, no running after bad guys for a few days. And you want to keep this clean and dry. I'll give you some antibiotic cream to put on it."

While I was talking, my gloved fingers absentmindedly drifted around his sutured palm, cleaning away blood that was no longer there with a wad of gauze. His fingers were a half-stroke away from touching my breast. I wanted to comfort him somehow and read his fortune all at the same time, hoping I could see myself getting caressed by this hand in the future. The feelings were overwhelming.

He sucked in another breath through his nose, jarring me from what I was doing.

"If you notice any redness or swelling, um, or if you should, if you should see any, any discharge around these sutures…"

His right hand caught my wrist, holding me gentle but firm. "You've got great eyes."

His own eyes were smoldering, capturing me in some tantric haze as ancient as the sun. Those full lips—so pink, so plump—made by divine intervention and created for very wicked things.

He sat up and dropped his feet off the edge of the bed, shifting me until I was standing between his open legs. I knew I should back up, put some distance between us, but my body refused to move and he didn't relent his grip on me.

"You should, um, see your family doctor if you have any problems," I managed to breathe out finally, a few mere inches separating us. He was so tall, the kind of which I might need to use my tippy-toes to reach that sexy mouth if I wasn't wearing heels, but sitting, he was darn near perfect height.

"Why don't I come back here, see *you* if I have any problems?"

My heart did a complete somersault in my chest. I took a half step back. "Why would you want to do that?"

Adam let go of my wrist, drifted his fingers over mine, and then snagged my open lab coat, hindering my full retreat. "Is there a reason I shouldn't?"

I swallowed hard, recalling an entire college course on medical ethics. I opted for light-hearted instead. "Well, yeah. For one, I charge more." I smiled shamelessly. *Am I flirting with him?*

"So, no discounts for repeat customers?" He sounded sort of hopeful. *Oh God, he's flirting right back with me.*

Unfortunately, his comment was heavily laden with repercussions. I looked up into his eyes. "I don't want you to be a repeat customer, Detective Trent."

"Adam," he corrected, licking some mysterious flavor off his bottom lip. Surely it was something decadent and sinful.

"Adam."

He smirked. "Can I ask why?"

I swallowed again, hoping not to say something stupid. "Because that would mean you were seriously hurt if you came back here again and I, ah… I don't want to think about you getting seriously hurt while you're— while you're protecting the streets where I live. That's why."

His lingering gaze seemed to search for something, a different answer perhaps, until his eyes leveled on mine. "I see your point."

I cleared my throat. "Your regular doctor will have to remove the stitches in about ten to fourteen days. By then… by then you should be all healed up."

"Nah," he said, dropping his hand to his lap. "I'll take them out myself."

I couldn't help but find the humor in his macho declaration. Of course he was the type of guy to pull his own stitches. He probably would have hand-stitched his wound with a needle and thread had they not brought him in by ambulance.

"What's so funny?"

I noted a few things in his file and signed his discharge papers. "You. For some reason I knew you were going to say that."

He shrugged his impressive shoulders. "Wouldn't be the first time I took my own stitches out. Probably won't be the last, either."

"No, I think this is the last time." Without thinking, I blurted, "I can take them out for you."

If I could have smacked my own forehead without looking ridiculous, I would have. *Oh God. I've completely lost my mind.*

That garnered another killer smile, showing perfectly aligned white teeth—perfect for eating me. "You willing to make house calls, Doc?"

"Erin," I corrected.

"I like calling you Doc," he said smoothly.

I gave up. "I don't normally make house calls, but I think I can make an exception."

Some emotion crossed over him; perplexity perhaps? Maybe regret? "It would have to be early in the morning or later in the evening. I'm on night shift five nights a week, sometimes six."

My schedule was tight, too. I shook my head, tossing some of the fog off my brain, trying to backpedal out of my asinine offer. "No, I mean yeah. That's fine."

The edge of his mouth quirked up. "That's not going to be a problem for you, is it?"

While I was hearing his words, the other half of my brain was trying to decipher their meaning. It was almost as if he was seeing if I was available, but damn, I didn't want to get my hopes up for nothing. It had been so long since I'd entertained the thought of a real date since ending it with Randy, I feared my exhaustion was misconstruing his questions. "You mean mornings?"

"Yeah."

"I'm a night owl. I'm here most nights anyway. No one ever wants the overnight shifts but I don't mind," I mumbled, smacking myself mentally for admitting that.

Adam wiped his thumb over my ID badge again. There was no doubt he was one hell of an intimidating cop. I wasn't even in trouble and my knees were knocking. I swear I could feel the roll of his thumb in other places.

"Me, too." He seemed pleased with that commonality.

I smiled. "Are you a night owl, too?"

His smirk told me *yes*. "You got a man at home?"

Damn, his bluntness surprised me again. I thought about the last guy I dated, which was months ago—that idiot Lab tech, Jeff, who thought a date meant watching him and his friends drink beer.

The truth spilled out of me in a heartbeat. "No. No man."

He raised an eyebrow. "Woman?"

I laughed uncomfortably. "Not my style."

He nodded once. His sweet smile was magnificent. "If I ask you to dinner sometime so I can thank you properly for stitching me up, you gonna say yes or you gonna shoot me down?"

All the saliva that was once in my mouth now clogged my throat. I swallowed hard, finding it almost incomprehensible that he was standing so close to me.

I felt frozen. "Depends," I managed to say, climbing my eyes from the noticeable dip between his pecs up to those smoldering long lashes of his.

"On?"

"If you ever ask," I breathed out.

His gaze seemed to center on my mouth. "Consider this me asking," he declared, his voice deep and husky. "Unless you're planning on turning into a jack on me."

My body was humming, abuzz from just the possibility of one day kissing this gorgeous man, but that would probably never happen. "I don't know what that means," I said with the last of the air in my lungs.

He tugged on my lab coat, causing me to rock forward onto the balls of my feet.

"What that means, Doc—"

"Erin. My name is Erin."

He scraped his teeth over his bottom lip. "What that means, Erin, is if I pursue you, are you going to run and make me chase you, or are you going to surrender willingly? I've got no time or patience for games."

My nerves went numb. *Is he really attracted to me? Oh my God. No way.* "You're going to chase me?"

"I was thinking about it. But we can start with a nice meal first. You okay with that?"

My brain seized, though my head managed to nod. My thoughts scattered to the gutter. "Are you going to cuff me again if I put up a fight?"

His finger traced the edge of my jacket. A sinister and yet very playful smirk turned up those luscious lips. "As much as I'd like to explore that idea in great length, I think we can discuss that some other time."

Again with the instant honestly for Officer Hottie. "Okay."

"What time do you get out of work?"

I looked at the clock on the wall and frowned. Time seemed to grind to a halt. "Not for another five hours."

He looked at his watch. It was silver and leather and manly. "You have someone to escort you to your car when you leave?"

I couldn't find my pen anywhere. I had just had it in my hand a few minutes ago. "My friend, Sarah, drove. The nurse."

When I met his gaze again, the deep frown was back. "The pregnant one?" He raised his bandaged hand near my head. I felt my ponytail tug, a few hairs pinch, and then I was looking at my missing blue pen. "This what you're looking for?"

He was a mind reader. Scary how he knew. I berated myself for violating my patient/doctor ethics so effortlessly. "Yes."

He bristled, instantly displeased. "Yeah, that's not gonna happen. I'll speak with Security before I leave. You won't be walking out unescorted."

Since when did it matter to him? I certainly didn't need him making issues for me on top of things. I started filling out the last bit of required information on his discharge paperwork, tersely replying to his meddling. "That's not necessary, Detective. I'm quite capable of looking out for myself."

He took a step closer, invading my personal space. "Yeah. I get that. Still isn't going to change my mind."

I held up his copy of his discharge information, shaking it to make some sort of point. "Yes, well. You are free to go. Do you have any other questions for me?"

"Dinner. Tomorrow."

"That's not a question."

He was smiling. What he found so amusing was beyond me, but I could stare at his smile all damn day. It sure beat the intimidating cop stoic glare he usually wore. "You work tomorrow night, Doc? Yes or no."

I nodded, reminding myself I had no life beyond sleeping and the ER at University Hospital. "Yes, *Detective*. At seven."

His lips twisted into a smirk. "Okay. Then we only have one option. Have breakfast with me."

CHAPTER 6
Adam

THE STITCHES IN my hand pinched as I slid into my usual booth at the Parkway Diner, making me wince from the annoying pain. The anesthesia had completely worn off, bringing back the throbbing ache and irritating reminder that I should have been wearing gloves last night. But my favorite leather gloves were in the trash back at the station, soaked with some other kid's blood from the night before.

I tossed my truck keys onto the table near the overflow of sugar packets and ketchup, resolving that there wasn't shit I could do about it now. It was what it was—a monumental screw up on my part and definitely one I wouldn't be repeating.

I took my ball cap off and ran my good hand over my head while Kathy brought me my usual cup of decaf. She gave me a motherly pat on the shoulder, her seven a.m. hurried smile, and a mutter that she'd be right back.

Man, what a fucking night. The kids running from the car they boosted really pissed me off. Amateurs—both of them—smashing out the back passenger window with a brick. It was crude but effective and gained them access quickly to take their little marijuana-filled joyride.

The one I chased was fast though; I'll give him that. But not fast enough. I still got him, the little delinquent. I gazed at my bandaged-up hand, noting what it had cost me, but it was worth it.

Or was it? Fuck.

I knew going back to the station when I left the hospital would be a mistake, but I wanted to get the paperwork over and done with. Hearing that I'd be on desk duty for a few days was infuriating but at least it would allow me some uninterrupted time to dig deeper into the Mancuso auto theft ring. I was willing to bet the farm that Mancuso's boys were the ones behind the diversion with the false call on the Doc's car and the high-end thefts, but I'd yet to confirm my gut instinct. I knew I needed to check up on a few of my confidential informants and find out what the word on the street was, but tracking some of them down was like trying to nail Jell-O to the wall.

My CIs walked a fine line between good and evil, leaning heavily on the evil side, but those were their choices in life—not mine.

I checked my watch, noting that my sexy doctor was running ten minutes late. Part of me was already resigning to the fact that I'd probably be eating alone again this morning, which was also starting to aggravate me for some reason.

I glanced toward the entrance one more time, spotting another one of my mistakes—the diner's newest waitress, Kara, who was scowling at me since I'd purposely sat in Kathy's section again and not hers. My father always used to tell us to never shit where we ate, and for the longest time I didn't know what the hell that meant—until now. Kara was twenty-something, cute, had been working the morning shift at the diner for almost a year, but unfortunately had zero goals in life. After dealing with Nikki's lack of ambition for so long, it became a character trait I was unwilling to compromise on going forward.

Even though it had been a few weeks since we hooked up that one time, I knew Kara's flirty smiles and glances were meant to entice me again, but that was a scene I had no desire to repeat. If I ever did decide to get serious again with someone, I sure as hell would strive a lot higher than some girl willing to give me a blowjob in my truck behind the diner where she works.

I did my best to ignore her but I knew what her longing looks meant. She'd been trying for weeks to make something more out of our superficial chats and meaningless encounter, find some comfortable acceptance that I didn't just use her when in reality, I did.

It was all I was capable of.

The stitches in my hand started to throb in time with my slight headache. The suits from the network would not be happy with another forced absence from the show due to this new injury, especially since they wanted to make me their show pony, but to hell with them. They'd just have to deal with a bunch of close-ups and commentaries outa me like last time when I got stabbed.

I took a sip of the ice water that Kathy brought to me. Hah. Who knew a trip to the ER in the middle of the night might get me laid.

No.

No, no.

Fuck no.

No, that gorgeous doctor wouldn't be just a lay. No. She'd be more, much, much more than a hit and run. That had long-term relationship written all over it.

Fuck.

And she even had the guts to take me on and call me on my shit when we'd pulled her over. Ballsy little thing. That alone did me in. She didn't hesitate jacking Ritchie up either.

When she bent over into that cabinet, I wanted to take her right then and there. Tight body, perfectly rounded heart-shaped ass, ample breasts that would fill my hands perfectly—made my mouth water again just thinking about them. I wanted to lay her across the fucking hospital bed and peel those light blue scrubs off her, see what kind of panties she had on under there while making those tits of hers ache with pleasure.

God, she was beautiful. Smart and independent, too. Wouldn't even let me pick her up from work, insisting she'd catch a ride to meet me here.

She didn't seem bothered that I worked night shift, either. Hell, she said she worked the same hours. That was a major bonus. Major. But they all say that at first before things come up to make my hours an issue. I so didn't need a repeat of Nikki, making me feel like shit for leaving her alone at night. There's only so much of that I could take. It's not like the bad guys commit their crimes at convenient hours. If a woman couldn't respect what I stood for and believed in, then I guess they weren't worth standing by.

Huh. Doctor Erin Novak. Who'd ever think I'd hook up with a doctor?

That long honey-colored, dirty-blonde hair tied at the nape of her neck—just begging for a hand to grasp onto it—was such a turn-on. I knew it made me a totally sick fucking bastard to think it, but the whole time she was stitching me up I couldn't stop fantasizing about holding onto it while guiding her mouth up and down on me.

I felt my balls tighten. It had been too long to remember what feeling real with a woman felt like. Even though I'd gotten laid since ending it with Nikki, it wasn't worth the time it took. But I knew going in that the girl was going to be nothing more than a few hours of fun, even though the generic sex didn't feed my needs.

Only a special kind of woman could satisfy that.

Ever since that fucking episode aired with me with my shirt off, things had been getting out of hand. All I had to do was pick any local club in Philly; girls started recognizing me, and it was like shooting fish in a barrel. But now this shit with these obsessive psycho fans, all the fan mail, bras, pictures, telephone numbers, girls coming to my damn house… Did these women actually think I'd relocate to Austin or bum-fuck Tuscaloosa for companionship? Grab one off my fucking front lawn? Yeah, like that would ever happen. The only thing their behaviors were doing was confirming my opinion that the world is full up of crazy people.

But Doctor Erin Novak didn't seem to have a clue who I was. She didn't have cable TV, either, which was another huge bonus, although I was surprised she didn't pick up anything from the newspapers, since our "Prowler Pack" was all over the local news as if we were the next best thing since those Jersey Shore douche bags.

I watched my waitress saunter over. Even in her early sixties, her hips still had the small diner sway that would garner more in tips. "You want some more decaf, Adam?"

I blocked her pour with my bandaged hand. "No thanks, Kathy." I bit back the throb that immediately shot into my wrist. It was as if my hand had a freaking pulse of its own.

Like a disapproving mother, she frowned at me. "What happened to you?"

I stared at the gauze, thinking how this night could have turned out much worse. I was slipping. Getting sloppy. But I wasn't about to explain myself so I shrugged it off. "Got cut."

She stood there waiting on the rest of the story but I wasn't in the mood for sharing.

Kathy tisked and then finally resigned to the idea that she wasn't going to get any more out of me. She tossed her chin. "Is it going to be on this Sunday?"

I scratched my forehead. How the hell would I know what scenes they edit and what gets prime time viewing? Considering I got hurt and Dumb and Dumber were ordered to follow me into the ER, all signs pointed to it being aired eventually. "I don't know. Doubt it."

"You want your usual?"

"Yeah, but not yet. I'm waiting on someone."

One very thin penciled-on eyebrow lifted. Why women shaved them off only to draw them back on was another one of those female mysteries I'd never care to understand.

"Should I be jealous?" she asked a little too seriously. As if I'd ever date a sixty-year-old at this point in my life.

"Should your husband be?" I tossed back at her.

"Touché. I'm glad you finally came in. I thought after… Well Kara's been moping around here for weeks."

Shit. Don't, just don't. I held up my hand. I was not in the mood for a lecture. "It was a mistake."

"I'm worried about her." Kathy sighed, leaning her hip on the back of the booth. "She doesn't seem to know that."

If I could kick myself, I would have. "A mistake that I won't be repeating."

"I'll talk to her," she said. "My grandson wants to know if you were serious about the offer to do that weight training with him."

"Yeah, of course. How's he doing?"

"Changing schools seems to have helped tremendously. He's far away from that old crowd he used to run with. He's seeing a drug and alcohol counselor every week too. Being away from Todd was the key, though, just like you said. Jerry and I told Crystal she could move back home too but she's not speaking to us anymore. She's blaming us for taking her son away and for believing Lucas instead of her. Threatening to come snatch him in the middle of the night. She can screw up her life but she's not going to take my grandson down with her. No way."

"You did the right thing. Crystal's an adult who's making bad decisions. And the courts gave you custody, so she doesn't have a leg to stand on. She tries to take him, that's a felony." I snagged a napkin and motioned for her pen. "Here's my number. Call me if you have any problems. I don't always answer, so make sure you leave me a message and I'll get back to ya."

She stuffed it into her apron. "You're an angel, Adam. I can't thank you enough for all that you've done."

I stood and gave her a hug, ignoring Kara's blatant staring from across the diner. "Don't worry. We'll work something out and get the boy on a better track. You keep believing in him and don't give up, okay?"

"Thank you." She sniffed, squeezing me. "Thank you. I better get back to the kitchen. Holler for me when you're ready."

As I watched her walk away, years of training and lack of trust for humanity had me eyeing the place, taking in every detail—what people were wearing, what they looked like—identifying, describing, and assessing them as potential victims or criminals. Kathy's grandson was only fourteen and had experienced the ugly side of people far more than any kid should.

Damn, when did I get so fucking jaded?

I'm sure Doctor Erin didn't view the world that way. All she saw were victims.

As soon as she drifted back into my mind, all I could picture was cuffing her hot, naked body to my headboard and violating her nine ways to Sunday. She'd definitely be fun to play with.

But the moment she came through the door of the diner I thought my heart was going to leap out of my chest. I caught myself grinning and had to remind myself to take my excitement down a notch.

Man, her smile is precious. That's enough to brighten the shittiest of days.

"Sorry I'm late," Erin said as she slid into the booth, sitting across from me. "Hope you weren't waiting long."

I probably would have waited all damn day for her. A vision of my grandfather smacking me in the head for not standing before she sat down flashed through my thoughts. Well, it was too late now. "Let me guess. You had an emergency."

She smiled. "Good guess. Um, compound fracture of the ulna."

"Ulna?" I asked, watching her fuss with her long hair. I was willing to bet her head was filled with all sorts of useful information.

She patted her forearm and then flicked a finger away from her skin.

I cringed a little inside. "Bone pierced the skin?"

"Yep. Guy fell off a roof. He said he was taking down his Christmas lights, but at four in the morning without pants on?"

"Yeah, that's highly unlikely." I'd seen plenty of derelicts in my lifetime so my imagination didn't have to stretch too far. I could only imagine what gore she'd seen with those soulful eyes. I didn't want to think about it though, spoiling my other visions of her. *Damn, she's gorgeous. I can't stop staring at her. Imagining her naked. Strapped down tight to my bed. My mouth on every inch of her. Her feet sliding over the sheets as she helplessly writhes in pleasure. Fuck, I want to have her in ways no one else ever has or ever will.*

This is not good.

I barely knew her and already she was getting under my skin.

You got to walk away from this, Adam, my inner voice warned. *This is going to be worse than Nikki. Even* she *didn't get you going like this. No woman is going to put up with your schedule or the fact that you're on goddamned television like some poseur wannabe, making it all that much worse. Decaf, some eggs, polite conversation, and get the hell outa here.*

Kathy came back, coffee pot in hand. "Coffee?"

Erin popped her head up from the menu. "No thank you. May I please have a tall glass of orange juice?"

"Make that two." She had the fullest lips with that hint of mischief set to them. My plan to eat and bail was diverted by imagining how sweet her mouth would taste.

"Do you know what you want?" I asked, shaking those thoughts out of my head while fighting back another bizarre desire to feed her with my fingers.

She seemed so peppy and excited by the simple task of picking out her breakfast, even though her lips were wrinkled with indecision. "Everything looks so tempting. I'm starving, actually. I'm thinking western omelet and whole wheat toast. Maybe some home fries too." Her grin was silly.

She was tempting. So very tempting. If she knew what I was really hungry for right now she'd surely reach across the table and slap me hard. I glanced back at the menu for the pure distraction of it while my desires and vivid images sort of blurred together.

I shifted, feeling tight all over. Fortunately I had a spare pair of jeans in my locker, replacing my bloodied cargo pants. Unfortunately, those jeans were constricting all sorts of new blood flow.

Kathy set our drinks down. "Are you ready?"

"Yes. For the lady, she'd like the western omelet and whole wheat toast and I'd like the Spanish omelet with whole wheat also. And a large plate of home fries and bacon." I handed the menus over, catching Kathy's approving smile while completely dazed by Erin's. She appeared to be a happy person, which was wonderful because I had enough shit to worry about; I didn't need to be the sole source of someone's happiness.

"I love bacon," she said.

I leaned up on the table. "Me too."

"How's the hand feel?"

I glanced at the meticulous job she did and flexed my fingers. "Feels fine, although I think wrapping it this good on my own might be tough."

I watched her lips pucker and brush the edge of her water glass, thinking it was one of the most erotic things I'd seen in a long time.

"What time do you normally start your shift?"

"Um, we have ops briefing at eight and then we're on the streets by eight-thirty. Why?"

She shrugged. "I'll be at the hospital at seven. I can re-wrap you, if you want, before you start your shift."

Is she giving me an in to see her or is she just being nice? Either way, I was thankful. "You'd be okay to do that?"

She didn't even question it. "Sure. You need to keep those stitches covered. While you're home, you can let them air, but while you're out there in germ world better to be safe than sorry."

She made me laugh with her little animations. "Germ world? That bad, huh?"

Erin nodded. "Yep. Trust me."

I leaned back. "Actually, I've been benched. Apparently stitches warrant a few days of desk duty."

"Well, you need to heal. How long are you benched?"

I shrugged, not really knowing. "A week? It's okay. Gives me time to dig into why someone switched your plate."

Erin fidgeted with her napkin. "That's been bothering me a lot, actually."

Thinking about some asswipe creeping around her car at night bothered me a whole hell of a lot, too. "I'm not completely sure, but my guess is that you were used as a diversion."

"A diversion?"

I nodded, reconsidering just how much I should divulge. Last thing I wanted to do was to scare her. "Several expensive cars on the other side of the city disappeared into thin air at the same time we were chasing you."

The look of abject horror I received told me she was completely innocent.

"Don't let it worry you, though. I talked with hospital security before I left and I got the number for their main office. I'll inform them that your car was tampered with on hospital property. But the fact they let you ladies walk out into that dark parking lot unescorted, well that's something they need to fix right away."

She frowned at me. "We've never had problems before."

Didn't matter if she disapproved or not. "I walked through your lot, Erin; it's dark, unlit, and unsafe. You ever have any self-defense training?"

"No," she admitted.

"Well then, you should never walk out there alone, especially when it's dark. I'll show you some self-defense moves. You should at least know how to escape if someone grabs you."

She gave me a measured look.

"I'm serious."

She smirked at me. "I believe you."

Didn't take long for Kathy to return with our food. I could have inhaled mine for how hungry I was. I let the subject of her safety drop and started scooping chunky salsa out over my omelet when I noticed Erin scrutinizing me. "Want some?"

"Salsa? On an omelet?" She was definitely questioning my sanity.

"You ever try it?"

She shook her head.

"Babe, you haven't lived until you've had salsa on an omelet. Here," I handed the small soup cup over to her, "give it a shot."

I was glad to see she was willing to try something new and even more relieved that she didn't get all righteous on me when I called her "babe." It had slipped out before I could stop myself.

One mouthful and she started grinning. "Oh, that's good."

I crammed a big bite into my mouth, nodding in agreement. "Told ya. Have some more."

She rubbed another spoonful over her food. "I think this is my new favorite thing."

"You think that's good, wait until I show you the proper way to eat French fries."

A lock of hair fell across her face. I wanted to touch it.

"Gravy on top?" she asked.

I set my fork down. "Aw. Who told you?"

"Are you kidding? I've known about gravy fries since I was old enough to speak the words. You know who has the best gravy fries?"

"Al's Tavern," we both said in unison.

"You've been to Al's?" I asked, completely shocked she knew about my favorite hole-in-the-wall pub.

She smiled that wholesome naughty girl grin again. God, I wanted to climb over the table and kiss her. *Could life be this poetic?* Something so benign and simple felt like a lifeline, gluing a piece of me back together. If she only knew…

"Yep. Many times, although it's been a while since I was there. Sarah and I used to go there all the time."

"Sarah?"

"The pregnant nurse that took your info."

"Oh. Yeah, I remember. The one who conveniently pointed out that we both live in the same town."

I saw her cringe a little.

"Yeah, your friend's not as subtle as she'd like to think." I shrugged. "I didn't mind. She gave up some very useful information."

I watched the blush stain Erin's cheeks. I wondered where else I might get to see her body flush with heat. The tightness in my muscles returned as well as part of my single-minded erection. "Don't be embarrassed. I'm not. I may even buy your pregnant tattletale some flowers for being so helpful."

"Seriously?"

I winked at her. That shy flush hit her again. "Yep. And I'm willing to bet she'd give up your phone number for a chocolate donut and a smile."

Erin's shoulders slumped, playing right along. "You'd bribe an eight-month pregnant woman with a donut to get my phone number?"

I didn't want to give away that I already had her cell number, her former addresses from when she lived in Baltimore and attended Johns Hopkins University, and that she had no priors and only ever had one speeding ticket in her life. The fact that she had no other aliases also brightened my shitty night.

Trade secret—all cops hooking up with new women ran their girl's information. That's because you never knew which hot babe was also a walking restraining order in disguise. It was a relief to find one without any priors.

Besides, I was sure the moment I left the hospital they had all of my medical records from the last four times I visited the ER up on their screen. Hell, there were even video clips from the show of the guys and me on the Internet. I wasn't feeling guilty in the least, but something about her whole vibe told me she hadn't cyber-stalked me yet.

"Yes, I most certainly would bribe a pregnant woman to give up your phone number, but only as a last resort."

I watched her take another bite, scrutinizing me. "Please don't torture my pregnant friend. Chocolate donuts make people do stupid things."

I set my coffee cup down. "Afraid she might tell me too much? I bet if I brought her a dozen she'd tell me all of your little secrets."

"I don't have secrets."

"Yeah right. All women have secrets."

I saw her spine stiffen. She liked the challenge. Good.

"And men don't?"

"I didn't say that." I shoved a piece of toast in my mouth.

"If I ask nicely, would you tell me your secrets? I promise to be open-minded."

Damn, she's good at this. I wonder how open-minded she'd be if we discussed my sexual depravities.

"Oh, no. I'm not falling for it. You want me to give up information? Not without a swap. One for one."

I wasn't sure if I'd like this game but I did sort of ask for it.

"Okay. Ladies first?"

As if I had a choice. I swept my hand for her to start, hoping like hell this didn't get out of hand.

"Ever been married?"

Easy. "No. My turn."

"Wait."

"One for one, Doc. Didn't give specifics on the amount of details."

And there went her enthusiasm and out came a pout. "Fine."

"Oh, the four letter death word," I teased, waving my fork at her. "I know what that word means in women speak, by the way. Rule Number One: you use that word on me, I get to call you on it."

And back came a bit of her perkiness with a smile wicked enough to destroy me. "We have rules now?"

I pushed one of my empty plates away and kicked back, enjoying the fun of riling her up. "Rules. Words to live by. Whatever you want to call it. I like rules. Keeps things clear."

Then came the sass with the ornery grin. "Fine."

God, she was hot.

"Fine," I volleyed. "My turn." I knew she'd never been married, so I didn't intend to waste my question. I had every intention to find out if she liked to be tied up during sex, so I tossed her an easy one. "What's the craziest thing you did in college?"

That made her lips pucker. Damn, even her little pout was cute. "Not fair."

"Hah! It's very fair. And by that reaction you definitely have to answer it now."

I wondered how long she'd take to think of an answer and how much of it would be the truth. Her eyes glanced up, to the right. I relaxed and waited.

"Okay, back in my sophomore year a friend of mine and I went to a frat party and somehow, after way too much beer, I got entered into the wet T-shirt contest."

I felt my eyes bulge and my throat tighten simultaneously at her honest recounting. Why the hell couldn't I have known her then? "For real?" This innocent-looking creature had a wild side. I knew it.

Erin nodded sheepishly. "Yep. And you want to know the best part of it? I won it, too."

Of course I had to look at her boobs now, wondering what soaking wet cotton would look like plastered against the lovely pair. *Hard, pink nipples begging to be warmed with my tongue. The left one, and then the right, sucking and tugging on them with my teeth until they're red and swollen, and she's moaning in my arms.* And just like that, my hard-on came back with a vengeance. *Damn, is she doing this to me on purpose?*

I tugged at the crotch of my jeans quickly, removing the denim seam that was impaling my dick.

Yeah, she knew exactly what she was doing to me.

"There may or may not have been a stripper pole involved as well, though I can't say. Was that crazy enough for you?"

I was so dumbstruck; all I could do was nod.

"My turn again," she said, way too enthusiastically.

"Wait. Is that something you might repeat anytime soon? Just curious."

Oh that shy, shy grin. This girl is going to wreck me.

"Why? Are you going to tell me you have one installed in your house or something?"

I swallowed hard just picturing that. *Don't think about the word "hard" now, Adam.* "No, but I'm thinking about buying one today if you're game, that's for damn sure."

"Well, you'll have to hold that thought since it's my turn again."

I waved for her to continue, fearing I was at risk for spilling my guts to her now.

"Since you obviously are a righteous man of the law, ever do anything that was illegal? *And...* if so, what was it?"

Look at her. She thinks she's got me. First rule of interrogation, sweetheart, trust no one and definitely never confess to anything illegal. I knew enough to know she was just trying to get to know me. There was nothing in my brief investigation on her to lead me to think otherwise as she had no record of criminal history. *Well, she doesn't need to know all of my dirty secrets in one sitting.* I took a few moments to think of a good story, something that would appease her curiosity.

"Okay, when I was seventeen, senior year of high school, I took the girl I was dating out to the lake that was a couple of miles from my parents' house. I spread out a nice blanket, had the radio playing, couple bottles of wine my brother Michael got for me, trying to show her what a class act I was. Well, it worked and there we were in all our glory goin' at it hot and heavy." I wiped my mouth just thinking about it. "I was quite preoccupied when the cops showed up."

Erin laughed. "What did you do?"

Why am I telling her this shit? Fuck it. Let her get a bit hot and bothered, too. "What could I do? We were totally busted. Chief cuffed me, butt-ass naked, tossed me in the back of the squad car, and remanded me over to my parents. Dragged me right to the front door of my house and threatened to shoot me. Guess he was pretty pissed that I was caught defiling his daughter or something—"

Erin covered her mouth. "Oh, no you didn't!"

I shrugged, holding back some. "Gave me a citation for public

TINA REBER

indecency and underage drinking, which was still cutting me a break because I was pretty wasted. I ended up having to do community service clearing all of the storm gutters for the entire summer."

"And that's when you decided to go into law enforcement?"

I nodded and scratched the scar above my left eyebrow I'd gotten as a result. "Actually it was a few days after that when Casper Cullis pulled a gun on me."

"*Casper* Cullis?"

"Her douche-bag boyfriend."

"Someone named their kid Casper? Isn't he the friendly ghost?"

I had to laugh at her, though the memory was far from funny. "No. We got into a fight, and then he pointed a gun at my head."

"He pointed a gun… at your head. Oh my God. What did you do?"

Images skittered through. "I knocked his hand away and broke his nose. And *that's* when I decided to be a police officer."

I watched her stab a piece of her omelet and followed it just so I could see her tongue again. It was a far better image than the one lingering from my story. "I believe it's my turn again."

She waved her fork. "Go for it."

At this point I fully intended to. "You look worried." I smiled, trying to ease her tension.

Erin laughed uncomfortably. "I'm not, really."

"Well don't be. I am curious though. Why the ER? I mean, you could probably set up shop in some cozy practice seeing head colds and skinned knees, no? But trauma? I don't know."

"Don't look at me like that, please," she said, admonishing my gaze.

"Like what?"

"Like I'm crazy. Are you questioning my sanity, Detective?"

"Maybe. A little. I mean, I've seen some gruesome shit in my lifetime, but I can't imagine doing what you do every day to fix them. Doesn't it give you nightmares?"

Her stalled response gave her away. "Not really."

Years of training had me reading her body language, and watching her twist her napkin, refusing to look me in the eye fully told me she was lying to one of us.

"Sometimes, but every day I'm presented with a whole host of new problems to solve. The mechanics of the human body just utterly

106

fascinates me. I love the challenge."

Her human body fascinated me. Watching her light up talking about it was like a gift.

She glanced around the restaurant and I wondered if she finally noticed the stares we were getting. Some people were just blatantly gawking.

She definitely noticed it. "I know it's a difficult field but it's my stepping stone."

"Oh? Where you stepping to, Doc?"

I could see the passion return in her eyes. "I'm trying for a fellowship in Toxicology."

I wasn't expecting that. "Toxicology? You mean, like poison and drugs and stuff?"

She nodded.

Great. A hot woman who'll know how to poison me when I piss her off. "Why?"

"*Why?*"

"Yeah, why? That's not something everyone aspires to be when then grow up."

I note her hesitance and the frown of sadness. "It's personal. I, ah, lost someone once and I want to make sure it doesn't happen again—to anyone."

"Understandable. You want to talk about it?"

She shook her head adamantly. "Maybe, one day, with you. Do you mind if that day isn't today?"

Damn. Someone hurt her. I wanted names, dates, details—*NOW*. But I couldn't. I knew she was holding something back, something painful by the looks of it, but I couldn't push her. There was nothing in her records that said she'd had trouble in the past. "Yeah. That's fine. If you don't want to talk about it now, I understand. As long as you don't have a collection of ex-boyfriends in a mass grave or something in your backyard."

Her lips twisted. "Not funny. By the way, how's your back? I may need help digging a new garden."

I knew she was joking, but I'd be more than willing to bury any fucker who'd come sniffing around her. "Back's just fine but my hand is out of commission for a few days though. You may have to hold off your plans for a week or two."

And just like that she reached across the table, taking my hand in hers to inspect it, tucking in some piece of the wrapping that we both knew was just fine. "Your fingers have good color. It's not too tight, is it?"

I flexed, enjoying the soft, almost sensual brush of her fingertips creeping under the edge of the bandage. All at once, I was very aware of my dick again. "Nah. It's perfect. Just glad I wasn't riding the bike." I let my fingers close up around hers, testing the waters.

She looked out the window, eyeing the parking lot, while doing a great job ignoring that I was holding her hand. "Bicycle?"

My gaze stayed locked on her. "Motorcycle." Her little butt wiggled, I suppose thinking about it. "You ever been on the back of a bike?"

Innocently, she shook her head.

"I can fix that, you know."

And just like that, playful Erin was back. "I bet you can."

This girl was dangerous to my health. But this hand—this hand I was holding—had a healing touch.

"Whose turn is it?" I asked.

"Yours," she breathed, pulling her hand back. "I just spent mine asking about your—um—bike."

For some reason I felt a bit disappointed. "That was hardly a question."

"No. It's your turn. I don't cheat."

I wondered if she meant something more by that, figuring that statement could cover a lot of areas. Regardless, it was good to know. I watched her struggle for a few seconds trying to open the ketchup bottle. I held out my hand.

"Would you?" she asked, handing it over. "My home fries—oh, wait, your hand."

I popped the top. "Here you go."

She met my reach. "Thanks."

"It's your turn, Doc."

She took a moment. "You mentioned you have brothers?"

Relief hit me that it was an easy one. "Yep. Three of them."

That seemed to surprise her. "Your poor mother."

"Hah! Yeah, she got a lot of gray hairs from us."

"You the oldest? Youngest?"

"I'm number two." She had me hooked deep and I was dying to know. "Seriously, are you dating anyone now?"

"No." That truth was instant and directed right into my eyes. "I wouldn't be sitting here with you if I was."

"That's good to know." I had to hide my smile. "Ditto by the way. In case you're wondering."

"I was," she answered honestly. "I find that hard to believe, but thank you for being so forthcoming."

Visions of me being forthcoming with my tongue in her mouth were dominating all other thoughts of reason. And yet, *was she serious?* "Why is that hard to believe?"

Her cheeks pinked again. "I would presume it's sort of obvious," she muttered.

Now I was completely confused. Did she know about the show? "What is?"

She waved her fork up and down at me, as if she was going head to toe with it. *Does she think I fuck everything that walks?*

I was searching for the words to let her know how way off base she was when a wall of blue uniform caught my attention.

Fuck. Not now. Not fucking now.

Last thing I needed was to deal with Ron Castoll, asshole cop from my old unit with a chip the size of Montana on his shoulder.

"Morning Trent. What happened to you? Cut yourself on a beer bottle?" Castoll snickered, adjusting the utility belt holding up his fat gut.

I wondered if this arrogant prick remembered that I possessed the skills and knowledge to kill him a hundred different ways with just my bare hands.

Surprised the fucker hasn't tasered his own nuts yet. Dipshit.

Didn't take him long to eye up Erin. Stitches or not, I wanted to punch him in the head just for looking at her, knowing what sort of dirty shit was already flowing through that pea-sized brain of his.

I noticed the squad car sitting out in the parking lot.

"Come for your donut fix, Castoll, or are you just here to creep out the customers?"

Bastard smirked. "Nope. Just doing my normal patrol. Wanted to make sure some lowlife wasn't in here causing trouble." He nodded at my bandaged hand. "I see the grapevine wasn't lying. Surprised they actually let you out in the field these days, Trent. Aren't you just for show now?"

It took everything within me to keep my hands from crushing his windpipe. "Well, you know how it is, Castoll. Someone's got to catch the bad guys while you're busy writing out all them parking tickets."

Erin couldn't hold back her laugh. One chuckle slipped out of her.

Castoll glared at her. "I didn't know your shrink saw you outside of her office. Be careful, honey. You may think he's charming but this one will screw anything with open legs—"

I turned on the bench seat to face him, fuming. "Do not fucking speak to her. Eyes on me."

His head jerked at my tone. So did Erin's, but I didn't care. This game with him was old and tiring.

"Careful, Trent."

Are you serious? Brushing your hand over your service weapon—here? "Or what, Castoll?" I tugged my badge off my belt and slapped it on the tabletop. "I've got one of them too, remember? You want to see *my* Glock?"

Castoll scoffed. "Surprised they even let you carry. What you've been doing is a joke, Trent. An embarrassment to the shield. You might as well be a whore—"

Fucker shrank a bit when I surged to my feet and got in his face. "I think it's best if you move on now. I'm about to lose my temper if you keep talking and we both know who will win if we throw it down."

Even though I was locked in a stare-down I still saw Erin move. *Please don't get in the middle of this, baby.*

"What's going on here, boys?" Kathy wedged her way in between us, grabbing a dirty plate off the table.

Castoll stepped back. "Just letting Trent here know some things, that's all."

She glared up at him. "Well I think you've made your point. Your order's ready. How about you quit making a scene and get back to doing whatever it is you're supposed to be doing."

He stepped back and tipped his head at Erin. "Miss."

"Officer Casshole," she returned with a grin.

I stood there fuming, making sure he left before I sat back down. Desire to put his head through the wall had me clenching and unclenching my fists.

"Hey, are you okay?" She reached back across the table for me but I just stared at her proffered hand until she withdrew. Fuck being consoled and to hell with the pain in my hand; I wanted to hit something. I knew withdrawing was a mistake, but I couldn't help it.

"You want to tell me what all of that was about? Why'd he say stuff about me being your shrink?"

Yeah, we so aren't going there. After what Nikki did, the choices she made without me. I swore then and there that I'd never get put back in that pain. And here I was, inviting that shit back in again with open arms.

This beautiful woman sitting across from me had the power to eviscerate my soul. I could feel it slipping away with every second I spent around her. Fun or not, that shit wasn't happening to me twice in one lifetime. Fuck that.

Kathy interrupted me. "How's everything? I see you're finished. Can I get you anything else?"

I looked over at Erin, catching her hiding a yawn. She probably looks like a little kitten once she's well sated and nestled in bed. Too bad I'd never get to see it. Erin shook her head.

I let out a breath I didn't know I was holding. "We're done. Take the check then, Kathy."

As soon as Kathy walked away with our dirty plates Erin said, "Adam, I need to know something. What was up with the camera crew? I keep waiting for you to tell me, but it seems to be a topic you don't want to discuss."

I felt my jaw crack. "You're right."

I knew when a woman was incensed, and the one sitting across from me was well on her way.

"I suppose it's for the same reasons that everyone in this place keeps looking at you. At first I thought it was because we live around here but they all keep gawking and whispering. That older woman over there has taken it one step further to pointing. I feel like everyone around me is in on some big secret and I'm apparently too lost to know what that is. So please, enlighten me. What's the deal?"

I stared at the tabletop, seeing patterns in the veneer, while I rubbed my hand over my head. Another reason this was a bad idea. I so didn't want to bring a woman into this shit.

"You a dirty cop?" she asked outright.

"What? No. *No*, I'm not a dirty cop." *How could she even think that? Once she finds out the truth though, I'm gonna be nothing but a novelty for her, just like the rest of the women that don't see me for me. Or worse—she'd become a target for hate, just like Marcus's wife. I'd be a selfish bastard to subject a woman I cared about to that. Girls were already camping on my front lawn.* "Can we just not discuss it right now?"

"Why won't you tell me?"

Something in me snapped. "Because I don't want to. Can't you just leave it the fuck alone?"

"Fine. You don't want to tell me." She fumbled through her purse and tossed a ten-dollar bill onto the table. "That ought to cover my meal. It's been a long night and I need to get home."

She started scooting out of the booth.

"Erin, wait."

She leveled me with a glare. "I knew just looking at you that you'd turn from someone I used to like a lot into someone I used to know but I'm surprised it happened so quickly. Congrats, you've set a new record. Take care, Detective."

Damn it!

"Wait a second," I ordered, expecting her to halt but like hell on fire she kept going. I chucked money on the table, took back her ten, and snagged my leather jacket.

I managed to grab a hold of her arm as she was opening up the front door. "Would ya hold on a second? Damn it, woman."

I spun her on her heels before she hit the door.

Her chin came up in defiance. "A few hours ago you said to me that you had no patience for games and here you are, playing games. I've got news for you, Detective, I've got no time or patience for games, either."

I took a deep breath. She was right; she deserved the truth but I knew once it was out there, things would change. Doctor Erin Novak deserved better than to have her life threatened or her world disrupted by prying cameras, and I had no plans to let her surgically remove what was left of my heart. I let her arm go.

"Sorry Doc. You're right. I, uh…" My mouth dried and a hollow burn started to fester in my chest. I wanted to run, to hit something, blow a few thousand rounds through my gun and annihilate the pain. She was standing there, that sexy mouth hanging slightly open, waiting on me to fix this disaster. "Let me give you a ride home."

She turned a shoulder. "That's okay. I can call someone or get a cab."

"I'm not going to let you do that, Erin. Come on."

Kara came rushing over, adding to my problems. "Adam? Baby, are you okay?"

"Baby?" Erin questioned. "Are you serious?"

Fuck.

"Yeah, and who are you?" Kara snipped.

I needed to get Erin out of here—FAST. Asking her to meet me here was quickly turning into a very bad idea.

"Who am I? Who are you?" Erin shot back.

"I'm his girlfriend," Kara announced.

FUCK! "No, she's not."

"Girlfriend?" Erin was obviously shocked.

"Yes, *girlfriend*. Adam and I are dating," Kara said, then turned to me. "You didn't tell her about us, did you?"

My head was about to explode. "There is no *us*, Kara. All right? Never was, never will be, so get that straight in your head right now."

Kara's face fell. "Why are you saying that? We've been together for months. You going to deny we had sex, too?"

Erin turned and shoved her way through the door.

Kara was yelling my name, but I ignored her and followed Erin.

She started walking through the parking lot, marching that pretty little ass again in a hurry to get away from me. Just like last time, I wasn't having any of it. I jogged to catch up and stepped in front of her, blocking her way. "I'm not letting you walk home or whatever the hell it is you think you're going to do, so turn around."

She defiantly crossed her arms as the bitter February wind tossed her hair around. Damn, I loved her fearlessness. Still… "Easy way or the hard way, but I'm driving you home."

She glared and then tried to step around me. That's when I snagged her by the arms, clipped her thighs and hoisted her up over my shoulder. I expected her to fight it and she didn't disappoint.

"Put me down," she growled, kicking her legs a bit. "Your girlfriend in there will see us."

"She's not my girlfriend. Never was. I told you I'm not seeing anyone." Erin scoffed.

I used my good hand to swat her ass, making her twitch and yelp on my shoulder as I hauled her to my truck. "Call me a liar again."

She gave me the death glare when I set her down next to the passenger door. "I can't believe you just did that."

"It's freezing cold, we've both had a long night, and sometimes I'm an asshole." I opened the door, motioning for her to climb in. "But I don't care how mad you get at me, there is no way in hell I'm letting you out of my sight."

The drive to her house was short and silent and I knew she was pissed. I didn't need anyone to clue me in on how much I'd just let her down. I pulled into her driveway, right behind her car, which I noted was still missing a plate. I needed to fix that.

She grabbed the door handle and in that split second I knew she wasn't even going to say goodbye.

"Erin, wait."

She had one foot out of the door with her bag in hand, and I felt like my heart that had been out of the equation for so long was being twisted and sliced seeing her go.

As soon as I had her eyes, words came rushing out like a confession.

"Last year, my unit was approached to do a pilot for a reality TV show. Things took off and now every Sunday night at nine o'clock I'm on television. The show is called *Car Jacked* and that's why I have a film crew following me when I'm on duty."

Her mouth was slightly agape for a second before crashing back into a hard line. "But you're really just a police officer, right?"

I'd hoped at least that much was obvious.

Those sexy blue eyes narrowed with unanswered disappointment. "Is that why half of the restaurant was staring at you?"

I nodded, rubbing my hand over my head, fighting back the animosity at being an unwanted center of attention. "Yeah, I suppose."

"Was that so hard to admit?" She shook her head. "Why didn't you just tell me? We could have avoided—"

"It's…" *Christ, what do I say?* I peeled my eyes away from her obvious frustration, as if the windshield or the roof of her tiny red brick salt-box house were going to give me a brilliant answer. "It's embarrassing. I hate it. It's turned me into some sort of fucking novelty." I glanced over at her, trying to read her, hoping she was getting what I was saying. "It takes away from what could be real… genuine."

I watched her lips mash together, frowning at me; not the reaction I was hoping for. She took a few moments to mull it over, and then, as clear as a bell, I saw it dawn on her. "You think people only want the TV persona now, don't you?"

Bingo. Smart and beautiful. I drew in a deep breath, praying that she'd understand. "It's not who I am. And now some of the wives of our unit members are getting harassed because of it. The cameras, the unwanted attention... I just... I just don't want to bring that on you."

She sat there in silence while each beat of my heart counted her time processing all of it. Something inside me needed her to know just exactly what she was getting herself into if she allows me to take this further. We hadn't even touched upon my perversions or any of my other issues and already I was shoving her off.

Erin turned in her seat, surprising me. I could see the hurt in her eyes and the unspoken accusations of me being a complete jackass. "How do I know if you don't even give it a chance, because an hour ago, I thought that's what we were doing with getting to know each other. Wasn't it?"

She stumped me with that one. Did I want to get tangled up in another woman after the last one gutted me so easily? Would she be understanding and strong enough to keep me from falling backwards into my old, numbing habits?

"Guess I was wrong," she muttered. I watched her gather her purse and backpack, knowing she was pissed. "Doesn't matter. I suppose that other cop back there at the diner said it for you. And the little waitress you're sleeping with. You apparently date a lot and I'm really not in the mood to get played, so I guess this is goodbye. Have a nice life, Detective."

She jumped out of my truck so damn fast, I barely got the word, "Wait" out.

Without turning, she waved me off, dismissing me just like she had on the night that we had pulled her over.

Internal instinct was screaming at me, telling me to move my ass and go after her again, but my fucking legs and wounded pride refused to obey. I punched the steering wheel with the flat of my good palm as the frustration got the better of me. By the time I fully resolved that I should, in fact, go after her, it was too late. She'd already gotten through her front door and closed it, clearly shutting me out.

I sat there for a moment rubbing my scalp, thinking of ways to fix this clusterfuck of my life, but I was at a loss. One thing was for certain: it was hard to describe how deep this woman I barely knew affected me. It was like I felt her already *in* me. In my blood. In my thoughts. As if some invisible force tethered me to her somehow, making me ache from the emptiness she'd left behind.

I stared at her door and pondered the mess I'd made, wrestling with the urge to go knock on the damn thing or even go so far as to tear it down, remove it off the fucking hinges so nothing separated me from her. But I knew that none of my actions would be well-received.

I pressed the heel of my hand over my breastbone, hating that I allowed another woman get to me this way.

But it was too late. The injury I inflicted on her was clearly visible in the gloss of her eyes. Banging on her door now would only infuriate her more and make me seem out of control, and I just didn't have it in me to fight. I put my truck in reverse and backed slowly out of her driveway. It was for the best, telling myself just to leave it alone, 'cause I sure as hell had no clue how to fix it.

CHAPTER 7

Erin

GOD, I HOPE there isn't a dead body in the trunk, was the first thought that passed through my mind when the red and blue lights started flashing in my rearview mirror.

Sarah had been chauffeuring me back and forth to work for the last couple of days, but by the end of our shift Thursday morning, my convenient ride had come to an end. Sarah had the next two nights off, leaving me without a way to get to work for my shift tonight.

Instead of sleeping after she'd dropped me off, I spent the last two hours studying while waiting for the notary office to open. My eyes, like the rest of my body, were tired and feeling blurry, but there was no mistaking the distinct siren and flashing lights ordering me to pull over.

"No. Not again," I whined out loud, squeezing the steering wheel. I knew better. Adam had warned me and yet here I was, driving without a plate on.

I pulled over to the first available spot of curb.

The police car pulled up right behind me.

Shit. It's not like I was doing ninety down the road.

Adrenaline was coursing thick through my bloodstream and I felt lightheaded. I knew I should stay calm, after all it was just a traffic stop, but getting caught made it worse. With my luck right now, he'd make me open the trunk only to find that someone *did* shove a dead body in there.

Why did a traffic citation feel like the onset of being hauled off to prison? On the bright side, at least six other steel-plated trucks didn't join in on the fun this time.

I rolled my window down.

"License and registration," the officer ordered. I was slightly surprised, considering this policeman had quite a paunch going on.

As soon as I looked up at him, noting the unsightly brown birthmark on his cheek and moustache that reminded me of a walrus's tusks, it registered that this was someone I'd already crossed paths with.

"Yes, sir," I responded, being as compliant as possible.

"Well, well, look who it is," he drawled. There was no denying that he recognized me from the diner where I had had breakfast with Adam. Just being this close to him creeped me out. It took him a few seconds to drift his beady eyes from my face to my boobs.

In my haste to avoid his unwanted leering, I grabbed the bottom of my purse, the contents of which immediately rained down all over my lap.

My wallet made a thud when it hit the floor. I bent to reach it and cracked my forehead on the steering wheel.

And that was it. The final straw. *Haul me off to prison because I'm about to lose my precious hold on sanity.*

"Is there a problem?" the impatient Officer Castoll groaned.

I rolled my planted face over the steering wheel to look at him.

The intimidating officer leaned closer to my window. "Have you been drinking, Miss?"

His partner came around to the other side of my car. I could see out of the corner of my eye that his hand was resting on his weapon.

That snapped me to attention. "No, officer. Never." And certainly not in hospital scrubs at nine in the morning. I left out the part, *and you're going to add points to my driving record, which means that I will mostly likely have my license suspended and I will not have a way to get back and forth to the hospital job that I'm going to lose once the videos hit.*

After the night I just had discussing removing Uncle Cal from life support and my nervous babble to the creepy cop, I couldn't stop the shakes. I'd finally succumbed to the stress.

My car door opened. "Step out of the car, please."

What? "Why?" I didn't care for the fact that his hand was hovering over his gun now.

"I *said* step out of the car, Miss."

I groaned and dropped my empty leather purse onto the passenger seat while the rest of my things rolled under my seat.

Officer Asshole walked me to the front of my car. "Hands on the hood."

"Wait. What?"

"Do not question me. Hands on the hood—now."

Jesus, what have I done? *Is* there a dead body in the trunk of my car? I was only kidding, although whenever I saw that in a movie, I never turned out so well for the driver.

I caught Officer Asshole snickering to his partner. Bet it got his little wiener stiff posing me out on my hood like this while his partner, Officer Very Skinny and Ugly, got his eyeful.

My wallet landed on the hood. What the hell was it with cops dropping shit on my brand new car? I winced, hoping the paint wouldn't get scratched by their macho asshole routine.

"That your wallet?"

No, it's the missing booster rocket from the space shuttle.

I figured sarcasm wouldn't go over very well right now so I answered, "Yes." I desperately wanted to attend to the hair that was hanging in my eyes but I dared not let go of my bent position.

I saw the black truck coming down the road, stirring new nervousness through me. It slowed down as it got near the cop car; I didn't have to look to know exactly who was driving.

I freed my license and handed it to the round cop.

He scrutinized the little plastic card. "Name?"

"Erin. Erin Novak," I said, purposely looking away from the black truck. No sense making eye contact with him while being embarrassed once again.

To my surprise, the truck picked up speed. Just when I thought he'd drive off, he made a tire-screeching U-turn at the end of the block and parked directly across the street.

My breath caught when he slipped out of his truck, all clad in black just the way he was the day I met him. "ATTF" was written in bright lettering across the pocket on his chest, confirming he was a force to be reckoned with.

I took in his dark, short hair, which was messed perfectly, the shadow of a beard on his face, and the angered glint in his eye as he approached.

Shit, he's pissed.

The other uniformed officer seemed like he knew Adam, too, and was none too happy to see him, either. Both of them looked nervous.

"Not your jurisdiction anymore, Trent," Officer Asshole said, puffing out his chest.

I felt Adam's dark eyes burrowing holes into mine. He didn't even acknowledge the two cops. Instead, he came straight over to me, took my hand in his, and tugged me a few feet away. "You okay?"

I gave him a one-shoulder shrug as I flashed my eyes over at the looming Officer Castoll. "I don't think so."

Adam drew in a leveling breath. I rubbed the spot on my forehead where the pain was starting to throb. "I was trying to get to the notary to get a new plate and then this happened."

He glared over at the other two cops, then back down at me. "You just getting home from work?"

I nodded, thankful that the blue scrubs I was wearing were fresh and clean.

"You drive this to work?" he asked privately.

I was glad my truthful answer was "no" or else I surmised I'd be in a whole heap of other sorts of trouble.

"Good." His hand softly cupped my cheek. "You look too tired to be driving anywhere, Doc."

Great. He's being all sorts of sweet and I probably have hideous bags under my eyes.

He leaned over, grabbed my wallet off the hood of my car, laced his hand with mine, and led me to my driver's door. "Come on, babe." He opened my door for me, his hand resting on my hip, slightly shocked by his outward actions. I swore I could feel his formidable chest through the back of my jacket. I may have been exhausted but my heart was thumping double-time. "Get in," he said near my ear. "I'll take care of this. It's too cold for you to be standing out here."

I slid into my seat.

"Just wait a second, Trent," one of the cops argued, stepping around the back of my car.

Adam closed my door, glaring at the other two. I rolled my window down. "Want to tell me why you pulled her over?"

"Got no plate on the vehicle," the skinny officer said.

Adam wasn't amused. "And you had her standing out here in the cold for what reason?"

The rotund Officer Castoll adjusted his utility belt, hiking it up. "Again, not your jurisdiction, Trent."

Adam ignored him. "Damn it, Stiles, just answer the question."

Officer Asshole seemed to like riling Adam. "Well, we were going to give her a sobriety test until you interrupted."

"Sobriety?" Adam said mockingly. "You're shitting me."

"This isn't your concern, Trent," Officer Stiles growled from the other side of my car. "Although you may be an expert here." Something was going down between these three and it sure as hell didn't appear to be about whether I'd been drinking.

Adam stiffened. "Well, seeing as you've pulled my girlfriend over and *falsely* accused her of driving under the influence after she just pulled another night shift in the ER, I'd say it *is* my concern."

Girlfriend? What? Why the hell would he say that to them? We were anything but!

Adam walked to the back of my car with commanding grace. He tilted his head as if he were inspecting where my plate had been removed.

"You *smell* alcohol on her?" he asked, knowing that they didn't. When the other two didn't answer, he continued, "Was she driving erratically? Hmm?"

Again, no reply.

"Just as I thought; you got nothing. Have anything else you want to say to me, Castoll? Might as well get it off your fucking chest now while you got the chance."

Oh shit. Now he's really mad.

I didn't hear the words they exchanged as they were growled and heated and were at the opposite corner of my car, but the second I saw the skinny cop dive in between them, holding them apart, I threw my door open and sprang out of my seat. This situation was about to explode. I needed to keep him from getting into a tussle because of me. I clutched his arm. "Adam, don't."

Adam grabbed my driver's license out of the round cop's meaty paw and handed it to me, glaring daggers at the gloating asshole.

I gave his arm a tug. "It's not worth it."

Adam didn't budge. "Just get back in your car."

"Not without you."

I was afraid to move so Adam did it for me.

"I'm sorry," I whispered up at him as he guided me back to my driver's door, his hand almost resting on my ass.

I barely knew the man but I sure as hell knew what that glare meant. A soft growl rolled up his throat. Angry Adam was scary but sexy as hell.

"Get in, Erin. Put your seatbelt on." He leaned in and nipped my chin with his fingers, playing the doting boyfriend well, putting on a convincing show for the two gaping cops.

The smell of his light cologne combined with something that was one hundred percent Adam Trent instantly woke me up.

"Wait for me to turn my truck around. I'll follow you home." He didn't need to say the word *"again"* aloud; it was obvious. I watched his fine ass in my side mirror as he spoke to the two patrolmen. Hand on his hip and one definitely resting on his own gun, he was getting me out of another mess. "We're done here. You're letting her go with a warning. I'm taking care of the missing plate so there's no need to intervene."

He didn't wait for a rebuttal. His word was final.

I drove with exceptional cautiousness the mile back to my house, even putting my turn signal on to pull into my driveway.

Adam pulled his stark black Avalanche with the nice chrome wheels in right behind me.

I knew I was in trouble the moment he sidled up to my car door. "I know you're pissed…"

His silence was unnerving. So was the little tick straining his jaw.

I was so tired I was running on fumes and now I had a pissed-off, gorgeous cop who was heavily armed in my driveway. I tried a different tactic. "Look, I know it was stupid to drive without the plate but I didn't have much of a choice."

His eyebrow arched.

"Sarah's off tonight and Jen is already at work and I…" I was rambling. "Doctor Mason offered but that comes with a whole host of strings attached to it and… Damn it, Adam, I need my car. I drive from here," I pointed at my spot in the drive, "to the hospital and back again. That's it. Without it, I'm screwed."

He made that gruff sigh he does when he's sympathizing with me. "I'm not pissed at you Erin, okay? I know you need your car. Did you get a copy of the police report for the stolen plate?"

Shit. One more detail I'd overlooked.

I had been at the hospital so much, I'd lost count, and I'd made several stupid mistakes being so distracted. Fortunately they weren't critical errors, but they were errors I normally didn't make. My uncle was steadily deteriorating and my parents were barely holding it together. And this man… this man just does too many things to me. Just when I think I've seen the last of him, he appears out of thin air, confusing me further.

I couldn't think straight anymore.

"Come on." He opened my car door and held out his hand.

Come on where?

"You're exhausted, Erin. Let me have your keys." He waited until I handed them over.

He unlocked my front door and held it open. The feel of his hand on my lower back, guiding me inside, was strange and elating all at the same time. Could fate be giving us another chance?

He followed me into the dining room where I normally stow my purse. His attention then veered to looking at his watch while he started messing with my keys. He took the key fob off the ring and pocketed it.

"I'm keeping this for now. Just so you're not tempted."

I groaned. I wanted to protest but something told me it would be a losing battle.

He glanced around, zeroing in on my kitchen. "When was the last time you ate?"

I stared at the small section of wall by the refrigerator, trying to remember.

That tendon in his jaw flexed again. "You need me to make you something?"

I glanced up at him. "Why, do you cook?"

He gave me his silent nod.

Visions of him wearing nothing but his skin and just-fucked hair while cooking in my kitchen flitted through my mind. Pity, I doubted I had any food worth making. I shook my head, knowing that would never transpire anyway. "I ate at work."

He sighed again. "Do I need to tuck your tired butt into bed or are you going to go on your own?"

For a split second Sarcastic Erin wanted to take him up on the challenge just to see if he would follow through on his threat, but then I clamped down on her. Just the thought of being able to drop onto my soft mattress was blissfully tempting, but the notion of having him join me was almost too much to deal with. Considering the room was slowly starting to swirl, I held my hands up in surrender. "I'll go willingly."

He seemed to like that answer.

"You work tonight?"

I nodded. "I have to be there by seven thirty."

"Got plans before?"

"Beyond sleep?"

I tiny laugh escaped him. "Set your alarm. Be ready by three thirty."

Again with the hands on hips bossy tone. "For what?"

He smiled at me, sauntered over to where I stood, and softly caressed my jaw with his thumb. "Go get some sleep, Doc. I'll be back."

I stared up into those warm, chocolate eyes of his, liking the way they looked back at me. "Do you ever say *please*?"

He smirked, and then with the most sensual of snarky comebacks, asked, "Do you ever say *thank you*?"

"Thank you." I truly meant it.

"Then *please* be ready at three thirty."

"I'm sorry… about the other day." I didn't know why I was apologizing. It just seemed like the right thing to do.

"I am too. It's not how I wanted things to go. At all."

"Truce?"

His smile was warm as he stood in my air space. The tips of his fingers captured mine. "I'd rather call it a *do-over*. That okay by you?"

A do-over sounded perfect to me.

I watched his fine ass walk out of my house, pausing long enough to make absolutely sure my front door was securely locked. Then I watched him through my front window as he climbed up into his black truck and backed out of my driveway, feeling very alone from seeing him go.

I set my alarm, wondering what was going to happen at three thirty. I snuggled into my pillow, picturing his crooked smile. That was the last thought I had.

THE BLACK AVALANCHE pulled into my driveway at three thirty on the dot. Damn, he was prompt.

And holy hell he was gorgeous, too: blue jeans made to make mouths water, black motorcycle jacket that hugged him as if the two were longtime faithful friends, his spiky hair still looking fresh and wet from a recent shower.

My heart stuttered a bit.

"Hey," he said, squinting at me when he stepped into my foyer. I felt his eyes brush up and down my body.

"Hey," I said, just as breathily.

He cleared his throat. "You look really nice."

The timbre of his voice reverberated right into my elevated pulse. I let my eyes drink in his tall, muscular frame, not caring that our time after our breakfast date ended so horribly wrong. *You look completely sexy and totally fuckable.* "So do you."

He seemed nervous, which was a surprise. "You're wearing makeup."

I immediately became self-conscious. "You don't like it?"

"No, no. I do. You... you look very pretty. I haven't seen you with your eyes done. It's... I like it. A lot."

I felt my face warm, marveling that I was able to get Officer Hottie to blush, too. "Thanks."

He tucked his fingers into his jeans pockets and stared at his feet for a moment. "Ready?"

For what? To jump you? To kiss you? To go to the store for milk? "I guess so. Can you tell me where we're going first?"

He gave me *the look.* "Get a new tag for your car, Doc. I don't want you to worry about that anymore. And then I'm going to take you to dinner."

I stood there for a second, not completely sure I heard him correctly.

"Something wrong?"

That's when I remembered to breathe. "You're taking me to dinner?"

Adam crowded my space. "Yeah. Why? You have some other place you need to be?"

I didn't want to lie, but I couldn't help but wonder where his sudden change of heart came from. "No."

"Okay, then good. Why don't you get your coat on and we'll get going."

I sorted through my front closet, looking for a nice jacket to go along with the new hope swirling about in my chest. That part of me that had felt empty and alone was being resuscitated back to life. My black mood had definitely been tied to that feeling of loss when our breakfast date ended so horribly wrong, compounded exponentially by the family stress of my uncle's continued deterioration.

And here Adam was, standing in my living room, breathing new life into me by giving us a second chance, too.

I had hoped he'd been thinking about me, but the niggling sliver of doubt that plagues all women had me convinced that he drove off that morning and never gave me another thought.

I pulled my tan suede coat with the fluffy cream liner off the hanger, relieved that he was proving me wrong.

Adam reached for my coat. "Here, let me."

I froze, wondering if he was for real, until he started to help me put my coat on. The subconscious version of my mother that lives inside my brain started cheering and doing a most annoying and very age-inappropriate jig at his act of chivalry. I knew the moment Christine Novak would witness any of his gallantry, she'd be rushing off to organize my wedding.

I paused on my front stoop while he made sure my front door was securely locked, spending a few seconds giving the knob a twist and the door a light shove to make sure it wouldn't open back up. The cynic in me wondered if all this was an act but these things seemed to come quite naturally for him.

I followed him to the passenger side of his truck in silence and felt another heart spike when he held the door open for me. He waited until I was set and then closed my door.

As soon as he climbed into the driver's seat, he pulled a piece of paper free from the visor. "Here, you'll need this."

I unfolded the paper. My heart skipped again. He had gotten a copy of the police report for me. I looked over at him, wanting to hug him for being so damn thoughtful. "Thank you."

He nodded once, winked, then backed his truck out of my driveway.

We made it three blocks before I had to kill the awkward silence. I figured since he wasn't talking there must be something still bothering him. Why he was taking care of my problems was beyond me. "Thank you for coming to my rescue this morning. I just want you to know that I'm really sorry."

He gave me a real quick, quizzical glance. "For?"

I took a deep breath. "You—having to intervene. I shouldn't have tried to drive myself to the title place. I'm guessing you're still mad at me, but I was a little desperate."

"I'm not mad at you, Erin, all right?"

Even though he said it, I wasn't completely convinced. "You almost got into a fight because of me."

Adam sighed heavily. "That had nothing to do with you. Trust me."

Again with the patronization. I'd rather he be honest with me.

"Hey. I'm serious," he stressed, gazing at me a few extra seconds to accentuate his point. "Assholes from my old unit… well, that's another subject. Nothing for you to feel responsible for. I'll just feel a hell of a lot better once we get a new plate on your car."

I nodded, wondering if I should ask about the strained relationship he briskly brushed over. "Thanks for taking me. I appreciate it." *More than you know.*

"Well, I can't have you breaking the law around me now, can I?"

I fought my private smile at his innuendo and the sultry sound of his voice as he delivered it. "I suppose not. So I guess knocking over a convenience store is out of the question then, huh?"

"Depends," he drawled, leaning up on the steering wheel to eye oncoming traffic.

"On?"

He slowed his truck behind an older brown minivan before stopping fully at the red light. "On how badly you want to wear my cuffs again."

The way his eyes glinted and the tip of his tongue wet his bottom lip when he turned that heated gaze my way… oh God; he knew just exactly how to make me squirm, blush, and feel alive all at the same time.

He measured me up and down, definitely waiting on a reply, one that I was afraid to answer truthfully. "Can I get back to you on that?"

That sly grin warmed his face. "Yes, please do. I'll wait." He made a right onto Fairfax Road, snickering to himself.

I left it at that. "So what happens if you find my original plate?"

"Well," he started, tapping his thumb on the wheel in tune with the music softly playing over the radio, "with any luck it will be attached to a stolen car. And if we're really lucky, the thief who stole the car will be driving."

Picturing what he would do once he found the car thief was all too familiar. I had to shake off the slight shudder. "Then *he* gets to wear your cuffs."

"Yep. Then he gets to wear my cuffs. And then he gets to have his picture taken, we fill out a bunch of paperwork, and he gets a special visit with a judge. But I highly doubt we'll ever find your plate. Just so you know."

I thought about how one idiot swapping my plate was the catalyst for Adam and I even meeting. "If you hadn't been driving by this morning, I'd probably be in that Officer Asshole's cuffs."

Adam growled. "Yeah, about that... You want to explain to me why he tried to get you for D.U.I.?"

I felt foolish all over again, recounting the circumstances leading up to me hitting my head on my own damn steering wheel. "I think he recognized me from the diner. He seemed to enjoy causing me grief—just like he did to you the day we had breakfast."

I saw the hint of anger on his face, though he was holding most of it in. "You want to talk about it?"

"Talk about what?"

"What his beef is with you?"

Adam's shoulder dropped slightly, hinting at that being a resounding *No.*

"It's been years since... Honestly, it's water under the bridge."

"Adam."

I saw his grip tighten on the wheel. He wasn't the first guy to give me the stoic silent treatment, making a career out of building walls.

"I can tell it bothers you."

"It really doesn't."

He was about as good a liar as I was, which was a dead giveaway.

He played it off as if I was digging for something that wasn't there. "You looking for a confession, or what?"

"No, I'm looking for honesty and openness. I thought we were starting over. But it's okay if you don't want to talk about it. It's your business and I respect your privacy." I had my own past to protect.

He drew in a deep breath while I broke this physical attraction between us down to nothing more than a doomed proposition.

"You don't pull any punches, do you? You go right for the deep shit."

I shrugged. "I tend to search for the life-threatening issues first. You know—the stuff that kills you."

He leveled his eyes on me. "You planning on trying to heal me, Doc?"

I didn't care for his tone. It was one that I was quite familiar with, laced with hints for me to back off. Pity for him it was a challenge to me and provided even more incentive to rise to the occasion. "If you need healing, Detective. I might have to tear a few Band-Aids off first. Don't quite know the severity of your wounds until you show me or let me look. Just so you know, some things are beyond my ability to fix, and subjecting yourself to receiving treatment is solely your option."

He snorted at that. "Sounds like this might come with a probing physical. Grab my ankles and turn and cough. So what is it you'd like to know?" he muttered low, reluctantly conceding.

I rested my elbow on the edge of the window while I watched the sitcom of my life go by at forty-five miles per hour. *Wow*. If getting him to talk about the simplest of hurts was this hard, any deep shit that would come up in a relationship would be grounds for sitting in separate rooms. "Nothing. I want to know nothing," I barely answered, hating the sound of the quiet resignation etching my own voice.

Randy never wanted to talk, either. Take me to bed and fuck me—yes. Litter my apartment with his shit while eating on my couch and using my pillows as napkins—yes. Talk to me or share emotions or anything that truly mattered—hell no.

I'd fair better if I'd just learned that those were things I'd never have in a relationship, as my past surely outlined that to be a hard and cold fact. Men were stoic and women bottled their feelings until they erupted and overflowed. Those were lessons Randy drove home repeatedly. He gave nothing while I drowned in silence.

Less than twenty-four hours ago I properly diagnosed Appendicitis, treated a ninety-two-year-old woman with a fractured pelvis, and brought a patient out of afib, but there was no medical diagnosis for this moment. *Stupidity, perhaps? Myocardial desperation? Don't recall seeing that one on the MCAT.*

It bothered me that every time I got involved with a guy the same crap repeated, even though my friends seemed to find men who didn't fit the standard mold. Just a few days ago, this gorgeous man sitting next to me convinced me that our encounter could never bloom into anything even closely resembling a relationship, and here we were, repeating it all over again. Maybe one of us should have listened.

I glanced at my phone, willing the damn thing to ring or chime a new message or give me a reason to disappear into my own protective world. But I knew it wouldn't ring. Those who truly cared about me were busy with their own lives. Perhaps being single had its benefits, as dealing with men was terribly exhausting. *Exasperating. Debilitating. No, not quite debilitating. What's the word I'm looking for? Annoying? Trying? Tiring?*

"I made sergeant," he said, surprising me that he spoke.

He glanced at me quickly and then resumed his vigilant attention on the road. "Before I was with the ATTF, back in my old unit. Castoll was up for a promotion, too, but I got it instead."

And with that detail, the grinding twitch in his jaw returned. I surmised that opening up to *anyone* wasn't something that Detective Adam Trent was comfortable with. Still, I was relieved that he was making an effort.

"Needless to say, he didn't take it very well. He had more years of service in than me and he made a point of reminding everyone of that every chance he got."

Being in emergency medicine, where some of my colleagues had huge egos, I could completely relate. "Well, apparently he didn't earn it or deserve it."

Adam let out a partial laugh. "Yeah, well he didn't see it that way. Having to report to me as his shift supervisor made it even worse. His friends didn't take it well, either. Shit got uncomfortable."

"Uncomfortable?"

Adam nodded.

"Like how?"

He stretched his neck. "It's not something I really care to rehash, Erin."

I could relate to that, too. There were some stories I'd rather never have to rehash, myself. "Okay. I understand. It's fine." I watched the buildings and storefronts pass by my window, streaking into a blur of glass and signs and messages.

"He tried to pin some shit on me." Adam ground his jaw again. "Even…" His head swayed and he let out a muffled curse. "It cost me my partner."

"What an asshole."

He blew out a long breath. "Yeah. Understatement. Castoll's held a grudge ever since, so when word went out that they were creating a new task force, I put in for the transfer. That was another strike against me, I suppose."

"Why? I would think that you leaving his unit would make him happy."

"Yeah, you'd think."

"And the skinny one? Stiles?"

Adam shrugged. "One of Castoll's supporters. Been his partner for years."

It was starting to make sense. "Did you get even?"

He turned to me, confusion painting his features. "For what?"

"Him trying to pin something on you."

Adam shook his head. "There was nothing to even up. He failed in his attempts to drum up trouble and I got the hell out of there before he had a chance to succeed."

I nodded to myself. "So how did it cost you a partner?"

With that, Adam's body tensed as he stared straight out the windshield. Tension wafted off him in waves. I was almost sorry I'd asked.

"I don't like talking about it."

"I can tell."

His eyes shot over to mine.

I held up a hand. "Listen, you don't have to tell me if you don't want to." I hoped he could hear my understanding and repentance. "I get it. It's apparent that it's a very uncomfortable subject for you. We can talk about something else. Really. It's okay."

We drove a few blocks while I tried to think of something, *anything* that would be more upbeat.

"It was during a traffic stop," he finally said, breaking the unnerving silence.

I turned in my seat to face him.

"Three guys in the car, driving way too fast. As soon as I got up on the driver door I smelled it; the car reeked of marijuana. I called for backup before removing any of them from the vehicle. Castoll and Stiles were the closest unit."

Whatever he was recalling was painful. I could see it in his eyes, his sullen expression, the way his chest rose and fell with each word.

Adam wiped his hand down his face. "Castoll and I exchanged a few heated words as I was removing the driver. I'd just cuffed the dude and was going through his pockets when I heard Tom yell and then them bam, a flash went off. Guy in the back seat had a loaded .45. Caught my partner..." Adam swallowed, his voice eerily monotone, "Caught Tom right in the neck and up into his skull. He was dead before he hit the ground."

I couldn't suppress my gasp. "Oh, Adam..."

His head rocked. "It happened so fucking fast."

I let him gather his composure while imagining the bullet's trajectory and the estimated damage it caused.

"Castoll told I.A. that he'd thought he'd seen me pocket the baggie I'd found in the driver's pocket and that's why his attention wasn't on the backseat passenger."

My heart immediately sank and twisted, aching for him—for his pain and his injustice. What he'd just laid on me was so much more than I had ever expected. It was beyond heavy, but I took it. I held it. I'd bear it for him. He needed that much.

I reached for his arm, for any part of him that I could touch. He'd made himself vulnerable at my petulant urging and whether or not he wanted comforting, he was going to get it from me because that's what you do when someone you care about is hurting. You listen, you empathize, you offer healing words whenever possible.

In one conversation, it was more than Randy had ever given me in the eight months we were together.

Adam's body was rigid. How long had he been dealing with the survivor's guilt?

He quickly glanced at me again. "So now you know. And that waitress, Kara? I went out with her once, months ago. Just once."

I nodded. "Okay. Thank you."

His shrug of indifference wasn't convincing.

I drifted my hand down to his wrist but Adam gave me his hand, opened and offered, beckoning my fingers to lace around his. He was letting me in, trusting me with some of his deepest wounds and scars. It felt so good to have that with him.

I could see it the grim set of his lips, in the crinkle of his sad eyes, knowing firsthand the destructive wrath of false accusations and the crushing weight of guilt.

Now, only if I could trust Adam with mine.

IT DIDN'T TAKE long to reach the strip mall where the notary services were located. He knew exactly where I needed to go without me having to direct him, and after his explanation, the silence was actually preferred.

Adam pulled into an open spot, cut the ignition, and then said to me, "Stay there."

Huh?

Stay?

Don't I go in there with you, too?

I watched him hustle around the front of the truck, coming over to the passenger door, opening it for me. He held out his hand.

Holy shit.

As soon as we touched again, I felt it. Warmth and strength and breath-rending anticipation mixed with a million other tiny impulses. I knew I wasn't going crazy.

Moth, meet your flame.

He placed his hand on my back, guiding me through the threshold when he opened the door.

I wracked my brain, trying to remember if any guy I'd ever spent time with opened doors like that for me. *Mark? No. He was a selfish asshole. Randy? Maybe once but it was probably by accident as chivalry was a stretch for him.*

"Hi! Can I help you?" some young girl with long, straight brown hair said, slightly bouncing on her toes and smiling at Adam as if he were dipped in sugary candy coating when we approached the counter.

Part of me considered giving her a tracheotomy with the pen lying out on the counter to lessen her buoyant enthusiasm. Impaling her in the middle of her forehead to drain her frontal lobe also sounded tempting. *Whoa.* The possessive, jealous feelings coming over me were disconcerting to say the least. I was just about to speak up, tell her why I was here, but Adam took over, handling it.

The moment he started speaking I sort of froze and rocked back on my foot. This was a new, unsettling feeling, and one I wasn't sure I was completely comfortable with. Usually I'm the one directing the team, giving instructions, orchestrating the chaos when a trauma patient comes in.

But as I stood there, doing nothing more than watching him handle things with clear and concise instructions, I felt a wave of relief wash over me, followed by a warm rush of feminine appreciation.

Oh, believe me, the urge to bark orders was simmering right there on the surface. Even the desire to move Adam's rock-solid cop body out of the way, point at the paperwork and say, "You need to do this—STAT" was there. But, for once, I didn't need to exercise any control over the situation.

In fact, the only control I needed to embolden was to silence myself and let him take the lead.

What a liberating feeling. I felt light, ethereal... almost giddy.

I knew my ER residency was taking its toll on me—dealing with unspeakable traumas and horrific wounds and trying to determine from a laundry list of symptoms what was ailing a patient. I just hadn't had a benchmark to compare it to—until now.

"Erin, need that paper," Adam said, stirring me from my self-analysis to hand over the copy of the police report.

While I filled out a required form, Adam hovered next to me. I thought he was scrutinizing my handwriting until he leaned even closer, giving me all of his attention. I felt the heat warming my cheeks. I wondered if we might be sharing some of the same illicit thoughts? *Does he feel the same attraction? The same unfulfilled sexual tension? Or is it just me? Perhaps I am just imagining it all.*

"Excuse me. Sorry, I have to ask. Aren't you the cop on the billboard near—?" the young girl started to gush when she stopped typing into her computer.

Adam cut her cleanly off with a curt, "No." He didn't even bother to look at her when he answered; he kept his eyes trained on me instead. Or maybe it was just my lips.

I couldn't help but smile at him. We both ignored her request to take a picture with him.

His finger brushed over the sleeve of my coat. "So, what are you hungry for?"

I felt the blush again, and held back my first instinct to answer plain and simple—*You.*

CHAPTER 8
Adam

I GLANCED UP at the familiar green awning over the windows, wondering if I was being one hell of a cheap, masochistic bastard bringing her here.

I may be far from rich but I could well afford a decent meal and to treat her properly, and bringing her here was *not* what I'd envisioned when I offered to take her to dinner.

I should have decided for us instead of giving in to her. Just looking at the front door of the place felt like bad déjà vu. "Are you sure this is where you want to eat?"

Al's Tavern used to be one of my regular dinner stops; it had that Irish pub feel and great bar food, but it was *far* from fine dining. It also added a huge undercurrent of unwanted temptation that I so didn't need right now, especially after dealing with Castoll this morning. I had thought of at least five other restaurants to take her to, but she had picked this place instead—quite enthusiastically I might add—and as much as I wanted to, I couldn't deny her.

Erin nodded. "I'm positive. You put the words *gravy fries* in my head days ago. I've been craving them. Please? Pretty please? We're so close, I can practically taste them."

I wanted to balk that French fries with gravy on top was on the opposite end of what I had in mind for our first nice dinner together, but she was giving me that beguiling innocent yet so damn provocative look, I caved.

Still, I wanted to show Erin some class and a bar pub was not on my list. I parked my truck and killed the ignition, thinking that this woman sitting next to me was my first real date since I broke things off with Nikki. We'd been together for so long, I wasn't even sure I knew *how* to date someone.

I gazed over at Erin, noting her easy smile, the way she permeated my wall with effortless ease, knowing that this woman would be worthy of putting forth an effort. Just the way her eyes sparkled at me turned me inside out and flipped me on my ass. I felt uneasy, inept, and unsure, wanting—no—needing her to like me. Shit, I hadn't felt like this in… hell, I couldn't even remember the last time I'd been this nervous. I just hoped to hell none of that was showing on the outside.

She gathered her purse and reached for the door handle but I wasn't going to allow that. I may have brought her here and let her get away with taking her expectations for a nice meal down a notch while I fumbled to manage this date, but that was as far as I was willing to bend.

This entire day had tested my patience, starting with that bogus traffic stop Stiles and Castoll pulled this morning. Bastards would have given her a sobriety test had I not driven by at just the right time. Castoll knew exactly who she was; I could tell by the smug look on his beady face when I stepped out of my truck that he was thoroughly enjoying messing with her.

And then that girl at the notary office trying to flirt with me with Erin standing right there? Unbelievable the way some of them behave with no shame. Hell if it didn't make my ego swell a bit when Erin glared her down. But there was still plenty within my control and sensing her independent eagerness to let herself out my truck was something that would not happen on my watch. Kind of woman like her deserved to be treated like a lady.

"Hang tight a second," I muttered, hoping she'd keep her lovely heart-shaped ass planted in the passenger seat without me having to repeat myself. She looked confused again as I spied her through the windshield, but I figured sooner or later she'd catch on to the way things are.

I held her hand, helping her climb out, watching those incredible legs and heeled boots unfurl to the ground. Some men love boobs, and as much as I loved to palm tit, I was a legs and ass man to the core. Visions of those luscious legs wrapped in some of my quarter inch red rope, trussed up like two candy canes and spread open for my pleasure made my dick twitch. I'd keep her tied up all damn day and fuck her when and how I wanted to then. *Patience, Trent.*

"Thank you," she said with a shy smile and it was easy to read that she was a bit uncomfortable with me, which made her all the more enticing.

We were ushered by a server I'd seen in here before to a booth in the back. Before Erin sat, I helped to remove her coat then nudged her gently, making sure I got the side facing the door. She arched a questioning brow when I stepped around her, then she narrowed those perplexed blue eyes as she slid farther into the booth.

"I never sit with my back to the door," I muttered, trying to explain away her confusion.

"Phobia?" she asked casually, dropping her purse down next to her.

Maybe, more like vigilance. "I don't like surprises."

She turned, checking the door once more. "What kind of surprises are you not expecting?"

"The robbery kind." *Or the ex-lover kind*, but I kept that one to myself.

"Ah," she said, understanding seeming to dawn until her eyes narrowed on me once more, inspecting my chest. "Are you...?" She started to point but quickly withdrew her hand and then leaned over the table, whispering, "Is that a gun under your coat?"

I had my personal Glock holstered under my left armpit since I had picked her up at her place. I guess she could see it now, now that I'd unzipped my leather. "Yes," I acknowledged, wondering where she was going with this.

"Why?" She motioned, pointing at it again.

"I'm a cop?" I figured that should be self-explanatory.

She fidgeted. "Yeah, but you're off duty."

She had no reason to be worried. "So?"

"So?" She looked sort of stunned. "Isn't it illegal to just carry a weapon into a bar?"

I tried to harness my slight annoyance at her naivety. "I'm a cop twenty-four/seven, Doc. I'm just off-duty. I never leave home without it." That answer didn't seem to be adequate for her, considering she was frowning at me. I had to ask. "Does it bother you?"

She traced her fingernail over some imaginary pattern in the wooden tabletop and then picked at the corner of the menu. "I'm not sure."

I set my forearms on the table, glancing at my bandaged hand for a second, knowing how much danger surrounds each and every one of us every day, though most folks walked around impervious to it all. Still, she'd given me a half-assed noncommittal answer, probably treading lightly around me. I had to shut down her unease.

I captured the tip of her finger with mine, stopping her fidgeting, and her mind from drifting to a wrong conclusion. "I've been a cop for ten years. I've seen enough in that time to know that I will never be caught off guard or unprepared, especially around here."

For reasons I could not explain, I needed her to know she could trust me, especially since I gave her plenty of reasons to be leery of me.

"You ever able to slip out of doctor mode?"

She brushed more of her fingers over mine, hesitantly at first.

"No, not really." She smiled.

We were testing the waters, feeling the boundaries, and if the sensations coursing through me from just holding the tips of her fingers were any indication, I wanted to grab hold and pull her into the deep end with me. I had to constantly remind myself to keep it in check, even though my body was pushing forward. Rushing into another huge head fuck with someone was nothing I wanted to jump into lightly. *Been there, done that.*

"I see your point and I understand your reasons, but I've also seen the destruction a bullet can cause to the human body and it's not pretty. Too many people end up being innocent victims. We treat a lot of gunshot wounds at University. So much of it could be avoided. It's senseless."

I pulled more of her hand into mine, relishing the connection that I'd finally found a woman who understood. "People make bad decisions every day, but if it comes down to them or us, I choose us."

The moment she sucked in the smallest of gasps between those enticing lips I knew I'd fucked up. *Shit. Shit, shit, shit.*

I could see as clear as day those womanly wheels turning at lightning speed, probably forming all sorts of ideas. I had to fix it before she started envisioning me in a damn tuxedo.

"I mean, not *us*, like in us-us, I mean *us* as in normal citizens. You know."

She gave me a nod, a forced smile of acknowledgment, and a "Got it."

138

And that's when I lost her hand and her attention to the menu. "Mmm, all of this food looks good."

I slid my plastic menu off the tabletop and congratulated myself for being a dick.

Erin glanced at her watch and then went back to scrutinizing the menu. "I'm running low on time, so I'll have to get something that won't take too long to make. I still have to put that new plate on my car before I leave for work tonight."

Yep, you're officially a dick if she thinks that she's going to be putting that plate on herself. "I'll put it on for you."

She disagreed, tossing those long locks of dirty-blonde hair, still maintaining the "it's all cool" act. "Oh, you don't have to do that. You've helped me enough for one day. I can handle a few screws."

I had no doubt she could but her sweet tone had a bit of a bite to it, and though I couldn't fault her for it, it still ticked me off. "Erin…" I waited until she peeked around the menu to finally look at me, "I'm putting the plate on your car."

Her spine stiffened and I had no doubt she was about to give me a hard time, but my attention diverted to the big guy wearing the white chef coat headed my way, effectively halting her rebuttal. His familiar face was grinning widely at me, pulling my gaze from her, creating a wide grin of my own.

"Adam! Yo, dude!" Kip roared, clasping my hand and giving me a one-shoulder friendly bump. "Amber said you were sitting out here at a table. No shit. How you doing, man?"

It'd been too long since I'd seen my old friend. "I'm doing all right, Kip. Good to see you."

Didn't take him long to eye up Erin, still smiling like the overgrown jock he was who'd taken one too many tackles out on the field. Thankfully he masked his surprise at seeing someone other than Nikki sitting across from me. I was in no mood to have to explain things. He reached to shake her hand. "Hi! Todd Kilpatrick, but my friends call me Kip."

"Erin," she said, dazzling him with her electric smile. "Nice to meet you, Kip."

I was glad that handshake between them didn't linger, as Kip appeared to be at a loss for words. Ten more seconds though and I would have had to intervene. "Kip's dad owns this place, and he and I went to school together."

"That's right. Played football together for many years, too. So where you been hiding out, Adam? Haven't seen you in here in months."

I glanced away from Erin to give Kip my private annoyance for pointing that out, while hoping for a decent response to manifest itself out of thin air. I couldn't bring myself to be honest, because blurting that I've made a life rule to avoid all of the places that remind me of my ex would be stupid and cruel. So I opted for simple. "Been busy."

Kip nodded. "I bet. I've seen the show." His quick pass over Erin told me he was measuring her reaction, too, trying to figure her out. "You guys are taking over the city, getting a lot of attention. Excellent. So, things good there?"

Yeah, I get to take shit criminals off the streets and the public gets insight, seeing exactly what we go through to accomplish that. "I can't complain."

"Maggie was all beside herself when she saw the article on you guys in *People*." Kip put his hands on his hips, taking a stand that showed he was planning on hanging a bit. "Maggie's my wife," he said to Erin, clearing her confusion. "You're a big-time celebrity now, ya bastard." He smacked my shoulder. "Just don't forget your roots."

"That'll never happen."

"Good. So what's up with the rest of the Trent boys? Your brothers all doing good?"

I found talking about them was an easier topic. "Mike is still in Florida but Jason's overseas again." I eyed Erin, watching her eyes widen. "He's a chopper medic in the army."

I felt her foot slide up against mine under the table while her soft pink lips parted, silently giving me the message that I had her support and comfort. Damn if it didn't feel good, too.

Knowing my youngest brother was a world apart in some god-forsaken hellhole was like a knife to the gut, slowing twisting in me every day. I saw her hand start to reach across the table but she checked herself and flinched back. It was all very subtle, nothing that the unobservant would have noticed. I was glad she wasn't in a rush to share public displays of affection, especially in front of one of my friends. She was so different from the other women I'd been accustomed to.

And with that, images of Nikki yelling at my brother Jason, calling him a stupid asshole to his face for being enlisted, drifted through my thoughts.

How she got up in his business, preaching and arguing with him about how he should give a shit about what was happening here in this country instead of fighting for other's rights. The two of them didn't speak to each other for a long time after that, and my family surely didn't want me to bring her around anymore.

Erin adjusted her foot that she was resting on mine, breaking my thoughts, rubbing as if she were nuzzling me. It took everything within me not to reach across the table and acknowledge her private messages in my own way. Her inner beauty was shining through, bright and clear, blinding me with her generous gifts. I'd be willing to bet the farm that Erin would never be the type to challenge one of my brothers or publicly humiliate them in front of the rest of my family on their choices.

"Shit," Kip breathed. "Doing another tour?"

I nodded.

"Afghanistan?"

Jason's orders were actually classified. "Some shithole like that."

"God, I hope he's safe. Middle East. That is *not* a place to be these days."

"Tell me about it," I muttered.

Kip shuttered. "Damn. Well, we'll pray for him. Oh, and speaking of the Trent brothers, my wife showed me a picture of Kyle the other day with that blonde actress… what the hell's her name from that movie? The one that all the women are going ape shit about? Aw hell, I can't remember."

Hell if I knew either. While I could only handle one girl at a time, Kyle liked variety. One thing was for certain—Kyle and I both had a weakness for blondes.

"He still in California?"

I gazed back at the gorgeous blonde sitting across from me, giving me her undivided focus and attention.

"He's all over the place, Kip. It's hard to keep up with him." I couldn't hold back my smile. My brothers might be dickheads sometimes, but they were still my brothers and we were all tight, even though we didn't take a lot of time to call each other. "My brother Kyle is a bodyguard. He's had a few high-profile clients lately."

"What, like celebrities?" she asked.

I nodded, aware of her tempered reaction.

"Wow," she uttered, giving me a warm smile. "Sounds like a very interesting career. I bet he has great stories."

I was glad to see her thoroughly interested but maintaining her enthusiasm. Last girl I told that to lurched over the table, pawing at me with such fangirl exuberance to find out dirty details, I was afraid, not to mention instantly turned off by it.

But not Erin. She had class.

My eyes focused on her sexy mouth, the pit of my gut sparked an all too familiar fire of want, and I found myself wishing Kip would get lost. "Probably, but we don't talk a lot about it. It's his business and he's usually pretty tight-lipped. His job comes with pages of non-disclosure agreements, so he's not one for long-winded discussions."

Erin readjusted in her seat, and that's when I lost her foot that was touching mine. I wished she'd put it back where it was. "Is Jason the one that's older than you?"

I shook my head, stretching my leg her way, trying not to kick her by accident. "No, he's the baby of the family. Mike's the oldest, then me, Kyle, and then Jason."

"What does Michael do?"

Gets into deeper shit than I do with drug cartels? "He's a police officer too, outa Miami."

Kip gave me another slap on my shoulder. "Badasses, all of them. Hey sorry to hear about your dad, man."

I let his condolences roll off my shoulder with a nod and took them for what they were—Kip being decent and respectful and a friend who still gave a shit.

"Is he doing better?"

Getting that frantic call from my mother last summer was something I could do without remembering. It was also one of the things that brought everything to a head. "Yeah. He's got a bit of a slur yet when he talks but it's a lot better and, well, he's still breathing." I met Erin's concerned stare. "He had a small stroke."

"Shit," Kip breathed out. "Looks like you've had your plate full, man. No wonder I haven't seen you around."

Considering I was the only son in town when it happened, that was putting it lightly.

"Adam's dad coached varsity ball our senior year. He's a tough son of a bitch," Kip said with a grin to Erin.

Erin brushed her fingers over the scar on top of my right hand, giving me her comfort again, but looking at that disfigured line that zigzagged across my skin was an unwelcomed reminder of being on the receiving end of his belt the night Nikki's cop father brought me home butt-ass naked. To say my father had a firm hand was an understatement. Raising four hell-raising boys took its toll on the old man.

Erin's face fell when she saw what I was focused on, and I could feel her wanting to give me her sympathy too, though I sure as hell didn't need it. The shit I went through to become a man wasn't anything out of the ordinary.

"How's your mom holding up?" Kip continued.

"She's got her hands full with him being home all the time. And it doesn't help that she's constantly worrying about all of us, either."

Kip nodded and pulled out his phone. "That's what moms do, man. Hey, I've got to get back into the kitchen, but it was great seeing you. You still at the same cell number? We need to keep in touch."

By the time the girl took our order and we got some soft drinks served to us, Erin had gone fairly quiet, eying me warily.

"I'm sorry about your dad," she said, tossing the topic back onto the table. "Was it recent?"

I felt my jaw clench, recalling that horrible moment. It happened right before Nikki and I split up. What she had done while I was dealing with one of scariest moments of my life was unforgivable. "It was last summer." June 18th to be exact, in the morning. "I was headed home from work. My mom called to tell me that she was having trouble rousing my dad from bed."

Just saying the words caused a shudder to roll down my spine. I'd never felt so helpless in all my life. And just when I needed someone the most, Nikki dropped the bottom out from under me. I know most of it was my fault, but damn.

I glanced back up at Erin, whose wheels were turning with what I could only surmise was filled with medical textbook passages, hospital experience, mixed in with a lot of womanly concern.

"I've treated a few stroke patients," she said assuredly. "Do you know if it was from a blockage or an aneurysm?"

Even though we were talking about my father, hence *my* inner wounds again, I had to hold back a smile. Her doctoring was cute as shit. "Blockage. High cholesterol runs in the family."

Her head popped up, scanning the entire area. "Maybe we should change our order then. You shouldn't be eating fried foods."

"Erin…" I grabbed her hand before she had a chance to even think about darting into the kitchen. "I'm good."

That brought her down a notch and her butt back down to the bench seat, but I still felt like I needed to hold her in place.

"Are you sure? I don't mind eating something else."

And just like that I thought about eating her—her lips, her neck, feeling the heels of her feet dig into my shoulders as I ate my fill. She'd wiggle in my hands, on my tongue. I felt the blood flow surge; my boys down below definitely wanted in on that entire scene. I cleared my throat. "You'd forgo eating gravy fries for me? For real?"

"Yeah. Please. Let's order something else that's healthier. Maybe the waitress can bring the menus back."

My chest tightened, pressing the emotions up into my neck. *Could she really be that concerned for me?* "We don't need menus. You wanted gravy fries—we're eating gravy fries."

"Adam, I'm serious."

"So am I. I swear… Healthy as a horse." Instantly, I had to fight back images of her riding me. Her hands pressing into my chest as I palmed her ass, guiding her up and down on me. *Fuck.* I shook my head. "I get regular checkups and donate blood every time we have a blood drive. My numbers are good, Doc."

She grimaced. "I hope you're being honest with me. I don't want to tempt you with bad food choices."

My lust-filled images were swept over with a tinge of annoyance. "Erin, I need you to get this in your head right now. I don't lie—ever. I'll always be straight up with you. Always. I may choose to keep things to myself, but omission is not lying."

Her eyes locked onto mine, searching, I supposed. "No man has ever said that to me," she said in a tiny voice.

That's because she's probably dated assholes. "Just so you know I expect it in return. I find that you're telling me a bunch of shit, it won't end well. We clear on that?"

"Crystal," she said with a nod. "And might I add—very refreshing."

I liked feeling her relaxing. Her hand eased into mine and most of the recent tension evaporated, allowing me to relish the fact that I was holding her hand again. Don't know exactly what was happening or how, but damn if I didn't feel that invisible tether winding its way through my hand, up my arm, making my pecs tingle.

I was far from a novice when it came to doing this dance with women, often feigning the interest to get the most out of it, but Erin Novak was tossing me way off my game, making me aware of everything.

"Why are you smiling?" She smiled back.

"You." I said it before I'd completely fleshed the reasons out in a rational explanation in my head.

"Me?"

"Yeah, you. I thought you were going to run into the kitchen and stop Kip from pouring gravy. I think it's cute you're all concerned about my cholesterol." If she was this concerned about me being tempted by fried food, I was willing to bet she'd be okay with my other issues. Well, at least I hoped she would be.

She was tickling the inside of my palm with her fingertip, and hell if I didn't feel that in other places again.

"I'm glad I amuse you," she said teasingly.

"You do."

"I can't help it," she admitted to the tabletop. "I'm a worrier. Always have been. Sometimes I can't sleep, knowing that I have people's lives at stake with my decisions. I try to be sensitive to the person I'm treating, but sometimes when it's crunch time and seconds count, I have to just detach and view them as nothing more than live human anatomy models and figure out why they're broken or else I drive myself mad. Oh God, I'm rambling."

"I like when you ramble."

She measured me, feeling me out. "Seriously?"

I nodded and took a sip of my Coke.

"I'm usually the poster child for controlled composure," she admitted.

I crossed my arms, resting them on the table. "Sounds like we have that in common."

Erin's head tilted. "You too?"

Totally, sweetheart. You have no idea. "Your mistakes could cost a life. Mine could cost the lives of innocent civilians, my team members, and myself. I take my job just as seriously."

She blew out a relieving breath. "It's like we have to be on our game twenty-four/seven. Sometimes it's utterly exhausting. Not too many people understand that."

"Well, if it's any consolation, I do. Very much."

Her glowing grin fell. "I'm sorry you had to experience that firsthand."

I was starting to think this woman was going to kill me with compassion. Wrap that around the notion of her fucking me to death and I couldn't think of a better way to go.

Even thinking about that day Tom took a bullet brought ugly pain back up in me.

"Something tells me there's more to it than that, but I won't ask."

Huge understatement. The fact that she was reading me so easily was also very unsettling. It was like she was tapped right into my thoughts, picking through the shit pile with effortless ease. I'd been out with plenty of girls in my time and none of them, not a single one of them, ever looked at me as if I were so transparent.

I could tell she wanted me to tear another patch off my inner festering wounds but I wasn't going to give it up. Not yet, anyway. I had to remind myself that Doctor Erin Novak's healing ways would have to endure some additional testing. We barely knew each other. But looking in those gorgeous sea-blue eyes and seeing my reflection bouncing back at me told me what I wasn't quite ready to face. I was a goner.

All through dinner I had to fight the urge to kiss her. The way she laughed at my lame recollections of the trouble my brothers and I had gotten into when we were kids, hanging on to every one of my words and giving me words of her own back, sharing those memories of skinned knees and adding gray hairs to our parents... It was all so easy and effortless that I felt like I'd known her a hell of a lot longer than a couple of days.

And when she talked about her sister, Kate, glowing with pride at her accomplishments in veterinary medicine, made me want to dial up one of my brothers and tell them to get their heads out of their asses and take the girl out because she, too, sounded amazing.

I'd never had a French fries with gravy sword fight before, but heck if she didn't make that one of the highlights of my month as well. Everything was just so... effortless. I didn't feel like I had to be on guard or measuring my words or pretending to be something I wasn't. I was just—me. Free and able to breathe again.

Even after three years, Nikki never got me. She tried to understand what made me tick, but so many times I knew with every fiber of my soul that the girl and I were on two very different pages most of the time. I'd try to explain and she'd only hear what she wanted to hear and then we'd argue.

But Erin was Nikki's polar opposite. She was funny and bubbly, teasing and playful, and just so down to earth that I found myself thoroughly at ease enjoying her company. I had gone into this worrying that she'd turn out to be somewhat of a snob; after all, she did go to several expensive colleges and was a trauma doctor for Christ's sake. I figured she'd be a bit more straight-laced and uppity, even when she let her guard down.

Instead, she was quite the opposite. For as obviously smart as she was, she was a bit insecure and unsure of herself around me, which was cute as hell. I liked it. I liked that a whole hell of a lot.

That meant she wouldn't treat me as if she were better than me, which was something—though I'd never admit it out loud—that passed through my mind while I helped her devour a plate of gravy fries and hot wings. Little by little I felt her wiggling her way into me.

I TIGHTENED THE last bolt holding her new license plate on the back of her car and gave it a tug, making sure it was on tight, and breathed out in relief that it was done. Now she could drive back and forth to the hospital without either one of us worrying about her being pulled over again. I put my tools back in my toolbox and locked them up in my truck, feeling satisfied. The anal part of me checked one more time to make sure the plate was securely fastened and that I had placed the new registration card in her center console. Things were golden when I saw it folded up with her insurance card.

I let myself in through her front door after knocking to announce my entry and found her in her kitchen, making what looked like a sandwich. I felt my breath stutter at the sight of her, that golden hair that was caressing a bit of cleavage that was peeking out from the white top she'd been wearing during our dinner, the way she was softly humming a song playing in her head. The entire package looked soft to the touch and completely consuming.

Her eyes lit up and, for a moment, I wondered if that was because of me. I felt something I thought was dead stir inside me. She smiled and then tilted her head my way. "All finished?"

"Yeah, you're all set."

Those lips that looked like pink candy curled up again. "Thank you," she sighed out, gazing at me as if I were some sort of hero.

I'd be a liar if I didn't admit that felt great, too.

In that moment I became acutely aware that there was a huge difference between a woman hanging on me making me feel wanted and one that was glowing with pure appreciation by a simple act of kindness, making me feel needed.

This wasn't my first rodeo and I'd had plenty of experience knowing that womanly appreciation eventually turned into expectations, but it was always a red flag when a woman started right off with entitled demands. The woman standing in front of me didn't expect anything. Hell, she had fought my intentions to put her new license plate on up until the moment I got my toolbox out of my truck.

And damn if that didn't make me more interested in her.

I noticed her kitchen sink had a slow drip, and my pushing down and jiggling the handle didn't stop it. The outdoor light above her garage door was burned out, too—those were just a few of the things a man should be taking care of for her. I added them to my mental list of future good excuses, because I sure as hell wanted to see her again.

CHAPTER 9

Erin

I WATCHED AS Adam glanced at his bandaged hand, flexing his fingers and picking at the wrapping.

"You got it dirty, didn't you?"

He nodded sheepishly, giving me a glimpse of how adorable he must have been as a mischievous child. "Tried not to, but I had to fight with one of the bolts."

"Come on," I motioned toward his hand, "let's go take a look at my handiwork."

Adam followed me down the hallway and up the steps, where I ushered him into my bathroom. "We going to play doctor?"

I grinned. "Yes, but not the X-rated version."

"Bummer," he grumbled under his breath.

I pointed to the closed toilet. "Okay, Detective Trent, have a seat."

Adam rested his elbow on the sink counter, offering his hand for inspection. I sifted through my medical kit, finding my thermometer. I saw his apprehensive, questioning look while I wiped it with an alcohol swab.

"Open."

"I thought we were just checking stitches, Doc."

"We are. I also want to check your temperature too, so open up."

He frowned at me. "Fine, but I'm not bending over for this."

What a big baby. "That's a shame." I smiled. "A low grade fever usually accompanies infection, so I'm checking it to make sure you're okay with a thorough exam. Now open."

I snapped on a pair of gloves, knowing he didn't have any allergies to latex.

The thermometer tipped up in his pinched lips and one gorgeous brown eye scrunched, leaving no doubt as to what he was thinking.

"You, officer, have a dirty mind."

"You're the one putting rubber gloves on, Doc."

I pushed the edge of the thermometer back into his mouth. "Hush."

"Yes, ma'am." He snickered.

I removed the damp, dirty gauze from his hand, hoping I wouldn't see signs of infection.

Ah, relief. "Sutures still look good." I cleaned them and put some antibiotic cream on a sterile cotton swab, noting with sheer exultation how his large hand dwarfed mine.

A man's hand... Proximal phalanges that articulate with the metacarpals... how would it feel squeezing my breast? Distal phalanges pinching, rolling my nipples between them, gliding down my body, touching me where I ache. Dipping and playing in the wetness that's gathering from just these thoughts?

"Still looks swollen, though," Adam mumbled, cutting right through my internal fantasies. Just as men get erections, I felt swollen myself.

I pulled the thermometer out of his mouth when the digital sensor beeped. If I didn't know any better, I'd have sworn he was eying me over with the same lascivious thoughts.

"What's the prognosis, Doc?"

Even the rumble of his deep voice set my body on high alert. "Your temp is normal. You're going to live."

I wished I could know what he was thinking. The way he regarded me with that speculative stare told me he was mulling a lot of things over in his mind as well, but what kind of things was still a mystery. Would he stick around long enough to make this a never-ending treasure hunt or would it be the cliff notes version of my sad, pathetic love life?

I wrapped the first pass of gauze around his hand, speculating that a man like him probably wasn't ready to settle down. The mischievous look in his eyes said it all. This cop was probably looking for a hit and run and I was far from bulletproof.

Though he'd been a complete gentleman so far, and had taken me out twice, so maybe... Wait... Did an omelet at a diner constitute an official date? Didn't matter; I wanted him and I was pretty sure he knew it. I was fumbling just trying to wrap the bandage on him.

Even if that other cop was just trying to be an asshole at the diner, there must have been some truth to his accusations of Adam being a player.

Sharp jaw, killer eyes and smile, biceps that screamed "you should see the rest of my body if you think this looks impressive" with that perfectly cropped bed-head hair; yeah, all signs pointed to trouble followed by that soul-squashing heartbreak.

While he looked amused, I fell apart inside.

This was typical. So freaking typical. My attraction to every wrong guy—starting with losing my virginity three weeks into my first semester of college to that idiot Dean whatshisname, stuck with me over the years like crap on my shoe.

I tacked on the last piece of tape, securing the end of the protective wrap, wishing I could bind my heart with the same. Would he play me for a fool? Distract me from my fellowship goal with meaningless sex while my feelings get tangled up? "There. Good as new." I gave him my trusty doctor's grin. It was a failsafe. "Try to keep it clean and dry at work."

"You're overthinking it," he muttered, sounding somewhat disappointed.

"I'm what? You need to keep the sutures dry and clean and—"

"No." Adam shook his chin slightly. "Whatever's rolling around in that pretty little head of yours that has your eyes looking sad. That's what I'm talking about. Not this." He held up my gauze-wrapped handiwork.

Could he read my mind? *Oh hell no.* "I'm not sure what you mean." I closed my med kit. "It's getting late. I have to be at work soon and traffic is going to be heavy and—"

Adam stood up abruptly, getting right into my space and staring me down. "You know what I'm talking about. Don't overthink it. I'm an open book, Erin. You've got questions, I got answers. It's best if that works both ways."

I fumbled with a comeback, feeling cornered and dumbfounded. Were my female insecurities that transparent?

He drifted his fingertips down the side of my jaw and, for a moment, I thought he was going to try and kiss me. God, I wanted him to so badly. That would shut down my internal musings.

That feeling of being let down washed over me when he stepped out of my bathroom.

I thought he'd be making a beeline for my front door; instead he lingered, scanning over my spattering of pictures, even picking up the one of me when I graduated from medical school.

"Johns Hopkins?" Adam questioned.

I nodded, stepping to his side. "That's my younger sister Kate in the blue dress."

"I see some resemblance. You've got the same eyes. How old is she again?" He handed the picture frame to me.

"Twenty-six."

"She's Jason's age."

I wiped a wisp of dust off the frame, staring at her smiling face. "She graduates from veterinary school in a few months. She's down at the University of Maryland. God, I miss her. But I'm sure I'll see her for the funerals."

"Funerals?"

I put the picture frame back on the shelf, straightening it. "My aunt and uncle were in a car crash a few days ago. The triple fatality on the Schuylkill that happened the night that you pulled me over?"

Adam's shocked gaze whipped over at me.

"My Uncle Cal is still in ICU but he's deteriorating and my aunt... my Aunt Karen was killed at the scene."

He eyed me over with something resembling abject horror, his face turning pallid. "You mean to tell me that the vics were related to you?"

I nodded. "We're all very close. This house is one of their rental units. They are, um, were like second parents to Kate and me."

Adam rubbed his forehead before covering his eyes, shielding them from me while his lips rambled a few silent curse words.

When he finally looked at me, his face was pained. "I am *so* sorry, Erin. Oh, God. I had no idea."

He was touching me, running his hands over my arms, feeling me as if I might be broken somehow. "You okay?"

I actually wanted to eke out a sob but refrained. Death was a fact of life, no matter how hard I tried to intervene. All we were capable of doing as doctors was delaying the inevitable. "I'm dealing. My parents are taking it hard, though. Really hard." I picked up the picture of them huddled around the slot machines from one of their trips to Las Vegas, smiling at the big "Win a Honda" sign over their heads.

Adam held out his hand for it. "Is that them?"

Just looking at the picture hurt. So many wonderful memories cut short. "Yeah. This is my mom and dad and that's Uncle Cal and Aunt Karen. The four amigos. She died at the scene."

A tear escaped the corner of my eye.

Adam seemed to take this information harder than I would have expected. His grip tightened on the frame and the oddest look came over him. "I don't even know what to say, Erin. I'm sorry you and your family are going through this. So much senseless violence in the world. So much I wish I could change." His hand shook a bit as he set the frame back down, adjusting it with the tip of his finger as if to put it back exactly where it once was. "…I had no control over it," he muttered, "God… have no control over any of it. The Manley brothers…"

I thought about all of the people who fought for their lives when they came through those ER doors, wishing I could fix them all, too, work some sort of miracle so that no one would have to experience loss or grief. "Sometimes I think our fate is just out of our control. No rhyme or reason to it. Bad people live; good people die. Innocent children fight diseases or suffer from the… the *malicious* mistreatment at the hands of their parents while drug addicts and gang bangers get to live on. It's crazy and it makes no sense."

I met Adam's solemn eyes. "But then there are people like you to stop them and people like me to fix them. And we do the best we can, knowing that we can't win them all."

He gazed at me for the longest moment; it was evident that something was troubling him. "Erin, I'm… Sorry, but I have to go."

His demeanor had changed so abruptly; I was confused by the sudden turn. But he grabbed his coat, looking lost, confused, and scattered, and hurried for my front door.

Adam barely looked at me before he gripped the doorknob. "See you later," he muttered and before I could stop him, he slipped out of my house.

And then he was gone. The blustering wind and winter chilled ice crystals swirling in his wake, leaving me just as cold and barren as the dark February sky.

I WAS GLAD Sarah had finally found other things to obsess about beyond my lack of a love life. Over the course of an emotionally trying solid week, her bubbly and excited, "Did he call yet?" daily questioning morphed into a somber, "Still no word?" with an extended bottom lip to show her solidarity.

No, he didn't call. He didn't ask for my phone number before he ran out my front door and unless he had police officer ways of finding my cell number, all points indicated to him never calling.

Believing I'd have a shot with someone so gorgeous—and locally famous as Adam was—well, let's just say I was fairly certain he didn't need my number. I'd be willing to bet women tossed their numbers at him daily and, if they got extremely desperate, they could always spray paint their phone numbers on the gigantic billboard advertising his television show that I'd discovered by accident yesterday near the underpass on Grant Avenue.

I was such a sappy ass. I even turned my car around so I could gaze at the ginormous picture of him. Adam was front and center with the rest of his team flanking him on both sides, looking all badass and sexy in their ATTF uniforms.

I parked in a space at the Dunkin' Donuts across the street, staring at a freaking billboard, wondering if I ever crossed his mind. Lord knows I surely couldn't get him out of mine. I couldn't stop the tears once they started. *Silent tears*, my grandmother used to call them—the kind that fall when you think there's no one who could possibly understand your sadness.

The stress from trying to follow my dreams was taking its toll. I'd achieved becoming a doctor—it was a blur of years mixed with spirit-rending days as a resident, barely existing while studying incessantly, balancing everything on the delicate precipice between killing someone and curing them. I'd made my mark, proved my competence time and time again, and gained the respect of my superiors and mentors.

But love? There was no pill or cure or pathology for that.

After ten minutes of reminiscing over something I never quite had while staring at his enormous likeness, I wiped my face with the backs of my hands, feeling stupid, foolish, lonely, and once again, not good enough.

Which is why on day six of Sarah's incessant questioning and my feigned happiness, I found myself calling an old friend, Tommy Rizzotti.

Six days of dwelling in my self-imposed misery spiral was enough. What I needed was to feel alive again. To at least feel desired, even if it was for meaningless sex. Tommy was my secret outlet when my limited array of personal pleasure products weren't enough to bolster my failing self-esteem. He had dropped out of med school his second year, returning to Philly and his first love of music. He was tall and lean, with a tiny birthmark on his cheek that accentuated a gorgeous face. Tommy was the lead guitarist in a rock cover band that was quite popular within the local club scene. He also had the dirty-blond unkempt bed hair and dexterous fingers of a decent musician, which made him one hell of a desirable package. This he used to his advantage, and finding his bed empty was hit or miss. One thing was for certain, Tommy may be a man-whore but he was vigilant when it came to wearing condoms.

And he was my man-whore standby.

And man, did I need his services—badly.

I felt sort of disgusted with myself that I'd have to resort to washing the residual hope of Detective Adam Trent away with a meaningless booty-call, but at least I wasn't crying inside anymore.

Tommy was unfortunately in Connecticut and wouldn't be back until the afternoon. He had a local gig Friday night at ten, but was willing to get a quick pre-show fuck in before it at eight. It was either that or I'd have to wait until after the show and then his options for bed partners would quadruple.

Must be nice to be in such demand that you could schedule getting laid.

Perhaps he was onto something; having your physical needs met without investing your heart and soul in the deal. It was actually a brilliant setup now that I'd spent some time analyzing it.

Tommy and I never had that emotional connection that brought about jealousy; he liked to fuck and was always willing to take me in like a sad kitten in desperate need for a meal, which made our encounters safe and manageable for both parties. It helped that he was one hell of a nice guy with the tongue skills of a madman.

I loved how Tommy managed to make the act of requesting meaningless sex over the phone as effortless as ordering Chinese take-out. *"Yeah, hi. I'd like to order the number two sex combo platter with extra cock. Does that come with one or two finger penetration with the oral? Two? Excellent. No, hold the post-sex awkwardness. Oh, can I get an extra helping of CumOfSomeYoungGuy? Thirty-five minutes? Perfect."*

These were the thoughts in my head as I drug my garbage can to my curb for its Friday morning pick-up, while contemplating whether or not I could pull off being a booty call for several men in between studying medical textbooks and reviewing toxicology studies. Would probably solve some of my tension issues without worrying that I might get hurt or have some asswipe do the foot-stomp on my heart.

I needed to get to the hospital and then get on with my clandestine arrangements.

"Yoohoo, Erin!"

Across the street, the widow, Mrs. Shumway, was waiving to me, pulling the front of her beige wool coat over her sunken chest. That combined with her grape purple pants that were too big and quilted black winter boots made for quite the fashion statement.

I put my plastic recycle bin next to my garbage can and waved back, noticing she was actually hailing me. I trotted across the street, avoiding the leftover snow and slushy puddles.

"Morning," she greeted, straining as she dragged her heavy-duty garbage can behind her. Even when he was in his eighties, that was a job that Mr. Shumway used to handle.

Her bright smile was never quite the same after he passed, forever altered by an irreplaceable loss. "Morning, Mrs. Shumway. Can I give you a hand with that?"

She cinched her coat tighter while I pulled her garbage to the curb. "Oh, thank you, dear. My hands aren't as strong as they used to be. It sure is cold out this morning."

I didn't need my medical degree to see the late stage Rheumatoid Arthritis crippling her. "Yes, it is. I heard we're getting more snow tonight. I'm ready for spring."

Mrs. Shumway's gaze turned distant. "Spring was always Frank's favorite season."

I saw her slipping away to some fond memory, one that was bittersweet. "I'm off this weekend so don't even think about trying to shovel on your own. I'll be over as soon as it stops so don't worry. Do you need anything at the store? I have to get to work soon but if I leave now I can run for you."

Her nurturing smile returned. "Oh, no, dear. That's sweet of you but I have everything I need."

"Okay. Well, I don't mean to be rude, but I should probably get going. I have a meeting this morning."

"Oh, then I won't keep you. I was just wondering if you were happy with the handyman you hired the other day. I have some work that needs to be done and I'm not sure who to even call. There are so many crooks these days, all wanting to take advantage now that my husband is gone. Frank used to take care of all of the maintenance around here." She waved a hand across her snow-covered front lawn. "But the old house has seen better days." She sighed, her weathered face turning quizzical. "Was he expensive?"

I was completely confused, wondering which one of us was getting Alzheimer's. "I don't know what you're talking about, Mrs. Shumway. I didn't hire anyone."

She frowned at me. "Well, you had a young man over there on a ladder a couple of days in a row. Fixed the loose shingles above your garage door on Tuesday and was tinkering around the place all morning on Wednesday. See my gutter?" She pointed and my eyes instinctively followed. "All that heavy snow is ripping mine off its hinges. If that comes down I'll end up having to replace the whole thing and I can't afford to do that. That's going to cost a lot of money and I'm on a fixed income."

While she went on about her late husband's measly pension, my brain fizzled, but sure enough, *my* gutter was fixed. So was the piece of vinyl siding that had pulled away near the roof peak and flapped against the house quite loudly every time the wind blew. *What the hell?* Why hadn't I noticed?

"Hmm. My dad must have fixed it." *But why didn't he call to tell me? And when the heck did he have time?* Between the hours of work and sleep, he was running my mom back and forth to the hospital. Maybe Chris or Nate had been by. It would be theirs to manage soon enough.

She squinted and shook her head. "Wasn't your father, Erin. It was a younger man, your age. Quite strapping, too. I wish these people would at least put a sign or something on their work trucks. You know, Frank and I lived on this street for fifty-nine years and they may not think that people are keeping watch, but I see everything that goes on around here. I'm home all day and television these days stinks. Nothing but talk show rubbish. Who is your baby's daddy and idiots who need a swift kick in the ass. How am I supposed to know if someone is here to fix things or to rob one of us? Would be nice to know. Just because he looked all clean cut doesn't mean he's not up to no good. They say it's always the ones you don't suspect that—"

My inner filter kicked in; the surge of information caused my nerves to spring. "He was in a truck?"

She nodded. "Yes. A shiny black one. The one day I saw he had the letters 'ATTF' on his coat but I couldn't find it in the phone book. I looked under *home repair* and *construction* too."

I swear I could hear the blood rushing through my body after my heart skipped a very long beat.

I TYPED MY password into the computer system, doing my best to replace my muddled thoughts with some sense of focus. I'd worked on three patients that coded, one stabbing victim, diagnosed a mysterious rash that turned out to be a severe allergic reaction to an ingredient in the patient's breakfast cereal, and kept some woman from overdosing.

You'd think that caseload would have been enough of a distraction.

It wasn't.

I'd repaired complex human anatomy, had brought back a few people from the brink of death, but for the life of me could not figure out why Adam had been at my house without letting me know. Why would he even come around if he didn't want to see me? And not just once but several times, according to my observant neighbor.

"Erin. Here, take this."

I looked up from the screen to see Sherry holding out a gel ice pack. "Thanks."

"She didn't break the skin, did she?"

I gave her my cheek, letting her inspect my injury.

"Jeez," she sighed. "It's swollen but thankfully there's no open wound. What the hell happened?"

I held the ice pack under my eye, hoping it would help dull the throbbing. "Heroin overdose. We pushed Narcan and Robert was bagging her when she came to. She completely freaked out. Took five of us to subdue her."

Doctor Miriam Vonore's annoyed throat clearing was hard to ignore.

"Doctor Novak, I understand that your intern had issues intubating the coding patient," she said, her condescension and disapproval making my head throb even worse. We'd worked on him right before the overdose came in. "If you can't intubate, it's better to manually ventilate. You should know that."

My guard immediately went up, but I couldn't let her see my defenses. I'd allowed the attendings to treat me like I was an ignorant dumb shit when I was a resident; I'd be damned to let any of them think they could get away with talking to me like that now. Enough was enough. And so much for her asking if I was all right after being kicked in the face.

"I'm well versed in airway, Doctor. The patient was combative, which made it more difficult, but Doctor Reyes was able to intubate him on her second try." I turned my gaze her way, giving her just a smidgen of my attention. She was lucky that she got that much. The woman was worse than that arrogant Doctor House from television. "I was right there supervising her technique, gave correction, and did not see a need to intervene any further. Besides, isn't that why we have interns? So they can learn just like we all did?"

Doctor Vonore's saggy jowls puckered. "The patient needed someone with more expertise in airway. Because of the delay, he's going to suffer."

I fought rolling my eyes, especially since she was trying to make something out of nothing.

My desk chair rolled a few inches when I stood up. "My patient's care was my top priority. As their attending, it was my call and I made the decision to allow the intern to try again. The patient's welfare was never compromised."

Doctor Jeremy Bond, tall, dark, and whistling happily, came around the corner, scrawling on a med chart. "Has anyone seen a leather notebook? It's dark brown."

Sherry slipped it off a workstation. "You mean this?"

"Yes," he said, relieved. "Thank you."

"No problem, One-Shot," Sherry teased.

His glare was amusing. "You all will never let me live this one down, will you?"

A resounding chorus of *"Never!"* echoed from the far reaches of the department.

I was glad for the playful distraction, although Miriam was far from amused. I could see her frustration growing from being ignored. "You should never have told them you got your wife pregnant on your honeymoon," I said to him. "You can't give them ammunition like that."

Sherry pegged me with a knowing glance, one that said *'if you would have dated him when he asked, you could have been the one who got pregnant on your honeymoon.'*

"Dayum, Novak. What happened to your face?" Jeremy asked.

"Heroin OD," Sherry said. She nudged my hand. "Ice. Face. Now. Doctors. I swear. You make the worst patients."

"Good news." He patted my shoulder. "Mr. Trujillo's surgery went well. You and your team did a great job." He nodded at Miriam. "Doctor."

I set my ice pack down, thanked Doctor Bond, and enjoying my moment of righteous indignation. I'd also owe Doctor Bond a favor or two for that save, but it would be worth it, seeing Miriam's maw gape like a confused fish. I turned my pleasantness back on her. "Unless you have any other constructive input, I have patients to attend to."

"This hospital doesn't need a malpractice suit. Remember that." She turned on a final huff and stormed away, probably a little self-satisfied she got the last word in again. She was always looking for a reason to make my life hell. *Bitch!* That sentiment was followed by a string of mental expletives. That woman had been riding my ass since day one, and my contempt for her ran as deep as hers did for me. Maybe even deeper.

That was it. My mind was made up. As soon as I left work I'd run home, shower, find some makeup to cover up the bruise blooming under my eye, and let Tommy have his way with my body. Hopefully he won't stare at my face while he's doing his thing between my legs. And while I was on a roll, screw Detective Adam Trent and his fickle bullshit, too.

When did I shave my pits last? Will I have time to stop for food and make it to Tommy's place by eight? Eating before I get there without brushing my teeth—yuck. Bad idea. I'll just shower and primp and then head over to his…

My pager chimed, vibrating from the pocket of my medical coat. The number displayed was for the ICU.

I slipped my cell back into my pocket after returning the page. Everything in my chest tightened, cutting off my ability to breathe.

I ran to the elevator, pushing the button several times, but it was taking too long. I sprinted down the hallway, slamming my shoulder into the door to the stairwell. I ran both flights of stairs up to the third floor.

The antiseptic smell of the ICU overpowered me, burning my nose as I jogged down the tiled hall. My sneakers squeaked on the floor with each step, breaking the relative quiet of the intensive care unit.

My father was leaning hard on the metal doorframe outside my uncle's room, looking as though he'd just had the wind knocked out of him. He had on a pale yellow long-sleeved medical gown covering the front of his body that was falling off his shoulders, exposing his street clothing underneath, and blue latex medical gloves that were protocol for all ICU visitors. He noticed me over his arm and slowly straightened; his face so sullen and anguished that it was almost unbearable to witness.

Dad held my face after he hugged me. "What happened? You're hurt."

I shook my head. "It's nothing. A patient—" My words cut off when the pool of tears dripped down his cheeks.

His entire body shook as he wept in my arms. I tried to be his strength but my own was waning fast.

My cousin Nate slipped around the curtain shielding the view of my uncle, exposing a sliver of an elderly man clad in all black. He read from the book held in his hands. Daylight from the window glinted off the beaded rosary dangling from his fingers.

Nate's wife Andrea hurried behind him. Both passed me, stopping only a few feet from the doorway. Nate covered his eyes and broke down into choking tears.

My own anguish roiled, sending a blaze of anguish throughout my chest and up into my throat.

"Kids decided to remove him... from the... the life support," my father stuttered into my shoulder.

I knew my uncle wasn't improving and one by one his major organs were starting to fail. There was no bouncing back at this point but I didn't know they'd be making the final decision of his treatment today. I tried to search for words of comfort. "I know it's hard to take, Dad, but it's for the best."

His breath stuttered. "I know."

I tried to speak through the burn and tears. "Uncle Cal would hate to be hooked up to all of those machines. You know he would."

I felt his cheek brush my hair, nodding in acknowledgement. "I know," he sputtered. "Your mom and I talked it over with the boys. Still, it's not an easy decision. I can't. I can't go back in there. Your mother…"

I rubbed his back, trying to sooth him. "I know."

Hearing my mom's muted wails from the other side of the curtain as she said her final goodbyes tore my heart to pieces.

I gave my dad one last kiss on the cheek before letting him go.

My mother and cousin were huddled together near the long spans of window. The bleak and cloudy backdrop of Philadelphia seemed so aptly befitting.

My mom had her face mashed into Chris's chest while hospital staff removed my uncle's breathing tube from the ventilator. Chris stood tall and rubbed her back, crying his own silent tears as he somehow found the last ounce of bravery within him.

"The Lord is my shepherd, I shall not want," the priest recited. "He maketh me to lie down in green pastures, He leadeth me beside the still waters, He restoreth my soul. He leadeth me in the paths of righteousness for His name's sake. Yea, though I walk through the valley of the shadow of death, I will fear no evil, for though art with me; Thy rod and Thy staff they comfort me. Thou preparest a table before me in the presence of mine enemies. Thou anointest my head with oil, my cup runneth over. Surely goodness and mercy shall follow me all the days of my life, and I will dwell in the house of the Lord forever."

Everything hit me at once, making me hyperaware of my surroundings, though it all seemed very irrationally unreal. The sight of my mother beyond distraught and falling apart crushed me. The anguish scorching my lungs was almost unbearable. My cousin Chris, who was just two years younger than me, suffering to keep a brave face clashed with my sudden anger. I knew both of my cousins had just made a very difficult decision, but my mother was too fragile to endure bearing witness to my uncle's final moments. She didn't need to be here like this, watching *this*. He needed to get her out of this room instead of facilitating it.

Uncle Cal's attending, Doctor Paul Webber, passed in front of me, his face impassive. I presumed he was doing his best to ignore the drowning feeling that surrounds you when a patient is dying in front of you and you can't do a damn thing to stop it. The nursing staff was working methodically, disconnecting my uncle from life support.

"Mom… come." I tried to move her. "You don't want this memory."

"No!" She refused to budge.

I wrapped myself around her, hugging any part of her I could reach, doing my best to comfort her.

Within moments, the constant monotone of a heart monitor no longer keeping rhythms marked the final process.

Doctor Webber hushed his voice to announce the official time of death and made a notation on the chart in his hand. He handed it to one of the nurses and then came over to us. I wondered for a moment if this latest loss had caused another weary line to permanently crinkle this doctor's face or take him one step closer to his own sad finality.

"I'm sorry for your loss," he said as passively as possible, adding the sympathetic smile they taught us to use when delivering such news. It felt as though a sledgehammer hit me in the chest. A bit of anger welled at his spurious sympathy.

Sorry? You're sorry? No, you're not! You're only saying that because you have to, you liar!

"Oh Erin." My mom reached for me, pulling me out of my momentary swirl and into her arms, back into reality.

Oh God, is this the way other families feel when I tell them that their loved one has died?

She crammed her nose near my neck and I felt her body shake with each sob, finding my own lifeline and renewed sense of strength and purpose in this tragedy. "I'm *so* sorry, Mom. *So* sorry. You'll be okay. Shhh. It's okay."

Father Connolly, the elderly Catholic priest who baptized every one of us, interrupted with his condolences.

I'd heard the familiar Bible passage he had read recited hundreds of times before inside this hospital, but tonight, surrounded by the people I love the most in the world, the psalm had torn through me like a knife through tissue paper.

I held my sobbing mother while my father's arms encircled us both, and let the pain and tears have at me.

I'D NEVER LOST a family member before, well, not counting my grandpa on my dad's side, but he had passed when I was young. The sorrow from losing someone you love was like a vortex of utter agony, pulling on my body so hard that it was difficult to walk back to the ER. My legs felt heavy, weighed down from the onslaught of emotional upheaval.

How would my cousins go on? Both of their parents—gone—just like that. No fair warning. No red flags. No months of mental preparation during a long-term illness. Thoughts of the day when *my* parents would depart this earth welled on top of the suffocating overload, making me miss them and fear the inevitable all at the same time.

I trudged past an exam room where a trauma team was tending to a patient. Fluids, chest compressions, orders being called out. Machines slowly beeped and hissed, while scrub-clad bodies rushed around me. The dread was turning into numbness. I felt internally abandoned.

I have to get out of here. I have to cancel meeting Tommy. Why can't I stop crying?

"Erin," the disembodied voice called out but it sounded muffled, distant, as though a figment of a possible delusion.

I was startled by the realization that there was a person blocking my way. My thoughts had to reroute themselves to realize that it was a woman, then they took a few extra beats to remember why this particular human with blonde hair irritated me so much. *"I want you to know Randy and I are seeing each other now. I'm being up front with you so you don't cause problems for us."*

"By the look of you, I guess you've heard," Mandy said.

Confusion rippled. Was she upset that she wasn't the first one to tell me that my uncle had just died?

"I figured you'd be disappointed but I didn't think you'd be this much of an emotional mess. God, look at you. You know things like this aren't within Randy's control. You can't blame him for what the board decides. I just hope you don't make things, well, *difficult* for him."

I felt dizzy, confused, caught in a cacophony of machine tones, alternating chimes, and a high-pitched ringing in both of my ears. "Wait. What?"

Mandy gapped at me as if I were stupid. For a moment, I was; at least I was oblivious to the point she was trying to make. Raw instinct was telling me to ignore her bullshit and just punch her. I'd dreamt about hitting her numerous times, even plotted when and how so I could get away with it, but no matter how many times I'd entertained the thoughts I just wasn't the violent type.

"The fellowship?" she tossed back.

I wiped a tear from my face. Damn she was annoying. "What fellowship?"

Mandy rolled her eyes. "*You* know. The one that you and Randy have been fighting over? I presume that's why you're crying. You've probably heard that Doctor Lawson told Randy that the fellowship is his. I hope you'll be an adult about this. He's worked just as hard for it, Erin. You know he has."

The meaning of her words hit me like a wrecking ball. "*My* fellowship?" *The fellowship I've worked my entire career for? The singular goal I've had in my sights since I was sixteen years old?*

Mandy narrowed her beady little brown eyes on me. "It's not your fellowship. Not anymore. Just…," she huffed. "Look, I don't expect you to be pleasant. Just please try not to be a total bitch to him. That's all I ask, okay?" Her lips twisted. She pointed at my eye. "You may want to put some ice on that. It looks pretty nasty."

I felt gut-punched. Gutted to the core. Unable to breathe. Unable to think. My vision distorted.

As I watched her shadow walk away, everything I've ever wanted, including my sanity and direction in life, left with her.

I grabbed for the wall, for something, scraping my nails on the wood trim.

"Doctor Novak!" a nurse called out as she jogged toward me, passing the retreating soul-stealer. Blue smears blurred into the medicinal white walls. Florescent lights streaked through the images, casting an eerie shadow over everything.

Gone. Everything. He's gone. It's gone. Everything—Gone. Oh, God.

"Doctor Novak, why aren't you answering your pager? What happened?" She urged me along. I think my legs moved though I wasn't sure. "We have a pediatric trauma coming in via Lifeflight. A four-year-old was struck by a car. ETA is seven minutes."

CHAPTER 10
Adam

I LEANED BACK in my chair and dug into my front jeans pocket for my money. I had a hundred on me tonight, which, knowing my luck at playing Poker every other Friday night, I'd probably just end up handing over to the grinning prick sitting on my right, but that was a risk I was willing to take for the love of the game.

"Hey, Adam, good to see ya. Oh, and congrats. Heard you got the Medal of Valor," Jack Gillis said, patting me on the shoulder. "Good job, dude."

Officer Jack Gillis was one of the good guys, funny as shit, too, but looked scruffy and unkempt like a street punk I'd normally haul away in cuffs. His look came with the job. He was undercover narcotics, part of Philly DEA, just like my oldest brother, Michael, though Mike was smart enough to move to south Florida and away from the harsh winter weather of the north to wage his personal war on drugs.

"Thanks, man." I peeled a twenty off the folded stack and tossed it across the table at my partner, Marcus. "My ante."

"Sucks you had to get stabbed to get a fucking award but hey, that's just part of the job," Jack continued.

I nodded and bit another hunk off my slice of pizza, washing it down with a swig of iced tea. Sometimes the smell of beer was tempting; sometimes it turned my stomach. Tonight, even the beads of condensation dripping down the brown bottles setting all around

Marcus's poker table were enticing.

I took another long swig of my tea, catching a chip of ice between my teeth, doing my best to tamp down the dry burn that was rolling up my throat.

I'd been clean for almost ten months, something that the men surrounding me at this table were well aware of; still I couldn't be a pansy asshole and ask them not to enjoy themselves just because I had a hard time stopping at one or two. That was all on me to manage.

We'd given up rotating houses; Marcus had recently refurbished his basement and bought a beautiful poker table inlaid with green felt. It was the shit, though the familiar surroundings and faces did little to ease my mind tonight.

The smell of homemade cookies wafting through the air was also making me slightly insane. Chocolate chip with extra chocolate—my favorite. But then again, Marcus's wife, Cherise, knew that. She also knew that I was in a funk the moment I stepped foot inside her kitchen and seeing as I didn't drink anymore, offered to drown my sorrows with her special cookies. Sometimes I wondered if the woman knew me better than I knew myself.

Well, maybe that's not completely accurate. I knew exactly why I was in a shitty-ass mood. Had been that way for the last week, ever since I left Erin standing alone in her living room, looking at me with confusion, as if she'd been the one to do something wrong.

Visions of her lovely face, of those amazing blue eyes that held me captive like a prisoner in my own mind, haunted my every waking moment. I kept doubting my reactions and intentions around her, knowing that all it would take would be one taste of her mouth and I'd drink her in and drown my sorrows. That alone made her hazardous to my health, but categorizing a treasure like that was totally unfair.

I stared at the cards in my hand, seeing a Jack of spades with its one eye glaring at me, telling me what an asshole I was being.

Erin deserved an explanation. No, she deserved the truth as to why I reacted the way I did, but no matter how many times I reached for my cell or thought about contacting her to explain things, I couldn't make myself do it. What would I say? *Yeah, about your dead family member… well you see, my team caused that. We fucked up and well, shit happens. Sorry. Hope you can get over it.*

Some stand-up guy I was being. I couldn't even man-up enough to be honest with her. Instead I skipped out on her like a big freaking coward and worked on her house while she was sleeping. Avoiding her seemed to be the easiest option.

Marcus studied his cards as if they were a tech manual, while his friend, a guy we secretly called Booger, dug his hand into the chip bowl. Todd Shifley was a pretty decent dude, our age, and on one of the local fire departments, but after seeing him pick at his nose and then spend time swirling his hand in the chip bowl, avoiding the unhealthy snack *Booger* touched became an easy fete. Fellow ATTF officers Nate Westfield and Mark "The Gribs" Gribble were sitting on either side of him, both just as disgusted. Some people had no class.

Who am I to judge? I have no class. I left a classy woman like Erin high and dry. I'm a classless train wreck.

"'Bout time you bring us some cookies, woman."

My head popped up.

Cherise had a tray in one hand, her other hand now on her hip, and a death scowl pointing directly at her husband. "You'll be lucky to get a crumb with that kind of attitude."

Marcus glared back, questioning her sass. "That so?"

She waved him off like only a black woman is capable of and brought the tray over to me.

"God, I love you," I said, eyeing the pile of cookies instead of her pretty face. Sometimes I wondered if Marcus realized how lucky he was. Not only was his wife sexy, she was smart as a whip, using her gifts to run one of the local Penn National Bank branches.

She pointed a long red fingernail at me. "And that's why you get cookies. Take a bunch. Not like Marcus will get any, not after that."

I took four of them, feeling the hot chocolate melting into my fingertips and all over my gauze-wrapped hand as they bent in half. Some chocolate smeared into the gauze, making the wrap look liked I'd wiped my ass with my own hand. I quickly palmed a napkin to cover it up.

Marcus smacked my arm. "Quit hitting on my wife."

I licked my finger, knowing that if he really meant it, his punch would have hurt. "Stop giving her a hard time and she won't be tempted to run off with me."

"That's right," she snapped. "Keep it up and it will be *you* sleeping on the couch in the den tonight." She put her hand on my shoulder. "Adam can have your spot upstairs."

Marcus clipped my arm again, gritting his teeth at me. Something told me my days of crashing at his house instead of going home to my empty one were numbered. "Touch my pillow and I'll shoot your ass."

It was all in good fun. I shoved the other half of the cookie in my mouth. "So much for vowing to protect my life and shit."

"Your ass goes anywhere near my bedroom and all bets are off."

I ignored him and gave Cherise another wink just for added effect. "I might as well go home then if you can't share."

Cherise set the plate next to my elbow, far enough away that Marcus would have to reach across the table for one, and winked at me. "It keeps snowing like it is right now and none of you will be going anywhere."

Nate took another cookie and looked at his watch. "Thought it wasn't supposed to start until midnight?"

I tapped my phone to see the time. It was only going on ten o'clock.

"Yeah right," she said. "News said we have a nor'easter coming now and by the looks of it, they just might be right this time. It's coming down fast. Supposed to be worse than the blizzard we got back in '06." She tisked. "Best get playing before Marcus has to quit so he can go plow the driveway."

He gave her an ugly glare and reached for the last cookie but I snagged the plate. Too bad he wasn't quick enough. It was fun to rile him up, and for the last few years it was my favorite pastime. He always got even.

My phone rang, vibrating on the round wooden table. I had no idea who would be calling me at this hour and for a moment a tinge of panic rolled through thinking that something might have happened with my dad again. I squinted, not recognizing number.

Marcus snagged the cookie out of my hand before I got it near my mouth. "Give me that."

I tried to decipher the local number, thinking maybe it was one of my CIs checking in. I had informants all over Philly—past criminals taking lighter sentences in exchange for providing tips on chop shops and stolen cars—and I'd been waiting for one to get back to me on a lead I was following. Someone had to know something about all the cars boosted that night we pulled her over.

Erin.

Those amazing blue eyes and soft pink lips came swirling into focus, along with a warm flush throughout my veins.

Part of me hoped to hear her voice on the other end of this call, answering my question of whether or not I had crossed her mind at all. The other part that flashed a healthy dose of panic hoped to hell it wasn't her reaching out; what the heck would I say?

The digits on my screen were foreign to me, making me wonder if Nikki was using an unknown number. It had been several days since she'd called last, trying to convince me once again that I'd made a mistake and she deserved another chance. I could easily hit *ignore*, which meant if she couldn't get a hold of me she'd send mutual friends to do her dirty work again.

What I did not expect was to hear my friend Kip's voice when I answered.

I was up on my feet before I realized it, patting my pockets for my truck keys.

THE ROADS WERE desolate, already covered with several inches of heavy snow, but nothing could keep me from making this drive. Two snowplows passed me going the other way; their yellow warning lights flashing, lighting up the darkened sky. Visibility sucked. I'd already fishtailed it around several corners trying to hurry. My wipers couldn't keep up and an annoying layer of frost was sticking on my windshield, making it even harder to see. Fortunately my route was well lit with streetlights. My tires slid when I turned into the parking lot adjacent to Al's Pub. My headlights flashed over two cars; one familiar vehicle was covered with snow. The other, Kip's truck, was mostly cleared off but a layer was quickly rebuilding.

I trudged through the snow, trying to keep it from getting down into the inside of my jacket, and banged my cold fist on the back kitchen door. Worry was driving me hard and heavy.

"Sorry, dude," Kip said, holding the thick steel door open for me.

I kicked the snow off my boots, trying to leave as much of it outside as I could, before I slipped past him.

"I wasn't sure if you wanted this call."

Actually, I was grateful he did. "No, you did the right thing. I appreciate it." I patted his shoulder while shaking off the rest of the cold. My cheeks stung from the sudden temperature change.

"I didn't know how tight you were with her." He shrugged.

I was still trying to determine that one myself.

Kip smacked me in the back. "Figured you had a vested interest at least. For what it's worth, I like that you've upgraded, but considering her current condition, I'm not so sure that it's a good thing."

Yeah, we weren't going to go there. Gut instinct was telling me this wasn't an everyday activity for her. I gave him a quick nod, hoping to hell I was right. "Where is she?"

"Sitting in one of the booths by the front door, waiting for a cab that ain't coming. How are the roads?"

I pulled my leather gloves off and shoved them into my coat pocket. "Slick."

"Speaking of slick, Benny was in here tonight."

The short hair on the back of my neck prickled. "Benny?"

Kip nodded. "He was sitting by her most of the night, hitting on her something fierce. He got a little pushy with her when I announced last call so I put her in my office until he shoved off."

My anger flared up hearing that. "Pushy?"

Kip drew in a deep, even breath through his nose. "He was trying to convince her to leave with him. Even yanked on her arm a few times. One of my boys intervened. We got him to leave."

"Thanks, man." At least I had friends out there watching my back. But Benny? I'd kill the weasel the next time I saw him. What he was doing sniffing around Erin was even more concerning. Could someone be tailing me, trying to use her to get to me?

Kip shrugged it off. "No problem, bro. I'm going to finish locking up. Try to make it quick, okay? I still haven't put my snow tires on."

I maneuvered out into the bar, catching a shock of long blonde hair that was resting on folded arms. The place was shut down for the night; only a few of the recessed lights were still on, which cast a dim shadow over her still frame.

"She asleep?" Kip asked.

She looked so peaceful all bundled up in her dark blue ski jacket and white knit hat, scarf, and mittens; her long hair obscuring most of her face. "Looks like it. How much did she drink?"

He shook his head. "Apparently too much. There were a few guys playing pool earlier who bought her a few, too."

My soaring anger spiked up another notch. He could have saved me from that detail. My molars started to hurt visualizing that scenario all too clearly. My stitches pinched when I balled my hands into fists. "Beer or mixed drinks?"

Kip tossed a leftover menu onto the bar. "Dude, I don't know. I think she had a mixture, probably a few shots. I was in the kitchen most of the night so I'm not sure. She seemed fine one minute and then pissed drunk the next, okay? She was sitting by herself for a long time. I thought she was waiting on someone, but I think she was crying, staring out the window most of the night. Anyway, I want to get the fuck out of here. Just take her home."

I slipped a long lock of her hair off her face, trying not to let the knowledge that she'd been crying kill me. I gave her a nudge. "Doc. Time to wake up."

She startled a bit, blinking up at me with heavy eyes. "Mhh, what?"

Yeah, there would be no way she could drive, even though we were only a mile or two from her place.

"Time to go."

She grunted, or was that a groan? "Adam, what? Why are you here? I called for um, a taxi. Just go."

Erin was great at waving me off. Don't know why it surprised me to receive it again. After the way I'd left her last time, I shouldn't have expected anything else.

"Cab isn't coming. Come on, Doc. I'm taking you home." I tried to pull on her arm, which got her to at least slide to the edge of the bench.

"I don't need you. I can drive. Just need coffee first." Erin tried to push me away which, after a couple of days of trying to convince myself otherwise, hurt a hell of a lot more than I wanted to admit.

Her anger and sadness was my doing, so I'd take the heat from her disappointment. "Roads are slippery, Erin. I wouldn't like the idea of you driving on them sober let alone drunk."

"I'm not drunk," she mumbled, searching through her purse.

Yeah, I think I'd said the same thing quite a few times. Flashbacks of others carrying my sad sack of a drunken ass out of a few bars—this one included—hit me hard. I must have been a huge disappointment so many times to my family and friends after my partner was killed. I tightened my grip around her waist. That's when I noticed her shiner. "What the hell happened to your eye?"

I tried to tilt her chin up to get a better look.

She covered her face. "Stop."

"Let me see it. Who hit you?" Thoughts of someone raising a finger to her blistered through me like wildfire.

"Just leave me alone."

"Not until you tell me what happened."

"I don't want you to see it."

"Too late, sweetheart. I've already seen it. Now tell me, who hit you?"

"Doesn't matter."

"Erin."

"What?"

I pegged Kip with a glare. "This happen here?" He'd better answer *no* because if this shit went down on his watch and he didn't call me the second it happened, we'd have another major issue to deal with.

He held his hands up. "Not in my bar, brother."

Back to square one. "Erin, one last time. Who hit you?"

She pushed my forearm away and then covered her face with her mitten. "I wanna go home now. I'm going." She tried to elbow me out of her way. Tried, but failed. "Move please."

The second she stood up, she swayed and then seized the table top.

"Come on, babe. I've got you." I swung her up into my arms before she had a chance to have an opinion. "Kip, get the door."

"Put me down! Fuck, Adam. Stop. I'm too heavy."

I felt his hand pat my back. "'Night, bro. Drive safe."

"Thanks, man. You too." The minute we hit the cold air, Erin and her leather purse shrank into my chest, shivering. She wasn't the only thing I felt shrinking in from the extreme cold and biting wind.

"Put me down."

"Why? So I can pick you up out of the snow?"

"Where are you taking me?" she chattered again.

I kept my eyes pinned on my truck, trying to keep my footing in the slippery snow while carrying a hundred and thirty-forty some pounds. With any luck, it should still be warm inside. I set her down on unsteady feet, opened her door, and urged her to climb in. "I'm taking you home."

I turned the heater up as high and fast as it would go, knowing that if I was cold, she had to be freezing. Her forehead was leaning on the window the entire drive and the way her head lolled about, I was wondering if she'd passed out. She surely wasn't talking to me.

"This isn't my house," she whispered gruffly when I started to turn into my snow-covered driveway, her words steaming up a small patch on her window.

I hit the overhead door opener; the light guiding my way in. "I know. It's mine."

Erin's head whipped in my direction, gaping at me. "You said you were taking me home." Her tone, still quite groggy and slurred, was now incensed.

I put my truck in park, shut off the lights, and hit the button again to close the garage door. "No, I said I was taking you home. Never said whose home we were going to."

I opened her door and took in her reluctant demeanor, wondering if I'd have to resort to lifting her out. She could be mad all she wanted; I just would rather she be pissy inside the house where it was warm. "Come on, Erin. It's cold out here."

I grabbed her arms and waist before she stumbled over my Harley.

"Whose motor…" She sighed heavily. "Motorcycle?"

I straightened her up. "Mine."

Her eyes narrowed. "You have a motorcycle?"

I gave the passenger door a shove. "Yep. Come on, Snow White. Let's get you inside."

"You didn't tell me you had a mo… a motorcycle."

Negotiating two bodies between the front end of my truck and my long wooden tool bench was tight. "Yes. I did."

She groaned.

Or was it a purr?

"I like motor… bike things."

That made me smile inside. "Good to know, Doc."

She patted my chest. "You'll take me for a ride sometime. Promise, Adam. Promise me."

Visions of her arms around my waist, her chest pressed to my back with those thighs squeezing on me, flashed so hard and fast that I didn't quite know what to do with them. Were they a glimpse at a possible future with her? Premonition? Thoughts of her becoming a part of my life happened all too easily every time I was around her, blasting right through the doubt and the months of counseling.

"I feel sick," she mumbled.

I had hoped she wouldn't puke in my truck, although she wouldn't be the first. I helped her into my kitchen, the warm air instantly leeching the cold from my bones. I had wondered for five miles of slippery, shitty roads whether or not she'd hold her liquor or if this was a typical way she burned off the stress, hoping to hell this was a rare occurrence.

Erin hiccupped. "Adam, I really… I don't feel so good."

I pulled off her knit hat and scarf and tossed them somewhere into my living room. "Come on. Let's get you into the bathroom."

I barely got the lid to the toilet up before she lurched for it. I stood there and watched her retch, hovering close to make sure she didn't choke or pass out. My mind whirled as I watched over her, *knowing* now with absolute certainty how helpless it feels to be on this side of the drunk. I bit back the automatic urge to gag and courtesy flushed the toilet, wondering what demons plagued her to go out drinking alone. I planned on figuring that out right after I gave her time to sober up.

CHAPTER 11
Erin

SOFT BREATHING COMING from behind me was the first thing I'd noticed when my eyes opened to the darkness. It was a gentle and manly snore—rhythmic, peaceful—something I hadn't realized my soul was parched without. He was definitely asleep and I couldn't help but want to savor the moment.

Adam.

Just the whispered thought of his name triggered the escalation of my heartbeat with flutters; unfortunately though, that moment of elation was immediately followed up by a Mariachi band tap dancing in my head. My throat was dry, sore, and hinted of an aftertaste that was very distinguishable and completely unpleasant.

One too many shots of pity-flavored tequila combined with beef gravy and deep fryer oil roiled through my stomach again, exacerbated by the recollection that I vomited profusely in Adam's toilet.

I closed my eyes, recalling how he'd hovered over me as I hurled my guts and my dignity. *Oh God, how embarrassing.*

I hadn't been that sick on alcohol since my freshman year of college when I learned the hard way that mixing alcohol inside your internal organs usually doesn't work out so well.

I ran my hand over the soft pillowcase and then over my face, thinking that taking the walk of shame was all that was left of another monumental catastrophe in my history with men. But damn, his pillow and this bed were comfortable. It was as if I were cradled in the soft pillow top of the mattress, giving my body the sensation of floating on a lovely cloud. I slid a foot, realizing that I was no longer wearing socks because I could feel the silky sheets without obstruction.

When did I lose my socks?

Oh cripes… my legs are bare, too. What the hell am I wearing?

The memories came back with painful clarity: Adam stripping off my socks and laughing without humor at my condition; him pulling a shirt over my head while holding me steady.

Oh God, how pathetic. I will never, ever, ever get that drunk again. What was I thinking? Oh, yeah… the four-hundred different ways my life sucked.

I'd been on this path for so long, this "I have to become a doctor and never fail another human being again" endless loop, that I'd stopped paying attention to everything else going on around me.

There's nothing worse to top a hangover than a healthy dose of self-loathing. I listened to Adam's steady breathing, wondering what his reaction to me would be when he woke up. Maybe I should just leave. Get dressed and sneak out, leave him undisturbed and avoid seeing him struggle for a subtle way to get rid of me. He'd been nothing but kind to me so far tonight, so I was betting he wouldn't be a complete asshole while washing his hands of the puking mess.

But it was still dark out, I was warm and toasty and comfortable, and maybe, just maybe I could get another hour of sleep in before slipping out undetected?

As I lay there thinking about my options, that urge *to go* hit me. My mind did the mental math trying to determine how long I could lay here before having to pee goes from necessity to urgency.

I leaned up on my elbow and squinted, mapping out a path to his bathroom in the dark. His window coverings were so thick, even the streetlight didn't break through.

A large hand slid over my hip. "Where you going?" he grumbled.

Shit. I cleared my rancid throat. "I have to go."

His hand gently clenched me through the covers. "No, you don't. Lay down, babe. Go back to sleep."

Was he worried I'd leave? A small simper erupted from hearing him call me "babe". "I have to use the bathroom."

His hand tensed, eased, and then quickly slid away. "You feeling sick again?"

"No, just have to use the bathroom."

"You sure?"

I nodded in the dark. "Yeah."

Adam took a deep breath and yawned. "Light switch is on the left, inside the door. Yell if you need me."

I glanced back at his darkened silhouette; one very impressive shoulder was bare and visible to the naked eye. He was on his side, right behind me. This was all so very confusing. He'd avoided me for what? A week? And now he's practically spooning with me?

And then he called me *babe*? Even after making an idiot out of myself, defiling his private space, he had a pet name for me? A chill hit my bare legs and feet while the residual drunkenness made me crave to lie back down. It made the need to pee even more urgent.

I gently closed the door behind me, squinting at the sudden brightness of the lights above the vanity. I flipped the next switch, finding the overhead fan. The third switch turned on the recessed lighting, which wasn't so hard on my bloodshot eyes. Now that I wasn't so ill, I was able to absorb more of his very nicely appointed bathroom.

He had a large, glass-encased shower with what looked like sandstone tiles in soothing earth tones that dominated the space. Two shower heads. *Nice.* The vanity was dark mahogany and looked like an oversized antique chest of drawers with a beautiful granite countertop and black metal loops for pulls that coordinated with everything. It was rustic and gave the room a very masculine spa-like vibe.

The entire bathroom looked brand new, completely remodeled, and made me think that my bathroom in my house was an outdated joke compared to what he had going on. A hot shower in that tempting space would certainly feel like heaven right now. A hot shower with someone as sexy as Adam in there with me sounded even better.

I rubbed my face, trying to push away the slight spins. I was glad he made me take aspirin before I tried to lie down. *Maybe he really does like me? He did leave wherever he was to come pick me up. That has to count for something. Doesn't it? And he called me "babe." Why would he do that if he didn't have some sort of feelings for me, unless I was just one of several babes. Could we be back together? Wait, we were never together. But I was just sleeping next to him in his bed. Is that?*

Are we? What does that mean? Oh my God, my head hurts.

I pulled the last five squares of paper off the roll. *Figures.* Everything was so pristine and yet there were no visible extra rolls? I leaned forward, catching the edge of the vanity door with the tips of my fingernails, fumbling and coming up empty.

I washed up, rinsed my mouth out several times, and contemplated whether searching for a new roll of toilet paper would be considered snooping.

I gingerly pressed the door handle down on the linen closet, peering inside for anything that resembled a roll.

Even his closet was neat. Well, the towels were shoved into a haphazard pile, but they were folded. Huh, a bachelor that folds stuff? I glanced back at the shower, noting two dark brown towels hanging over the top of the glass.

He had a few rolls of paper wedged under another pile of towels that required shifting the load off of them. That's when I noticed the pink, green, and baby blue swirl on the edge of a box.

I pulled the box free, my bleary eyes taking in the words "plastic applicator" and "fresh scent."

Disappointment cracked into my chest and up into my skull like a lightning strike. Sure enough, there on the shelf right next to the empty space where the box had been was a ladies' deodorant stick. *What the hell else does he have in here?*

I wanted to go on a complete tear through, looking for more evidence, but a brand new box of thirty-six tampons was pretty much all the proof I needed.

I shoved the box back in its spot, berating myself for once again falling for the suave bullshit. I may not be the most experienced when it came to the shit guys keep in their bathrooms, but tampons were definitely not one of them. Reminded me of the time I found a discarded birth control pack in Randy's apartment. He never did give me a good explanation, either. Bastard.

I left the bathroom light on and cracked the door, illuminating his bedroom enough for me to find my clothes and get the fuck out of there. My ten-minute fantasy was just shot to hell and I had no desire to stitch it up or even confront him with it.

We didn't have a formal relationship and I had no right making a big to-do out of the fact that he obviously has a steady woman in his life who parks her fresh-scented shit in his closet.

I found my jeans and one of my socks; the other sock was missing somewhere and if it meant that I'd have to stay here a second longer looking for it, the sock would end up a casualty of war.

I shucked his shorts off and crammed my toes into a sock, balancing precariously on one foot in my hung-over irate state.

A light flicked on, freezing me like a deer caught in headlights.

"What are you doing?" Adam grumbled low.

Shit. I curbed my frustrated anger and went for an innocent smirk and a *"quiet walk of shame with as much dignity as possible"* moment.

"Oh, sorry. I tried not to wake you. It's, um, late, and I have to go."

The covers slipped down his bare chest when he propped his head up. "Go?" He glanced over at his clock. "It's five twenty-two in the morning, Erin. You got someplace to be?"

My mind blanked. "Yeah."

His eyes narrowed. "Now? You have someplace to be at five thirty *a.m.*?"

I nodded while ineptly cramming a leg into my jeans. I nearly fell over; my balance was shit. "Yeah, I have this thing. But thanks for…" Saying *everything* at that moment seemed so cheesy. *For holding my hair while I puked?*

When he sat up, the sheets dropped, exposing his deliciously bare chest and those incredible arms and sexy-as-hell rope tattoos that wrapped onto very impressive pecs… making me wonder for a second if I was being too hasty. He should arrest himself for being so insanely sexy that it should be illegal. But knowing my luck, his woman would be coming home soon anyway.

"Hold up. Five minutes ago you were sleeping. Now you're running a race to get the hell out of here? What the fuck happened from the time you got out of my bed to now?"

Do I accuse him? *Nah.* Best if I just leave without making a spectacle of myself. I'm wiser now and he can play all the games he wants with the next hopeful who crawls into his bed, but that won't be me. No way was I going to get fooled twice.

"Nothing. I just have to go."

Adam frowned. "Bullshit."

I could tell that I'd angered him.

"You have to go to work or something? Pretty sure they won't appreciate you coming into the hospital in your condition."

"I don't go in until Sunday night," I blurted, inadvertently wasting my only plausible excuse.

He craned his neck, glancing at the dark window in his bedroom. "You hear that?"

I stopped moving, concentrating on some mysterious noise.

"That's the sound of heavy snow and sleet hitting the window. You aren't going anywhere."

"I'll be all right."

He gazed down at my bare foot. "With one sock and no car? What the hell, Erin?"

Oh, you want to be grumpy with me? "Are you even wearing any clothes under there?"

He flopped the bedding back, exposing what looked like dark cotton sleep pants riding dangerously low on his beveled hips. "I usually sleep naked." He was out of bed and in my face three seconds later. "What's going on with you? The truth."

I watched him cross his beefy arms over his chest, waiting. We were at a draw and I was in knots, just like the braided artwork on his body. Fine. He wanted to know so damn bad, I'd tell him. "I shouldn't be here."

His brow tipped up. "No?"

"No."

"Who says?"

I wanted to laugh. "I wasn't snooping."

"Excuse me?"

Gah! I wished I had my full wits about me. I knew my words would not come out of my still inebriated brain properly. "I used the last of the toilet paper."

"And?"

"And I needed more. Listen, you obviously have a girlfriend and I don't want to go into the many reasons why I need to go."

"Wait. Hold up. I have a what?"

I wanted to shove him for playing dumb. "A girlfriend. A wife. I don't know. Whatever. I got a new roll of toilet paper out of the closet and that's when… You have an entire box of tampons and shit in there, Adam. Girl's deodorant and hairspray and stuff. Listen, it's cool. Thanks for helping me out but I'm in no condition to defend myself when your woman gets home."

He gave me such an angered look, it shook me a moment. "Do not move," he ordered harshly before turning for the bathroom. I watched him shove the door out of his way; another sound told me he was in his linen closet.

He walked back with the box gripped in his hand. "This what you found?"

I nodded. "Listen, Adam. It's cool. You don't owe me any explanations, really."

"Well, now I think I do, seeing as you are running out of my bedroom like your ass is on fire, willing to go out in the middle of the night *into a blizzard* to get away from me."

He had a point. *Blizzard? Shit.* Guess I'll be moving out to a couch for a few hours instead of walking home.

He held the box up and took a deep breath. "Box is still sealed, right?"

I looked at it until he dropped it in my hands. The box was still glued shut. "Yeah. Really though, Adam. Seriously, you don't have—"

"Still sealed. Untouched. Guess I never thought about it until now, but do those things have an expiration date on them?"

"I don't know." I turned the box over, trying to read the small print in the dimmed light and answer the question while he turned this confrontation into a quiz.

"Doesn't matter. They upset you, they're gone." He snatched the box back and tossed it blindly across the room without regard. "They belonged to someone who used to live here. She left. I couldn't see throwing a new box of anything away, especially since she used my money to buy them. Shit in my bathroom closet is all new, too. Figured it might come in handy one day if somebody was here who needed that stuff."

"Oh."

"Oh," he mimicked and sighed, his frustration waning. "You have any more questions or can we go back to bed now?"

"Adam…" I felt like a fool.

He gazed passively at me. "Bed's new, too. Bought it the day after she left. That was last June. Only person's been in it is me… and now you."

My eyes roamed over his totally cut body and incredible abs, finding that extremely hard to believe.

"You look like you doubt me."

I waved a hand at him, pointing out the obvious, losing my track of thought when I zeroed in on that delicious "V" that disappeared into those sleep pants. "I don't want to, but... but you said you'd never lie to me."

He nodded. "I have no reason to lie. It's pointless." He tipped my chin up so I'd meet his eyes. "And know this: if I didn't want you in my house or in my bed, you wouldn't be. You need any girl products, there's some shit in my closet that's untouched. Use it. Got new toothbrushes in the top drawer, too. But right now I'm tired and you've obviously been out partying with a variety of alcohol. I'm not up for arguing over nonsense."

His warm hand glided up over my cheek. "We good?"

All I could do was nod. "I'm sorry."

His hand slipped up the back of my neck; his thumb skating along my jaw line. He leaned down and placed a soft kiss on my forehead, which warmed my entire body. "Apology accepted. Now let's go back to bed," he muttered on my skin. "You can lose the jeans, Doc. No need to sleep in them. I'll give you some privacy to change again."

I thought he would try to kiss me, but he let go and stepped back, giving me a heated stare after nudging me toward the side I'd been sleeping on. I watched his sexy ass retreat into the bathroom.

I curled back onto my side under the lukewarm sheets and stared at the window, tracing imaginary patterns in the dark curtains, feeling like an absolute drunken fool filled with regret. The bed dipped when Adam climbed under the covers a few moments later. He had his back to me while he turned out the light.

I heard the sheets shuffle as he got comfortable, breathing out an audible breath from his nose. As we lay there in uncomfortable silence, I actually reconsidered leaving, but the wind was howling outside, rattling the window in its frame, making that thought a very foolish and perilous option. I was stuck here and we both knew it.

I couldn't blame him for being guarded; after all, I brought this on myself again. At least he was being a gentleman and not tossing me out into the cold and...

He rolled over and slipped his hand over my stomach. "Stop overthinking," he muttered, honing in on my thoughts so accurately it sent another chill through me. He urged me backward toward the middle of the bed. "C'mere."

His warm body molded around my back, pulling me into his chest, sending a wash of elation through me. I felt his breath, his chest rising and falling, the confusion and arousal from skin touching skin. My mind whirled from the close proximity of his parts near mine. He placed a soft kiss on the nape of my neck and tightened his arm around me. "I want you here, Erin. That's all you need to think about." He snuggled even deeper and slipped his arm under my pillow. "Get some sleep, babe."

I WAS IN the throes of a familiar reoccurring dream—the one where I'm back in high school of all places, and I've obviously forgotten to wear shoes again. My feet are bare and the industrial flooring is cold, and I am becoming more and more frantic because I can't remember my locker combination. Random numbers barrage my brain as I spin the dial on the lock, but none of them seems to be correct, and for the life of me I can no longer even remember the PIN for my ATM card. An older woman with shellacked blonde hair clears her throat and informs me that I've missed a few important tests and therefore I'll have to repeat my last year of high school because I haven't technically graduated.

Somehow I know this is all so preposterous and untrue but I can neither stop the dream from unfurling or from letting it upset me. I knew I shouldn't have argued with the strange woman because now the police have come to remove me from class. People are staring, some in shock, others with glee.

The cold steel they place around my wrists echo their frigidness down into my fingertips, making them as numb as the rest of me. A chill blasts down my spine. I wish I had shoes on; the floor is so cold. They don't care that I didn't do it. My words fall on deaf ears. Mrs. Morton is crying, pointing a finger at me, screaming accusations of murder that are untrue! Blue vomit dripped from the lifeless body clutched in my arms. Someone make her put down the chainsaw! Please!

I woke on a gasp, pulled right out of the fog of sleep. Despite the black-out curtains covering the solitary window, bright sunlight was still beaming down from the edges, casting a warm, ethereal hue over everything.

It took me a few moments to realize that I wasn't in my own bed. My bedroom walls were still painted their original sterile white, not soothing sandstone. After three years, I still hadn't gotten around to changing the color or making my mark on the place. The harsh reality was that my place wasn't really mine. It didn't belong to me.

I blinked a few times and rubbed the sleep from my eyes, rationalizing that the loud machine noises were coming from outside and not from the inside of my inebriated skull. My chest muscles felt strained from having expelled the contents of my stomach, but the pounding headache seemed to have mostly subsided. I didn't even want to think about the complexity of toxins poisoning my system.

Shit, Erin. Let's not do that ever again.

My head felt like it weighed a lot less resting on the mound of soft pillows. I was warm, cozy. Adam's bed was super comfortable, cradling my body in some invisible layer of cushioned protectiveness. The soft blankets covering me held enough weight to keep me snuggled in though they did nothing to prevent the onslaught of reality from slamming into my thoughts.

Visions of my mother crying, utterly devastated, melded with the sounds of the rest of my family member's painful reactions from yesterday. I'd been preparing for this outcome since the moment the extent of his injuries were assessed, and from a medical standpoint, was surprised my uncle had lasted as long as he did. Uncle Cal's passing was probably for the best. A vegetative state was no way to live.

My own body felt in a vegetative state, lethargic and weak. I rubbed my face, trying to make the barrage of unwanted thoughts go away, and rolled over slowly, only to find Adam's side of the bed rumpled but empty. I closed my eyes, imagining what it might be like to wake with him beside me on a regular basis.

Outside, faint voices were drowned out by the whirl of snow blowers and the scraping sounds of shovels. Apparently last night's storm was over and Adam's neighborhood was digging out. My eyes were still heavy, though the clock on his nightstand indicated it was after ten.

My car. That thought had me tossing the covers off.

I found the light switch on the wall in the bathroom and winced at my haggard reflection in the mirror. The purple and yellow crescent-shaped bruise under my eye didn't help. I needed a hot shower and clean clothes and most definitely a toothbrush. Adam's baggy florescent green T-shirt was okay but not…

Wait…

What?

I held the shirt out, seeing the image of what appeared to be a martini glass and a car key in the center of a circle with a slash across everything.

I felt my eyes go wide with astonishment.

And here I thought Adam was just the strong, silent type. Apparently he had a wicked sense of humor. I found my jeans and pulled them on but my black, long-sleeved shirt was missing. I searched everywhere, even under the bed. Next to his bedroom was a hallway closet and two smaller bedrooms; one containing a desk and makeshift office and the other barren except for some tools, some cans of paint, a canvas tarp covering the floor, and strips of white molding. Would he hide the rest of my clothes on purpose? It made no sense.

I had just found my hat and scarf on the floor in his living room downstairs when I heard Adam come into his kitchen, his alarm system announcing his arrival. The mechanical grind of a closing garage door reverberated behind him. That moment of awkward silence hit me—the one where you're not sure if the guy really wants to see you hanging around in his house the next day or if I should ask where he put my coat so I could scatter quickly.

He eyed me warily, which did nothing for me to be able to read his mood.

"Hey. Didn't think you'd be up yet."

I ran a hand through my hair, hoping he wouldn't be appalled my haggard appearance. "I heard the snow blowers." I pointed toward the windows. "I was going to come help you but I can't seem to find my coat or my other sock."

Adam gave me a soft smirk when I tugged up my jeans and wiggled my bare left foot.

He shrugged out of his heavy tan-colored work jacket and hung it over the back of the chair at the counter at his huge kitchen island.

"My shirt seems to be missing, too."

Adam rubbed the back of his neck. "What's wrong with the one you have one?"

I grabbed the hem. "I see you have a sense of humor."

His boyish smile was devastating. "Figured it was appropriate considering…"

I found I couldn't hold my smile either. "Dressing me in a Mothers Against Drunk Driving shirt—how apropos."

He tossed his gloves onto the kitchen island and for a moment I was lost, drinking him in from head to toe, watching his methodical movements. The man surely filled out a pair of jeans. A tinge of sexual intrigue hit me; I wanted to bury my nose in the space where his gray thermal Henley grazed the nape of his neck and see if he smelled as delicious as he looked.

His soft chuckle blended perfectly with his rosy cheeks and strong shadowed jaw. "I thought so." He slipped his black knit hat with ATTF written in yellow letters off his head, patting his hair down. "Your shirt is in the washer."

I followed where his chin indicated, catching the thrumming sounds of a spin cycle. "You washed it?"

Adam nodded. "It was a casualty of your, ah… overindulgence. You got some yuck on it when you got sick."

A burst of extreme embarrassment made my head spin for a few seconds. My grand show in his bathroom was not something I cared to relive. "I'm so sorry. I'm…" *Feeling humiliated, mortified, unsure of how to move.* "Thanks for… taking care of me last night. I appreciate it."

Adam's pleasant demeanor vanished, washed away with a frustrated scowl and a discerning glare. Every nerve in my body itched to disappear. Not only did my world come crashing down yesterday, the one man I could actually see myself spending time with was assessing me as if I were an experiment gone terribly wrong. I couldn't look at him anymore. It was too awkward. I noticed my purse on the leather recliner chair in his living room.

"It's um… I should probably get going. Are the roads okay?" I pulled out my cell, wondering who I could call to come and give me a ride.

"Sun is out. Snow is starting to melt."

His low, grumbling voice set my body on high alert.

"Good, okay." I scrolled through my phone, seeing a missed text from Tommy: *"What's up? You coming?"*

A stabbing piece of my headache returned. After having lost a family member and my hopes for a fellowship decimated, meaningless sex was no longer on my agenda. And now the man I had hoped to accidentally run into last night was eight feet behind me, getting an eyeful of me at my worst.

Maybe if I don't look directly at him, he'll find some compassion. "Can I ask you for one last favor? Think you can drive me to get my car? I'm sure you have things you have to do, so the quicker I can get out of your hair—"

"Your car is in the driveway."

Um, what? "What?"

He pulled keys out of his jeans pocket; my silver "E" initial dangled on the ring between his fingers. "It's in the driveway."

My heart skipped a beat. Was he just that extremely thoughtful or in that much of a hurry to get rid of me? I opted for being grateful nonetheless. "Wow, you ran for it?"

He gave me a quick chin nod. "I told Kip I'd move it before he opened. They were plowing the lot."

Well there was a partial answer. "Oh, yeah. Okay. Thanks." The after-effects of my evening of debauchery tossed a renewed wave of nausea over me. "I think it will be a while until I show my face in his bar again." Visions of Kip harassing Adam about picking up some drunken girl's car toppled over the nausea.

Adam tipped a brow, silently agreeing. I presumed that also meant he'd never take me back there again as well.

"How did you get there?"

Adam pulled another set of keys from his pocket, setting them on the edge of the granite countertop. For a bachelor, he had a killer kitchen, which was also a surprise.

He ran a hand over his short spiky hair. "My partner Marcus picked me up."

"Really? Wow."

So much for small talk.

Something was bothering him; that much was obvious. I watched him glance around at everything but me, rubbing his neck, deliberately avoiding me as he did his thing. I tried to determine what he was looking for while presuming he was searching for a nice way to tell me to get going. I'd seen the same behaviors from other guys before him. It was the *morning air of regret* waltz. He may have felt one way last night, but the indecisiveness I'd come to learn about him was swirling like a tornado around the room.

Well, before he had the opportunity to make me feel like shit I figured I'd make it easier on him. I may be a lot of things, but a lingering inconvenience is not one of them.

"Thank you. And please tell your partner I said thank you, too. I… I really appreciate it."

Adam nodded.

"So um… I guess you want me to… I should get going…"

Adam pulled my keys back before I could grasp them. "Not so fast."

I stopped in midair, shocked.

He crossed his arms, effectively tucking my keys away. "I need to know something."

I braced, sensing I was about to be interrogated.

"Last night, drinking like that. Is that something you do often?"

Hung-over or not, I knew a displeased accusation when I'd heard one. Even shaking my head was enough to make me never want to take another drink again. "No."

His eyes narrowed. "No? You sure?"

I straightened, feeling weak and dizzy but strangely annoyed at having to be on guard. "No. Never."

His small scoff didn't go unnoticed, either.

"So you're telling me this was a one-time thing? Because I've got to tell ya, that sort of thing does *not* sit well with me. Last thing I need in my life is a party girl who gets smashed every weekend."

My throat felt as raw as my emotions. "Believe me, I don't make a habit out of it, but it looks like you don't believe me so…"

Adam's head swayed. "You know how I feel about lying, Erin."

"I have no reason to lie to you, Adam." I shoved my knit hat into my opened purse, incensed by his false assumptions. "I have no life. Haven't had much of one for years. It's not like I even have opportunities to go out anymore. All my friends are…" *Busy, married, making babies.* "I just completed my medical residency. Do you even know what that means? I work, study, and barely sleep. Whatever. I don't know why I'm bothering to explain myself. I can't help it if you choose not to believe me."

I wished my boots would magically appear on the other side of his overstuffed brown leather chair. "*Everything* else in my life has turned to shit, might as well add you to that list, too. If you tell me where you put my coat and the rest of my stuff I'll gladly get out of your hair." I pulled my purse up over my arm and held out my hand. "Can I have my keys now?"

"You make a habit of walking away a lot. You're a jack."

A what? "A what?"

"A jack rabbit."

Was he equating me to one of his petty car thieves? He made my head spin. "You've got to be kidding me. You ran away first, Adam. No, actually if I remember correctly, you *pushed* me away several times and then the last time I saw you, *you* ran out of *my* house like *your* ass was on fire. So screw you. Can I have my keys, please?"

Adam sighed. "You're right. I did. But you're here now."

My coat was nowhere in sight, adding to my agitation. "To which I still don't understand why. Can you tell me where my boots are?"

He took a step toward me, frowning at my bare foot. "All public transportation shut down last night, Doc. You would have been waiting a long time for a cab."

"So? I could have walked or waited in my car until I felt okay to drive. I didn't ask you to come get me."

"What? And let you drive home as drunk as you were? I don't think so."

I took a leveling breath. "Is that what's bugging you? I'm sorry, but I had no intentions of ruining your evening and I'm sorry if I did. Honestly, I'm surprised you came for me or that you even care."

His eyes turned even darker.

"And to answer your question, yes, I do walk away. I have no reason to stay where I'm not wanted. Been there, done that, Officer. You can't pretend to care one minute and not give a shit the next. It's confusing."

His hands balled into fists. "Who said I don't give a shit?"

"Oh that's right. You'd rather sneak around and stay anonymous than see me. Please tell me where my boots are so I can go."

"What are you talking about? Sneaking around?"

Annoyed blood thinned out with tequila was thrumming through my veins. "You know exactly what I'm talking about: my loose siding, the shingles that were peeled up, the burnt out light over my garage that suddenly works now. My neighbor told me yesterday that a mysterious guy in a big black truck has been stopping by with a ladder and tools all week, performing all sorts of random acts of kindness. Know anyone with a black truck, Adam?"

He shrugged. "I fucked up. Won't do that again."

His reply hit my like a physical blow. "And what? I wasn't supposed to know you've been the one fixing things around my house? Why would you do that, Adam? It's the most thoughtful thing *anyone* has *ever* done for me and yet I don't see you? Or hear from you at all? I'm just trying to understand."

His eyes narrowed. "Why did you pick Al's? Out of all of places to go tie one on—"

"I don't have time for this."

"Why Al's?"

I glared back. "It's close to my house."

"Bullshit. This town isn't lacking for bars."

"And they have good food. And I was home on Tuesday, by the way. And Wednesday, too."

He sighed. "I know. You worked the night shift again."

"And you couldn't knock on my door?"

He cast his eyes to the ground. "I did, sort of. The hammering didn't wake you up and you never came out to investigate, so I figured you were avoiding me or sound asleep."

My brain felt close to imploding. "So you admit to being at my house?"

"Why Al's, Erin?" he asked. His words were soft but definitely demanding an answer.

I wanted my boots and coat now more than ever. "For your information, I didn't intend to *tie one on*, either. I just so happened to have one of *the most* shittiest days of my life yesterday and then someone bought me a drink and then before I—"

"I know," he interrupted. "His name is Benny Deets and he's one of my snitches. He's a piece of shit and nothing but trouble. Been in jail more than he's been out of it. So answer my question. Why did you go to Al's?"

My skin pricked with fright. I remembered talking to a cute guy who, by Adam's accounts, was dangerous. Well, if Adam was looking to make an issue about my bad choices, I wouldn't give him any fuel. "I don't owe you any explanations. I don't owe you anything."

"Erin!"

"You want me to say it?"

I could see the weight of his plea in his eyes.

He nodded stiffly, once.

"Not sure you deserve the satisfaction." I stepped around him, searching for the rest of my things, hating that my attraction for him had turned into another Spanish Inquisition. "Why did you bother to come and get me anyway? I sure as hell didn't ask you to drive there last night, or were you just conveniently patrolling the neighborhood again?"

He snagged my arm. "Why Al's, Erin? Fucking answer me!"

His words cracked me like a whip, casting an instant icy chill through the air. My hands started to tremble. I was barely holding it together as it was, feeling wrung out and stripped of my stability. Without recourse, I pulled out of his hand and snapped. "You! Is that what you want to hear? That I was hoping to find or see... *you*. Okay?"

I swiped an errant tear, hating that I'd been reduced to this emotional mess. "My... my uncle died yesterday. So did a little four-year-old girl who was doing nothing but playing in the snow. *She* died right in my fucking hands." I heard my own voice crack, pinched with renewed pain to the point where I could barely speak. The sights, the sounds, the feelings of utter failure from yesterday barraged me all at once. "You satisfied now?"

I watched his face fall.

"They took him off life support and I watched him take his last breath." My purse slipped off my shoulder and thudded on the floor. "I didn't... I didn't know where else to go."

His feet ate up the space between us. Seconds later, I was in his arms, his warmth seeping into my skin from his intense embrace. His hands pressed into the center of my back, into my hair, pulling me in even closer. It was hard to tell where he ended and I began.

"Oh, babe, I didn't know."

Even his warm breath on my hair felt like a soothing balm on my tattered spirit.

He hugged me tighter, placing kisses on the top of my head. "I'm sorry. So fucking sorry."

I hated that my cheek fit perfectly on the broad plane of his chest. Desperation for some much-needed sympathy had me gripping his shirt as if it were a lifeline.

"I just thought you went out to party last night. I didn't know something bad had happened. Oh, babe, forgive me. I didn't know. I swear. I'll get you through this, though. I promise. We'll get through this."

I wanted so badly to believe him. "Please don't make me promises."

Adam heaved out a sigh. "I should have knocked on your door, Erin. I wanted to." He pulled me back far enough to look down at me; his eyes were so sincere. "Know that I wanted to so fucking badly, okay?"

Harsh reality was warring with my need for comfort. I knew I should leave but I was too busy crying. "Yeah, but you didn't."

Adam's eyes closed. "I know I owe you some explanations."

"I figured you were done with me or that I did or said something wrong."

"Far from it. This is all on me." The pad of his thumb skated lightly over my cheek. "I'm sorry I got angry. It's just certain things bring up bad memories."

Boy, could I relate.

"Tell me how you got this bruise. Did you get into a fight or something?"

I needed to rest my head back on his chest. Things just seemed so much better there. "No. I got kicked by a patient. A drugged-up hooker, actually." I sniffed, catching a wonderful whiff of Adam at the same time. "Her tox levels were so high I'm surprised she was able to move at all."

Adam's thumb wiped away some tears. I heard his tiny laugh, though I knew he wasn't laughing at me.

I rubbed the spot on my face where his fingers just were. "She caught me with the front of her boot."

"Her hooker boots?" He chuckled softly.

"Yeah, her crack-whore hooker boots," I mumbled into his chest. "It's not funny."

"I know." He twisted all of my hair into one roll and moved it out of his way.

I melted when his fingers massaged my neck, running along the sore tendons like a seasoned pro, lulling me into an instant stupor. I had to get away from him before he eviscerated my heart. "I need to go home."

"I want you to stay."

"I need a shower," I grumbled, wiping my cheek.

"So go take a shower."

"You have my car keys." The sensation of his thumb pressing harder into my achy muscles felt like heaven. "You keep doing that I'm gonna fall asleep."

"So go back to bed," he murmured near my ear.

"Why didn't you knock on my door, Adam? You were there."

I felt his chest rise and fall. "I don't know. I've been trying to figure that one out myself."

His words crushed me. *I can't keep doing this to myself.* I pushed off of his chest, trying to put some space in between us. I had nothing left in me. The last guy to tell me he needed to *figure out* our relationship was fucking a Radiologist while he did it. "I have to go."

Adam pulled me back in, gripping me by my upper arms. He was so much stronger than me and, in my weakened state, his hold was unbreakable. "I'm done letting you go, Erin. Made that mistake too many times now. You want to go back to sleep, go crawl back into my bed. You need to chill, pick one of my couches. But you're not walking out that door without a fight."

"Please don't mess with me." I was close to cracking. "I can't take much more."

Adam's hand rested on my throat; his thumb pushed my chin up. I had no choice but to look at him. His eyes searched mine. Something heavy was weighing on him, too. "I came for you last night because I can't stop thinking about you, no matter how hard I try. You're not just some girl to me and honestly, I just needed some time to figure it out."

His answer sounded reasonable; still it was a bit unsettling. I'd read enough self-help books and seen enough sappy movies to know that a guy who's truly interested in you makes time to be with you or at least makes his presence known.

Adam did neither.

The hopeful romantic inside me that twined daisies and paper hearts together all day jumped with glee, elated to hear that he had set me apart from any other. The other part, the sobering, rational, and skeptical part, was telling me to run before it was too late. What would happen if he changed his mind again?

Another half-assed relationship with someone who couldn't commit to it was the last thing *I* needed. "We've had two dates, Adam, neither of which ended very well. I don't know what's left to figure out. You've just said you've been trying to forget me. That sort of says it all."

The implications of that admission hit me like a physical blow to the chest, ripping the protective shell around the insecure woman inside, cutting a fresh wound across my heart. He wasn't the first man to make me feel unwanted. I felt the tears of rejection pool in my eyes. "Being with someone shouldn't be such a hard decision. I get that you're not sure. Neither am I. It's too risky to take such leaps of faith with someone you don't really know. And I sure as hell haven't asked you for anything, but either you want to see me or you don't. It's just that simple."

I stepped away from him, but he stopped me. "I just told you I do."

I tried to wriggle out of his hands. "Sounds like you're still trying to convince yourself."

His fingers constricted into my arms just deep enough to tell me he was serious. "Go ahead and try to leave if you want to test me."

The rebel in me tested his hold instead. "What about what I want?"

His fingers relented ever so slightly, but still he didn't let go. "I know what you want. It's what every woman wants."

His arrogance annoyed me. "You think you have it all figured out. Well, you don't. You have *no clue* about what I want."

He grit his teeth. "Like hell I don't. The question really is if you're the one I want to give it to."

I jerked my arm back. "Well let me know when you've made up your mind."

He snagged my hip and threaded his other hand into my hair, bringing us nose to nose. "You're not the only one in the middle of a head fuck. Your yesterday was *far* worse than mine, but that doesn't mean we both can't take the time to think things over. I've never met anyone like you before, Erin. I needed some time to process that. And before that smart mouth of yours hits me with another comeback, how's this for a final answer?"

I was stunned for all of about two seconds, trying to determine if he'd just given me an admission or a confession, before his head tilted and his lips covered mine.

The messages his mouth conveyed drilled right into my core. It was want and desperate need and unbridled desire mixed with a plethora of unspoken promises all worth exploring.

Adam's fingers tightened on my scalp while I took every one of his throaty moans and gave back my own.

The need to protect my heart didn't seem so important anymore as I clutched his shirt in my hands. He was giving me an answer and shutting down my worries all at the same time, making a serious effort to make his point irrefutable.

And that's when I realized when he was kissing me, none of the senselessness seemed to exist. It was as if he had the power to erase all of the doubts he'd placed in my mind and replace them with the promise of hope.

My mind began to feel cleansed of all its pain and sorrow, allowing me to simply *be*.

CHAPTER 12

Adam

I WANTED TO argue, plead, tell her we were both wrong, but instead I cupped her face in my hand, pulling her into my chest with the other. Her unspoken argument disappeared on a gasp when I let my actions speak for themselves.

I felt off balance. Hungry, confused, twisted up inside. This amazing woman was in my house and mine for the taking, and hell if I'd let another opportunity to let her know it slip by.

She only fought a second, giving me a weak shove not really meant to push me off, before she surrendered and melted into me. I released her lips long enough to wet mine so I could kiss the shit out of her, holding her fast so she'd get my meaning.

She made a few soft whimpers as I tested her willingness with the tip of my tongue. I deepened the kiss, demanding more, needing more, *dying* for more. I drew in her sighs, her tongue, the way her moans curled around my own. I wanted to drink her in, devour her mouth, spend hours getting to know every square inch of her body. I tangled my hand in her hair, branding her memories with my flavor.

Erin's hand brushed over the day-old stubble on my face, curling her fingertips into the edge of my jaw, doing her own form of branding on me. Holy hell, she had me deep, searing her name all over my bones, owning me inside and out.

I felt like a teenager all over again, getting that all-encompassing rush of excitement from kissing the girl, feeling that strange pressure in my chest and limbs. Arousal also flooded into my cock, indenting it painfully into the zipper on my jeans.

I'd kissed plenty of girls since... but none of them had me panting like this.

Not even...

I palmed Erin's ass, squeezing out the memories of that other female as quickly as they came in to spill their poison on this moment. The wind gusted outside, sending a frosty haze of white crystals across my front window, but it didn't matter, because inside I was burning up. Erin, however, quivered in my arms.

Our lips rested as our breath blended into one. Her hair was all tangled around my fingers.

"I wanted to do that since the first night I met you," I whispered quickly, taking her mouth again. Getting to feel this much from just kissing someone was worth the risk of having myself gutted if it didn't work out.

Never before had I felt this passionately connected to someone. *Never*. This woman was stripping me of my self-protective shields one by one, wiggling her way past my defenses.

"I thought you didn't—" Erin managed to say before I cut her words off with my tongue, letting my overwhelming desire for her answer her questions.

She whimpered again, wrapping her tiny hands up the back of my shirt.

"Spend the day with me," I said on her mouth, unwilling to separate us that far.

Her hands did a slow slide up my back, grazing her nails lightly over my skin. "You really want me to?"

I scraped my teeth over her top lip, sucking on it, thinking about kissing her like this for the next twelve hours, at least, while she scored my skin with her fingernails. "Most definitely."

She tore her mouth away and gasped, leaving me out of breath. Her chin dipped down. "I wish... I wish you would have knocked."

I pressed my lips to her forehead to keep our connection, guessing she still doubted my intentions. It was frustrating, but I tamped it down, knowing I had the power to change her perceptions. Girls were always worried about being used, and I suspected Erin was no different in that respect.

I tilted her face up. "Make no mistake; this is me knocking now, okay?"

I locked eyes with her and stared her down until she nodded. "Okay," she whispered.

I sealed our small agreement with a soft kiss, sensing she wasn't ready for much more.

Her hand gently closed around mine, wrapping herself deeper.

She tugged on my bandaged hand, raising it up to inspect it. That little crinkle formed between her brows, followed by her disapproving frown. "This should be changed."

I sighed with relief knowing I'd managed to crack into her tough outer shell. It may have been a small tear into her protective lining, but at least she wasn't running out of my house anymore.

"Just so we're clear, all these dark spots are *chocolate*. I had a few cookies last night. They were fresh from the oven and still hot."

Her brow tipped up. So did one side of her luscious mouth. "Chocolate?"

Just seeing part of her smile return was enough to make me high. "I'm serious. My partner's wife made them. Stuff melted all over."

"Well, I need to rewrap it before you get any more food in your stitches."

Her teasing me was cute as shit, however separating her body from mine was the last thing on my mind. I warmed the edge of her jaw with my mouth. "I'd appreciate that."

She left out a breathy "okay" before both of her hands pushed slightly back on my arms. A moment of sanity slipped in on top of my thrumming heart, reminding me to slow the fuck down.

Her brilliant blue eyes flashed down my body before a tinge of shock registered on her face. The smug bastard inside me smiled. *That's right, babe. Check it. I'm hard as a rock because of you.*

There was no way I could hide it, either, not that I wanted to. I gazed at her until she looked back up at me, amused that she was so intrigued.

She tugged on her T-shirt and tried to smooth her hair. "I, um…"

Seeing her flustered, her soft cheeks flushed, wearing one sock and a dazed look in her eyes made her even cuter. I took her hand and gave a tug. "Come on." She followed me back up the steps without objection. By the fifth step I contemplated stripping her bare and messing the bed up even more, see if we could dislodge the sheets, let her feel *exactly* how much I was turned on by her.

But her hand felt so fragile in mine and the weak hold she had on my fingers was enough to tell me she was probably still feeling the aftereffects of a night of binge drinking. I could completely relate to that shitty state of being all too well. The body aches, the sour stomach, the debilitating lethargy. Making love to her would have to wait.

I towed her right into my bathroom and closed the lid on the john, giving her a place to sit.

I don't know why, but the first thing I noticed when I opened up my linen closet was that fucking box of tampons. I fought the urge to crush the box, squeeze it flat, and get them the hell out of my house. I shoved it to the side. Erin had to have put them back in there because I surely didn't.

I stifled my curse, knowing she restored things to how they were before she stumbled onto them, as if she didn't want to upset me or my world.

I pushed some towels over it, searching for my new roll of gauze, knocking over a bottle of hair spray that used to belong to Nikki in the process. It landed on my foot.

Two new bottles of women's body wash and some other girl products were also glaring at me. I wanted to swipe it all off the shelf, toss it all in the fucking garbage, and eradicate every trace of Nikki from my house. I should have done it sooner, but I resolved that I'd throw it all out later when Erin wasn't sitting two feet away watching me get pissed off.

"Here's shampoo." I pointed, purposely not looking at her, knowing that I'd probably see her disappointment all over again. I set the purple bottle in the shower and turned the water on. "Why don't you take a shower? I'll leave some clean clothes on my bed."

"Wait. What about your hand?"

I glanced back, masking my attitude with a smile, and flashed the roll of gauze between my fingers. "I'll deal with it."

I pulled the door closed behind me, getting out of there before I lost my shit. Nikki and I were done. I needed to get rid of her crap. Pronto.

I had thought seeing Nikki's stuff used by another woman would give me satisfaction, but in reality it turned my stomach, thinking of her lingering memories touching Erin's skin.

Erin was beautiful inside and out.

She didn't deserve to be soiled by my past.

She deserved better.

She deserves better from me.

ERIN CAME INTO my kitchen with her hair still wet, wearing one of my black ATTF T-shirts and my Temple University sweatpants. My chest started to ache. The shirt was fairly new, but those sweats I'd had since my freshman year. The logo running down the length of her right leg was as well-worn as my memories. Knowing Erin was the first woman I'd ever allowed to wear them gave me a renewed sense of satisfaction.

A ghost of a smile tilted her lips but her lingering sadness was visible, like a heavy weight crushing down on her shoulders, making me wonder if there wasn't more to her depression than she was letting on. I knew without a doubt I had something to do with her mood, but the loss in her eyes was unmistakable.

I'd lost plenty of people in my life. I'd been through my share of death—friends, relatives, my partner. It hurts, it sucks, it takes a while to get over, but whatever it was that she was carrying was more than that.

I turned the burner off on the stove. This was as good of a time as any to defrost some homemade chicken soup. "You hungry?"

She nodded and pulled out one of the island chairs. "It smells good."

I slid the sandwiches I'd made out of the pan and sliced them in half. "Hope you like grilled cheese." It had always been my failsafe meal after a bout of heavy drinking.

Erin was still trying to shield that crescent-shaped bruise under her eye. Her hand covered what wasn't hidden by strands of wet hair.

It was time to break her of her self-consciousness. I tossed my damp dishtowel over my shoulder, set her plate in front of her, and met her on the other side of the island.

I tipped her face up. "Let me see it."

She tugged her chin away. "No, just don't look at it. Please."

"It's not as bad as you think."

She didn't seem to agree. "It's hideous, and huge."

I took her face in my hands. "Doc, look at me. Seriously, it's a small bruise. It will disappear in a couple of days. I've got a two-inch gash in my hand that's tied up with your stitches. We're just having a row of bad luck."

Being this close to her, catching the all too familiar fragrance coming off her clean skin, it was as if she'd branded herself just for me, bathing her entire body in my scent. Curiosity and base male instinct had me sniffing her hair next.

"Something wrong?" she asked.

I couldn't suppress my groan. "You smell like me."

She looked apologetic. "You told me to take a shower."

"I thought you'd use the girl stuff."

She shook her head; long wet strands swished back and forth, tickling the backs of my hands. "Decided against it."

I couldn't hide my smile. "Yeah?"

Her shoulder tipped up. "I didn't want to smell like a reminder of someone else." She sniffed her arm. "I'd rather smell like you."

Holy shit. I think I'm in love.

That was it.

Her five simple words tipped me right over the edge.

If *want* could take human form, it just possessed me from head to toe and clouded my every thought. And now I wanted to possess this woman as much as she'd possessed me—inside and out. Gone was the guy who questioned how far I was willing to overlook her drinking binge while freezing his nuts off for two hours this morning shoveling heavy snow and ice.

Those vibrant blue eyes gazed up at me, glistening with anticipation, rimmed with a hint of fear but open to trust, calling on every carnal instinct deep within me to own her heart.

I wanted to dive in, take what I wanted so desperately, but I restrained myself, using her reactions to gauge if I had an open invitation. I had never forced myself on a woman before and I sure as hell wasn't starting now.

But her soft pink lips parted, her eyes darted from mine, down to my mouth, then back up to seeing right into my wretched soul. That was all the invitation I needed. Her stretching to meet my mouth halfway caused that winded feeling to blast my chest, taking away my ability to breathe.

Excitement flashed through me like a million tiny shards of sheer energy, tensing my muscles, tingling down my spine, driving me to that point where everything and nothing merge and consumes you. The soft brush of her beckoning tongue pushed all of my doubts and lingering fears right out the fucking window. Nothing in my life had ever felt so right as her lips on mine—

N o t O n e T h i n g.

This woman, this luscious creature, had been haunting my every waking moment and much of my unconscious ones since the moment I met her and by some dumb luck or twist of fate here she was, in my hands like a precious jewel, letting me show her exactly how I'd been feeling but unwilling to admit.

Her teeth scraped over my bottom lip, sucking and pulling and just as hungry, echoing that same sensation right into the depths of my jeans. If just kissing her was this mind-blowing then making love to her would surely be the death of me. I'd been bleeding inside for so long, missing something I couldn't quite name. It was hard to hide just how desperate I was for her to heal me.

Her fingertips pressed into my sides and curled, tugging and gripping my shirt in bunches. I tangled my fingers into her damp hair, hanging on for dear life, marking her memories so she'd never want to think of another man ever again.

I'd been down for so long, I forgot how it felt to be happy. I'd been doing time, not living it. A prisoner of my own doing. Erin was a breath of freedom and a lifeline of sunshine and damn if she didn't taste like perfection.

…mixed with my mint toothpaste.

Our kiss slowed, our lips rested, our breaths both came out in pants. It was the best and scariest feeling, like the exhilaration that comes from jumping out a plane and landing in a safety net piled with pillows and knowing you'd survived the wildest ride of your life.

If I go in for another kiss, I'm not coming up for air.

And fuck being afraid.

Or hesitant.

Or unsure.

I held her jaw, hoping she could see all I wanted to say to her but wasn't quite ready to say out loud.

Not yet. That would have to wait, and be earned.

But this kiss, it was enough to seal our fate. At least for me it was, because I could see so many unsaid words flashing in her wounded eyes, basically asking the same thing.

Will you hurt me if I let you in?

Can we go forward without being torn apart inside?

I want to want you.

And I'm scared, too.

But I'm drunk on you and I need you to feel this high again because if this is how you make me soar from one kiss, imagine what else we can feel inside.

And yes, you've turned this hard-hearted bastard into a poet.

Most of the time, when I'm kissing a girl, I feel nothing. Well, not exactly nothing. More like physical horniness mixed with a bit of deviousness, plotting the quickest way to getting the woman naked and my balls emptied. That had been my only goal since ending things with Nikki. Make no ties with anyone who crossed my path, have no worries. Things were simpler that way. Manageable.

But Erin was different. I don't know how but I could just feel it inside. I felt different with her, as if she had this invisible hold on me, tethering me with renewed purpose.

The hold Nikki once had had on me was nothing compared to this.

The granite top of my kitchen island was looking to be the perfect height for me to crawl up inside this amazing woman, but I won't. Erin isn't the type I want to fuck and chuck to the curb. I knew that for sure now. All my senses were telling me that would be a waste of a good woman.

A small "wow" slipped out of her wet mouth when I rested my forehead on hers. I had to agree.

I knew I should back up, re-evaluate, slow the fuck down, but that seemed too far away from her and I just didn't want that separation yet.

The smile I felt burning on the inside came out on my face.

Part of me considered whether or not I should just toss her over my shoulder, carry her to my bed, and continue this until neither of us could walk or move. My mind had wrapped itself tightly around that single notion. My hard-on definitely loved that idea too, even giving me a standing ovation for being brilliant.

But the weight of her sadness was still lying heavily around her despite having new things fluttering around her busy mind. She didn't need to say it; I could feel it.

I skimmed my nose over hers, wanting to stay locked together somehow. "Sorry. Couldn't help myself."

Her fingers slipped up my back, sending another shiver through me. Erin's shy approach was beyond sexy.

"Is that so?" she whispered.

I shrugged. "I'm just saying."

She smiled coyly. "You're just saying?"

"Just saying." Playing with her was such a turn-on.

Her fingernails scraped over my sides again from my small taunt when I faked backing away, unwilling to relinquish her hold on my shirt. Hell if that wasn't a turn-on, too.

I went in for another kiss. Carrying her off to my bed and fucking her stupid crossed my mind again, this time with clearer, more vivid pictures.

Pictures I'd hoped to paste around the entire inside of my skull and keep the leftovers in my wallet.

Erin's lips let go first.

Another time, perhaps. I tried to back up, get out of her space. It was after I kissed her forehead that it struck me how natural that felt. "Eat your sandwich."

I set two bowls of soup down and sat next to her, dipping half of my sandwich right into my hot broth, trying to get my hard-on to subside. No sense putting on false pretenses. I was glad to see she was able to eat, even though she was taking small bites. There was nothing worse than rot gut from a hangover. Been there, done that.

"Your stomach feeling better?"

She nodded, puckering her lips to blow on another spoonful. An urge to snag the spoon away from her and kiss her again came on like a sudden hurricane.

"This is delicious. You make it?"

I finished the last of my grilled cheese. "Nope. This is mom soup."

She leaned back over her bowl. "I love mom soup."

"It cures whatever ails you. Well, that's what we were raised to believe."

And just like that, my favorite doctor curled into herself a bit more. It was tiny but noticeable. Over at my stove, I filled my bowl back up to the top. She was still in her protective ball when I sat back down.

"You're killing my ego, you know."

She glanced over at me. "I am?"

I stirred my noodles around with my spoon. "Yep. Usually a woman isn't so sad after kissing me. I fear I'm losing my touch."

At least she smiled.

"You're not losing your touch. Trust me."

"Well, that's a relief." I took another bite of my sandwich. "You want to talk about it?"

She looked back over at me. "Talk about what?"

"Whatever it *is* that's weighing heavy on your mind."

"I wouldn't know where to start."

I set my spoon down and turned to face her. Something was telling me I was still partly to blame here somehow. I'd spent my entire life conquering things that tried to break me. A few situations got close to wrecking me for good, but I had to keep reminding myself that there was nothing that I couldn't overcome.

Guilt, however, was laying its heavy hand on my shoulder, weaving its malevolence up into my thoughts. The fact that I went from avoiding Erin, to accusing her of being a drunk, to making out with her in my kitchen, wasn't lost on me. Last thing I wanted to do was mess with her head. Time to own up to my mistakes and take the heat.

"Start by talking."

I noticed her hand trembled slightly when she scratched her eyebrow. She probably feels like wrung-out garbage being hung-over.

"I lost a pediatric patient yesterday. It's… it's hitting me hard."

My body jerked, ready to console her. Misty blue eyes hesitantly glanced over at me and just like that I was rendered helpless, feeling powerless to fix whatever was causing her such grief. Maybe that's why I found myself over at her house so many times this past week, unable to ring her damn door, but repairing everything else I could get my hands on beyond the rift I'd made between us.

"She was only four years old. Four. Her entire life was in front of her."

Oh shit. My hand landed softly on the curve of her shoulder. None of the words of comfort that flashed through my mind seemed appropriate or fitting.

She dipped her face down. "She had long blonde hair, and curls… I tried not to look at her face while we worked on her. I just couldn't. That was someone's baby. Someone's daughter. I lost her before we could get her into the O.R."

I rubbed her back while feeling her pain. It was all too familiar for me.

"I've worked on injured kids before, too many to count, but I never had one die on me." She drifted her eyes over to me. "Losing a geriatric patient is one thing. It's still ha... hard, but I just try to tell myself that they've lived their life, that they've loved and lost and made their mark on the world. But babies? Babies aren't supposed to die, not like that. I can't shake the fact that I let her down."

Words my counselor once told me came to mind. "You can't blame yourself, Doc. I know you want to because it's easy to do, but deep down inside you know it's not your fault."

Erin shook her head in disagreement. "I was upset and unfocused and had no business working another severe trauma. I didn't have my head in the game and that's all on me."

I held my breath for a moment, recalling the days when I had to rip my own wounds apart. "Circumstances aren't always within our control, Erin."

"I know. It... it's just been a lot to process for one day."

I could only imagine how many of those cases were causing the massive trauma to her soul. No wonder she sought solace in a bottle. There were only so many ways to purge your system of the ugly crap and I was all too familiar with her chosen outlet. Seeing how torn up she was about losing a child caused a twin echo to burn into my chest. The lump in my throat suddenly became hard to swallow.

"I'm sure you did everything you could." I wanted to take her hand in mine. "A very wise man once told me that sometimes it's not within our power to stop bad things from happening."

I heard the words come out of my mouth; if only I could keep remembering that myself.

Erin pushed her soup bowl away. "I should get going. I need to make some calls and get back to the hospital."

Shit, she was running again. "Thought you had the next two days off?"

"I do but there are some things I need to do."

I snagged her wrist before she could walk away. "Hold up. I get being a workaholic; been one myself on occasion. I also get that you're upset and feel the need to fix something. But what I know for a fact is you have to take time for *you* every now and then or else the job eats you alive. Look at me, babe." I turned her to face me. "What's so important that you have to go in on your day off?"

This defeated woman in my hands was not the self-assured go-getter

I'd seen in her personality before and it was killing me to see her this way.

"You wouldn't understand."

I held her firm. "Try me."

She sighed, trying to hide that her lip was quivering. "I lost my fellowship yesterday, Adam. I need to see if I can fix it before it's too late." Her eyes were filling with unshed tears, which instantly brought back that burn in my throat. "I don't know what I'm going to do now."

Her voice was barely audible, barely above a whisper. Well, she was partially right; I didn't understand what that meant but sure as hell could tell that it was hurting her beyond a level I was comfortable with. At least I could do something about that. What, though, I had no clue beyond helping her search for what she'd lost. "Was it because you lost the little girl?"

She shook her head no.

"Then sit. Explain it to me."

She wiped her face with her fingertips. "It means that *everything* I've worked for since I was a teenager was stolen out from under me by a thieving bastard who doesn't deserve it."

I tore a paper towel off the roll and handed it to her, stiffening at hearing the words "stolen" and "thieving bastard." "I may not fully understand what you mean by fellowship, but I have plenty of guns and tons of bullets and a lot of experience hunting down thieving bastards."

That at least generated a partial laugh, which was what I was aiming for.

Erin dabbed her eyes. "If only it were that easy." She exhaled hard. "I'd probably have to resuscitate him before I go to jail. Might as well take out his evil girlfriend while I'm at it."

"Now you're thinking like a predator." I pulled out her chair so she'd sit and calm down. At least she was talking, which kept me from thinking about taking out whoever stole from her. "Come on, Doc. Sit. Tell me; what did this thieving bastard do exactly?"

She slid back onto the chair. "The hospital only gives out so many fellowships a year when you finish your residency. I thought the toxicology fellow was mine, but apparently I assumed too much. I don't know. Maybe I can find another program at another hospital. That would mean I'd have to leave University, though. That's going to suck." Her fingers landed in her hair, tugging on the long strands. "Guess I don't have much of a choice now, do I?"

I hated seeing the vitality sucked out of her like this. I wanted to go find this thieving bastard who stole her happiness and punch him in the head a few times just for a warm-up. "That's a shitty thing for your boss to drop on you on the same day you went through a family loss, Erin. Nothing like kicking you when you're down. Maybe you would be better off working somewhere else."

She finger-combed her hair back. I tried not to think about how sexy that was but it was difficult. She was chewing on her lip too, which also did nothing to aid my concentration.

"He wasn't the one who told me. The thieving bastard's girlfriend delivered the news. She even went so far as to ask me to be *nice* about it. God, I wanted to punch her. Sorry, I'm... it's just talk. I've never hit anyone in my life but man I wanted to hit her."

Several images of me helping to make that scenario possible flashed through my mind. I'd reflect on how her hurt made me hurt too, but later. The bitter bite of resentment in her words was unmistakable; so was the hot flare of my own jealousy that flashed up the sides of my neck.

"Thieving bastard's girlfriend? I take it you and this dude have history?"

Erin's lips twisted while her guarded expression gave her away. Last thing I wanted to worry about was someone I was gonna be dating hooking up in some dark hospital room with a readily available supply of empty beds.

"It's in the *past*, correct?"

She nodded once. "Yeah, it is. Been over a while."

That was a relief, but still my fingers itched to lock him away for something and make it permanent. "You still work with this guy?"

Erin shrugged. "Not all the time. But yeah, I do. We both started out as interns together."

I felt the muscle in my jaw twitch. "Invest a lot of time in him?"

Her hair shook. "About a year. He was never serious about it. I thought that wanting the same things out of life would be a good foundation until I found out he wanted the *exact* same things. Then it turned it into a competition. Guess I know who won in the end."

Yeah, apparently this asshole gutted her along the way, too. "You still in love with this guy?"

"No. I pretty much despise him. At the time when we were together, I think I was in love with the idea of love. You know what I mean? Does that constitute love? I don't know."

I had no idea, either.

"What about you and the girl who left her box of tampons behind?"

Wait. When did this become about me? Dredging up my past was not something I was keen on doing. "Her name is Nikki. It didn't work out."

"Oh. Were you together long?"

Fuck.

"A while."

The edges of Erin's mouth curled down. "Sounds like you were in love with her."

Actually she drove me crazy. My cell dinged; a number I didn't have programmed had sent me a text.

> **Thinking about you** 🖤

What the? Jesus, I don't need this. I deleted it and tossed my phone aside.

Erin sat up. I could see the thoughts ricocheting around her head, ready to pinball her out of my kitchen when I didn't answer. "What time is it?"

I glanced at my microwave. "Eleven thirty."

She slipped off her chair. "I need to talk to Doctor Wilson."

Somewhere in my living room, a cell began to ring. I watched her fish her phone out of her purse, finding relief after hearing her say hello to her mother.

Erin's body was silhouetted by the sun streaming in through my front window, giving her a golden glow. Her hair was mostly dry now, with each strand taking on a slight curl. The back of the T-shirt she was wearing was bunched up around the waistline of my gray baggy sweats and tied into a knot, amplifying a mouthwatering, heart-shaped ass hidden in the fabric. Even the floppy white socks she was wearing were mine.

Watching the way she chewed on her thumbnail as she held the cell to her ear, the way her body swayed while she gave her mom words of comfort mesmerized me. I didn't know things could feel this strongly with someone. I couldn't quite put my finger on what it was about her that was like the center of gravity, pulling me in. I felt weak and vulnerable and tough and virile all at the same time. In all the time I was with Nikki I never felt this attracted to her like I did with the woman in my presence right now.

Instead of centering on herself and her own problems, Erin was calm and confident, making plans to handle things that had to do with upcoming funerals, taking that burden off her grieving mother and adding more onto her own plate. Never once did she complain about her own problems or even mention what she was dealing with. *Man, she's selfless.*

My chest swelled with pride. At the same time, I wanted to wrap her in my arms and give her my strength too, knowing that after what she'd shared with me, she needed it. She probably never burdened anyone with her problems.

My body moved before I completed that thought, first checking if she'd shy away from me. When she didn't budge, I pulled her back into my chest, letting her say her "okay, moms" while I held her.

Despite her convincing telephone act with her mother, she was on the verge of a breakdown.

I could see it; sense it.

Sure enough, as soon as she ended her call, she turned in my arms and tangled her hands into the back of my shirt. It started with sniffles before it turned into a full-blown cry.

I held her tightly and gave her every bit of strength I had.

I MANAGED TO move her into my kitchen without letting go of her and tore another paper towel off the roll. "Sorry, it's all I have."

Erin dabbed her eyes and wiped her face. "Thanks. I'm sorry I fell apart like that. It's not… I never… And I got your shirt all wet."

I'd be willing to collect all of her tears—just as long as I wasn't the reason she was crying. "Not worried about the shirt. You okay?"

She nodded but didn't look convincing. Her eyes were puffy and rimmed in red. She wiped her nose. "Funeral is Friday at ten o'clock. My cousins had my Aunt Karen cremated. It's what she wanted. Oh God. I have to order flowers and help them find a hall to have a luncheon afterward. They are going to have a memorial service Thursday night. My mom wants me to come up there and help her bake, too."

"Where is *there?*"

"Plymouth Meeting."

My inner navigation clicked in, mapping out the logistics. That was a thirty-five minute drive north. The natural detective in me questioned the bigger picture. "Wait, why were your aunt and uncle driving the Schuylkill Expressway that night?"

She tried to mask her bruise with her hand again while she talked with me but I stopped her, pulling her hand into mine. "They were visiting my cousin Nate in Cherry Hill."

East. Just below Philly in New Jersey. The Schuylkill would have been the most direct route.

Fuck.

I tried to banish visions of the chase from that night—the lights, the glare on the wet roads, the adrenaline that coursed through our veins tracking that stolen Nissan. It would do me no good to rehash it now. "I'm all about family, but you can't do it all, Erin."

She was exasperated. "I'm the one who gets things done, Adam. It's expected."

Yeah, we'd see about her being so accessible to everyone once I had a say about it. "What about your sister?"

Erin's hair swayed again. "Kate's got her own challenges. It's always fallen on my shoulders."

I could relate to that. I was forever cleaning up after Kyle's and Jason's antics. "So what are you going to do?"

Her bottom lip puffed out. "I hate to bake."

I grabbed my cell and scrolled through my calendar. Suits from the network wanted me to come to the main office for a meeting with the bigwig but that wasn't until the following week. "What time is the service Thursday?"

"Why?"

I looked up. "Why? Because I want to know what time to pick you up, that's why."

Her head started shaking again. "You don't have to do that."

I'd need to take Friday off, too. Could they make it any more difficult to type on these damn phones? How did I end up in next year? Back. God damn it. Not June. These buttons aren't made for men's fingers. She said Thursday. "What time, Doc?"

"Adam, you don't have to go. It's family and everyone will be upset and—"

"What *time*, Erin? It's not up for debate."

She looked stunned. "You really want to take me?"

God, how many men have fucked with this woman's head? "I don't say things I don't mean. Going to take you to the funeral, too."

"There's a church service before the burial."

I shrugged. Been in plenty of churches before.

"A *Catholic* church," she added.

Was she really that set on me not going, trying to dissuade me? "Just so you know, all four of the Trent brothers were altar boys at one time or another. And no, we weren't sexually assaulted or anything like that. Well, maybe Kyle was. Would explain a few things. I'll have to ask him next time I see him."

It felt great to see her smile again.

I took her by her hands and pulled her up off the counter chair. "I'm driving you, so no arguments."

Those big blue eyes gazed up at me, capturing my complete attention. "My mother expects me to stay overnight."

I slipped my hand over her cheek. "So I'll sleep on the couch or something. It's not that far of a drive, either. We'll figure it out as we go, okay?"

Erin nodded. "Okay."

I leaned down to kiss her again, wanting to wipe the worry from her mind. I knew she was hurting but I couldn't stop myself. "What time, Doc?" I asked, probing her for answers.

"Six," she whispered. "Starts at six."

Her answer made me smile. She made me work for it. The sadness making her eyes still heavy, however, was instantly sobering. "How about we go relax and watch a movie?"

I seized her moment of hesitance. "Come with me."

"What about the dishes?" She pointed.

"Leave them." I didn't let go of her hand as I led her down the stairwell, the old steps creaking under both our weight.

I'd been working on renovating the basement for the last few years. The walls were framed and dry walled and I'd used some of the money from the show to buy a huge sectional sofa and a large flat screen television. I had hoped she wouldn't notice the steel eye-hook bolted to the exposed ceiling joist in the middle of the room, so I pulled her down to sit next to me as quickly as I could. Though it hadn't been used in well over a year, it was still something I wasn't ready to openly discuss. I debated taking it down. The last thing I wanted was for her to fear me, especially since I was finally taking a chance with someone.

She was sitting on the very edge of the couch, tension and apprehension and that womanly consternation making each of her movements very deliberate. I kept reminding myself to take it slow, test the waters, see how receptive she was.

One step at a time, Adam.

I grabbed the remote and slid behind her, sprawling out on the wide couch. I wanted to feel her close to me. The dying man inside me was starving for it.

I grabbed a few pillows and crammed them under my head, making sure to make a spot for her. "You've been through enough. Kick back. Relax. Let's watch some TV."

She turned to look at me. "I should get going. I have to figure out why I lost my fellowship."

Thinking about her running out, running away, nearly set me into a panic. I wasn't willing to let her go just yet. "Your boss going to be there?"

"No, but maybe I can get answers somewhere else. Maybe one of the other committee members is in. Why they told Randy, Doctor Mason, first and not me... I don't know. I just have to get to the bottom of this."

I held her firm. "I think it's shitty that they didn't give you an official reason. Hearing something so important second hand, well... So how did this other woman find out before you?"

Erin gazed at the floor. "Good question."

"I don't know how things work with hospital administration, but unless I hear it directly from my commanding officer, it's usually just rumors. People running their mouths."

She rubbed her forehead. "And I just talked to Doctor Wilson about it a few days ago."

"Doctor Wilson?"

"My boss," she said. "Review committee isn't supposed to even meet for another few weeks, that's why I'm so confused."

I nudged her back, getting her to lean on me. "Sound like that nurse or whatever was feeding you a line of bullshit."

Erin nodded. "I think you're right."

"I usually am."

She rolled her eyes. "Doctor Wilson will be in on Monday. I'll just have to wait until then, I guess."

I grabbed the blanket off the back of the couch and shook it open. "Good. Then you'll get answers on Monday. So for now, just relax. C'mere." It took a tiny bit of coaxing, but she relented pretty quickly. I pulled her down, curling her body into my chest, feeling her warmth seep into my aching soul. I wasn't sure who needed who more here. Her or me?

I tossed the blanket over us, making sure she wasn't going anywhere, not while I had her finally in my arms. I twined my fingers with hers and placed a small kiss on her shoulder. It felt so natural. "Rest, babe. It will all work out. I promise."

CHAPTER 13

Erin

FOR THE FIRST time in a long time, I couldn't remember my dream. I wasn't sure if I even had one beyond feeling as if I'd been floating on a cloud; the sweet nothingness was such a relief. The large flat screen TV was on, though the volume was very low. I tested my unwilling legs, giving them a needed stretch, feeling something rigid underneath my feet.

A warm body stirred behind me, a pair of legs shifted with mine, and I remembered I was far from alone. I didn't feel that private ache deep within my heart, either—that hollowness that stemmed from wondering if I'd ever be here, like this, within the tender embrace of someone special.

His deep exhale was followed by a large hand tensing on my ribs and sock-clad feet brushing over mine; and though I couldn't see him yet in the soft light and the haze of my unfocused eyes, it sounded as though he was waking up along with me.

When I laid my head down on this pillow, I knew I'd be safe and cared for, despite the troubles that plagued my mind.

Adam's arms were holding me just tightly enough to let me know that the man behind me didn't want me to go anywhere.

I tried not to think about anything else but the incredible body pressed against mine, the slow hand sliding over my stomach, the unsaid messages he was conveying with a careful touch.

That little voice of doubt most women harbor tried to remind me not to read into this too much, not to get my hopes up, for I knew how quickly the presumed bliss could turn to cold abandonment. I tried to squash her, that annoying niggle, because the soft kiss he'd just placed on my exposed neck was enough to engulf me.

I ran my hand over the top of his, feeling the warmth of flesh and the roughness of his manly skin and a million tiny impulses of our growing connection, and as if he could read me, our fingers slid together, his thicker digits curling around mine.

Could I dare to allow myself to hope once again?

Adam's cheek nuzzled my hair, his lips brushed the edge of my ear, and my entire body tingled to life. I needed to see him, to know if he was real and not just some very vivid fantasy concocted in my lonely brain.

Sleepy milk-chocolate eyes greeted me, and his gaze was so focused, so sincere, so filled with what I could only hope was desire, I was lost in that sense of falling.

His hand softly brushed my hair back while he just looked at me, and I felt stripped bare and open to the possibilities and wondering if this amazing feeling could last a lifetime.

I wanted him to kiss me and was thinking about making the first move, but he beat me to it. Just the mere thought of his amazing mouth on mine took my breath away.

His kiss was light at first, full lips coving mine, but it was enough to pull me under his spell. His soft suck on my upper lip, a wordless call, made me open my eyes. His eyes were opened too, speaking a thousand silent messages just for me.

Before I could capture my next breath his lips were back on mine, hungry—starving actually—just like mine were for him.

My fingers threaded through his short hair, tickling my skin, while the rest of my body lit on fire. His tongue was hypnotic, luring me to plot how I could get more of him inside me without appearing like an easy piece of ass.

Part of me didn't care.

The part of me that had been starved for this passionate affection wanted to pull his shirt off and wrap my legs around his hips and take my fill.

My mother's ancient words of buying cows and getting milk for free and lectures of never cheapening myself swirled about, making that ridiculous girl inside my thoughts question how far this might go. I hated that my insecurities chose this moment of all moments to make an appearance and dampen the overpowering lust swirling about.

Adam's hand slid over my hip, cupping my rear.

I could feel his erection in his jeans; it was hard and ready and probably pulsing in time with my heart. His fingers found the opening where his T-shirt separated from my stomach and just the simple touch sent jolts of awareness right through my body.

His hand eventually stopped directly below my breast and that's where it stayed while he kissed me. Just his close proximity to the underwire of my bra was driving me slightly insane. I'd never been this turned on, this alive, this needy, and the way he devoured my mouth made me wonder if he wasn't in the same exact spot with me.

I wanted to feel his hands on me; willed it, actually. As if he could sense my unspoken need, the tips of his fingers brushed lightly over my breast, and my body instantly bowed.

"Is this okay?" he asked while rolling a fingertip around my hard nipple over and over again, pausing his kiss long enough to check for my answer but never separating his lips too far from mine. His soft, teasing touch sent wave after wave of heat down into my core, rendering me unable to breathe let alone speak.

"Yes or no, Erin."

His polar question left no room for ambiguity, while his fingers continued on their path of sensual assault, lacing my body with many promising outcomes. I nodded.

"I want to hear you say it," he softly demanded, rolling and tugging my nipple between his thumb and fingers.

Sensations zinged, awakening more need. My answer came out in a breathless rush. "Yes."

Adam smiled right before his head dipped; his mouth moved to kissing the lower part of my jaw. His tongue circled mine again, luring me in. "I want to touch you," he said in my mouth, "and taste you. And fuck you senseless."

The wanton whore inside me loved that idea.

"But I don't want to rush you."

My body arched into his hand while several years of gross anatomy had me questioning whether or not it was possible for all the nerve endings in my breast to be directly connected to my vagina. He had set my body aflame; how could I possibly not feel rushed when my insides have turned into a live wire screaming for release?

"You have the power here, Erin. You get uncomfortable, just tell me to stop, okay?"

The last thing I wanted was for him to stop. It had been too long. I put my hand atop of his, warring with myself whether I should encourage him or slow this down, hoping he'd just take away my choice and lead me to places unnamed, to where this pleasure would never end.

My shirt pushed up; the cup of my lacy bra was pulled down, and talented fingers tugged and pulled and twisted while the pressure built to unmanageable levels.

Careful, lust-filled eyes scanned over my face while he put my bra cup back into place, making me wonder if he was second guessing this turning into more. His hand slid down my back and under the drawstring waistband, cupping my bare ass, pulling my leg over his.

"No underwear?" he growled, moaning in my mouth.

I shuddered when his fingertips brushed over the seam of my ass, delving farther and deeper.

Oh God.

"I didn't have any spares," I confessed.

Adam definitely liked that answer, laughing lightly. His fingers worked deeper, skating through the wetness from my extreme arousal, circling, swirling, driving me insane with need, until he shifted underneath me, pulling my leg and lifting my hips so I was straddling him.

He rolled his stiff erection back and forth under me, working our hips in unison. Didn't take him long to pull my shirt up and off. He cupped my breasts, teasing them through the black lace, slipping the straps of my bra until they fell off my shoulders.

He pulled me down for a kiss and effortlessly opened the clasp, raking the fabric off with his fingers.

"I want you. All of you," he said in my mouth, flinging my bra to the floor.

Adam sat up enough to pull his shirt off, exposing his tight stomach and those erotic tribal tattoos. Black ink intricately designed thick braids of rope, which coiled around both biceps like hungry snakes. I wanted to trace them with my tongue but as I started, he grasped my breast, taking my nipple in his mouth.

I gasped from the onslaught of sensations, drifting further when his hand found its way back into my sweat pants.

Hearing him moan while toying with my body was such a heady turn on. With little effort, he rolled me next to him, my foot landed on the large ottoman behind me. His finger slipped up inside me, spreading me open for his bidding, fucking me slowly while he took my mouth. His thumb drove me to madness, circling my clit, working my body into an all-out frenzy.

It didn't take long. My orgasm ripped through my body, making me cry out in his mouth as he kissed me.

I collapsed onto his chest with his fingers still inside me, milking every possible bit of overwhelming sensations.

God that felt *so* good.

He gave me a lascivious and very self-assured smile, then pressed my head to his warm chest. His hand felt so soothing as it stroked lightly over my naked back while I listened to the soft cadence of his heartbeat.

My own heart was still hammering in my chest.

Adam placed a lingering kiss on my forehead before commanding my lips again. "You okay?"

No. Yes. I was far from okay.

My body was still twitching with aftershocks.

I was also mere inches away from the zipper of his jeans and the very tempting bulge lying in wait.

Adding to my list, this gorgeous man named Adam Trent was sprawled out underneath me, partially naked, very, very hard, and in complete control of both my body and my heart.

I tried to catch my breath and managed a sated "yeah" instead.

Adam's smile was devastating.

"Good." He kissed me quickly and urged me to get off him. "Let's get up."

No! I didn't want to move. I was cozy and comfortable right where I was, swirling in my post-orgasm haze. His sweatpants fell down my hips when I crawled off and stood. I scrambled to pull them up, suddenly very aware of my nakedness. I looked around for my discarded shirt, wondering why he disrupted our interlude.

"Come on," he said, reaching for me. I retied the drawstring at my waist and grabbed my shirt and bra up off the floor. He left me no time to dress, towing me toward the steps.

I slowed him down before he could climb the first stair. "Where are we going?"

"My bedroom," he said without regard. I covered my chest with his shirt, wondering if I was ready for all of this.

I think he sensed my subconscious hesitation. Concerned but thoughtful chocolate-brown eyes gazed down at me. "I wanted you from the first moment I set eyes on you, Erin. And the first time I make love to you isn't going to be on a couch."

My mouth fell open.

"If you don't want me like that, say so now. Otherwise I'm going to keep walking up those steps and I'm not stopping until you're completely naked and giving yourself to me."

His directness made me smile.

"That's what I thought."

I had to hurry behind him to keep up.

He closed his bedroom door behind us and stalked toward me. I felt trapped, caught in the lion's den, about to be eaten. He stopped in front of me and gave me a light kiss. "Give me a minute."

A rush of exhilaration whirled through me just watching his commanding gait as he walked off into his master bath. It seemed as though everything Adam did was with either purpose or conviction, making me question if he's even aware of his masterful presence. Doubt, as always, crept back into my thoughts, leaving me to ponder how I got so fortunate to be this intimately close with him. Surely he has flaws, doesn't he?

It would make me feel so much better about myself if he did. I'd been weak-kneed and all doe-eyed since that first kiss, and as a reminder I touched my lips.

I heard the toilet flush and the sink water running, and my nerves pricked in anticipation. I quickly threw his black shirt on, feeling too vulnerable, too exposed. I tugged the shirt as long as it would go, and then tugged once more for good measure. Needs of another kind spurred me into action now, glad that he was finished in there. His sudden smile at seeing me was enough to level me where I stood.

"My turn," I said, making light of the fact that I needed to pee in the worst way and then assure myself that all of that, from before, didn't funk up the works down below.

His fingers lightly drifted over my arm before cinching me in place. His nose drifted over mine. "Don't take too long, Doc."

"I'll try not to."

Deft fingers pulled the drawstring holding my sweatpants up, and I felt frozen, unable to move, mesmerized under his intense gaze.

If only I could live a thousand years in his eyes.

His fingertips skated over my bare hips, down the slope of my ass, sending a ripple of goose bumps all over as he uncovered my skin.

God, I want you.

"You won't be needing these," he said as he pushed the soft jersey away. A tangle of sweat pants pooled around my ankles while the sudden nip of fresh air on my legs made me shiver.

His foot landed between my legs. "Step," he instructed.

I pulled my feet out one foot at a time.

He took my bare rear end in a possessive hold and drifted his mouth down my neck, nipping my collarbone with his teeth while I untangled myself from my discarded sweats.

"Hurry," he whispered across my lips.

Behind the closed bathroom door, I was another story, needing the separation to calm myself. *"Here I am, Adam, all naked and ready to be fucked!"* seemed like a bad way to start off our first time together.

First time.

Just those two words alone set things in motion that once done could not be undone. The pre-med version of myself skipped back into view, wagging her finger at me to not be such an easy slut like we were that day virginity made her final exit.

I'd had a few *first times* with a couple of other guys since then, and although I'd felt wanted and desired by them, those encounters paled in comparison to the intensity at which Adam conveyed those messages.

Adam had put me in motion, making my body respond to his every command, taking away my need to choose.

There was a part of me that was actually relieved by that. Like when we were getting my new license plate, Adam just took control. He was bossy. In charge. Strangely though, I liked it. No, I loved it. Randy never took command; he sort of fell on my sofa and just made himself at home.

The first time Randy and I had sex we were a bit drunk. We'd been out partying with a couple of other residents and a handful of ER nurses, blowing off steam drinking beers and tossing back endless rounds of shots while listening to ear-pounding music.

It was awkward—that first time. We were sloppy, smacking our heads together in our hurry. Every encounter with Randy after that was a race to the finish, never taking the time to really appreciate the journey. He never took the time, which left my confidence shattered that I wasn't worthy.

Ever since the trial fourteen years ago, I'd been living with guilt, feeling punished and isolated and heartbroken. How many lonely nights would I have to spend atoning for my sins? I'd poured every ounce of energy into my studies and career goals, hoping one day I might be able to redeem myself and find forgiveness, save an innocent life before it was too late.

If I couldn't save them, how could I save myself?

I glanced at my reflection in the mirror, wondering where the last eight years of my life had gone. Med school and residency had taken their toll, rushing time in fast-forward, putting everything else in my life into second place. Wanting a relationship now and actually achieving one were also two *very* separate things. Adam was like a decadent dessert I didn't quite deserve but so desperately craved.

Something lightly thumped on the other side of the door and then I heard his voice in conversation with someone but I could only hear his side. I turned out the light and cracked the door ever so slightly, giving a furtive glance. The last thing I wanted to do was to walk into the middle of an awkward situation in his bedroom.

His incredible muscular back was facing me, glistening with a golden hue from the last of the day's setting sun that was peeking through the opened curtains. One hand was stuck roughly in his hair. The top edge of his boxer briefs was exposed underneath his hanging blue jeans. He was on his cell.

I glanced around the doorframe once more before taking another step.

"That's the thing, Turk, none of the cars have resurfaced. I've been investigating this for the last nine months," Adam said to the caller. "We had another ten boosted in the last four weeks. No, no GM products. They were all high-end taken right from the dealerships and a few right from the owners' homes. No, I'm lead on this investigation down here."

Adam glanced back and motioned for me. He put his hand around my hip and gave me a soft kiss, locking me under his arm.

"Can you email me the list that you've compiled up there? We're looking for new rentals of warehouses along the Delaware that might have access to shipping and rail but that's like finding a needle in a haystack. And now our search area just got a hell of a lot wider.

"Check EZ Pass tolls; see if there's a connection. Yeah, I think they're shipping them in containers and right out of the country because not one of them is showing back up on the streets in the States. No, GPS devices have all been deactivated, so we're looking for some high-tech hackers here, too. Yeah, of course we'll keep in touch with NYPD. I'll be making a few calls Monday to some of the task forces in Jersey, see if anyone has any leads on the drivers. We've got some leads we're following here, but nothing solid. Few nights ago, twenty cars parked at a local hospital all had their plates switched. Yep. Bogies. We actually got a call on one that we ended up pitting, but it was just a distraction. Yeah, same night two hundred grand of new vehicles disappeared. Word on the street is that this all goes back to Mancuso. I've compiled a list of all his known associates here so I'm getting very familiar with his players but if you have more intel than that send it my way. Yep. Now we just need to catch one and convince him to flip on the rest. No, no, not today," he laughed lightly.

Adam glanced down at me; his dark eyes smoldered. How he managed to render me immobile was both intriguing and disturbing. His tongue slid over his bottom lip. "I have other pressing engagements I need to attend to. I'll send you files on Monday. Yep, talk to you then."

He didn't even say goodbye to whomever he was talking to. He tossed his phone over onto the rustic leather chair by his dresser and pulled me into his chest.

"Police work?"

He nodded. "We're very similar, you and me. Sometimes it's hard to shut the job off." He combed a few strands of my hair back. "But right now, you have all of my attention. You are so beautiful, Doc. Not sure how I got so lucky."

Funny, I was just thinking the same thing about him. His words, though, made me slightly uncomfortable. It had been a long time since someone complimented me, especially when I was mostly naked. "I don't think you got lucky, yet."

Adam tipped my chin back up. His smile was devastating. "I think I have. The rest? Well, I'm crossing my fingers."

Thoughts of being an easy lay warred with my desire. My eyes darted to the ominous bed and then back to the intricate tribal tattoos outlining his incredible body. "Guess it's too soon to wonder if you'll call me tomorrow."

He gave me a sardonic grin and an admonishing sigh while he palmed my ass with both hands. "How about I just cook you breakfast tomorrow? Then you don't need to worry about anything. We can talk over coffee instead."

Adam pivoted me, herding me backwards.

"Oh, you're good. Do you practice these lines or do they just come naturally?" I felt the mattress touch the back of my thighs.

And then I was sitting.

"Don't think you're going home tonight, Doc. It's not looking good for you."

He loomed over me, urging me to scuttle back on his king-sized bed. His hands slid under my shoulders, his forearms holding most of his weight. The look on his face was so serene, so loving and full of emotion, taking my apprehensions completely away.

"I'm serious about breakfast," he said, adjusting himself to move a thick lock of hair off my neck. He followed his statement with a kiss so powerful I felt welded to the bed, my heart running its own marathon in its wake. Adam's kisses turned soft, playful, taunting even, with little nips of his teeth on my lip, but his face was very serious. I felt cherished just seeing how he looked at me.

I raked my fingers into his hair, our union taking on a new passion, filled with a level of intenseness I'd never felt before. Adam wasn't in a hurry, taking his time to stroke my body with his hands, making a meal out of just kissing me.

He slid down my body and rolled my shirt up, one kiss at a time. I raised my hands above me while he shimmied the shirt over my chest and over my head, leaving the tee binding my arms. His flat tongue licked right up between my breasts, and then he took my mouth.

His bare chest rubbed over mine, sending wave after wave of tingles throughout my body, driving my need to exponential levels. I wanted to touch him but his forearms had me pinned while his tongue made agonizing circles around my nipple.

I thought the feeling couldn't get any better until he sucked—hard.

I tried to get an arm free but he wouldn't relent, taking his time to explore every inch while slowly driving me insane. By the time he was done with my right breast, I was more than ready. His mouth continued to assault my body, gliding over my ribs, placing kisses and sensual bites along the way.

Adam circled back up, and just when I thought he was going to kiss me again, he didn't. He just hovered over me, gazing at me so adoringly, and for a moment I thought he was about to tell me he was falling in love.

I pulled an arm free, desperately needing to touch him. Sometimes in the throes of passion it's easy to mistake lust for love, but the softness in his gaze, the way it seemed he was looking beyond what was visible on the outside, spoke of far deeper things than simple desire.

I hoped I wasn't misreading him because I was feeling it too, but it was far too soon to entertain those notions or utter such things aloud.

The sensations of his mouth, of his tongue weaving its way and commanding mine to follow, conveyed emotions that words alone were incapable of saying. It consumed me.

Adam made his way down my body, leaving no place unattended. Between tender kisses, soft bites, and the rasp of his shadowed jaw line, he was discovering erogenous zones I never knew I had.

When he lifted my leg and his lips reached my ankle, those smoldering eyes met mine, silently informing—not asking—his intentions. I knew I could say no and stop him, but he'd awakened my deepest desires, leaving me dying for more.

He didn't need to ask permission; I was his for the taking.

Strong forearms slipped under my thighs, lifting me from the bedding, as he adjusted my hips to his liking. I felt his warm breath tingle over me as he spread me open and then instantly bowed when he let me experience his tongue.

Hearing his throaty moans while he devoured me was all the reassurance I needed. I had just closed my eyes to enjoy his attentions when I heard my name being called out.

"Look at me," he ordered, his tongue still on my flesh. His bandaged hand slid over my ribs and covered my breast, staking his claim and owning me. I brought his wounded hand to my mouth, knowing he had to be hurting, needing to worship and heal him, too.

Feeling his finger enter me was my undoing. A second finger followed and I was lost in the abyss. His commanding strokes and expert tongue worked in tandem, taking me to the edge and beyond to the stars. Air stuttered in my lungs while his bandaged hand clenched onto my thigh. My hand flew to the top of his head, scoring his hair with my fingernails, wanting to ride this incredible wave to the ends of the earth, but fearing I couldn't take much more of it.

When he was satisfied he'd gotten every last quake out of me, Adam swiped his chin and crawled back over me, letting me taste myself on his mouth. I gazed into his open eyes, seeing and feeling only him. Nothing else existed.

I opened the top button of his jeans and carefully lowered his zipper, needing to feel all of him.

Watching him rise to leave the bed and remove his jeans was akin to having a front-row seat to the best show in town. He was wearing black boxer briefs and a sly smile.

He retrieved a foil packet from his nightstand drawer, pulled his boxers off, and crawled back onto the bed.

Seeing Adam partially naked was a delectable feast for the eyes. Seeing Adam completely naked was enticing beyond all comprehension. His erection stood long and heavy, almost touching his bellybutton when he rested next to me. The smatter of hair that lightly dusted his chest and blazed a thin trail to his groin beckoned to be touched. I wanted to pleasure him, to ruin his thoughts of ever looking elsewhere for satisfaction. I placed slow, languid kisses on his neck, using his soft moans to map out his erogenous zones, adding each subtle nuance to my memory.

Adam combed my hair away, watching me draw the tip of my tongue around braided rope tattoos that decorated the edges of his chest. He let out a small hiss when I sucked his nipple into my mouth.

Adam rested on his back and let me explore at my own pace. I hadn't been with someone in a while, and the newness and unfamiliarity made me uncomfortable and hesitant. His hips curled in when my hand neared his cock, silently urging me to touch.

My fingers tentatively drifted, feeling the smooth skin of the plump head and down the full length. His hand tensed, tangled within my hair. Our kiss became breathy and aggressive. The desire—irrefutable. He sighed in my mouth when I wrapped my fingers around him, stroking him up and down with growing confidence.

"God, that feels *so* good," he groaned. Hearing his throaty moans, watching him watch me, it was a heady combination.

"I need to be inside you," he said on my lips. "You on birth control?"

I nodded. "I have an IUD, but…"

He paused and then grabbed the condom off his nightstand. My eyes followed his reach, relieved I wouldn't have to ask him to wear one. He probably had a hell of a lot more lovers than I did, and the last thing I needed or wanted was a sexually transmitted disease.

Adam positioned himself between my thighs while kissing me fervently. He stared at me with such intense reverence while he rolled the condom on. My breath hitched from the slight pinch as he entered me.

Adam stilled, bracing himself above me. "You okay?"

I nodded, pulling him in tighter.

He lowered over me, wrapping me in the protective hold of his arms. Nose to nose, he kissed me, breathing hard with me, making his mark on my body and my heart with each stroke.

"You feel so fucking good," he whispered on my throat, his hand lifting my rear to angle in deeper. I wrapped my legs around his hips, gripping his muscular shoulders to keep him buried within me.

I'd had other lovers before but none of them compared to what I was feeling for Adam. He gazed at me so intently, making every stroke, every grind of his hips, every sensual touch and languid kiss seem like an unbreakable promise. He stilled inside me, making love to my mouth instead.

This wasn't just sex.

I'd had plenty of *just sex* over the years with a few select men who made me feel more like a receptacle than a counterpart. The way Adam was constantly gazing directly in my eyes, the way he poured his entire existence into being with me, was so vastly different from anything I'd experienced before.

No, this wasn't *just sex.*

This was the physical manifestation of an unspoken vow.

Adam kissed me one last time and then slowly withdrew, leaving an aching void in more places than I cared to admit. He moved next to me and onto his back, urging me to straddle him, and pulled my mouth back to his.

In one move, he'd surrendered and given me all of the control, to take whatever I wanted, whatever I needed from him on my own terms. He met me beat for beat, going slow or pounding into me, grinding deep while he worked my hips back and forth. Whatever I asked for, he gave it to me.

Adam's hand cinched around my wrists, binding me like an iron shackle. He pressed my hands flat to his chest, holding me in place, while his thumb rubbed me. Within moments, the quickening accelerated, taking my breath away as the pressure built. I gasped. "Adam."

"Not yet, babe," he uttered, sitting up abruptly, taking me with him.

He rolled us over, adjusted us onto our sides, pressing my spine to his chest. Strong, thick arms with killer braided-rope tattoos wrapped around me, holding me fast, while tender lips made their way up and down my neck.

And then he was back inside me, wrapping his arm under my knee, taking his fill and filling me all at the same time.

"Look at me," he ordered, drifting his command over the shell of my ear. I turned my head, wrapped my hand around his neck, and he took my mouth and my heart all in one swoop.

Adam's large hand fanned over my pubic bone, pressing down, tilting my pelvis while the tips of his fingers played a perfect melody.

He was everywhere all at once. Lips, tongue, fingers, weaving his way around my soul, touching me in places inside where I'd never been touched before. New sensations struck me, seizing all the oxygen in my lungs. I grasped his shoulder, at every part of him I could hold on to, unable to breathe, unable to think. I felt split apart and slammed back together as the massive orgasm struck and rolled throughout my body.

"That's it, baby," he said, railing into me with everything he had.

Adam let out a lengthy groan, stuttering into me, following me over the edge. His warm breath fanned over my neck, up over my cheek, cooling wherever it touched the trickles of sweat beading on my skin.

I held on, clutching his damp head to me. Our breathing came out in labored, winded pants, while the final tremors rippled throughout our bodies.

His fingers drifted over my cheek and tangled up into my hair. His adoring gaze and loving expression gave way to the possibility of having a future with someone—something I hadn't dared to hope for in a very long time.

In that moment, hope didn't seem so out of reach. Neither did the possibility of falling in love.

His hips pressed up one more time, a final message that he was still very much in me, owning me. His mouth quirked up into a pleased smile. I couldn't help but relish how gentle he was with me. Even his kisses were sweet. "You good?"

I swallowed the dryness forming in my throat and drifted my fingers over the tiny birthmark near the corner of his eye, up through his tousled hair, trying to find the words that could encompass all that I was feeling. I opted for a simple, "I'm very good. And you?"

"I'm definitely good." He placed another tender kiss on my lips and shifted, slipping out of me.

I rolled to face him, needing to cuddle up with him and share this incredibly intimate moment. We lay there in silence for a long time, drifting, smiling, Adam softly stroking my cheek. Then his eyes narrowed, seeming to concentrate on the spot under his fingertips. His breathing changed and his lips drew together and something that resembled sadness or frustration etched his demeanor.

And then he rolled out of bed.

The sudden loss of his body heat caused a chill to snake over my skin. Being this exposed, all sprawled out in the middle of his bed, was also causing self-conscious discomfort. I searched the floor and snagged up his T-shirt, trying not to gawk at his incredible shape while he discarded the used condom in his bathroom.

I sat on the edge of his bed, waiting for what felt like ten minutes, slowly morphing from post-coital bliss to confused concern, watching his head hang down as he leaned hard on his bathroom vanity in the dark. Body language usually spoke truths that the mouth was unwilling to admit and something equally as dark had just taken him over.

My worry was confirmed when Adam walked past me, avoiding making eye contact, and snagged his boxers off the floor.

I took a deep breath and threw self-preservation out the window, tired of walking on eggshells around moody men. "Everything okay?"

His deep breath was answer enough as he pulled his boxer briefs up. It was the sound of inhaled regret. I felt stupid.

Stupid, stupid, stupid.

As much as I'd hoped otherwise, I did misread our entire encounter. It was *just sex*, passionate, mind-blowing, life-altering sex, but regrettable sex for him, apparently. I heard the snap of his elastic waistband and then the bed dipped next to me.

He rolled his forlorn gaze over at me, that adoration I'd lost myself in was gone. "Listen," he said hesitantly, "there's something I need to tell you."

I could tell whatever he was about to say wasn't going to be something I'd want to hear.

He took a deep breath, obviously searching for the best way to let me down gently. "I know I owe you an explanation." He rubbed his face, wiping his fingers over his lips. "God, this is hard. I should have been truthful with you before we…" His eyes flashed between us to the rumpled sheets, to me, then the floor. "I don't want to hurt you."

I waved a dismissive hand and braced for the worst, wishing I had my keys and coat and an exit strategy. Just admitting he didn't want to hurt me was hurting me. Anger welled, hating him for ruining the best love-making encounter of my entire life. Disappointment scorched on top of that. I should have known better. Someone as gorgeous as Adam was probably a fantastic lay with *whomever* he was fucking. That incredible experience wasn't meant for me to take personally. "You don't owe me anything, Adam."

My jeans were draped over the chair in the corner. My heart broke into a million pieces just thinking about having to put them on, but I'd be damned before I let him or any man see me shed another tear.

Adam snagged me by my wrist when I tried to step past him. "Where you going?"

I steeled my shoulders and tried to jerk free. "Getting dressed."

His eyes narrowed and his hand tightened. "Why? Erin, sit."

"I need my clothes."

"Erin." His voice was severe, so was the grip he had on me.

Gone were the soft *"babes"* and other whispered sentiments. We were back to the formality of first names.

"Why? So you can give me the 'it's not you, it's me' speech?" A small chuckle erupted, though this constant reality of my sad love life was far from humorous. "Save it. We both have busy lives and it's cool. I understand, believe me."

He huffed in frustration, glaring at me. "*Jesus Christ*. Jumping to

231

conclusions pretty fast, don't ya think?"

I tried to tug away. "Just say what you're going to say."

"You gonna sit the fuck down and listen?"

I gave him my "I don't think so" glare.

He tugged me again, this time with some force, pulling me across his body until my butt was sitting on the bed next to him.

I wanted to find my coat before he had a chance to go on.

"Listen, just hear me out. The other night... Damn it. I wasn't prepared. I didn't expect..." His head swayed. "This morning, I was angry. In my mind, I thought you were different, and then you went out and got fucked up on alcohol. I can't have that in my life, Erin."

None of this made any sense. "Wait, are you still mad at me?"

"No," he declared. "No, I'm not. I have no right to be upset with you. This is my problem. It's me that has to deal with it, not you."

He stared at me for so long, making me feel like I was missing some obvious point. "I'm confused," I whispered.

Adam pried my fingers apart, lacing his with mine.

Is he placating me?

His head dipped, gazing at the floor instead of just gutting me with the obvious truth. The span of silence was almost deafening, waiting, imagining a thousand different responses that might tumble from his lips to spear me through the chest. It was almost too easy to imagine a young Adam, guilty and unwilling to admit to his mistakes, hoping that some dimpled-cheek charm might spare him from the repercussion of his misdeeds.

"After sharing what we just shared, I want you to know me, Erin, and that... well, that includes the ugly parts too. I can't... I can't bring you in or ask you for more, not without you knowing all of me. You have the right to know what you're getting yourself into before we go any further, no matter how much I want you. It's only fair. I care way too much about you to do that to you." He drew in another deep breath. "But I know once I tell you, things between us are going to change."

Now he was scaring me. "I don't understand. What—?"

"I'm trying to explain. *Shit.*" He muttered another curse and then looked me straight in the eyes. "I have a drinking problem, Erin. Ever since my partner was shot, it's been... rough. The job. The stress. It was hard to deal with it all. But I'm sober now. Been sober for ten months."

Reality hit hard. "You're an alcoholic?"

Adam shrugged slightly. "Hate that word. Hate thinking that something like that got the better of me. Some days are harder than others. But I'm working on it. I'm keeping clean, avoiding temptation. Channeling my frustrations with other things that are giving me back a sense of control. But that label is going to follow me and haunt me and spill over on whoever I'm with."

My hair started to tingle from absorbing all of this at once. "You go to meetings?"

Adam let out a small sigh. "Not the public kind but yeah, I see a counselor twice a month. It's part grief and part addiction, since things tipped when my partner got shot."

"So no AA?"

"No," he uttered.

Substance abuse was rampant in Philly; all of the doctors on staff were well versed with addiction and treatment plans. "Why not?"

He bristled at that. "Listen, when I say I'm dealing with it, you have to trust me on that. There's no way I'm going back to that. No way." He eyed me warily. "See, this is why I didn't want to bring anyone into this; it already cost me too much. My shit forces the people around me to make choices and sacrifices, and that's not fair. Not fair to you."

He stood up abruptly. "I want this, Erin. I want you and I want to see where this goes because I think we could have a great thing between us. But what I want and what you need are two different things," he muttered. "I thought you of all people would understand the crush that comes from the overwhelming stress of our jobs. Day in and day out, it's never pretty."

I watched him reach for his discarded jeans, fishing in the front pocket.

"Fuck. Here are your keys. I'm going to take a shower. If you're still here by the time I'm done…" He dropped my keys in my hand and then raised my chin up. "Well, I hope to God you stay, but I understand if you can't deal with it. At least I have the peace of mind knowing that you know. That I was honest."

I was stunned. Utterly stunned. My mind was spinning in its own tornado of confusion, further muddled by the look of regretful despair on his face. What I had thought he was going to drop on me turned out to be a multi-layered confession. He flicked the light on in the bathroom, leaving the door cracked a few inches. I could see the well-defined triceps of one arm, then a gloriously bare ass as he tugged his boxers back off, leaving me in a perpetual state of lustful want. I sat in a stupor, hearing the shower water raining onto the enormous glass surround.

Did he think that having a character flaw was a deal-breaker for me? Was it? My head started to throb, but my heart didn't feel like it was being ripped out of my chest anymore.

I could easily leave—leave him to his demons—though Lord knew I had my own legion of demons plaguing me. After all, I did wind up at a bar by myself and got drunk trying to get over the crushing stress.

I replayed his words—well, the ones I strategically picked out of his monologue—paying particular attention to the ones that described his current feelings for me.

The last twenty-four hours had been absolute hell. I hurt. My heart ached. But now I just felt angry.

I shoved the bathroom door out of my way and flung the shower door open, catching him with both palms flat against the tiled wall, the shower water raining down on his head.

Adam rolled his gaze over and shoved away from the wall. "Erin—"

"So that's it? You fuck my brains out then give me an ultimatum?"

He swiped his hair back. "Not an ultimatum. A choice."

"A choice?" My voice came out a bit higher than I wanted it to. I also felt the need to give his dumb-ass a shove. "So that's why you were being such a jerk this morning? Because you think I'm some raging party girl who gets fucked up every Friday night?"

He gave me a curt nod. "I admit when I'm wrong."

My eyes zoned in on his face, doing my best to ignore the water rippling down the contours of his body. "Do you get violent?"

"*What?*"

"Do I have to worry about you getting violent? Doing stupid shit, like punching walls and stuff?"

"No," he said emphatically.

I crossed my arms. "Do I have to be worried that you might get abusive or hit me?"

Adam scowled at me. "I've *never* hit a woman in my life, Erin. Never."

I stepped into the shower, water pelting me, soaking into my tee. "So if I get up in your face like this, you going to get rough with me? Continue to be an asshole to me?"

Adam growled, seized my upper arms, and spun me; my back pressed flush with the tiled wall. "You get up in my face like this, I'll get rough." As soon as he let go of my arms, my wet shirt was ripped up over my head and my intimidating cop was back in full force. He pinned my wrists to the wall above my head and cut off the rest of my rebuttal by shoving his tongue in my mouth. "I want you, Doc," he announced on my lips, water pouring down both our faces. "More than anything I've wanted in a *very* long time. From the moment I first laid eyes on you, you're all I fucking think about."

"You already said that," I reminded.

He hands held me captive. "Maybe you need to hear it more than once."

I tried to wiggle free. "Maybe, but—"

He pressed harder. "Then hear this. You're in my *veins*, Erin. Understand? You're twisted in deep now. I'd never hurt you. *Never*. Not even if you ripped my heart out."

"Let go of me," I ordered.

Adam's hands instantly opened.

I wrapped my arms around his neck, needing his mouth back on mine. He gave it all back to me, biting and sucking my lips with equal force and desperation, sliding his hands all over my body.

I may be in his blood but he was my air.

He palmed my ass and lifted my leg, impaling me on his newly formed erection, connecting us from the inside out.

I should have cared that he wasn't wearing a condom, but I didn't, needing him just as frantically.

Just when I thought I'd be broken again, left to fall apart and wither to dust, Adam put us back together again.

CHAPTER 14

Adam

IT'D BEEN A long time since I felt this type of peace, this semblance of serenity. The soft *tick, tock* of the clock in my bathroom seemed to match the cadence of the heart beating steadily against my side.

Erin's cheek was pressed to my chest; her arm was draped over my abs. I was twisting a piece of her long blonde hair around my fingers, feeling every muscle in my body finally relax. The index finger of my other hand was busy circling the tiny freckles on her upper arm. If things kept up at this soothing rate, I could make a career mapping out each dip and swell of her body, kiss every fine nuance of her skin.

This morning, I wasn't sure how I felt about this woman lying in my arms. My mind had gone round and round in an endless circle, making up reasons why it would be best to keep her at arm's length. Letting her in meant I'd have to break down some of my walls, but history showed that leaving the fortress vulnerable never worked out for the inhabitants.

Earlier when she broke and told me all the things making her sad, I felt like a complete bastard. Here I thought she'd just gone out to get fucked up. Boy was I mistaken. Years of bad experiences had me jumping the gun, letting the shit poison my mind.

Erin nuzzled in deeper and let out a soft, contented sigh. Without thinking, my body responded, holding her tighter. She was settling in, giving me her trust, her affection, and after the grief I'd given her over the last week, I wasn't sure I deserved it.

But there she was, patching the holes in me without even knowing it. I thought she was the broken one but it was actually me that needed saving.

Erin's mouth moved over my chest, breaking our silent moment. "Adam?"

I dipped my chin. "Hmm?"

Her fingertip glided over my bicep, following the path of my ink. "Did all of this hurt to get?"

"What, my tats?"

Her finger trailed down my arm, sending tender sensations right through me. "Yeah. They're so intricate. Must have taken a while."

I rolled my arm. "Took a couple of sessions. I think I have about nine or ten hours in so far. I have a bit more to go yet 'til it's finished."

She looked up at me, squinting her eyes. "Was it painful?"

Compared to some of my past pains, it wasn't even close. "It hurts a little. You get used to it after awhile. Why you asking?"

Erin shrugged. "I always worry that I'm hurting people when I have to inject them. I think it's one of the things people fear the most about doctors. I can't imagine having to do it repeatedly."

"It's not so bad. And you did a fantastic job when you worked on my hand. Why, you thinking of getting one? I've searched your entire body, so I know you're a blank canvas." I squeezed her in my arms. Just hearing her playful laugh made me smile.

"Maybe. One day."

In a flash, I thought about tattooing my name on her ass. "I hear women have a higher tolerance for pain. I'm sure you'd be able to handle it."

"I'll think about it."

"You do that." I envisioned her getting a pretty butterfly or something hanging off the "A" in my first name that I'd have inked on her luscious behind. Maybe put a warning back there too that says "If your name isn't Adam, I'm gonna kill you for attempting to fuck my woman." *That might be too many words though. "Property of"* might work.

"Why the rope?"

"Hmm?"

"The rope? Just curious as to your choice of artwork."

I shifted underneath her, not sure how to explain the lengths I've gone through to keep myself together, whole. "It's a reminder. Hard to explain."

Erin propped herself up on my chest, giving me her full attention. She didn't ask me to go on. She didn't prod or make faces at me either. She just studied me, silently assuring me that I'd be safe if I shared my reasons. I combed her hair back, finding myself unable to deny her much of anything. If she only knew how hard this was for me.

"I understand. It's okay." She kissed my chest right above my heart, cracking the last bit of my stubbornness.

I blew out a breath. Naked and vulnerable were never a good combination. "I've been a cop for over ten years, Doc. I've seen things, horrific things, just as I'm sure you have. Kids, drugs, violent crimes, violent criminals. I thought… I thought once I became a cop I could put an end to it, ya know? Make a difference. But no matter how hard I try it's like pissing in the wind. That accident you and I worked together? That was just one of many I'll never be able to forget."

Erin's head tilted, spilling her hair over her shoulder. I twisted another lock around my finger, concentrating on how soft it felt instead of the unrelenting demons that plagued my mind. "Sometimes I can still hear the gunshot." A phantom pain flashed over my temples. I'd never admitted that to anyone; not even during counseling. "Back then, after I… after Tom was killed during that traffic stop, I stopped caring about a lot of things. It took me a while to realize that that was an empty, lonely road."

Her fingers brushed over my arm. "Is that when you got these?"

I nodded. "I got the ink on my arms when I gave up drinking. The only person who could throw me a lifeline back then was me. These tats are my lifelines."

She rested her cheek on my chest and blew out a deep sigh, as if she'd been holding her breath in as long as I'd had. "I know exactly how you feel."

I felt the jolt when her words passed right though my walls. "You do?"

"More than you know. It's like no matter how many medical miracles I perform, I'll never be able to keep people from dying. Everything I do, everything I try is nothing more than a temporary fix. I love what I do, but sometimes it's discouraging. Some days it feels like for every person I patch up, there's an endless line of people falling apart, waiting right behind them."

"Exactly. I put one bad guy away and five more crop up to take his place." Her finger was still softly tracing my tats, lazily blazing her heat down my arm. "The rope reminds me that what's inside of me is my first priority. I can't lose me. I can't lose my sanity to the ugly. If I do, then I'm done."

She sighed, nuzzling even deeper. "Maybe I need some rope tattoos." Her fingers tickled down over my ribs, circling over the tats that ran down the side of my stomach. "What about these? Are they Chinese?"

More like hidden messages to myself scored into my skin. I nodded, answering her.

"What do they mean?"

I felt my muscles tense as I cleared my throat. "That one is 'Remember'. Second one is 'Truth' and then 'Trust'."

"And this last one?"

It was the one I had the most difficulty with. "It's 'Forgiveness'."

She rested her lips on my skin, patching another unseen hole. "I've had my fair share of breakdowns, too. You got to see my embarrassment firsthand."

Oh, baby. Don't go there. My fingers tensed in her hair. *It's just between us, sweetheart.*

"I love what I do but sometimes the pressure is… it just builds up and gets to be too much. I see enough gore in one shift to leave most folks scarred for life."

"I bet you do."

Her head tilted up. "I bet you do, too. I guess not too many people can relate to what we go through on a daily basis. Most of the people who come into the ER are far from happy and sometimes they yell and scream and add mental abuse to the physical and emotional strain. And you," she tapped my chest, "you get the added pleasure of them pointing guns at you. Maybe we should go into selling bathroom fixtures or something. Can't be too much stress in doing that, right?"

She made me laugh. "Could be fun, but now I'm thinking of taking you back in the shower."

Erin smiled broadly and just like that, she gently bit my nipple for being a smartass. Fuck, that felt good. No… great. *That's it, use your tongue. Heal me, baby.*

I ran both hands through her hair. "It takes a special kind of person to do what you do, Doc."

Erin's head popped up, grinning. "You like calling me Doc, don't ya?"

"I do. It fits. Why, does it bother you?"

She seemed unsure. I hauled her up my chest. I was done talking. I needed to kiss her again, to feel that heated connection to this amazing creature who was consuming me like fire.

She drew my top lip into her mouth and then pulled back to study my face. "How would you feel if I called you *Cop*?"

Her feistiness was such a turn on. I pulled her leg over my body, making her straddle me. I was glad the rest of her came along for the ride. She climbed right on and owned me.

My mind was certainly up for another round; I was just hoping my dick would support the idea. "Cop a feel. Cop a squat." I pressed my hips up. "You can call me anything you'd like, Doc."

"Is that so, dear?" She giggled on my lips, showing her newfound dominance by wrapping my head up in her arms.

I palmed her fantastic ass. "No, see now I have to draw the line. You can call me anything but that."

Erin grinned. "No *dear*?"

I gave her a squeeze. "Absolutely not, Doc."

"Never ever?"

"Never fucking ever."

"Okay, dear," she teased.

"Now you're just looking for trouble."

She placed a soft kiss on my neck. "No. Not looking. Found."

The feelings she invoked by just playing with me were enough to take my breath away. I locked my fingers into her hair and held her against my skin, enjoying every second of her attention. And that's when it hit me—just exactly what I'd been missing, and it *wasn't* having a gorgeous, naked woman sprawled out on top of me, although that was definitely a bonus. No, this was *very* different and very specific, as if a gigantic sign had just lit up in front of me and smacked me in the head, showing me word for word where I'd been going wrong.

I could actually describe it now, put a name and reasons to what I'd been lacking.

Why Nikki and I would never, COULD never work out. She could never understand the stress that came with my job. She could never empathize, not that I needed her to, but the girl had zero compassion.

Erin wasn't just another naked woman on top of me. She was a kindred spirit, just as jaded, but maybe not quite as ruined.

"You are so fucking beautiful," I whispered, combing her hair off her face, hating that that sounded like a bad movie line but no other words were more perfect to say what I was feeling. My spirit had been missing this sunshine, this brand of beauty, making me question if I ever really had it in my life before. One thing was for sure, I knew how rare it was to find it.

Erin instantly shied and dropped her face to my neck. Compliments made her humble and uncomfortable, which made her even more attractive.

"Not just on the outside." I drifted my hand over her jaw and then tipped her chin up. "Look at me." I waited until I had her complete attention; my fingers trailed down her neck to the hollow below her throat to the top swell of her breast. "In here, too. You're beautiful inside and out."

Her fingers sifted through my hair. "You're not too shabby yourself."

I cupped her ass in my hands, wanting to get her as close as possible, dousing my smile with her lips. I needed to climb back inside of her and rest my weary bones in a safe haven before I cracked.

I wanted to make love to her, to show her what I saw when I looked at her, to let her know how free I finally felt.

She tore her mouth away, pressed her cheek against mine, and rode the length of my new erection. "You need to get another condom."

I couldn't hide my happiness at that. "You up for another round?"

"Ten four, Officer," she chuckled.

I wrapped my arm across her back. "I think I need to take you into custody and lock you away for a *very* long time."

She shrank back. "Why? Am I breaking the law or something, or are you just looking for a reason to cuff me again?"

I really didn't want to move, let alone reach for another condom. I was in her once without one when we were in the shower, though she was adamant I didn't finish that way. Still, feeling her without one on was so much more preferable. Condoms sucked but were necessary evils. Both of our jobs required periodic blood tests, of that I was sure, so it would just be a matter of time before we felt comfortable enough to go without them. I'd surely see to that happening sooner rather than later.

I did, however, consider relocating her for a minute to get a set of cuffs. My partial erection was back to full on just on that thought alone. "You enjoy taunting an officer of the law?"

Erin kissed my cheek and then started to suck on my neck. "Why yes, I do believe I do, Detective."

I flexed my hips, falling into the sensations of skin gliding over skin. "Either you need to roll off me or I'm going to take you bare. I'll handcuff you some other time. Right now, I want you to have the use of your hands."

I felt her teeth on my earlobe. "Why? You gonna ten eighty-eight me or are we gonna ten sixty-nine?"

That was it. I was done. I spun her over onto her back. "Ten eighty-eight means I'm going to lunch." I glanced down her body, enjoying the entire package. "Or dinner. Whichever."

"Looks to me like ten eighty-eight means I'm in trouble."

I pinned her arms. "Oh, you're in trouble, all right. I'm going to ten eighty-eight you until you scream. Guess it's time to show you my happy version of *officer down*."

MY BODY FELT heavy but well rested, and unusually warm in places that used to feel vacant and cold. I nuzzled into the warmth, embracing it completely like a long forgotten blanket. I was absolutely positive the serenity flowing through me had everything to do with the woman sleeping peacefully against me. She'd rocked my world repeatedly last night, giving herself to me completely.

She didn't hold back either; well, not that I could tell. We twisted together and tangled the sheets, made each other sweaty and winded, and somewhere in between, climbed into each other's hearts.

Well, at least I can say with certainty she climbed into mine.

I felt her steady breaths and saw her eyes flutter under closed lids and I wondered if she was dreaming or just finding her own moment of peace in the chaos that threatened to engulf us.

It had been a long time since I woke to a woman in my bed. It had been *years* since I woke to a woman snuggled up tightly to me like this. Nikki hated cuddling. She'd yell at me and throw a punch if my feet came anywhere near her while we were sleeping. I definitely didn't miss that.

But this? I'd forgotten just how enjoyable the middle of the bed could be since I'd spent my entire relationship with Nikki hovering near the edge of my side just to avoid the possible altercation. After a while, those three feet became wider than the Grand Canyon.

I shut my eyes, trying to force out the comparisons. I didn't mean to do them; I just couldn't seem to stop them when they came. Maybe it was my subconscious trying to scrub itself of the past, to justify my choices and actions and make them into decisions I can live with. One way or another, I felt like my entire world was shifting, that wrong was turning right, and the darkness was finally lifting.

Erin was still naked, just the way I liked her best. Future visions of her wanting to wear my tees to crash out in also peppered my mind. All in good time, I supposed, but after making love to her last night, we just pulled the covers up over us and stayed naked for movie night.

I rested my nose near her neck, imagining more naked Saturday night movie nights with her.

My Doc.

Erin's back was pressed up against my chest, her ass was resting on the top of my thighs, and my arm was crammed under her pillow, though the stitches in my hand were starting to throb. I pushed back the nagging pain; the rest of me was too warm and comfortable to give a shit.

Well, with the exception of one other part that was stiff and in need of relief, urging me like a barking dog to get the hell up.

I hated the idea of leaving her to even go take a piss, but the more I thought about it the worse it became. I kissed her bare shoulder and tried to gently pull my arm free, but she still stirred.

"Mmm… morning," she purred softly.

I kissed her shoulder again. "Morning, Doc."

She snickered and laced her hand with mine. "Morning, Cop."

I bit her shoulder hard enough to make her giggle. "You want some coffee?"

"Cop coffee? Mmm… Sounds yummy."

I drifted my hand over her cheek, not wanting to kill the mood with morning breath. "You want to shower first and then have sex or do you want sex now and then some coffee after a shower?"

Her soft laugh was like music to my ears.

"I think I've created a monster," she joked.

I could definitely eat her for breakfast. "I think so, too. That's okay. You like me anyway."

Her eyes narrowed. "Who told you this?"

Her luscious tits were too much to ignore so I sucked the closest one right into my mouth. I sucked hard too, proud that I made her hiss. Her hand wove right into my hair.

Point made. I finished off with one swirl of the tongue. "I'm just guessing."

The need to fuck her again was warring with my need to piss. The bathroom won out.

She rubbed my stubble-covered chin with a hungry look in her eyes that said "don't take too long." I playfully bit at her fingers, just as hungry. I wondered if I'd ever get enough of her.

As soon as I came back to bed, she hurried off to the bathroom. Part of me was hoping she'd brush her teeth too so I could kiss her until one of us stopped breathing. I had a partial erection on that thought alone; wouldn't take much effort on her part to make me full-mast.

I heard her turn on my shower instead.

I tossed the covers off. Fuck needing an invitation for that.

ERIN SAT DOWN on one of the island bar stools with the coffee I'd poured for her, watching me work.

"I hate to be presumptuous," she started, "but it would be nice to make this into a tradition."

I tossed the scrambled eggs over once more in the fry pan, making sure they weren't runny. "What's that?"

She glanced at me over top of her coffee mug. "You, wearing nothing but black boxer briefs, making me breakfast on a Sunday morning."

I turned the burner off and smiled. "Is that so?"

Erin shrugged, brightening up my entire fucking world with her shy smile. "Just sayin'. I had a great night's sleep, fantastic wake-up sex, you washed my hair *and* my entire body, and now you're feeding me."

I scrapped the eggs onto two plates, grinning hard. I could still taste her on my tongue, on my lips. Addictive. "Are you telling me that I'm spoiling you already?"

Her happiness was infectious. "So far, this day is better than Christmas."

She made me laugh, though the idea of making every day with her better than Christmas was one I could totally get on board with. I pointed toward the counter. "Santa will put you on his naughty list if you don't get up off that luscious ass and go butter some toast."

She hopped off the chair and sauntered over to me. "Oh really?"

I wanted to give her the spatula treatment and then climb inside her again for the challenge. "Really. But I've got bacon to attend to. And I'm mostly naked, so I have to pay attention."

Erin's fingers drifted over my bare shoulders, sending shudders all over my body. "We wouldn't want you to get first degree burns, although I am medically qualified to treat your wounds."

I'll treat your wounds. "So you're saying after breakfast you want to go play doctor? I'm there." I opened the drawer containing my silverware, letting her know where things were located.

She grabbed a butter knife. "I most definitely created a monster. A cop monster."

I pinned her to the counter and swept her hair aside. "This from the woman who is parading around my kitchen wearing nothing but one of my tanks and a pair of *my* boxers?" I dipped my hand inside the elastic waistband while zeroing in on her neck. "I can't help myself. It's coercion. There isn't a court in the world that would side with you on this one." I felt myself getting hard again. What was it with this woman? She was like living Viagra.

Erin giggled when I bit her earlobe. "I think your bacon is burning."

"I don't care."

"Fire department might have other opinions about your cooking techniques if you burn your house down."

"Fuck the bacon." I spun her around and captured her mouth with mine, unsure if I was falling or if I'd fallen already. No matter how many times I kissed her, it would never be enough. She was my end and my new beginning.

The bacon made a loud pop, bringing me back from losing myself in her again.

"Bacon," she said out of breath.

"You're lucky," I growled and kissed her once more for good measure.

She jumped when I gave her ass a swat.

I layered the bacon on a bed of paper towels and pulled out the stool next to her at the counter. She was like a vision of pure sunshine sitting there, warming my day. I leaned down and kissed the side of her forehead before I sat down. "So, Doc, what would you like to do today?"

My cell rang, flashing numbers I didn't recognize on my screen. I set it aside, uninterested in being bothered.

She took a sip of her coffee. "Not sure." She shimmied in her seat.

I went with my hunch, teasing her. "You sore or something?"

Erin tried to shrug it off. "Not really. Well, maybe, just a little; back of my thighs ache a little."

I couldn't hide my grin. Mission accomplished. I put another spoonful of salsa on top of my eggs. After all, I earned it. "Good."

Her fork stopped midair. "Good?"

I finished chewing. "Well, not good because I plan on having you for lunch, but if you're sore, that means I did something right."

She knocked her knee into mine. "You must be so proud of yourself."

"I am, actually." I was also thinking that bacon is right up there with sex.

"Well, don't be. I'm not *that* sore."

I knocked my knee into hers. "Liar!"

"You're lucky I like you," she teased.

I stirred my coffee while disappearing into the beautiful depths of those blue eyes again. Everything about her held such promise. I was so very fucking lucky. "I know." My cell pinged with a new message, but her smile was more interesting.

The second ping pulled my attention. I read the new message then reached over for my laptop on the corner of the counter.

"Checking email?" she asked.

I held my fork between my teeth as I punched in my password. "Yeah. My contact from the NYPD just sent me some info on the case I'm working." Several mug shots and a few surveillance pictures littered my screen.

"Are you supposed to be fighting crime today?"

I watched her drag her fork slowly out of her mouth. Don't know if she was trying to make the move sensual and erotic but it was working nonetheless.

Erin's eyebrows arched up, calling me out on my promise to make our weekend as relaxing as possible. But I only had a few more pictures to look at and then I'd be done.

"Adam?"

"Hmm?"

"Question. I caught part of your phone conversation yesterday. My car wasn't the only one tampered with, was it?"

Fuck. I glanced over at her. "No."

"How many cars?"

I sighed, sipping my coffee instead. "So far, twenty. That's all that's been reported. Could be more."

Erin started chewing on her thumbnail instead of eating.

"Wanna see what the bad guys look like?"

That perked her up. "Are you allowed to show me that?"

I shrugged. "Don't see why not. It's not like medical records. Arrest records are public."

She leaned, sliding closer. "Okay, then sure. Show me. Wait, is that a woman?"

I enlarged the photo on the rap sheet. "Yep. Yolanda Dukane. She's been a busy girl. Felony possession firearm, carrying concealed, possession of drugs."

"Motor vehicle theft. Burglary," she read over my shoulder. "Holy crap. I didn't know women steal cars. Well, I know they steal cars, but I'm just surprised."

I had to laugh a little. "More often than not car thieves are male but it's not uncommon." I scrolled down the screen, reading the long list of offenses. "And this one, she's been at it a long time by the looks of it. See, there's a difference between the street punks who boost a car because they're too lazy to walk to this kind of criminal." I studied the face on my screen, from the hollows under her eyes to the telltale acne scars of a meth addict.

Erin shuddered. "She's scary looking. You can also see evidence of drug abuse. My guess is crystal meth."

My head whipped her way. Was she reading my mind now? "You can see that?"

"Yeah," Erin said, pointing. "Her face is covered in skin lesions and see how they extend down to her neck and throat area? She's developed a formication disorder from prolonged use."

"Fornication?" I teased.

Erin nudged me for being a smartass. "*Form*ication, not fornication. She's got the creepy crawly itches from compromising her central nervous system. Look at the big welts she's left on her neck from scratching."

I hunched when she started tickling my neck in retaliation. "Easy, woman. You tickle me, I get to tickle back. You've been warned."

I closed the email, enjoying Erin's attention much more. "So you *are* ticklish," I surmised when she stopped immediately.

I grabbed her by her waist as soon as she tried to step away.

"Please don't tickle me." She giggled, struggling.

"I won't." I pulled her into my chest. "Promise. I'll save this new knowledge for another time when you're not expecting it."

She smiled back at me, resting her hands on my bare shoulders. "You love your job, don't you?"

"I do."

"I'm glad you do. I want you to be happy."

She made me happy. "I am."

"Good. So tell me… what else do you normally do on a Sunday besides studying rap sheets, Cop?"

I loved that she enjoyed fucking with me. "Well, *Doc*," I slipped her cell across the counter and handed it to her. "As soon as I program your number in my phone, we can figure that out."

I typed each number in carefully; tiny icons were getting harder to see. "H-o-t D-o-c," I joked.

"You seriously did not add me in like that, did you? Is that in case you forget my name?"

"*Erin Novak*—" I enjoyed watching her private smile when her phone rang in her hand. "My phone, my rules."

"Fine. Be that way." She bumped into me. "S-e-x-y C-o-p," she spelled, leaning on me while she did it.

I set my cell down. "You done?"

"Why? You going to ten fifteen me now?"

I slipped the phone out of her hand and pulled her between my thighs, needing to kiss her in the worst way. My hands were in her hair again, my tongue riding hers on a newfound high. I swear my cock felt like it was Christmas, too. "I like that idea." I locked her in my arms. "Prisoner in custody. Mine."

She giggled at first and then pulled back. "I may need a ten twenty too."

She followed my glance around. "You're in my kitchen, although I think we should move our location back to my bedroom. I have more *ten* codes I can teach you." I squeezed her luscious ass.

"Now you're just making shit up."

"You dare doubt an officer of the law?"

My doorbell rang, not once but twice, surprising the heck out of me and rudely interrupting my plans. *Who the fuck would be at my door on a Sunday?* I hoped to hell it wasn't some ballsy fans of the show coming to get their eyeful.

Just as I completed that thought, the person outside started banging on my door. One glance out my front window was all it took to see whose car was parked in the driveway behind Erin's.

Fuck.

"Erin, come with me." More knocking came from the impatient bitch outside. I towed Erin up the steps to my bedroom.

"What's going on?" she asked.

I tossed her jeans over to her and pulled mine up.

"Adam?" Erin asked again, yanking her jeans up.

I grabbed the green tee Erin wore the other day, still smelling her scent on it, giving me strength to go deal with the bullshit banging on my door.

I also grabbed my Glock and holstered it in the back of my jeans.

Erin froze. "Adam, what's going on? Tell me right now."

I took a deep breath. "Nikki's at my door."

"Nikki?" she questioned.

"My ex."

Erin snagged my arm; both of us slightly distracted by the continuous banging. "You need a gun to answer your door?"

I held her face in my hand. "Things got ugly between us. I have no idea why she is here but I will not be caught off guard. Not while I'm in my own fucking house."

The doorbell rang again and again.

"Stay here. I'm going to see what she wants and get rid of her." I kissed Erin softly. "I won't let this ruin our day. I promise. She's history. Okay?"

Erin nodded; her eyes were wide and showing fear. "Is that *tampon girl?*"

It hurt just having to answer that. It hurt worse seeing her so scared. "Yes. I'm going to fix that, too." I held her gaze so she'd see how serious I was. "Stay here, babe. I'll be right back. You copy?"

I nodded. "I copy."

I hoped to hell she'd stay upstairs, but my gut was telling me she wouldn't.

Nikki was calling out my name with each thud of her fist.

It was time to bury some old ghosts once and for all.

CHAPTER 15
Erin

THE FACT THAT Adam armed himself to go answer his front door was beyond unsettling. Knowing it was his ex-girlfriend pounding on his door *and* that he felt he needed to be armed was downright incomprehensible.

Even though he told me to stay in his bedroom, curiosity and concern had me sneaking to the top of the stairs, but not before I snagged Adam's hammer from the pile of tools in the spare bedroom. I stopped on the third step down with hammer in hand—well within hearing distance but out of sight. Any farther and she'd be able to see me through the wooden railing.

I had no idea what this woman could be capable of. Adam armed himself, but I still felt the need to be able to defend him.

"What do you want?" Adam asked brusquely.

"I need to talk to you," the female voice replied, a hint of an urgent plea etching her voice. "Please."

Great. She's playing on his sympathy, sounding desperate.

"You alone?"

"Of course," she insisted.

Italian, maybe? Definitely a South Philly-accented attitude.

"You have two minutes, then I'm closing this door."

"Can I at least come in? It's freezing out here."

The hinges creaked and then the front door shut, echoing the change of pressure throughout the house. I tried to see their reflection in the glass on the large print of whitetail deer Adam had hanging on the downstairs wall, wanting to know what she looked like in the worst way.

"Were you sleeping?" Nikki asked, straining to hide her annoyance.

He sighed. "No."

"Then why did it take you so long to answer?"

I could hear him draw in an impatient breath through his nose. "I was busy."

"Oh. Is someone here?"

"What do you want? Why are you here?"

"Whose car is in the driveway?"

Adam didn't answer.

"What, did you get another new car or something? It's okay. You can tell me." She chuckled. "Looks expensive. Must be nice. I mean, things must be going really good for you."

What a…! Could you be any more condescending?

"It belongs to a friend. You've got one minute."

"Jeez, Adam. Chill."

"Nikki, I got shit to do. Get to the fucking point."

"Wow. Can't you even be civil to me anymore? It would be nice to be able to talk to you without you biting my head off."

I heard him groan.

"How have you been? You look really good. I mean, you look great."

I craned my neck, trying to hear them better.

"Time is ticking," he said flatly. "You gonna get to the point of this visit anytime soon?"

She let out a long sigh. "Can't we just talk, you know, like we used to?"

"Why? I've said everything I needed to say to you a *long* time ago. There's nothing left to talk about."

"I thought maybe we could try again. Come on. Please? I miss you so much."

"Don't start."

"Four years, baby."

"I'm warning you, Nikki, do *not* start this shit with me."

"I made a mistake. A terrible mistake. Please! I was scared and confused and I didn't know what to do. Half the time I tried to talk to you, you were either too drunk or too tired to be bothered. What did you expect me to do?"

"Jesus. I expected you to fucking talk to me instead of lying to my face. That's what *I* expected."

"I know and I'm sorry. Please, please don't throw away everything we had. I know in your heart you still love me. I know you do."

We both waited for an answer that didn't come. I felt my heart sink and twist.

"God, how many times do I have to tell you I'm sorry before you forgive me?"

"I don't have time for this. We've been through this shit already."

"I know, but—"

"But nothing. How many times do we have to keep rehashing this shit? Huh? You need to get it in your head. I'm done! It's over!"

I shifted, becoming uncomfortable hearing them argue.

"Don't say that. Please. I thought if I gave you some time… I thought you said we could try again?"

"When the hell did I say that?"

"On the phone last week. You said that you'd talk to me later, or was that just bullshit?"

I could hear him getting frustrated.

"Nikki, I'm… you need to get this straight, okay? What you and I had is done. It's gone. You killed that, not me. I've put it behind me. I suggest you do the same. You need to move on, all right?"

"Is that what you've done? I'm sorry, but I'm having a hard time doing that. I can't erase all the years we were together as if they meant nothing. I thought since you're sober now we could try again. I promise I'll be different. I swear. Don't you remember all of the promises we made to each other? All the fun we used to have? Making love to each other?"

"That was *before* you went and made decisions without me," he growled.

"You telling me you don't miss anything? That after everything we've been through, you don't love me anymore? You think you're going to find another woman who will put up with you drowning your sorrows in beer and whiskey while sitting here night after night all alone?"

"Do not throw that in my face. I've apologized too many times. And I worked nights before we met. You knew what you were getting into."

"Yeah, that's right. I did. But maybe if you'd just try to get on day shift a few times. For *me*. Is that too much to ask?"

"Why are we even having this conversation again?"

I heard her footsteps crossing his hardwood floor. "I miss you, Adam. So much."

"No, Nikki. No. This is not gonna happen. You're wasting your time so just stop."

"You think you'll find another woman who will stand by you like I did? Brush your ego like I did?"

"Brush my ego?"

"Yeah, *you* know," she kidded, placating him, "playing your stupid kinky games with your rope and shit?"

"You're unbelievable. You call what you did to me *standing by me*? You fucked me over in every possible way *every* chance you had. I came home from work and found my entire fucking house emptied out!"

"You told me you wanted me out, so I left," Nikki retorted like an insolent child.

"*You*, not all my stuff. You. Took. Everything. Even the food out of the fucking refrigerator!"

"You knew I had no money when you kicked me out."

"And that justified… You know what, it doesn't matter anymore. I'm done with this."

"Hey, I had just as much of a hard time dealing with things as you did. But did you give *me* your understanding and forgiveness? No, you didn't. I did what you wanted me to, Adam!"

"You don't get it. I'm a cop, and on top of everything else, on top of everything you pulled, you brought drugs into my house."

"It was one time!"

"Bullshit. Do not stand here and lie to my face. Instead of looking for another job you spent your days getting high. You knew after Tommy's death that I was under investigation and *still* you brought that shit into my house. Christ. I'm glad you went to that butcher. Fucking relieved. Showed me your true colors and saved me a lifetime of misery."

"Oh, but getting drunk and strapping a gun on your hip is okay?"

"Was it even mine?"

"You know the answer to that," she groaned.

"Do I? Never once did I stray on you. Never once. Can you look me in the eyes and say the same?"

The silence stretched.

"Just what I thought," Adam snapped. "Listen, I'm not playing this game with you anymore. I haven't touched a drop in months, so that too is behind me. You made your decisions. I've made mine. You need to move on."

His voice was low, tight. Definitely trying to send a message.

I heard her sniff. "What about the wedding?"

My heart clenched just hearing that word. *Oh my God. Were they engaged to be married?*

"What about it?"

"I thought you would call me. You told Jesse to mark down two people."

"I have a date."

"Oh really? You're taking a stranger to Ellie's wedding?"

Her contempt was more than apparent.

"All of our friends will be there, Adam. What am I supposed to do? Not show up?"

"Christ. They're not your friends."

"Ellie is, and she invited *me* to her wedding."

"Good for you."

"Can't we just try again? Please? We *both* made mistakes. I promise things will be different."

Adam snorted.

"You need me, Adam. Cancel your date. Let me show you how much you still want me. I bet your cock misses me."

Her pleading with him was wearing down my resolve. Hearing that he had a date planned with someone else made my throat burn. I wondered if he even knew I was standing here listening.

My car keys were in his bedroom. My coat and car were in the opposite direction. My right foot was on one step, my left foot on another. I didn't know which way to go.

"You're delusional," Adam said, huffing. "Don't fucking touch me."

"Why? Is someone upstairs?" Nikki asked, her voice seeming to get closer. "Do you have someone up there?"

I darted into the first bedroom on the tips of my toes and shrank into the wall, unable to keep the floor from creaking under my wake.

I heard the front door open. "It's time for you to leave."

"Whose car is out there?"

"Nikki, leave."

"Not until you tell me whose fucking car is out there!"

"It's none of your business. Leave," he ordered.

"You have some whore in my bedroom?"

"That's it." Something banged into the wall.

"Ow! Let go of my arm. Adam, let go. You're hurting me," she shrieked. "Come down here! Show your face, whore. I want to see what you look like."

"I asked you nicely, now I'm showing you out." They both cursed and then something crashed and shattered to the floor. "Nikki! Jesus Christ!"

"Come down here, you skanky bitch! Show your face! He'll *never* love you. You hear me, bitch? Never. I'll fucking kill you."

My heart was racing, knowing they were having a physical scuffle. She was cursing at him something fierce until the front door slammed. Both of them were still arguing, though their voices were muffled and distant outside.

I scrambled back to his bedroom and paced. Then I sat on his bed and waited, unsure of where to go from here. I wanted to leave. A big part of me wanted to stay. My heart wanted to fall in love with the man who I woke up with a few hours ago and who made me eggs and bacon and kissed me sweetly and made love to me so many times I'd lost count.

His ex-girlfriend, however, was too much drama for me.

She was the *scary sort of drama* kind of girl.

The front door open and closed again. Adam's feet pounded up the steps and then his bedroom door opened wide. He stopped in front of me and dropped to one knee.

"Erin." His hands landed on my knees. "Doc, look at me."

Too much drama.

His eyes were solemn and crinkled with concern. "Sorry you had to hear all of that. You okay?"

I wasn't sure how I was feeling actually so I just said, "I'm fine."

He chuckled. "I told you once before that if you ever tell me you're fine I get to call you on it. Talk to me. You have questions, I can tell. I can see it."

"You still love her?"

His head started shaking immediately. "No, I do not."

"You sure?"

"Positive."

"She cleaned out your house?"

Adam nodded. "She took everything, even the butter and fucking ketchup. Told you the bed was new."

How a woman could do that to someone was almost too much to comprehend.

"Except she left her tampons behind."

His eyes closed for a moment. "All that shit is going in the garbage. I swear. I don't want any of it touching you." His head tilted. "If I let go of your knees, are you going to run?"

I couldn't tell if he was serious or if he was joking, until it registered how truly scared he looked.

"I'm sorry you had to hear that. I'm sure it wasn't easy for you."

"It wasn't."

I leaned back when he tried to kiss me.

His broad shoulders slumped. "Doc…"

I held up my index finger. "I like you—a lot. I do. But I've got a lot going on in my life right now and I can't afford to be derailed by crazy drama and a broken heart. If you're seeing other people, you have to tell me right now."

Adam's face twisted up. "What?"

I hated being taken for a fool. "I heard everything. Sorry, I didn't mean to eavesdrop but I was worried when you strapped a gun to the back of your pants."

"Is that why there's a hammer on the floor here?"

I nodded.

He took a deep breath, picked it up, and then tossed it gently aside. I wanted to follow the hammer out into the hallway, hating confrontations of any kind.

I tried to calm myself, glancing at the wrinkled sheets.

Adam laughed to himself. "Amazing. The woman I *don't* want to be with is banging my door down while the one woman I *do* want is always ready to run away. That's why I'm holding your legs, in case you're wondering."

I couldn't help but smile at him.

"I'm only seeing one woman," he said, swaying me with his killer smile, "and she's right in front of me."

It was nice to be able to almost breathe again… Still, words were just words. "You told your ex that you had a date planned. I don't want to get tangled up if you're dating other women, Adam. Seriously. I'm not interested in standing in a line or getting jerked around."

Adam glanced up at me, squinting one eye. "One of the guys in my unit is getting married in two weeks. I'm hoping you'll be able to go with me. I was going to ask you about it today over breakfast, but we were interrupted."

My spirit instantly warmed.

"No one else, Erin," he stated, his voice deep and raspy but unmistakably stern. "We do this, it's just you and me seeing where this goes. I don't share and I don't roam. We clear?"

I put my hand over his, taking in the severity of his tone, my mind veering off his serious expression to unwanted visions of Randy and his excess roaming. No matter how attractive Adam was on the outside, he needed to deliver a lot more than a few well-intended words and outstanding orgasms to get my whole heart. Until then, I was keeping myself well guarded.

"We clear?" he asked again.

"We're clear."

"Good. Then we can get back to eating breakfast."

I nodded though I wasn't hungry anymore.

He didn't move. "You gonna kiss me now, or do we still need to talk shit out?"

The fact that he was determined to clear the air made me more confident. I hated stupid misunderstandings. Still, I didn't want his incredible kissing abilities to distract me. "I can see why she is so desperate to get you back."

"That's never gonna happen."

I believed him. "Regardless, I can see why."

Adam stood. "Well, that's good, I guess, but it doesn't change anything."

I stared down at his bare feet. Even his darn toes were appealing.

"You went outside barefoot?"

He put his hands on his hips. "I wanted to make sure she left without doing anything stupid."

I looked up at him. "Stupid?"

"She knows that the silver SHO in my driveway belongs to the girl I'm seeing. From now on your car goes in the garage when you're here. I'll move my bike so you have room to pull in."

My skin started to prickle again. "Is that why you have a gun in the back of your pants?"

Adam drew in a deep breath. "I trust very few people, Erin. I've also pissed off more people than I care to count. Some people don't take too kindly to you putting them in jail." His fingers brushed over my chin. "I will always be able to protect myself and the people I care about, even if that means I have to take out people I used to care about in the process. Know this. I never answer my door unarmed. Whenever I leave the house, I'm armed. There are guns hidden on every floor of this house. It's just the way things are."

"Are you that worried?" I asked gently.

He shook his head. "Not worried. Prepared."

I watched him open up his nightstand drawer and pull out another black gun. He took the bullets out and handed it to me. I felt like he was handing me death.

Adam frowned. "You afraid?"

Afraid was mild to what I was feeling.

"It's unloaded. Take it. See?" He pulled the top back and showed me an empty cavity. "Chamber is empty."

It still looked dangerous.

"You ever fire a gun before?"

I shook my head so hard I was afraid I might shoot myself accidentally just by holding it in my palm. "I've pulled plenty of slugs out of people though."

He stared down at me for the longest time while I fought my budding anxiety. "You want to learn?"

Did I? I'd thought about shooting plenty of people over the course of my life but that was always in the *hypothetical daydream sense*, not the actual *pull the trigger* sense.

Adam set the gun down on his nightstand and then took me by the hands, pulling me up. He worked his arms around me. "I think step one in learning to trust me starts now." He tipped my chin up and gave me a very sweet kiss.

I spent the next half hour musing about him being mostly naked while watching him buzz around his house packing for our next adventure.

"BREATHE OUT," ADAM whispered into my ear. "Then squeeze."

It was difficult to ignore his instructions; they affected my entire body, setting every one of my nerves on a heightened level of awareness.

His arms were supporting mine, holding them up to help me aim while giving me his patience and expertise. I'd listened carefully when he had demonstrated how I should stand, how I shouldn't fear the cold steel gripped in my hands. I knew my fears were unfounded, based solely on seeing the aftermath of what a bullet could do to the human body. Still, I needed to do this.

Every move Adam made was executed with commanding precision, adding a new level of sex appeal that I hadn't been quite aware of before. How he was completely at ease with a lethal weapon in his hand, making him appear even more foreboding, was also a sight to be appreciated.

His hips shift as he widened my stance; the hard wall of his chest pressed into my back and braced me as I tried not to outwardly tremble.

It was important to Adam to make me feel safe and "empowered" as he emphatically stated in his truck on the way here, and seeing this additional glimpse at how enthralled he was bringing me to the indoor range where he trained was infectious.

"Use the dots, line up your sights first." He adjusted my arms higher. "Remember; bring the gun up level to your eyes, not your eyes down to the gun."

It was nearly impossible to concentrate while feeling the stiff ridge of his pants brushing the seam of my ass. "It's hard."

"No it isn't," he quickly admonished, missing my point but brushing his against my butt again. "Don't doubt yourself. We've gone over the mechanics. You know how to load and unload it and work the slide."

My inner dirty girl was having a field day with this. "That's not what I meant. Well, not completely."

"Adjust your grip. You're squeezing too tight. Relax your fingers, babe. That's better. Nice and easy. This finger stays on the trigger."

The size of the gun alone was making me nervous. His lips mere centimeters from my neck was even worse. His partial erection brushing my ass was making concentration damn near impossible. "I still think I should start out with a smaller gun."

"It fits you perfectly."

I wasn't sure we if we were even talking about firearms anymore. I rested into the reassuring safety of his chest again, enjoying the many freedoms that came along with being intimately familiar with someone. Innocent contact wasn't so innocent anymore, but more of an inalienable right. I brushed my butt over his package once more just because I could.

He sucked in a quick breath, followed by a throat-clearing groan and a reciprocating press into me. "You have seven rounds in the magazine so when you're ready you'll chamber it and aim just like I've shown you. When you're ready." He let me go and pulled the headset up off his neck and placed them over his ears. I was on my own with Adam in full-blown teacher mode.

I was glad that the only other guy inside the range left so we had the entire place to ourselves. I felt awkward at first, like I should have had prior gun knowledge before stepping foot in this place.

The black circles on the paper human target were just twenty feet away, but felt looming nonetheless.

Adam folded his arms across his chest and gave me an encouraging nod, like an overindulging parent.

I tried to focus, aim, and breathe, while the only sound I could hear under my headset was the constant thrum of my own heartbeat.

"Doc."

I looked over at him, instantly reacting as if he'd called out my real first name. He was smirking, holding one muff off his ear. "You look sexy as hell holding my Glock. I know the minute you pop your first round you'll be addicted, *begging* me to bring you back here. Don't overthink it. Just relax and enjoy it. It's a hell of a stress reliever. Trust me."

His small phrase repeated in my mind, evoking both my comfort and apprehension while I replaced the brand name of his gun with visions of his cock. "You say *trust me* a lot, you know that?"

His smile widened. "I just put a loaded gun in your hands. There's a *tremendous* amount of trust going on here. Besides," he shrugged, "trust is the basis for everything. Without it, relationships are superficial."

I focused back on my target instead of his sexy mouth and the potentially meaningful words coming out of it. "You feeling awfully poetic, Cop?"

Adam laughed. "Gotta say, watching a hot doctor fire one of my weapons *is* pretty fucking inspiring."

I fought my smile. "Quit distracting me."

"You need to learn how to block it out. Now relax, remember to exhale, and squeeze. Oh, and you might want to chamber the round first before you pull the trigger."

Shit. I'd forgotten. I wanted him to do it.

He put his hands up. "Oh no, no. This one is all you."

I set the gun down on the ledge, pulled my hearing protection off, and motioned for his hand.

"What?" he asked.

"Your hand. Let me see it."

"You're stalling."

I scowled at him. His wellbeing was more important to me. "I am not. Give it. Please?"

He pulled the headset off his ears, rolled his eyes, and held out his right hand.

"No, the other one. The one with stitches in it."

As soon as he placed his hand in mine, my suspicions were confirmed. "You popped a stitch."

He pulled his hand back and inspected it. "Yeah, I know. Happened in the shower this morning as I was taking you up against the wall."

My mouth fell open; his turned up into a wicked grin.

"It needs to be restitched. It's all red. It's open here."

"Nah. I'll live. Besides, I think we should remove the rest of the stitches that way. Would make it a lot more interesting, don't ya think?"

I wanted to yell "hell yes" but opted for stunned demureness instead. "As your doctor, I cannot advise that. You'll run the risk of infection."

"As my doctor, I'll let you give me a complete physical later. You can examine anything you want." Adam took my chin and kissed me. "Now quit stalling," he said on my lips, then turned me toward the target. "You can fix it later if it bothers you that much."

I eyed the target. "Good, because it does."

Adam chuckled indulgingly and turned his ringing cell phone off.

"You get a lot of calls."

He was busy looking at the screen; his brows were pulled together. "Not usually." He shoved it back into his pocket. "Put your ears on." He wrapped a finger on the headset gripping my head.

I readied myself and pulled the slide back like he'd shown me. There was no turning back.

I took a deep breath and exhaled.

I didn't expect the crack to be as loud as it was or for my wrists and arms to tingle after absorbing the recoil, but it wasn't nearly as scary as I thought it would be. I actually flinched afterward but Adam was right—the power was heady. He helped me aim, taught me how to use the sights and I pulled the trigger six more times, each one more powerful than the last.

For a moment, I felt invincible. Well, at least seriously badass. The shot of adrenaline flowing through my veins created an instant addiction, clearing my mind of everything but the weapon in my hands and the release it created.

Adam pulled his headset off; his concern that I'd been injured somehow clearly painted all over his face. "Are you okay?"

I wanted to hug him for giving me this experience. I set the gun down and threw myself at him.

"Whoa!" he chuckled, rocking back on his heels. He patted my butt, hugged me tightly, and kissed me. "Yeah, you're good." His smile was laced with pride. "Let's see how you did."

The paper target sailed toward us on the mechanical track.

He pinched the paper in his fingers. "Not bad, Doc. You blew his kidneys apart with this one. You're aiming a bit low though."

I was thrilled that I actually hit the paper, but I did a lot better than I'd thought. "I want to do that again."

Adam slung his arm over my shoulders and dipped his head for another toe-curling kiss, effectively stopping my excited bouncing. "I've created a monster." He laughed on my mouth.

He'd created more than a monster. In the course of a weekend he'd created an addictive package that is sweet and fascinating and makes my blood feel alive in an entirely new capacity. I was completely drawn to him; there was no denying it now.

"You keep looking at me like that you'll get me permanently banned from here for lewd and lascivious behavior." I got another encouraging squeeze and a smack on the butt. "Come on. Practice makes perfect." He set an entire box of bullets on the counter in front of me. "Hit the target seven more times and I'll buy you lunch."

I checked the small box, disappointed by his limiting challenge. "Only seven? There's like fifty bullets here."

While I tried to count the brass rounds, I found myself pinned, pressed between the counter and the unyielding wall of Adam's chest. He peeled my headset off and set it in front of me. His temperate breath brushed my neck. Strong hands covered my stomach. "Weaving your way deeper, Doc." His warm lips slid up and down the column of my throat. "Mmm, I want to do you so bad right now."

His playful growl tickled my ear. I wanted to kiss him in the worst way. I turned my head so he'd grant my wish.

"Christ. Get a fucking room, Trent," a man's voice boomed.

Adam's fingers tightened before he released me, his body tensing as he tucked me behind his back. I peered around his shoulder, getting an eyeful of the man putting Adam on high alert. He had a short crew cut and a smug attitude that looked like he could become an asshole easily with the right incentive.

Adam held me behind his body. "Sidel," he said tightly.

Another man, shorter, very thin, with a dark, greasy comb-over and pockmarked face came through the door behind Sidel. I thought they might be together as there seemed to be an air of familiarity there, but as soon as he spotted us, he came to an abrupt halt, hesitated while trying to appear inconspicuous, and then with a barely perceptible chin nod, set his gear down at the first booth.

The man Adam addressed as Sidel glanced back over his shoulder; his cocky smile faltering quickly. Adam scrutinized the man at the far end, tilting his head slightly as though there was some recognition.

"Surprised to see you here on a Sunday," Sidel said to Adam. It was my guess that it wasn't a pleasant surprise for Sidel, either.

I didn't need to be a mind-reader to sense Adam wasn't too fond of this guy.

Sidel was eying me over; his blatant leering made me feel violated. "So, who you got with you? One of your adoring fans?"

I saw the instant when he recognized me. "You! No shit!" He turned his smug look to Adam and then pegged me again with his attention. "You're the doctor woman we pulled over a few weeks ago. Trent, you sly dog. You actually hooked up with her? Unfuckingbelievable."

"Exercise some couth, Sidel," Adam ordered low.

Sidel ignored him and held out his hand to me. "Brian Sidel. Nice to see you again."

My manners insisted I greet him back. Adam's posture was anything but relaxed, making me question whether touching Brian Sidel's hand would be a poor judgment call on my part.

Adam glanced back at me. "Sidel is in my unit."

My manners won out after that. "Hi. Erin."

I swore I heard Adam growl the second Sidel touched my hand.

The weird man at the far end of the range periodically glanced our way, making me slightly uncomfortable. Adam backed up, backing me up with him. He was wearing his Glock on his hip, which he touched briefly. He picked up the gun I was shooting, popped the magazine out, and fished out another from the carry case. This one contained a full row of bullets.

I swallowed hard when he slapped it back in and chambered the first round.

"Teaching her how to shoot?" Sidel asked, doing a poor job at masking his amusement.

I was hoping he'd go off and mind his own business, but no such luck.

Adam handed the loaded gun to me, keeping it pointed down, but he barely took his eyes off the two men while he did it. "Just enjoying some time at the range, like you."

Sidel nodded and set his gear down on the floor. "Well, let's see what you got, sweetheart," he said to me, raising his eyes expectantly. He exposed the gun under his jacket when he put his hands on his hips.

Adam read my hesitance. He stepped back even farther; I presumed so his back would never be vulnerable. I was starting to understand him better, too. Gone was the playful folded-arms posture he had when we'd arrived. Adam looked ready to enter a quick draw contest. I imagined he would win it, too.

"Go ahead, babe," he said with a nod.

I put my headset back on while Adam floated a new target back out.

All eyes were on me as I lined up my sights. I exhaled and pulled the trigger. I took my time, shooting until it was empty. I wanted to see how well I did but Adam nudged me safely out of the way, putting his body between Sidel and me again.

In one fast swoop, he drew his weapon from his side and without hesitance, pulled the trigger once. He put his gun back in the holster on his hip and locked eyes with Sidel as the target floated back to us.

I could see the light shining through several holes on the paper. When the target stopped, one hole stood out.

It was the one dead center in the target's forehead.

"Who's your friend?" Adam asked Sidel, casually noting the direction with his chin.

Sidel glanced down the range, seeming bored with the question. His lips twisted. "No idea. Don't know him."

I may not have a PhD in human behavior, but I was cognizant enough to know a lie when I heard one. Adam's throaty "hmm" told me he thought that answer was bullshit, too.

Adam pulled the target down and nudged me privately. His apprehension was palpable. He made a point of looking at his watch. "Shit, it's getting late. We need to get going. We'll come back again when we have more time. Load this empty mag; I'll do the other one."

While we worked, I leaned closer to him, taking another bullet out of the box. I knew we had plenty of time to goof around, so I gathered his outward comment wasn't really meant for me. "You're going to explain this to me later?" I whispered.

His expression was impassive though his eyes never stopped scanning. "Yep."

I didn't question him further. I finished up and put my coat on.

"Leaving already?" Sidel asked, forming his question with a big brush of underhanded sarcasm.

Okay, I was *really* starting to dislike this guy.

Adam didn't buy into the baiting. He even smiled at the ass. "Got other things to do before shift tonight."

Sidel raised his brows, sliding his eyes my way. "I bet you do. You gonna film that for the show, too, or just add another one to your private collection?" Sidel leaned to speak directly at me, as though he was sharing a secret. "He's got quite the fan girl following, you know."

I didn't understand his maliciousness. "Why would you say that?"

Adam grabbed my hand and shot Sidel a warning glare. "Come on, babe."

"Have fun, Trent," Sidel jeered.

As soon as we hit the parking lot, Adam walked so darn fast, it felt like we practically ran to his truck. He opened the door locks and held the passenger door for me, urging me to climb in. I waited for him to get us on the road and for him to calm down a little before even attempting to say anything. Luckily I didn't have to.

Adam kept shaking his head. "I don't believe it. I would have called somebody a liar if I didn't just see that shit for myself."

I rubbed my cold hands together and then slipped my sunglasses on. "So what did just happen back there?"

He glanced over at me quickly. "Fucked-up shit, that's what just happened. Sidel? I just... Erin, I have no words. Yeah, he's a dick most of the time, but a rat? Thought he was a cop to the core."

"What do you mean, he's a rat? He was pretty arrogant and I'm not sure because I don't know him, but he seemed a bit jealous of you, too."

Adam shrugged. "That's his issue, not mine. We used to be good friends." I could clearly see how much the divergence hurt him. "Ever since we started filming this show, things steadily got worse. All the other guys in my unit are rolling with it but Sidel seems hell bent on digging me every chance he gets. Still, I can't believe it."

His face was twisted with mix of anger and disbelief. "The guy that came in behind Sidel? I know who he is."

CHAPTER 16
Adam

"SO YOU THINK this Salvador Mancuso is the one running everything?" Erin asked, swirling the spoon in her coffee while she analyzed my dilemmas.

One cream, two sugars. I committed that to memory, trading my blinding rage and visions of dirtball criminals for sweeter things that didn't make my blood pressure skyrocket. My woman liked her coffee on the sweet side. It totally fit.

Huh. My woman.

Somehow in the last few hours something inside me had claimed a stake on her and, strangely, I was totally at ease with that.

I glanced around the restaurant, assuring myself no one was listening, and gave her a single nod. I shouldn't have been discussing this with her, but when I'm around her I have no restraint. She was one hell of a great listener, helping me think this entire operation out rationally when all I wanted at the moment was vengeance. "Now you see my concern."

She concentrated on her cup of coffee, her eyes narrowed and contemplating. "But what's the motivating factor for Sidel to be seen in public with Mancuso's brother? Sidel has to be getting something major out of it to be putting everything at risk like that."

I shrugged. "People do all sorts of stupid shit for money."

"Yeah, but he'd be in big trouble if he got caught. Would the money be worth it?"

"No amount of money is worth risking your career and going to jail, because that's where he'll be going if I find out he's taking part in this operation. I'll put him behind bars myself. Cops serving time don't do well in gen pop and it would be my pleasure to see him suffer if he's involved—"

Erin held up her hand, halting my tirade. "Why would a police officer meet up with his criminal friend in a public place where he might be seen by other cops? Would Sidel risk exposure like that? No, I'm not buying it. It's too risky and frankly, enormously stupid." I watched her finger slowly circle the rim of her mug, wishing that coffee cup were me. I could almost feel it echoing on my skin, lulling me into a trance.

"He may come off as a jerk," she said, pulling back my attention, "but my gut tells me he's a lot more calculating than that. Besides, if they needed to talk, there are a million other places to meet where no one would see them together."

She had a point. A *very* good point. One that months of my growing animosity toward Sidel was refusing to let me see. "Yeah," I scratched my brow, "but none of our team has seen *Vincent* Mancuso's face. Well, not exactly all of them." I started compiling a short mental list, which included my captain and my partner, Marcus.

"Well," Erin continued, "until you have definitive proof, everything is just speculation. You'll figure it all out."

Her brush of confidence dropped my blood pressure a few notches. The waitress brought our salads and hot rolls, making my stomach growl in appreciation. I unrolled my napkin and snagged a fork. "You'd make a very good detective, Doc. You're very levelheaded."

Erin smiled shyly and nodded at me, covering her mouth with her hand. God she was gorgeous when she was being humble—another trait that I admired tremendously—even when she was trying to downplay my compliment with a well-crafted distraction about being a medical detective.

That sense of peaceful contentment I hadn't felt in such a long time washed over me, almost making me feel lightheaded in its wake. I wanted to concentrate on the rage skimming around the edge of my thoughts— form a plan to lock Sidel and his criminal cronies away for a very long time—but the blistering anger simply vanished every time I looked at her. One thing was for certain. *She* was the source of the light snuffing out the darkness within me.

My senses were tingling even before my headlights hit her car and confirmed my suspicions. Part of me expected to see fans camped out in front of my house, but the harsh winter weather and mounds of snow were quite an effective deterrent. Pain lanced right into my gut when I saw Erin's car sitting lopsided, and as I got closer, my temper skyrocketed.

I knew it. I fucking knew it. I should have locked her car in my garage before we left, but like a dumbass, I didn't. *Son of a...*

"What?" Erin asked.

I pulled into the driveway and hit the button to open the garage door, hoping to park before she noticed the damage.

I shut off the ignition and held out my hand. "Let me have your keys."

She dug in her purse. "Why? What's wrong?"

Erin followed me out into the driveway. "Adam?"

The cold wind blew a gust of snow crystals over us but the frigid weather only seemed to ramp up my fury.

"Shit," she whispered. I avoided looking at her pained face as the damage registered.

Shit was putting it mildly. Red was blistering my vision seeing that both tires on the driver side had been flattened. A quick check on the other side had me releasing the breath I was holding; the two on the passenger side were still inflated.

I halted Erin as she tried to follow me. "Stay back. This is a fucking crime scene."

She stopped dead in her tracks and gasped. The wind rustled the bare branches in the large elm that bordered my driveway, stirring more of my senses. It was still light and sunny outside; the suspect could still be in the vicinity.

I took her by the waist and backed her into the safety of my garage, tucking her in front of my truck onto the padded stool at my workbench. "It's cold and you're shivering. Stay here."

"I'm okay."

I leveled my gaze on hers. "I'm not." I sat her down and got the flashlight out of my truck.

Erin nodded woodenly; the shock was doing its number on her. "I have to work tonight."

I shut my passenger door and eyed her over the hood. "I know."

She started to stand, not fully understanding the severity of the situation.

"I'll drive you myself if it comes down to it, but right now I need you to stay put." She got my meaning, sliding her rump back onto the stool without argument.

Aggravation was burning deep in my gut as I did a careful walk-around, scanning the paint on her car, looking for damage or signs of forced entry. The drive was clear of visible footprints; only a bit of wet slush remained, leaving no clue as to who may have done this.

My neighborhood was quiet, insulated within layers and piles of powdery white snow. The street was typical for an after-storm dig out; small rivulets of water were interspersed within random ridges of ice and snow created by dozens of tire tracks. As I looked around for any shred of evidence, I tried to calm myself enough to form a game plan without putting my fists through something. I crouched back down next to Erin's car; each of her tires had one very distinct straight slice in the sidewall.

I couldn't suppress my growl. A guy wouldn't do this kind of damage unless he was tied to Erin somehow. Still, a jealous ex wouldn't strand her under the care of another man if he were trying to make a point. The tires on her ride were expensive.

I glanced around the neighborhood again. Rick's green pick-up was dirty, but sitting on four full tires in front of his house across the street. Jeanne's dark blue Passat was untouched in their driveway. On the other side of the small bushes separating our yards, Vic's brand new red Camaro, his gift to himself when he retired last September, had a stack of snow on its roof. There were no footprints in the snow in my yard, either. House, windows, everything appeared untouched.

My eyes scanned back to Erin's car. No, this was personal.

Someone trying to send me a message would have been more creative. Even roaming punks would have jacked her car up and stole them before wasting the effort of stabbing them for the fun of it. Most of the kids in the neighborhood knew I was a cop, which seemed to deter them from getting into trouble around here.

Slashes were vertical and close to the top. This had anger and female scorn written all over it.

"I have to call this in."

Erin nodded. "Will I be able to get them fixed?"

I wanted to squeeze the fuck out of my cell as I dialed dispatch. "No. We have to buy new ones."

"It's Sunday," her voice broke. "I can't let my father know about this. If I have it towed back to his dealership he'll never let me hear the end of it. He needs to stay focused on getting my mom through the funerals. Maybe I can call Rudy to come with the flatbed."

My molars were starting to hurt. I didn't know who the fuck Rudy was, but Hell would have to completely freeze over before I let some other guy take care of this. "Yeah, this is Detective Adam Trent, I need a unit dispatched to my residence."

I could see the stress taking its toll on Erin as I moved my motorcycle into the corner. "Once we file a report, I'm going to pull your car in here and then I'll take the tires off. I want it garaged while we're gone."

Nikki had definitely crossed the fucking line with this one.

Erin watched me work, and I was thankful she wasn't asking questions or bitching out loud like most women would do, even though she had every right to pitch a fit. I risked a glance at her. "Why don't you go inside? Go get warm."

With a simple shake of her head, she declined and instead, wrapped her arms around herself, braving the cold.

I set my tools down and stepped between her knees, needing her to know I was here, sharing the burden. Knowing she was upset was driving me crazy. Knowing someone did this damage because of me was pushing me toward a blinding rage. "You're shivering."

"I'm okay. I just… I don't understand. I work so hard."

I knew she was close to crying. "Look at me. I'm going to fix this." The pain I saw in her eyes slayed me.

"Who would do something like that? Why?"

My list of possible suspects was short. "Because some people just have too much ugly in them, Erin." The burn of guilt rolled up into my throat. My inattention to detail had put her in harm's way. It was a mistake I'd never let happen again.

Red and blue lights bounced off the back window of my garage. I tucked her cold hand in mine as I walked her out into the driveway to meet the arriving squad car.

SHE RESTED HER forehead against the window as I backed my truck out of the garage. Her car looked just as wounded as she did, though only one of them was propped up on jacks and missing two wheels.

"Do you think your ex did this?" she finally asked, rolling her fingertip through the mist clouding the edge of her window.

Good question. I pressed the Bluetooth button on my steering wheel. "Call Nikki cell."

Erin's attention whipped my way but I ignored her concern and her disapproving glare.

"Adam?" Nikki's surprised greeting threw me for a second, making me question my level of hostility. My jaw clenched. No, this was just another one of her tricks, manipulating the situation to her advantage.

Just hearing her phony bullshit made me borderline homicidal. "You crossed the fucking line today, Nikki."

"Are you serious?" Nikki's disembodied sigh was annoying. "You never answer your phone. How else am I supposed to talk to you?"

My hands tightened around the steering wheel. "You wanted my attention; you *got* my fucking attention now. Your childish stunt was totally uncalled for. I just filed a police report on the damage."

"Oh my God, what damage? I rang your doorbell. *You* knocked the picture off the wall when you pushed *me* out the door, remember? Can you be any more melodramatic?"

"Melodramatic? After what you did?"

"Jesus. I didn't do anything. You broke that ugly-ass picture, not me."

"Do *not* fucking lie to me, Nik. Not now. I'm in no mood."

"Why are you so pissed? It wasn't even worth ten bucks. Jees, Adam. Arrest me."

"You know exactly why I'm calling."

"*You* may think so. What's got your panties in a twist? Did your new piece of ass find your bag of ropes and shit and leave you or something?"

I bit back my reaction to tear her apart, but the loud rumble that erupted from my throat was something I had no control over. It'd been coming out of me the entire last year of our relationship. Still, my need to wound her surfaced. "She's not as shallow as you, Nik."

"Shallow? Nice, Adam. Thanks for that. Well, maybe you can tell me why you're so pissed and being such an asshole to me again, because despite what you think *I don't* know what you're talking about."

"Don't play dumb with me. You know exactly what I'm talking about. I thought slashing tires was something you and your bitch posse did in high school. You're lucky I don't press criminal charges."

"For what? I didn't do anything. Are you accusing me of something? Because if you expect me to apologize for coming over to *my* old house to see you, you're crazy," she snapped. "Being on TV has gone to your head. You think everyone is out get you, like it's all about what Adam is doing. That's your problem. You only care about yourself. Our friends are going to be laughing at me at Ellie's wedding and you don't even care."

Nikki's ploy was making me lose my temper in front of Erin, and although I knew there might be a possibility that one day Erin might see me lose my shit, today was definitely not going to be that day.

Nikki may have made it a personal goal to bring out my mean side but Erin most certainly did not. And through months of counseling with my fucking therapist I'd come to realize that my uncontrollable anger was a form of poison that had no business in my life.

I had a choice: let the shit fester and eat at me or figure out a better way of handling the never-ending mountain of bullshit. The festering had caused the binge drinking, my way of seeking some semblance of peace in the constant turmoil. But times like these, it would be just so easy to explode. I took a leveling breath.

"If you feel people are going to laugh at you, then don't come to their wedding. I don't give a shit. Is that why you sliced two very expensive tires on the car in my driveway?"

"Wait. What? Somebody slashed your new whore's tires? And you think I did it? Hah. Wow. Um... Ellie told me things were getting bad with the fans harassing the unit but I didn't believe her. Oh well... Maybe your new pussy should be careful or she may get hurt."

It took everything in me not to point my truck toward Nikki's apartment and call in an extra unit for backup. "Careful, Nik. You know I don't deal with threats. And we both know who's to blame here. I know you did it and I'm telling you right now, this shit repeats and I will not be gentle."

"I didn't do it, all right? I've been at my sister's shop all day, right after you tossed me out, so quit accusing me. You're the one with the psycho fans, not me. Probably one of them did it. I told you doing that show was a stupid fucking idea but you never listened to me. You think some new girl is going to put up with that kind of bullshit? I mean, I know how to handle it but it's not for everyone, especially when they see how dangerous your life is. How many nights I worried that you might get shot on the job. That's hard for a woman to deal with. I still worry about you, baby."

"I'm a doctor. I'll fix him if he gets hurt," Erin snapped. "And he's not your baby anymore."

I almost slammed on the brakes, hearing Erin speak her mind. I knew she had teeth but unlike Nikki, Erin was reserved.

"Oh, you think so, bitch? Let me tell you—"

"Enough!" I cut Nikki off. "Stay off my property. Do not come to my house anymore. I catch you sniffing around and I'll have you arrested for trespassing. We clear?"

"Whatever, Adam," Nikki snipped back. "It's just a matter of time 'til you get tired of this one and come running back to me. You always do. You'll never love—"

I killed the phone connection. *Fucking delusional bitch.*

Erin crossed her arms as though she was just getting started to let Nikki have it. I rested my hand on Erin's thigh; the spark from feeling her budding possessiveness swelled in my chest and snuffed out all of Nikki's bullshit. I could also clearly see that Nikki's words were marinating around in Erin's brain.

"What she said, it's not going to happen." I knew enough about how women think, and the crinkles around Erin's eyes meant she needed reassurance. I glanced over at her, making sure she saw the truth in my words.

Erin's little nod of assent wasn't very convincing, well, to me at least it wasn't. I took her hand in mine, giving it a squeeze, trying to keep her walls from slamming me out. I relaxed a bit more when her fingers tightened around mine.

"I'm starting to think your ex is not a very nice person."

Understatement. I laughed. "She's not."

"She also seems to go from one emotional extreme to another. Is she... do you know if she's on drugs?"

Erin's astute perceptions amazed me. "She's ah... she's actually mildly bipolar. She's supposed to take meds every day but, well, I'm not her keeper." I looked over my shoulder for merging traffic.

"I heard you earlier this morning when you had your argument at your house. Is she doing illegal stuff?"

"Don't know, and honestly? I don't care."

Erin cleared her throat. "Was she your first love?"

I wasn't prepared for that but my answer came quickly and with absolute assurance. "No."

It was hard to make Erin see my sincerity while driving in traffic. The truth was that even though I may have said those three little words to women in the past none of them brought out this side of me before. Just being in Erin's powerful but unassuming presence made me want to be a better man, though my spinning thoughts were churning my jealousy. "You ever tell some guy that you love him?"

Erin's fingers flexed but never released their hold. "Yes. Once." She stared at our hands on her lap; a weak smile twitched her lips but the sadness there was as plain as day. "He didn't say it back."

Fuck. Guy must have been a total idiot and asshole.

She scratched a fingernail over her bottom lip and I could see she was trying to rally back to happier thoughts. "And you?"

If we weren't doing sixty on a major roadway I would have pulled over and kissed the sadness right off that bottom lip. Then I'd kiss the top one just for good measure. "Nope, never told another dude that I loved him, unless we're counting family, then I'm probably guilty of saying it a few times."

Erin tugged my arm. "That's not what I meant."

At least I gave her a piece of her smile back. "I know." I put my thoughts to getting us safely into the right lane to turn into the mall instead of her expectant retort. The tire store would be closing in thirty minutes. Her fingers clenched around mine again—a silent urging for me to get back to point—but there was no good way of answering that question.

No woman ever wants to hear that she might be the third or fourth recipient of "I love you" and I sure as hell wasn't going to spoil it for her.

I couldn't.

I wouldn't.

I gave her hand a gentle squeeze. "Past is the past. You being here should tell you how all that worked out. Let's just leave it at that, okay?" I pulled her hand to my mouth when she nodded. The simple brush of her skin on my lips sent visions of a dozen beautiful possibilities with her, each one deserving my undivided exploration.

I cut across the vast mall parking lot to get to the tire store. We were running low on time and I needed to focus on the goal. Erin sifted through her purse and pulled out her wallet.

"Okay, good," she muttered to herself.

I spotted the credit card in her hand. Did she really think that I wouldn't take care of this? Her lack of faith in me was maddening. "Put it away." I don't know why her brows knit together, questioning me. I parked in a spot near the entrance. "You don't need it."

"But I need it to buy new ones."

"Erin." This day had stressed the limits of my patience, and if she thought I'd allow her to pay for the damage, she was crazy.

Her mouth popped open slightly, no doubt to dispute my intentions, but the glare I gave her needed no explanation. "I know you're independent and self-reliant but this here," I waved my hand between us, "changes that."

Erin leaned back into her seat and sighed, resigning only so far. "I don't expect you to pay for the tires, Adam. It's my car. They're probably going to be expensive."

I took a calming breath, not wanting to argue and needing to choose my words carefully so I didn't come off as an asshole. "You're missing the point. You get a flat while going to work, I'll take you for a new tire or I'll plug it myself. You have shit damaged on *my watch* and at *my house*, that is not yours to fix, it's mine."

"I appreciate that but I've never been a user, Adam. I don't expect you to pay for everything. That's not how this works. The tires... What happened—it's not your fault. You're not responsible. I'm not—"

I cut her off. "I get that, Doc. It's easy to see you aren't a taker and I respect the hell out of that. If you were, believe me, we wouldn't even be having this conversation. But it's my job to make sure you're safe and protected and *that is* my responsibility. And I hear ya, but it still doesn't change things between us or that I want you to put your credit card away."

Her eyes widened briefly and then narrowed, assessing her options. "Is that your final answer, Cop?"

I thoroughly enjoyed seeing her bend to my will. That and her tease amused me to no end. "Yes."

"I take it you usually get your way once you flash that smile."

Usually. "Don't know. Why, is it working?"

Her answering smile was quite seductive. "Like you have to ask."

No, I didn't. I'd learned a long time ago how to sway life with a bit of charm. All the Trent boys knew the tricks, born with smiles that worked like magic. Where Michael's techniques were slow and stealthy, Jason's sway tactics were almost lethal. My little brother could bend the toughest of nails with little effort. Kyle used his charm to separate hundreds of girls from their underwear. I turned mine Erin's way. "Not really, but it's still nice to hear. And now that I know it works on you, I'll be unleashing it quite often."

"That's not fair."

Her pout was adorable. "All's fair in love and war, sweetheart."

The moment the "L" word slipped out of my mouth, I froze. I caught Erin shifting slightly in her seat, undoubtedly drawing her own conclusions.

Shit. Should I do damage control? What would I say? Asshole. Say nothing or you'll just dig a deeper hole. I shoved the gear shift into park. "Your smile is pretty potent too, you know."

My cell started to ring over the system on my dash. Once again, no number was showing.

"You need to take that?" Erin asked.

I shut my ringer off and shoved it in my pocket. "They can leave me a message."

Squaring Erin away was the only thing on my mind.

CHAPTER 17
Erin

I WAS STILL furiously pissed off by the time I pulled onto my street. I parked at the very edge of my driveway, held the wheel with both hands, and cursed the mounds of snow blocking my way.

I closed my eyes and turned the stereo up. Every word, every note playing through the speakers wrapped perfectly around renewed thoughts of Adam and the two amazing days we'd spent together this weekend. It was as if I could find bits and pieces of him in each song, but it still wasn't enough to calm my raging anger.

Knowing someone was out there with so much contempt in their heart to commit such a violent act as flattening my tires became secondary to the conversation I'd just had with Doctor Sam Wilson in his office.

I'd waited for him to finish his Monday morning staff meeting before asking to speak with him privately. The second I posed my question about the fellowship, I felt foolish for even asking. I knew the committee wouldn't be meeting for a few more weeks and yet I allowed that bitch Mandy to poison my mind with her false bravado. Randy had apparently gotten his information from an unreliable source.

Sam confirmed my suspicions that no decisions had been made and that the likelihood of both of us getting denied for the program was unlikely, though he again did his best to convince me that emergency medicine was where I belonged. This information was the driving force that had me storming down to Radiology. I knew I shouldn't be reacting emotionally as nothing good ever came from that approach, but the scorned part of me demanded instant retribution.

Fortunately for one of us, Mandy wasn't in. Neither was my ex, Randy. The bastard who'd said he'd cover shifts for me so I could attend to my family's double tragedy decided to take several days of vacation. How convenient. Proof once again that his words weren't even worth the air that he wasted expelling them.

All of this emotional upheaval was exhausting. So was the eight inches of crusty snow waiting to be shoveled out of my driveway.

I retrieved my shovel and started clearing a path, finding the task and chilled air mind-numbing. Each heavy load had me wishing for a snow blower or a strong boyfriend willing to dig me out of this snow-covered world.

Adam.

I could still feel his passionate kisses echo on my lips, the feel of his incredible back muscles and ass under my hands as he ground his hips into me over and over again, making me slightly sore in all the right places. After another ten hours on my feet, two hours of lecture and meetings, and now moving heavy snow, I was feeling Adam's mark deep in my muscles.

I tossed another shovel full of snow while the lingering memories of his presence manifested into my achy thighs. If his actions this weekend were any indication, he'd given me plenty of reassurance that he was into me. Way into me. I couldn't hide my renewed smile, even though anyone watching me grinning like an idiot probably thought I'd finally lost my mind.

Maybe I could convince Adam into taking a look at my broken garage door, although my days living here were probably numbered. Surely my cousins would be forced to liquidate all of their parents' assets once they started divvying up the estate. I dreaded the idea of packing and moving into a new place, as finding a place like this within my budget would be difficult.

After fifteen minutes of pushing snow, my muscles were starting to revolt. I was halfway up my snow-covered front walkway when Adam's black truck gunned down the street, grinding to a halt over the salt and cinders behind my parked car.

He came directly from work to see me? Oh my God, he did!

I felt like jumping up and down with delight. I kept my abundant giddiness in check but couldn't keep my happy smile hidden. He made me feel so fucking alive.

"Hey you," I called out to him.

My smile dropped, watching his body move with concerned purpose. He was still in full ATTF uniform, clad all in black down to his scary black gun and attitude. I'd seen enough sides of him to know when he was unhappy and the scowl he was wearing wasn't budging as he trudged up over the slushy snow.

He stepped up onto the front landing.

"Hey. You okay?" I asked, rising up on my toes to give him a kiss hello. I'd had his mouth all over me for the last two days; I figured we were at least at the *kissing hello in public* stage.

His lips were rigid and barely gave me a proper greeting, though I did get a short "hey" out of him. I pulled my keys out of my pocket. "I didn't expect to see you today."

Adam held my glass storm door open, gazing down at me. "No?"

His one word held a bit of a bite. Worry rattled right through me, causing my hand to tremble slightly when I tried to get the key into the lock.

"Is there a problem?"

"You're making me nervous."

His chest pressed into my back, his hand covered mine. He held my hand steady and slid the key into place. "You should be," he whispered ominously.

I almost fell into my entryway.

I set my gloves down and saw him out of the corner of my eye, staring me down as he locked my front door.

I debated taking my coat off. "Are you hungry? I can make some breakfast."

Adam stopped in front of me. "Don't need food right now, Doc." He snagged my hip. His other hand twisted around my disheveled ponytail, tugging gently to tilt my chin up. "Seems as though I have to refresh your memory," he grumbled, alternating between giving my eyes and my lips his heated glare.

Just as I was starting to say I didn't understand, his mouth cut my words off. I'd definitely misread his look before.

That wasn't anger. It was absolute determination. His tongue making its point to clarify.

Adam backed me into the wall and shrugged his heavy black coat off, never breaking our kiss. Deft hands stripped me right out of mine. My coat slid down the wall, pooling behind my calves.

"Show me your bedroom, Doc."

It was hard to swallow.

He seized my hips and then one hand slid around to cup my ass. His mouth was unrelenting. "Either you lead or I will carry you."

Having a cop in full cop garb following me up my steps was slightly nerve-wracking. He had his gun strapped in its holster on his hip with his array of cop stuff dotting his utility belt. We barely passed the threshold of my bedroom when Adam stopped me, turned me, and grabbed the hem of my top.

"Scrubs have to go, Doc." One fast tug and it was up and off. I wanted to reach for the gold badge he had hanging from a chain around his neck, but he wasn't to be deterred from his mission.

Adam slid his hand across my neck, dug his fingers into my hair, and seared my lips with a kiss so powerful I forgot how to breathe. I had to grab his arms to keep from falling over.

"Turn around," he ordered.

He held my shoulders back, pressing me to his chest, rasping pinprick tickles from his shadowed beard over my skin.

Soft nips on my collarbone.

"Remember my mouth on you?"

Teeth scraped over my neck.

"Not liking your short-term memory, Doc."

His confusing statement pulled me out of my dreamy haze. "What?"

Hands squeezed both of my breasts, kneading, pinching until my nipples were achingly hard.

"I'm gonna fuck you until you have no memory of anything else."

Sounds perfect. "Want to take a shower first?"

His tongue marked a spot before his teeth grazed me. "No."

Not the answer I was hoping for. "I just worked twelve hours. I'm feeling dirty, Adam."

Ten strong fingers rolled down my back and opened my bra, discarding it to the floor. "You're about to get a whole lot dirtier.

We'll take a shower later."

His hands returned to teasing my breasts. *God, that feels good.*

"You trust me?"

Did I?

"Yes."

His right hand drifted away while he placed sensual kisses my shoulder. I heard a snap pop and then something metallic jingled. He had my wrists gripped behind my back and within seconds, before I'd realized what he had done or could properly fight it, I was handcuffed.

"Adam," I began to protest, feeling the bite of cold steel.

He wrapped me in a protective hold. "Shhh, it's okay. I want you to trust me and this is just another step. I'd never hurt you, Erin. Never." He kissed my neck then grazed his teeth. "You have nothing to fear."

"Am I under arrest?"

His hands returned to torturing my nipples. "Not under arrest, just being detained for questioning."

So apparently my moody cop liked kink. Still, I was unconvinced. "Questioning?"

He rolled, pinched, and pulled, sending pulsating waves right into my vagina.

"Yes, but first I need you to know something."

It was hard to concentrate. "What?"

"I'd never hurt you. I'd never put you at risk of getting hurt either. No matter what. Okay?"

Adam had been super gentle with me the entire weekend, giving me no cause for worry. I had no choice but to give him the benefit of the doubt, so I nodded.

He pulled harder, ebbing toward a wee bit of pain. It felt even better than what he'd been doing before. "I want to hear your words, Doc. We have to be on the same page here. Do you trust me?"

He had me so hot and bothered, almost to the point of panting. "Yes. Yes, I trust you."

"Good," he whispered on my neck.

I was trusting that he wouldn't give me a hickey.

He pulled away for a moment and I heard the rustle of snaps and clothes, and then something heavy thumped onto the floor. Then his warmth returned; his chest pressed up against me.

His pants rasped over my palms; his erection strained inside.

"Feel that?"

Yes. Yes, I most certainly could feel that.

Adam pulled his zipper down and a moment later I had hot veined hardness brushing over my hands. I tried to wrap my hand around him; I wanted more.

"I see your memory is coming back," he hissed, flexing his hips to glide through my fingers.

"How could I ever forget? You've been on my mind all night. It was virtually impossible to think of anything else."

Adam's hand slid up the column of my throat, his teeth nipped at my jaw. "Oh really?" he muttered. "That so?"

I managed to cup his tightened balls, rolling them around in my fingers, knowing that would make him shudder too.

"Yes. One of my patients caught me zoning out."

He pushed the length of his erection up through my hand, tisking at me in the process. "I was worried you'd forgotten me already."

I gripped him harder. "Impossible."

"Then why didn't you answer my calls?"

My eyes opened. He was a guy who called afterward. This was a major revelation. "You called?"

Adam's embrace tightened. "Sent you a text and called you but got your voice mail. Thought you'd call me back."

Of all times to go to work without it. "I didn't have my phone." He pinched and pulled my nipples, twisting them with just enough pressure to ebb on pleasurably painful.

God, how I love that.

"Oh really?"

I gasped from the sensations, only able to nod. "It's, oh fuck that feels good. It's over there, on my nightstand. I... I forgot it last night."

I felt his gaze shift as he rolled his cheek over the back of my head.

It was becoming hard to breathe. "I was so busy thinking of other things that I went to work without it."

I heard him take a relieving sigh and mutter something unintelligible under his breath. "I'm going to make you come so hard, Doc. Kick your sneakers off."

I used my toes to peel them away.

Adam made quick work of removing my scrub bottoms and underwear, leaving me standing in nothing but white ankle socks and handcuffs.

He pulled the laces on his black boots, kicked them off, and tossed the pair near my dresser. His cargos landed next to his utility belt.

I held my foot out, needing help. "Socks?"

"You can keep them on. I'd hate for you to get cold feet."

The handcuffs were uncomfortable and brought back all sorts of unwanted memories. "Okay. Are you going to take these off of me now?" Viewing a very naked Adam in my bedroom made my skin hot.

He grasped my upper arms somewhat forcefully and tenderly kissed my shoulder. "No." It was direct and absolute and very much non-negotiable.

It was hard to swallow. "How am I…?" I was trying to work out the logistics of how we'd have fantastic sex with my arms pinned behind me when Adam crossed his forearm over my chest and slid his fingernails up my throat. His other hand cupped me, locking me in place and rendering me immobile while he explored.

"That's not for you to worry about," he whispered. His index finger drifted over my mouth and bottom lip, silencing me.

His actions made my legs open farther, willing him to take whatever he wanted. My head fell back onto his chest while he turned me into a panting mess.

"Feel me," he said, swirling his fingers back and forth and around in circles. My breathing became more sporadic, labored, feeling and thinking about nothing but what he was doing to me. "I know what you need. You never have to question that."

My knees began to quiver.

Strong thighs nudged the backs of mine; the dusting of hair on his legs tickling where they touched. "On the bed, Doc."

I did as he requested and fumbled my way, noting his eyes narrowing—almost daring me to speak—when I opened my mouth. It wasn't an easy fete to maneuver without the use of my hands.

My arms hung slightly off the mattress when I finally managed to lie on my side.

"Look at me," he requested, brushing the hair off my face.

I had no doubts this man was working his way to becoming the center of my world. That in itself was unsettling.

His kiss was filled with passion and promise, needing me just as much as I needed him. Maybe even more. The rest of my stress and worries withered away when his hand spread my thighs apart.

Oh, God.

"That's it, ride my fingers."

He was unrelenting. His mouth, his mastery and attention to detail… it didn't take long for him to unravel me. The massive orgasm slammed into me, taking away my ability to breathe. His hand continued to work, getting every last shudder out of me, until I couldn't take it anymore.

The bed jostled as he rolled away and then he dug into his pile of belongings on the floor.

His glorious muscular frame made my mouth water. So did his unattended erection. I felt it brush over my fingertips when he opened the handcuffs.

Adam relieved one wrist, gently massaging it between his hands. He leaned over me and took my mouth again, giving me a devilish smile. My right arm was guided toward the headboard and then he cuffed me to the rail.

"Adam." I heard my own voice crack as I tugged on the handcuffs.

He stroked his erection and then tore a foil condom packet open. "Shh. I'm not done with you yet. Just curbing your tendency to run from me." He winkled. He climbed over me and caged me in with his formidable presence.

I swallowed hard. "I'm not running."

His nose brushed over mine. "That's because I've taken your choices away." He placed the softest of kisses on my lips and then looked me dead in the eyes as he parted my thighs, making himself right at home. He didn't stop until he was fully seated inside me, rending all the breath from my lungs.

I thought about my penchant for walking away instead of fighting for what I wanted, for the man that I wanted. I gazed up into his glorious face while he showed me all those things that words could not convey. His intensity as he rolled his hips into me, making me feel protected and adored. It made me realize that Adam was a man worth fighting for.

ADAM UNCUFFED ME and gently massaged my wrist, placing tender kisses on the slight redness that appeared from me twisting and tugging while he made love to me. This encounter between us was quite different from the weekend. Perhaps it was the added kink of the handcuffs that made it so much more erotic and exciting.

Regardless, I thoroughly enjoyed it. For once I didn't have a guy fumbling, mumbling that lame "do you like that, baby?" crap while trying to figure out how to pleasure me. That was such a turn off. Adam never asked; he didn't require me to tell him what I wanted or needed.

He just knew.

I don't know how he just knew, but he did.

Adam gave. He took. He didn't need instructions or me calling out orders and orchestrating the team effort to eliminate the chaos and potential errors.

And that's the moment I realized I was more relaxed than I had been in years. The man lying on the pillow next to me, working on calming his own erratic heartbeat, was simply amazing.

He gave me a sweet kiss, then rolled off the bed and headed into my bathroom. I took great pleasure in watching his muscular ass indent as he discarded the used condom.

How'd I get so lucky?

"Doc," he leaned out of the doorway, "Shower? Or are you ready to crash?"

There wasn't one muscle in my body willing to move. Even blinking felt like a momentous effort. But my brain, on the other hand, was working overtime, though I still managed to utter, "Sleep."

Adam's lazy smile was devastating when he added it to his casual *naked in my bedroom* swagger. One knee hit the edge of my mattress.

"You look gorgeous all sated like that," he said, grinning down at me, apparently enjoying his mastery of ruining me.

"I had several *amazing* orgasms."

His smile widened. "Good to know."

He climbed back into bed, taking care to tuck us both under the warming layers of blankets. I closed my eyes and tried to ignore my thoughts, but something had been bugging me. "Adam?"

"Hmm?"

"I need to ask you something."

His eyes opened, giving me his full attention.

"Your ex… Nikki…"

His mouth curled down. "Yeah?"

"Yesterday morning she said something about your kinky rope games?" I felt ridiculous for asking.

Adam diverted his attention to the stitches in his palm.

"I didn't mean to eavesdrop. You know that, but I can't help but wonder what she was talking about."

I could see him clearly contemplating how he was going to respond, mulling his answer over carefully.

"She said rope, Adam, more than once. I need to know. Are you into S&M or whatever it's called?"

He snorted. "No. I don't get off inflicting pain on women. I haven't hurt you so far, have I?"

My wrist was only slightly tender, but other than a bit of kinkiness, he hadn't inflicted any pain whatsoever. "No. Well, except for the torture you've put my nipples through."

Adam's devilish smile widened. "You've enjoyed everything I've done to your nipples." He brushed my hair back. "I know you have. I listen to the sounds you make, to the way your fingers grip into my hair, the way your breathing increases and you arch into my touch. Believe me, I'd know if I was hurting you."

He took a measured breath. "Be honest. Did you like the cuffs? It seemed to me like you did but I want to hear it from you."

I nodded. "Yeah. It was strangely liberating."

"Liberating?" His head tilted. "Explain."

That was easier said than done. "I head up trauma teams every day, Adam. I have to be in control of everything, all the time, making decisions, instructing several people, telling them what to do. I don't want to have to dictate what happens during sex. No woman really wants that, well, none of the women that I know do."

"So you liked the cuffs," he deadpanned.

I gave him a nudge. "I've answered that already. Now answer mine."

"Which was?"

Was he stalling on purpose?

Adam took a deep breath and held it a few beats. "Neither of us is ready for that conversation, Doc. Ask me some other time." He patted his hand on my hip, placating me. "Let's get some sleep. I'm tired. You wore me out."

I sat up on my pillows, watching him nestle in deeper and close his eyes. I wasn't happy that he got to be the one to decide that this conversation was over.

Adam sighed again. "Come on, Erin. Don't do this right now. We'll talk about it some other time."

I reached for my cell phone, taking my own stand on the subject. "It seems like a pretty significant topic to me. I let you handcuff me, and, well, that was hard for me to do, so if there's more—"

He gazed up at me. "Really?"

I nodded, not wanting to go into my history with cops handcuffing me and why. I needed that to stay in my buried past. "I think we've made it to a certain level of honesty after that." I checked my missed messages since he seemed resigned to dropping the subject. There was one text from Adam.

One tap on the screen was all it took for him to take my breath away. Five simple words in a gray text bubble.

> Can't stop thinking about you

Adam let out an exasperated breath. "Have you ever heard of Shibari?"

I lowered my cell. "Who?"

He laughed softly. "It's a *what*, Doc, not a *who*."

I considered searching Google. "Um, no."

I lost his gaze for a moment. He leaned up on his elbow and then studied my face. "It's Japanese rope bondage."

My nerves tingled at the myriad of implications those words evoked.

"Before you get all worried, it's not as bad as it sounds."

I set my phone down on the nightstand. "Then explain it to me. You going to make me call you *Master* or something and humiliate me?"

Adam frowned and sat up next to me. "Not into any of that, Erin. Shibari is an art; it's not ass paddles and whips. I'm not into giving or receiving pain, *at all*, so just get that out of your head right now."

He tucked a few pillows behind his back and pulled his knee up, resting it on top of my thigh. "There's a difference between sex and exploring the boundaries of control and surrender with a partner, Doc. Anyone can have meaningless sex. It's nothing more than a physical release without a connection."

I nodded, intrigued by the simple movements of his lips.

"Sometimes sex is mutual; sometimes it's selfish and one-sided. Shibari, on the other hand, is more than that. It's sharing so much more than just the act of sex. It's a give and take."

He studied my face.

"When you're bound, like you *just were* with my cuffs, you put your trust in my hands, knowing I will do everything in my power to make it so much more than just a release. Be honest, did you or did you not just enjoy what we did?"

I had to be truthful, though doing so was almost admitting to liking it dirty. "Honestly, I enjoyed it very much, although it was a bit scary at first."

He gave me a confident grin and then snagged my hip, encouraging me to snuggle down next to him. He laced our hands together. "I can awaken parts of your sexuality you didn't even realize you had," he said. "I don't need you to tell me what you like or don't like. I can tell just how your body reacts under my touch to know what gives you the greatest pleasure. Read you like a book, open you at my whim, just waiting, anticipating my perusal. Will I? Won't I? That's not for you to decide. I take those choices away from you, just like I did earlier. Your part is just to feel and enjoy and know with every fiber of your being that I will take you to places you've never been. Touch you in ways you've never experienced." His eyes leveled on mine. "So to answer your question, Doc, yes, I want to do so much more than just have sex with you. But that will come, I hope, in time. The rest we'll experiment with later, when we're both ready."

I needed to digest all of that while feeling his words settle in my most sensitive places. "So you want someone you can tie up?"

He drifted his lips down the back of my hand. "No, I want you, Erin. But yes, from time to time I would like you to let me take complete control of how you receive your orgasms. Sound doable?"

"Just a little kink?"

"Don't take it to a dark place, babe. It's just a little surrender every now and then."

My body naturally softened. "Then why did Tampon Girl make it sound so horrible?"

Adam chuckled, his gaze warm with his amusement. He pulled the blankets up over us. I laid my face on his arm and cuddled deeper into his chest, my body sated with fantastic sex and heavy with exhaustion and mental overload. Yet, content.

"Because," he said, "*Tampon Girl* has a way of twisting everything and finding a way to be miserable about it. But you…" He folded our hands together and pressed them to his chest. "You are just the opposite."

He kissed me sweetly and slowly, letting me know the depth of his feelings without saying a word.

"One last question," I managed to say.

Adam pulled his face back.

I let my fingers sift through his soft hair. "Is this Shib… rope stuff the extent of it? The truth."

He smiled softly, pressing into my touch like a pampered lion. "It's Shibari, and yes, that and seeing you in my cuffs is about the extent of it. You look worried."

Part of me was.

"Think rope swing, okay? And maybe being tied to my bed for a few hours while I make you come over and over again."

I liked the sound of that very much. "Why rope?"

Adam shoved at the pillow under his head. "I like it. I like the feeling of control it gives me, Erin. I don't know how else to explain it."

I could sense I was making him agitated and I was too tired to properly analyze it all. My fingertip traced the ornate rope tattoo that wrapped his upper arms. It made sense as to why he decorated his body with the symbol that gave him a sense of stability. His spirit was just as vulnerable as mine.

Life, death, crime, control… it was all so very exhausting. I snuggled into him and closed my eyes, but Adam was restless.

"Hey," he said softly.

I stirred. "What?"

"My bed is much more comfortable than yours," he whispered. "Just sayin'."

I smiled, agreeing with him. My old mattress felt like a rock compared to his.

Adam let out a deep yawn.

"Just sayin', Cop?"

He smiled, kissed my forehead, and tucked me back under his chin. "Just sayin', Doc."

CHAPTER 18

Adam

I PULLED MY black cargos on and zipped them, going commando underneath, my cock as deflated and tired as the rest of me. Erin had slept peacefully for about six hours. The first half hour of which I'd just laid there and watched her instead of sleeping.

I'd been too restless, too worried after my disclosure to sleep. Too many variables played out in my mind, all surrounded by one central fear, if I truly self-analyzed it. She'd let me cuff her and surrendered without a fuss, but would she be truly open to taking it further?

I remembered when I first tried to bind Nikki with rope. It was an experiment, an attempt to fix some of the problems we were having. Too many things weren't adding up, leading me to believe she was messing around with someone else behind my back. She'd vehemently denied it and I didn't have solid proof, but once the seed of doubt was planted, it slowly ate at me.

I didn't know what else to do to build the trust back up between us or to give myself a sense of control again. My life had been a speeding train headed on a collision course with an immovable mountain, everything in fast forward and careening out of control.

I needed to find my center, my focus.

I'd practiced Shibari with a few girls back in college; I'd taken classes with local rope bondage artists and, over the years, perfected my techniques until I'd mastered it. It was fun and a hell of a rush, and filled a need inside me that nothing else was able to meet.

When I tried to introduce Nikki to Shibari, she had laughed in my face for a good portion of it, stating repeatedly that I was being a controlling ass amongst other demeaning names. My counselor said I was feeling emasculated. I actually looked it up on Google to see if I could agree with that assessment.

It wasn't too far off the mark, actually.

We'd tried it again a few times after that but each of those encounters had left me more frustrated and fractured than was smart or healthy.

I ran a hand through my wet hair and sat down on Erin's bed to pull my socks on. At least this time I didn't wake up shaking after hearing the echo of gunfire. No, this afternoon I felt pretty fucking fantastic for once.

After stirring Erin with some kisses in bed, I'd woken us both up completely in the shower with some soapy foreplay. Waking with Erin, feeling her hand twine with mine, her naked body resting comfortably against me, I was finding it hard to remember what life was like without this feeling in it.

This was the kind of connection I'd kill somebody to protect.

I'd given her two more orgasms after that and, considering how hard I'd taken her, I highly doubted I could get another erection right now even if I tried.

I knew I'd have to stop by my place and change before driving to the station, but the thought of leaving Erin had me dragging my feet. Throwing an extra change of clothes in my truck would definitely be in order.

"You want some dinner?" Erin asked, slipping a pair of pale blue panties up her legs and under the towel she had wrapped around her.

What I really wanted was to crawl back in bed and make a blanket out of her naked body. Since that wasn't an option, I supposed nourishment was in order.

"Sounds good. What time you have to be at the hospital?" We both looked at her alarm clock.

"I've got almost two hours."

I rubbed the sore spot blooming on my elbow. Her fucking tub shower was so narrow it wasn't even funny. I'd really whacked it good, catching the corner of the interior towel bar. Trying to fuck her properly in there wasn't easy, and after I almost busted the damn glass in its track, we gave up, finished showering, and I took her back on her bed.

I could still taste her flavor on my tongue, which was something I hoped would last a few hours, at least, to get me through the night. "You find out about your fellowship?"

The astonished look on her face surprised me. "Yeah, I did."

I really wanted Erin to stop going through her laundry basket as seeing her in nothing but a bra and matching undies was turning me on. I lost my heavenly vision when she pulled a tight blue top up over her head.

When she didn't go on, I tugged on her hand until I had her standing in front of me. I nudged her thighs until she was straddled up over my lap, right where I wanted her. "Now then." I held her hips, making sure I had her complete attention. "Tell me."

Erin held my shoulders and then moved them up my neck. I wanted her to feel comfortable with me and I found myself craving it, leaning into her touch.

"You were right. It was bullshit."

Thank God. "Good. And the woman who started it? You confront her?"

"No," she sighed. "She wasn't in. Probably a good thing too because I was really mad. I can't risk getting into trouble at work. I'm trying to convince myself that she's not worth it."

I didn't like the idea of people upsetting her. It pissed me off. "That kind of frustration is good to take out at the range." My cell pinged, probably reminding me of my conference call later tonight with John Turk from the NYPD. I had a lot of shit to do between now and then, but the incredible woman spanning my lap was my top priority. I could tell just by the way her breath was uneven to know there was more to her story. I held her gaze. It was my best interrogation technique. Most females would continue talking if you just gave them your full attention or stared at them until they cracked.

"I should have known better not to believe her," she admitted.

My patience paid off. "You didn't know. It's something that's very important to you."

"My boss keeps trying to convince me to stay in the ER. It would be a huge pay cut to take the fellowship."

"Huge?" I asked.

Her nod was quite confirming.

"What are you going to do?"

Erin shrugged. "Sometimes I'm not sure."

My hands tightened on her hips, wishing I could give her the answer. "Back when I was in college I debated going to law school. I had the grades."

"You wanted to be a lawyer?"

I adjusted her on my lap, rubbing her bare legs resting next to mine. "Considered it for a long time but then when I graduated I had to decide, do I pursue a career capturing them in the act and putting them in jail or do I study my ass off with the hopes of making sure they stay in jail?"

"Well, at least you wouldn't have had the risk of getting wounded."

I felt my stitches tug. "Yeah, but I could have gotten paper cuts."

I loved hearing her laugh.

"They hurt!"

"And they're not covered by most insurances either." She snickered.

I combed her hair back over her shoulder. "My point is that I realized I needed to be where the action is, not sitting behind some desk. I can't stop them sitting on my ass."

I saw her eyes become distant while the contemplation took her attention.

"What's more important to you? You never did tell me why toxicology is a goal."

She tried to climb off my lap.

Evasion. Avoidance. I'd seen all the non-verbal cues before—many times. *Not so fast, sweetheart.* I held her hips and yanked her back. "Talk to me."

I saw the mask cover her features.

"Not much to talk about." She shrugged. "It fascinates me."

I'd interrogated hardened criminals who broke easier than this. I also recognized half truths when I heard them. I thought about pushing for more; it would be easy to play her and get her to confess.

I tried not to get pissed that she was holding back from me. I had to talk myself down before I let the anger invade, because despite what I was feeling, this was new to both of us. In some ways, it made me respect her more. She was so independent, self-contained. I let her climb off of me, but this conversation was far from over. I'd give her time, but eventually I'd break her.

She was quick to want to rip my Band-Aids off. Watching her finish dressing, I silently vowed I'd return the favor and rip all of hers off just the same.

THE LAST TIME I'd kissed Erin, it was Monday early evening and we were both heading our separate ways to go to work. The fact that she worked most nights like I did was fucking beautiful.

It was something I'd feared—getting involved with another woman who would spend her nights loathing me because I was on the clock.

I sat at my desk in the station, handling paperwork and following tips and leads while watching the nighttime sky turn to dusky pink and then to yellow with the rising sun, but maintaining focus on anything for more than ten minutes was sketchy.

I couldn't recall ever missing someone so much that it turned into a physical ache.

I was physically aching to see her again.

We'd talked and shot some texts back and forth but I was trying to play it cool and not turn into some lovesick whipping boy. Every fiber inside me wanted to seek her out while the rational part of my thinking told me to chill and give her space. Around midnight on Tuesday I'd lost my hold and almost begged her to meet me at my place after we both got out of work. It didn't take too much convincing on my part.

I knew it was from the newness of our relationship driving this insurmountable lust but it didn't matter. As soon as her car was safely locked away in my garage and she was in front of me again, I had her out of her clothes. I had my cock in her by the time we got to my living room, fucking her over the arm of my leather chair. I'd chased her up the stairs soon after that and flipped her around on my bed while pounding in and out of her like a starving lunatic.

And now I was finally at peace, holding her head in the crook of my elbow while enjoying her incredible mouth on mine.

"I missed you," I confessed. Fuck it, the words just rolled out so I might as well be honest.

She smiled and tangled her fingers in my hair, needing my mouth just as much.

"I missed you, too," she said softly, sucking on my upper lip.

"I didn't sleep for shit yesterday," I added. *Fuck*, I was turning into a lovesick sap, divulging my weaknesses. No wonder I lost so much money when I played poker with the guys.

Erin nuzzled her face on my shoulder. "I passed out reading Molecular and Biochemical Toxicology."

Even the words were too much for my brain to take in right now. "Is that like porn for doctors?"

She squeezed me for being a smartass. "Yes. It even has pictures and graphs."

"Ooh," I teased, then kissed her forehead for being so smart and perfect.

"You find out anything from your informant?"

"Are we talking shop in bed?"

Erin gripped my bare ass. "Yes, Detective. You're purging."

I grinned. "I just purged inside you five minutes ago. You need more purging? Because we can see about bumping you up to a fourth orgasm."

I felt her smile on my skin. "Will I have to move?"

"Participation *is* encouraged."

Erin answered me with laugh that turned into a deep yawn.

I pulled the sheets up over her shoulders. "I think I'll let you rest."

"You wore me out," she said, snuggling in deeper. "And you didn't answer my question."

"Talked to him yesterday. Got me a lead on a suspect who's supposedly been boosting cars for Mancuso. We're going to set up a bait car next week. See if we can lure in a thief."

"Bait car?"

"Yeah. DEA has a few high end cars that were seized in recent investigations. We're setting up two of them with tracking and surveillance equipment. It's really cool. Everything's computerized. We can control the entire operation remotely, record footage of the driver, even shut the car down and lock him inside with the click of a key. We need to get someone within the organization to work as an informant."

"You love your job, don't you?" She grinned.

I pulled her back up to my mouth with my arm. "I do. Very much."

Erin's little follow-up kiss on my chest resonated all through me.

"What about your night, Doc?"

She shrugged. "Nothing to talk about," she murmured.

"Nothing?"

"It would bore you to death and then I'd have to revive you."

"So you've got nothing to share?"

She closed her eyes and let out a sigh. "No."

Guess she was done purging; too bad the only thing she purged was me.

CHAPTER 19
Erin

DECORATIVE VICTORIAN LAMPS hung from the statuesque pillars outside Baylor Funeral Home, illuminating the evening sky with a soft, ethereal glow. It was as if they were trying to soften the dread building in my stomach with a false sense of serenity.

Adam backed his truck into a spot at the edge of the parking lot near a sedan I didn't recognize, but directly in front of us next to the walkway was my dad's current dealership car. I stared at the *Novak Ford* emblem instead of the other apparitions violently swirling about in my thoughts.

I felt Adam's gaze. "You okay?"

My heart swelled even more, taking in the breathtaking sight of him dressed up in a new suit and tie. I brushed my fingertips over his freshly shaven jaw. His familiar cologne scented the air, wrapping me in a sensually comforting cocoon. I was so glad he was here with me, just like he had promised. "You are so handsome, and you smell really good, too."

Adam's smile warmed me. "Glad you like it. I couldn't decide between Smelly Garbage or Wet Dog. I went with Wet Dog."

I burst out laughing. "That's from, from, from Monsters, Inc., right?"

He winked at me. "Figured I'd be meeting your family tonight, so I thought I should smell it up."

I snorted. "That's funny, Cop."

"You know once you name it you'll start getting attached to it."

300

My belly actually started to hurt, but in a good way. "Is that your favorite movie?"

Adam shrugged. "One of them."

"I love that movie too, although *The Incredibles* is still my favorite. 'I never look back, darling, it distracts from the now'." I took a few sobering breaths after our mutual laugh. "You're going to meet my family at a viewing. My mother is never going to forgive me."

He captured my hand and pressed it to his lips. "You worry too much."

As soon as he released me, he gently nudged my elbow so he could get into his center console. I watched him pluck several tissues out of a box, fold them, and slip them into his suit pocket. The console lid fell back in place with a thud. "Ready?"

My chest felt heavy as I nodded. There was no delaying the inevitable.

Adam held my hand as we ascended the five steps up to the front entryway. I tugged my black skirt into place.

"You look beautiful," he said, pausing to kiss my cheek before opening the ornate door.

I can do this, I chanted silently, taking his warm hand in mine.

"You lead," Adam murmured, though he never wavered from my side.

I signed my name in the guest book resting on the podium next to a lavish floral arrangement. The sickly sweet scent from the roses perfumed the air, churning my stomach from their attempts to disguise the smell of embalming fluid. Adam swallowed noticeably when I handed the pen to him. He hesitated, nodded once, and then signed his name under mine.

Even though we were fifteen minutes early, a line had already formed. Several people held conversations; a few hugged and rubbed hands over backs in solidarity. I spotted my sister, Kate, wiping a tear from her eye as she chatted with some friends of the family.

She looked thinner, as though her inner mourning had wilted her somehow. The moment she spotted me, she politely excused herself and rushed over to me. I pulled my sister into my arms, feeling her sadness mirroring my own.

"Oh, E." She sniffled on my neck.

I squeezed her harder, wishing I could take on her pain, too. My baby sister had endured enough obstacles in her life; she didn't need any more. "I know, hon." I swept Kate's blonde hair back so I wouldn't cry on it.

That's when I noticed three distinct black and blue marks in a vertical line up her neck.

"What are these? What happened?"

Kate quickly backed away and covered her neck. "Oh, it's nothing," she dismissed. "Struggled with ah… an animal… a dog during labs."

"A dog?"

Kate nodded and scanned the growing line of mourners. "He was a handful. Got me good."

Her feigned disinterest was what gave her away. I hated pretenses, especially from her. I glanced around, trying to spot her current boyfriend, the one that made me tense up the moment I met him. "Is Prick here with you?"

"Prick?" Adam questioned.

Kate flit her eyes, incensed. "His name is Nick."

My sister may be brilliant veterinarian in training but she was a lousy actress and a worse liar than I was. "And no, he's not. He, um, has a paper due. I drove up by myself this morning."

My sadness turned to angered disappointment hearing that her boyfriend couldn't adjust his own agenda to support her. I reached for her shoulder. "Kate."

She brushed me of and fixed her silk scarf so it would cover her neck, and then wiped under her eyes. "I'm serious. Stop looking at me like that. It was a dog. Mom's been waiting for you to get here. She's a mess. They had Aunt Karen cremated and put her remains in with Uncle Cal's body." She shivered and then became entranced by Adam.

"Kate, this is my… Adam. Adam, my sister, Kate."

Adam offered his hand and a warm smile. "Nice to meet you, Kate. I'm her Adam."

Kate smiled shyly, letting her long bangs drop over the scar that ran from her temple to her cheek. Her coping mechanism instantly reminded me of my failures.

"Nice to meet you, Erin's Adam." She eyed me speculatively. "I didn't know you had an Adam, sis."

I hadn't told anyone I was dating him; why set false hope? "I just got him a couple of days ago."

Her eyebrows rose.

I went for distracted levity. "Macy's was having a sale."

Adam laughed lightly and recaptured my hand in his.

Kate's eyes followed his gesture, her smile wavering. "And you didn't get one for me? Lousy sister."

"I was the floor model. She got a discount," Adam joked.

It almost felt sacrilegious to be sharing a small laugh at a funeral.

Kate scanned him from head to toe. I could read her mind as clearly as my own. "I'd say she got quite a bargain. Have Mom and Dad met your Adam yet?"

I shook my head. "Not yet."

Kate gazed up at him again. "And you're meeting our parents for the first time at a funeral?"

Adam shrugged and gave me his attention. "Seems so."

"You wouldn't happen to have any single brothers, or do I have to run to Macy's?"

Adam squeezed my fingers. "I've got three single brothers, actually."

"Three?" she said, her voice etched with hope.

I don't think she was expecting that answer. "I can't let Nick ever know that." Her hand shook a bit, reaching back up to fuss with her scarf.

I immediately started cataloging her appearance and outward symptoms. I hadn't seen her in a few months, but she surely would have told Mom if she'd had another seizure. "Have you been feeling okay?"

"Huh? Um, yeah. Yeah," she stammered and then blanched that I'd even ask.

I caught Adam scrutinizing her too, though I suppose there were detectives ingrained in both of us. I could see our concern was making her uncomfortable. She was retreating into her own protective bubble. I was used to it, as it was a trait we both shared. Adam, however, was surely questioning my sister's demeanor.

"Mom will want to know you're here."

"Maybe we should get in line," Adam suggested, motioning with his head.

"I'll see you in there then," Kate murmured. "It was nice meeting you, Adam." She quickly leaned in to kiss me on the cheek, barely making eye contact with Adam as she hurried back through the pillared threshold.

Adam was quite cordial and charismatic as we made small talk with the older couple in front of us. It was easier to distract myself that way then to watch my mom sitting front and center across from Uncle

Cal's open casket, weeping.

The burn in my throat was becoming unmanageable.

Adam put his arm around my shoulders and turned me so I was facing the heavy floral draperies instead.

I took a calming breath when I felt his lips press into my forehead.

"Thank you for being here."

He leaned his ear closer. "Sorry. What?"

I looked into his eyes, hoping with every fiber of my soul that his sweetness wasn't just a cruel ruse. "Thank you for being here."

His receptive smile warmed me but then it quickly faltered. "No problem."

I leaned into him and chewed on my thumbnail, wishing I could disappear into the protectiveness of his broad chest.

Adam shuffled us forward a few steps and pulled my hand from my mouth, holding me firmly by the wrist. "You keep gnawing like that you're going to make yourself bleed."

But I was frustrated and bordering on emotional overload. "There's something fundamentally wrong with how we parade ourselves past the dead like this."

"I know," Adam murmured and rubbed my shoulder. "It's all about closure. Sometimes it's just not enough."

I studied everything while trying not to focus on the gleaming black casket adorned with an abundant spray of red and white roses. As soon as I spotted it, the ripping sorrow came back with renewed force.

I got that we needed to have closure; we need to have that final moment where denial and anger turns into acceptance, but for many, including myself, this experience was like pouring acid into the gaping wound.

Adam nudged me again to move us along.

I held my breath and the urge to sob, taking my moment to say my final goodbyes to a man who'd been like a second father to me.

I touched his graying hair, feeling how cold and still he was beneath my fingertips. How many deaths I'd witnessed in the ER, never allowing my mind to go beyond the clinical to the aftermath. "I'll miss you. Watch over us, Uncle Cal. No more suffering." I reached to touch his exposed hand; that's when I noticed the slender, ornately carved wooden box clutched to his chest.

He was holding my Aunt Karen's remains next to his heart.

My stoic façade crumbled, taking my knees out with it. Adam seized me around my waist, supporting me with his strength. He, too, was becoming emotional, appearing both extremely sorrowful and yet somehow resolved.

As I stepped into my mom's embrace, I thought I heard Adam say, "I'm sorry we failed you." I thought he was greeting my father, so I was surprised to see his head bowed, gripping the edge of my uncle's casket.

I WAS LOST in my thoughts while the miles of highway clicked by; the streetlights' glow fractured by layers of growing fog hovering in the dark sky. I presumed Adam could sense I was in no mood to converse; I gathered he wasn't either. We'd exchanged a few glances but that had been the extent of it since we left the funeral home.

My parents had accepted Adam with open arms, which I knew they would. His presence actually provided a wonderful buffer, giving my mother not only a reason to smile but a renewed sense of hope that all was not lost with the love life of her eldest daughter. While he'd been open and receptive to meeting a good portion of my extended family, Adam had been in his own sullen mood, making me worry that maybe this was too much on our new relationship.

He didn't seem to appreciate being introduced as my *friend*, either, frowning or doing a small eye-roll each time, but I didn't know if he'd run for the hills if I started to publicly refer to him as my boyfriend. Men were so fickle and I was used to walking on eggshells. The combination made me leery to place a label on us. After all, every guy I'd dated in college who just wanted to "chill" or "hang out" really meant they wanted a label-free relationship with a clean exit strategy. And Doctor Randy Mason had been the last grand reminder that even months of sex did not equal a future.

I'd mentally cataloged every one of my relationship mistakes, adding each new discovery to my list of "do not repeat."

"Your parents are great," Adam said, breaking our comfortable silence.

I was relieved to know he felt that way, considering that meeting the parents was usually the beginning of the end. Mentioning them meant it was in the forefront of his mind, which in itself was instantly alarming. It was one thing to be a teenager meeting your girlfriend's parents. It didn't have the same underlying meaning of the possibility of a future and/or marriage intentions like meeting the parents of your thirty-year-old girlfriend did.

I glanced over at him, diagnosing just how long this new relationship had before expiring from the acute stress of growth. "Thanks. Sorry my dad talked your ear off."

Adam smiled. "He's a nice guy. I actually learned a few things from him tonight."

"Oh?" *Oh God! What did my dad tell him?* They were locked in conversation toward the end of the night for over an hour. Did he tell Adam about my past? I was afraid to ask.

He glanced over. "Well, beyond hearing that you once thought a Ford Mustang was a horse and your favorite color growing up was hot pink? Yeah, we had a great chat. He's really easy to talk to."

I held my breath.

While Adam recapped his conversation about anti-theft devices in new cars, my heart pounded like a bass drum in my throat. My dad was a car guy through and through, which, much to my relief, melded perfectly with my auto theft detective. But did my father share too much? My family never talked about my arrest anymore; it had become taboo to dredge it back up, just like we never talked about Kate's accident. If we didn't acknowledge it, it didn't happen.

I didn't think my dad would share, but he was emotionally strained and vulnerable. Anything was possible.

Just when I thought Adam would make a right onto Landsdowne Avenue, he drove straight. "Um, aren't you taking me home?"

"Yeah," he glanced over, "just not your home."

ADAM PUNCHED IN his security code, reset the house alarm, and tossed his truck keys onto the granite countertop. I hung my dress coat up on one of the hooks on the wall in his laundry room where I'd learned all coats go.

I was also learning the many moods that made up Adam Trent, but unfortunately was at a complete loss for the one he was currently wearing.

"You okay?" he asked.

After having been asked that question over two hundred times tonight, I was done hearing it. "I'm *fine*."

He held up both hands. "Easy. You didn't cry tonight, that's all. I'm just checking."

I was particularly proud that I hadn't. Someone had to hold my family together.

"I thought you would," he continued, taking the folded tissues out of his pocket.

"I'm sorry if I disappointed you."

His irritated glare set me back a half step, making me instantly regret my snappy retort.

"You getting short with me, Doc?"

My head was starting to hurt. "Sorry. I just have a lot of things on my mind right now."

"Like?"

I shook my head; I wouldn't even know where to begin—not that he would care.

He rested his hands on his hips. "You want to talk about it?"

And make you dump me faster? I don't think so. "No. That's okay. You really don't want to hear my problems."

"I don't?"

I needed to crawl into bed and hug a pillow. I'd thought about asking him to drive me home; I was tired and torn between wanting to be alone and needing the comfort of his company. "No, you don't." And that's when residual echoes of Randy telling me to *"Just shut the fuck up already. If I wanted to hear bitching I'd have stayed at work!"* roared through my brain. It was a hard lesson learned, and one I'd never forget. "I'll work it out on my own. It's okay."

Adam scowled and then scanned the corners of his kitchen. "I don't think you're on your own here."

"I'm fine, or at least I will be."

He muttered a curse. "You're fine?"

"Yes."

"You don't look fucking fine, Erin."

"They're my problems, Adam. I'll figure it out. You don't need to pretend to care. Really. It's okay. Believe me; I know guys don't want to hear women whining and bitching about stuff. I learned *that* lesson a long time ago, so I'll spare you."

I heard his unmistakable scoff. "Unbelievable. You'll *spare* me."

Great, now I've pissed him off.

He stormed around the kitchen. "What's bugging you?"

"Nothing. Just drop it, okay?"

He stared me down, puffing like a bull ready to charge. "You trust me?"

I felt off-balance. "Trust has nothing to do with it."

"Do you trust me?" he asked again, punctuating each word.

"Why? Are you going to give me a reason not to?"

Adam grabbed my hand and hauled me through his living room. I had presumed his assertive gait meant we were headed to his bedroom, so I was quite confused when he led me downstairs.

"What are we doing?"

He stopped abruptly at the bottom of the stairs. "You're done questioning me."

His tone cracked me like a sharp sting from a whip. "Listen, I'm sorry."

"*Sorry* has nothing to do with it," he tossed back, echoing my words as he pulled me past the edge of the couch to the center of the room. His grip on my wrist tightened while he glared down at me. "Do *not* move."

I watched him cross the room, my feet frozen in place with what I could only surmise was curiosity mixed with a bit of fear—fear of angering him further. He fetched a large black duffle bag from the closet built under the stairs, which he deposited at my feet. He stuffed something into his pocket and then stepped up onto the ottoman and clipped something to the ceiling.

Adam stripped off his suit jacket and laid it over the back of the single chair; his jaw hard and tensed. His necktie was the next item to go. He stretched the black paisley silk to its full length and moved behind me, grasping my shoulders firmly as he draped his tie over my neck.

I couldn't calm my heart rate. "You're scaring me."

He peeled my black cardigan sweater off, gliding his fingertips over my bare arms. His lips touched the edge of my ear. "Good. You'll come harder that way."

My breath hitched. *I'll what?*

Adam tossed my sweater onto the couch. "You don't get it, so I'm going to explain it to you." He seized my wrists, cinching them together with authoritative efficiency. Instinct to flee warred with paralyzing panic.

I felt his breath on my neck. "I asked you to share and you chose not to, making assumptions instead. That does *not* sit well with me." The plastic noose around my wrists tightened with a final tug.

"Adam—"

"Right now I don't want to hear another word out of your mouth unless you're answering my questions or moaning my name. Are we clear? Nod if you understand."

I wanted to kneecap him but was frozen in emotional overload. His words crackled with commanding authority. He rolled his shirt sleeves up, exposing his corded forearms that were as tense as his focus.

"What are you—?"

He unzipped the large duffle bag. "No. You had your chance to talk." He retrieved a coil of bright red rope and started unwinding it, running each inch through his hands, meticulously inspecting it. "So we play this my way. After all, aren't you a little curious?"

Damn him. I was, but now was *not* the time.

He folded the rope in half. Firm hands guided my body, swiftly wrapping me in his cording. His control seemed effortless, as though the motions were practiced and ingrained. I should have balked at the idea, put up some sort of resistance, but his focused attention was too liberating to pass up.

"The red looks gorgeous against your skin."

Anticipation made my throat constrict. With a couple of passes and measured tugs, both of my arms were bound together behind me with soft cotton, from my upper arms down to my wrists.

I staggered on my high heels as the tension in my muscles increased. "Adam."

"Always in control, my doc is. Always fighting what's inside her head." He snipped the plastic band off my wrists and then tied the rope off. "Let's see what we can do about that." He removed the necktie from my shoulders. The soft silk drifted over my eyes, slowly over the slope of my nose, brushing the scent of his cologne and his focused presence into my senses. Silk tickled over my cheeks and separated my lips. I felt helpless and nervous when he tightened it enough so it would stay in place.

"There we go. Much better," he whispered right next to my ear, sending shivers of unbridled anticipation rolling through my body. "You can keep your silence. Now then, where were we?" He tugged my sleeveless blouse up with painstaking casualness, slowly pulling it out of my skirt. Firm hands slid over my stomach, warming my skin, and then left me feeling bereft when deft fingers opened each button. My mind went hazy when he cupped both of my breasts.

He squeezed my nipples, rolling them within the lace of my bra. The pleasurable pain jolted throughout me, replacing angered apprehension with heightened awareness. "When I ask you a question I expect the truth, and not some bullshit about how you think I don't want to hear what's bothering you."

His words and teeth grazed my neck. He pinched harder. "Does this feel like pretend to you?"

I couldn't stifle my moan through the necktie gag, even though my shame and penitent heart were weighing heavily.

"Have I given you any reason to think I don't care about you?"

I snuffled hard and shook my head.

He pulled and squeezed, zinging another wave of arousal through my darkness. "Have I?"

I shook more fervently.

I felt his deep sigh as he dropped his hands, leaving me cold and empty and strangely alone inside. The rope tugged between my shoulders, jostled my wrists, and then he threaded the end through the clip in the ceiling.

My sleeveless blouse hung open, the air chilling my exposed skin. I felt like a side of beef dangling from a hook, raw and bleeding. It was aggravating, not to mention slightly uncomfortable.

He set a pair of silver sheers on the end table and stood in front of me. A gentle hand softly caressed my cheek. "I've thought about this first scene between us a lot. Everyone always placing demands on you. I've wondered how you would handle being bound. If you'd be able to free your mind."

I wanted to kill him with my eye daggers. After several hours of standing at the viewing tonight, my high heels had moved beyond constricting and into the second level of pain. I thought about kicking them off and aiming for his head, maybe even put an early end to the budding humiliation, but then I'd probably be forced to dangle here on my tippy-toes. I groaned my displeasure.

His head tilted. "Do you want me to leave you alone with your thoughts?"

Damn it, he was frustrating.

I tried to slouch; my legs were aching, but every time I let the rope take some of my weight, my arms would pull and send registers of pain into my shoulders and spine.

"Stressful night." Adam unbuckled his wristwatch. "Kind of night when I could really go for a drink." He rubbed his wrist, carefully massaging his skin, and set the heavy timepiece on the table. "I know all about stress."

He sat down on the couch and crossed his feet on the ottoman. "Instead of managing it, I let it get the better of me. One drink led to too many. Took me a long time to realize I was choosing self destruction instead of dealing with things." He glanced over my body. "But that doesn't seem to be a problem for you, Doc. You don't need any help, just like I didn't. I get that you want to keep that all bottled in. Worry about everyone else but yourself. It's cool. You don't have to share if you don't want to. You're right—most guys don't give a fuck."

Sheer determination had me fighting this every step of the way but gravity was hammering me hard. So were my tattered emotions. What did he want from me? Didn't I just deal with enough grief and sadness for one day? I was starting to hate him. I closed my eyes so I wouldn't have to look at him. This was not love. No, this was torture and he was all smug and content and relaxed and comfortable while I dangled from the fucking ceiling.

If he wanted to explore his fetishes, pissing me off was the wrong way to go about it. I shifted from foot to foot, unable to stand in one place for very long, despising him even more with each agonizing second that passed. What had probably been only minutes bound up and tethered began to feel like hours. My ankles were beginning to ache more than my squashed toes.

I started to sway. Thoughts were barraging my mind faster than each pounding beat of my heart. Pain, anger, regret, sorrow, hate, contempt all swirled into a vortex of agony. Sobs started to break. I squeezed the tears from my eyes while my saliva soaked into the silk between my lips. I had to remember to breathe through my nose. *What did I ever do to deserve this?*

Strong arms braced me, keeping me from falling over. He tipped my chin up. "I've got you. What you're feeling right now is how I feel. You don't trust me enough to share more than your body with me. I get that. I want you to trust me, Erin. Trust *in* me. I'm here, baby. Right here. For you."

I was becoming as distressed and crazed as a cornered cat. Mascara and exhaustion mixed with anger and unshed tears, burning my eyes. That's when I'd noticed the room had gone silent and his white dress shirt was gone.

He loosened the knot at the back of my head and pulled his tie away from my mouth. I could see his regret and sadness as clearly as my own. "Please. Talk to me."

My hair hung in my eyes, while his desperate plea resonated through my stubborn stance. Worries that had been plaguing my mind all night flooded my throat and bubbled up out of me. "I'm waiting for you to run."

"Oh, baby, no."

I focused on the floor. "It's just a matter of time. You'll be sick of me."

"Sweetheart, no."

Adam quickly released the tension tethering me to the ceiling, holding my weight. He walked us backward and sat down on the couch, slipping my skirt up so my legs could straddle him. He brushed my hair back. His eyes never left mine. "No, baby. I'm not running."

"You will."

"Hard to run with you sitting on me, Doc."

"You know what I mean. It's too much. Too fast. Sooner or later... Men don't want drama."

"I'm here. Right here."

Years of inadequacies stood like gatekeepers, prepared to discount his words, while the rationale behind my current breakdown sealed my fate. Surely he'd see me as an unstable female—unworthy of his time—just like his predecessors.

"Hey. Hey." He held my face. "Look at me."

His request was difficult. I was afraid of what he'd see.

Adam's eyes searched mine. "I'm not running, Doc. I'm falling."

My heart pushed out a soft whimper. "You are?"

He bit his bottom lip and nodded.

I leaned forward just as he pulled me in, relishing in the relief of his mouth on mine.

I rested my forehead on his and drew in a deep breath.

"It's just you and me here." He caressed my cheek. "Talk to me."

"I'm worried about my sister. I think... I think her boyfriend is abusing her."

"I think you may be right," he said softly, brushing my hair back. He slipped my shoes off, dropping them to the floor, relieving some of the physical pain, but the mental anguish had far surpassed the body. As if he could read my mind, his hands held my face and seemed to hold the heaviness of my thoughts, too.

My eyes stung. "It's my fault." Three simple words, spoken aloud. An admission of guilt once again. The weight from letting a piece of my darkest secrets out was almost crushing.

"Oh, sweetheart, no," he admonished. "Why would you even think that?"

"She doesn't feel good about herself."

"And so it's your fault she's letting some guy hit her?"

My rationality said "no" but my guilty conscience said, "Yes, it is."

His thumbs brushed my cheeks with soothing strokes. "How? How are you responsible for his actions? Or hers?"

"I bought the alcohol for her that night." The memories ripped through me, fresh as if they were from yesterday, but oddly I couldn't seem to stop myself from confiding in Adam. "I'd just turned twenty-one. Kate and her friends were underage. I thought they were staying in but they took it to a party. She'd called me three times begging me to come get her but I didn't want to leave my dorm and drive all the way back up here. Don't you see? If I would have just gone and gotten her she would have never been in that accident. She would never have gotten into a car and tried to drive. She was perfectly healthy and I ruined that."

"Oh, babe. No. It's not your fault." He swallowed hard and pulled me to his chest. "It's not your fault."

"The scars… the seizures… She's letting that bastard abuse her. I saw the marks on her neck. I know what strangulation looks like, Adam. I've seen it before." My breath hitched. "Women… at the hospital… I've seen it before."

"I'll take care of it."

"How?"

"I don't know, but *no* woman deserves to be hit. I'll make some calls and do a background check for priors. Whatever it takes, babe." He ran his fingers through my hair and kissed my face, my forehead, soothing me. "Whatever it takes."

"My mom had enough to worry about tonight. Kate, my cousins, my family." I sniffed. "She didn't need to be worrying about me, too."

"Sweetheart, you can't carry the weight of the world on your shoulders. You can't. That shit will break you. Trust me, I know. It broke me. Look at me." He held my face. "I'm here. Right here. You're not alone in this."

His eyes were laced with sincere concern. His hands skated over the ropes binding my arms, inspecting. "Are you in pain? Is the rope hurting you?"

I shook my head and wiggled my arms. "It's not that comfortable but no, it doesn't hurt. You can untie me now."

He brushed my hair away from my face. "You mean a lot to me, Erin." His fingers slipped underneath the bindings at every point where they wrapped around my arms. "I want this. Us."

I let his words soak in, trying to erase my dejected emotions with the admission he just laid out. "I want it, too. I do." I also wanted to believe he was interested in something more than playing with me until he'd had his fill and I would be left a broken shell of a woman again. "I've never told… anyone… about Kate's accident." It was hard to speak; my confession was choking me. "No one knows I bought the alcohol for them." *She didn't want me to go to jail again.*

"We all have secrets." Adam wiped my face with his fingertips until he covered my mouth with his. His fingers fanned into my hair, holding me fast, as though he was taking in my pain as his own. "It's okay. It's not your fault. You know that, right?"

No matter how I painted it, it was and always would be my fault.

"I want to hear you say it out loud."

"I can't."

"Say it," he ordered, his fingers pressing into my scalp. "It's not your fault."

Oh, but it is. I *provided the booze.* I *put her in peril.* Our foreheads rested together, but I was still trapped in my own head, hearing my mom berating me for not being there for Kate when she needed me. Little did my parents know…

Adam gently sucked my top lip between his teeth, stopping my head from shaking. "Say it."

I relinquished my hold, albeit reluctantly. My lie sputtered out in a sob with my deeply embedded regret. "It's not my fault." *But it is and always will be.*

His fingers tensed behind my ears. "That's right. It's not." His grip gentled and he drew in a deep, steadying breath. "It's not mine, it's not yours. We didn't pull that trigger. They did. It was *their* decision to do that, not ours. Not ours, baby. Understand?"

His breathing became slightly erratic, making me acutely aware that he was no longer talking about my sister. His burdens flowed from his lips right into mine, both of us needing a lifeline to keep from drowning in our sorrows. I nodded, forcing myself to agree with him, wanting for just a second to let go of the guilt.

My poor, wronged man.

His tongue slipped over mine, replacing the isolating loneliness with a flood of unbridled need. His hands were in my hair, on my neck, squeezing my thighs, my rear, washing my pain away with each touch.

He pushed my skirt up, bunching it around my waist, squeezing the fabric in his fists. I felt his desperate hunger right through the indents he was making on my skin. It mirrored my own.

I was so aroused. It was difficult to breathe. I wanted the use of my hands. "Untie me."

Adam's mouth skimmed my jaw. "No."

It was a firm, yet playful answer. His tongue swirled with mine, cutting off my ability for rebuttal.

His hand slipped between my legs, rasping glorious friction back and forth. Back and forth. Pulling me into this glorious world where I didn't have to think. I've lost control to what he does to my body. My head lolled with heaviness; it was hard to focus on anything other than where he touched me. How he touched me. My body was his to do with as he pleased. He continued to heighten my arousal over the lining of my stockings, over the additional layer of underwear beneath, both of which I was starting to loath.

"Adam…" I needed more, more of this exhilarating euphoria. He had me aching for it and yet I couldn't do anything about it.

"Shh. I know," he whispered on the edge of my mouth, rolling his fingertips with maddening precision. He had me panting, swirling in a whirlwind of sensations while the quickening started to form into a path of glorious relief. It was like being on a Merry-Go-Round, spinning and spinning and then screeching to a dizzying halt when his hand slipped away.

He gripped my waist and sat up. "Stand up."

An order? A simple request? It didn't matter. My body was on autopilot, answering him autonomously as I scurried back. He helped me to my feet, guiding my hips to hold me steady. Warm chocolate eyes gazed at me with sheer determination. His focus narrowed with what I could only describe as heated reverence while he slowly unzipped my skirt.

It was difficult to swallow; I was slightly lightheaded.

Adam hooked his fingers over the waistband of my black tights and tugged, dragging my underwear off with them. Feeling his soft kiss on my hip, his hands pressing down the backs of my thighs, made me unsteady on my feet.

As soon as he freed me from my undergarments, he pulled me back over his thighs and adjusted my knees to his liking. His thumb drifted, skating over my leg, making agonizing passes very close but not where I needed it the most.

"So beautiful," he murmured, taking his good old time trailing his hands all over my body, painting imaginary lines and heavenly swirls. Even though my arms were bound he somehow made me feel like I was an extraordinary present, a gift he'd been waiting to open his entire life. Each patch of flesh he exposed was something to be felt, appreciated, and savored. His fingertips tickled, radiating the awakening.

"All mine," he said while slipping my opened blouse over my shoulders. He ran his hand down my throat, over my sternum, and down to my pubic bone, blazing a path of inner destruction. His fingers skated over the top of my left breast, down and around, slipping the cup of my bra out of his way.

"Nice," he whispered, drawing circles around my nipple. Watching him enjoy himself as he uncovered my other breast was an exhilarating experience, knowing I had the power to make him this way. He was mesmerized, enthralled, and yet completely focused.

He wet the tip of his thumb, preparing, luring me with want, making me clench in anticipation.

He shifted my thighs apart and went in for the kill, rolling the pad of his rigid thumb up and down and around in agonizing circles over and over again while he filled his mouth with my breast. My body was tensed and yet languid and electrified; I lost the ability to control my lungs when he pushed his finger up inside me.

Adam unbuckled his leather belt and lowered his zipper, shoving clothing down and out of his way. His thumb stilled while our breath mingled together. "Shit, I don't have a condom down here." He nipped at my jaw. "Fuck."

Insane need drew our mouths back together, as if we'd suffocate without each other. Thoughts of having to stop, to separate and disconnect, had me groaning at the interruption. His eyes questioned me. Do we/don't we? I couldn't bear with the idea of losing our intensity.

"It's okay," I breathed. I sucked on his lip, my body primed for a leap of faith.

His tongue reached for mine. "You said… IUD?"

"I do. Please." I didn't know what I was even asking for. "Just don't, inside me."

"Okay, I won't. I promise." His hand gripped the back of my neck, holding me fast to his mouth, while his teeth scraped where his lips just sucked. His kiss alone had the power to make me forget all of my worries, falling further for him with each kiss. His tongue wrapped around mine, absorbing my gasp when he penetrated me with his finger. He rubbed inside me, in and out, in and out, barraging my body with sharp sensations and sweet melodies. He was unrelenting, building the quickening inside me.

I groaned when his hand slipped away.

Adam stared right into my eyes. "You sure?"

I nodded. "Yes."

His breathing was rough, his eyes speculative, as though he was expecting me to change my mind. I really wasn't sure but I was in a near state of frenzy, my need eradicating all rational thought. He was right. Shibari was completely liberating.

The only thing I cared about was getting him inside me, binding us together once again.

He narrowed his focus and gripped himself, rubbing the plump head of his cock around in my body's natural wetness. His strained determination softened when he was fully seated inside me.

"Erin," he whispered. It was more than my name; it was an utterance of a promise, the shared feeling of comfort and serenity that only coming home can invoke.

Home.

He guided our bodies as we gave in to the need and connected us in ways that no other dance could ever do.

There was no walking away anymore—not without leaving a huge section of my heart behind.

CHAPTER 20

Adam

I RESTED MY head on the couch and rocked her hips back and forth, needing to get deeper inside her while she rode me.

Her silk blouse was hanging back onto her shoulders like a birthday present ripped open in unrestrained haste. Her arms were gloriously bound together in my red rope, giving me the gift of her unconditional surrender wrapped neatly with a red bow. I slid my hand down the column of her throat, feeling her quake under my touch.

Her pleasure was mine for the taking, mine to dictate and master. I may have pulled her on top of me, letting her assume some measure of control, but this was my show. I rolled my hips up into her with extra vigor, watching each fine nuance of her heightening enjoyment twist her expressions.

She was my fantasy and my dream; my end and my beginning.

I pulled her mouth back to mine, my head spinning each time she raised her hips. Her fast lifts mixed with my slow grinds, driving me out of my mind. She gave me exactly what I needed without me having to ask. I wanted to disappear inside her and never surface.

I'd never been…

Never felt…

Fuck. Spots were forming in my eyes.

This had to be a glimpse at Heaven because there was no other explanation for it. Partial words and guttural noises escaped with each of my breaths, making absolutely no sense but somehow she was right there with me, answering me right back.

I held on, feeling my internal damage healing every time she looked into my eyes, every time her wet mouth rested on mine, through every breath we shared. *I'd* been guarded, but *she* was stripping me. I could only hope I was stripping her just as bare, that my perseverance would eliminate her reservations.

We may not have known each other very long, but I knew with absolute certainty that we just fit. Physically. Emotionally. It was beyond want. I needed her.

I slid down and spread her thighs farther apart, needing to keep these incredible sensations sustained. Being inside her like this, fucking her skin on skin, was so much better. Each glide magnified, each internal squeeze and flutter better than the last. I pressed my thumb down on her clit, needing her to come before I did. I could tell she was getting tired and I was getting close; just watching my cock sliding in and out of her was making my balls tighten.

I took her with short, fast strokes, keeping my cock buried as deep as I could go, watching her hair fall over her beautiful face as the orgasm took her breath away. I fucked her with everything I had, slamming up in her with the singular focus to take her to places she'd never been before, prove some point to both of us that she didn't need to run or worry or fear opening herself up to me. She could relinquish control to me and trust I'd always do right by her.

Always, baby. Always.

Watching Erin unravel was my undoing but I needed to feel every flutter, every internal convulsion to make sure her orgasm was complete before letting go myself. I pulled out just in time, catching most of it between my fingers as I finished stroking off.

A trickle of sweat ran down the side of my cheek while Erin rested her face on mine, steaming up my neck. I tugged her hair, putting her mouth back on mine where it belonged.

But as much as I wanted to just hold her, come down from this incredible ride by kissing her, my right hand and stomach were coated. I needed to clean us up before I made more of a mess.

Worry that she'd been bound too long and might become injured in some way was adding to my restlessness. I kissed her once for good measure and patted her ass, letting her know without saying the words how I was feeling.

"Need you to get up, Doc. Easy. Go slow."

I helped her off of me without touching her with my sticky hand, hating the frown that marred her post-coital bliss. I kissed her forehead, appreciating her. "Let me clean up quick." I checked her arms, her wrists and fingers, and then her eyes for any signs of distress. Meeting her physical and emotional needs also made me completely responsible for her care. Rope play was not something to take lightly, and I was already fucking up her aftercare by not being prepared with a towel. I urged her to sit down, holding her steady. "Are you okay like that?"

Erin rolled her shoulders. Strands of hair hung across her face, masking me out. "Yeah."

I hurried, yanking my boxers up along the way. Untying her was top priority, right after I washed my hand off.

I sat behind her, untying my knots carefully, murmuring soft words of encouragement. As soon as I had her undone, I rubbed over every place my rope had touched her skin. I was gentle but could feel the distance growing between us when she pulled away. I knew she needed time to process our first rope bondage encounter but I couldn't let her slip too far. It was scaring me.

As soon as she stood to retrieve her discarded skirt, I knew I had to act fast. I tugged the black fabric out of her fingers and snagged the fleece blanket off the back of the couch. She was in my arms within the next breath. I bundled her up and urged her to relax with me, locking her between my body and the back of the couch.

"I hope you enjoyed that as much as I did. Please don't withdraw on me."

A small giggle followed, but her smile was measured and forced and didn't quite reach her eyes. "I won't."

She was far from convincing. Every muscle in my body started preparing for the worst, fighting against the desire to collapse after an amazing session of fucking the shit out of her. But bondage came with rules, ones that I needed to see to immediately, especially since she was coming back into her own headspace. I played with her fingers, needing to keep the connection.

"I need to know something," I asked, checking her arms again, assuring myself that the rope didn't mar her skin. She seemed okay but I kissed her softly anyway because *I* needed to. I was physically drawn to her—that was a given. But the emotional pull was becoming just as natural.

"Hmm?"

A little redness remained, but she wasn't chaffed, thank God. I wanted to see the truth in her eyes. "Why did you think I wouldn't care to know what's upsetting you?"

Her mouth curled down, and I lost her gaze to the back of the couch.

"Erin."

She shrugged. "Most guys don't. You've done so much for me today, I didn't want to push it. Too much heavy is never a good thing." She actually looked worried. "It's a recipe for disaster."

It was hard not to get pissed off. "Is that what the last guy had you believing?"

"Last guy?" She laughed. "Try every guy."

Did she actually believe the words coming out of her mouth? *Maybe I should kiss her; derail her from this path.*

"Come on, Adam, you can't honestly tell me that you want to deal with the heavy emotional stuff."

She shifted, trying to sit up, but I had her pinned. "You serious?"

She looked at me like I was cracked. Maybe I was.

"What is it you think we're doing here, Doc?"

"I don't know. Dating? Getting to know one another?"

"And how do you figure we'll do that? What? You just want to fuck and keep it at that?"

"No, but isn't that what all men want?"

I wiped a hand down my face. "Christ, Erin."

"We just started dating. I wasn't sure we were ready for *things.* I mean you met my entire family at my aunt and uncle's viewing tonight. Any normal guy would have—"

I tipped her chin back up when she quit talking. "Would have what?"

"Just forget it," she muttered contritely.

Now she was just testing my sanity. Her sharp inhale told me she was reading me correctly.

"Would have bolted by now."

"I told you I'm not running, sweetheart."

"It's only been a week."

"You know it's been longer than that. You make it sound like we just hooked up last night."

"I know, but—"

"But what?"

"Maybe I'm not ready to mess up a good thing."

"Don't *what if* it, Doc."

"I can't help it. Let's just say I've learned my lesson the hard way. And we're just getting to know each other's moods. Like for instance, do you realize both times you've *restrained* me you were mad at me?"

I concentrated on my breathing while the reality of my actions slowly came into focus. She had me again. *Is that the way she's seen it from her end?* "As much as I like that you call me out on my bullshit, I may have restrained you twice, but your safety has always been my top priority. And it was for both of our benefits. Besides, it beats the alternative."

Her brow tipped up. "Which is?"

I untangled the thin, gold necklace pinched around her neck, slipping it away from her throat. "Not giving a shit. Would you rather have it that way?"

Her chin dipped. "No."

"Good, 'cause I dealt with that crap before and I want no part of it. Not with you." I leaned into her hand when she cupped my face. "Both times it effectively sorted our shit right out and—"

"And built trust?"

"You're catching on." I smiled.

"It's not something I'm quick to give."

"Me neither. But know this. When I want answers, I get them anyway I can. You challenge me. I challenge you. You'll piss me off, and I'll aggravate the shit out of you. I'm pretty sure that's how this all works."

I felt her soft giggle settle my worry; her smile warmed me right into my bones. I looked into her beautifully expressive eyes.

"Erin, I've never used Shibari quite like this before. But I know its power… ability… to enable your mind and your emotions to open up. This wasn't just for you; it was for both of us. I want that with you."

I kissed her arm when she reached to run her fingers through my hair. It was then, when she was gazing at me with all those things unsaid, enjoying the comfort and reassurance of her affection, when I realized how easy it was to breathe.

"I want that, too." Her eyes searched mine. "But I don't know how things are supposed to work."

"Guess we'll just have to figure that out as we go."

"I take it you like me then."

The way her breath hitched around her nervous laugh was adorable. I had to remind myself that this was new to both of us, but for now, I couldn't keep my lips off her. Just the sweet scent of her hair alone had become something I craved. Her neck was equally as enticing.

"I think you already know the answer to that."

Her fingers wove into my hair. "It's still nice to hear."

The way her eyes lit up and sparkled when I looked at her made showing my hand worth it, though I still enjoyed toying with her. "I'd rather show you."

She smiled back at me. "Just sayin'?"

I'd have to save telling her I'd already fallen for another day. "Just sayin'."

GRAY SKIES HOVERED above us from the moment we woke, setting the tone for a very heavy, somber day. My shoulder pulled a little from the weight when we lifted the casket containing Erin's uncle and the cremated remains of her aunt, but I bore it.

It wasn't a burden, it was my atonement; my way of making some sort of amends for this senseless tragedy. So was enduring the cold bite of metal on my right hand from the lifting bars on the gleaming black casket. I considered wearing gloves but decided against anything that might give me comfort while I served my penance.

Erin and her parents had been surprised at first, but when the funeral director asked for pallbearers this morning I immediately volunteered. It was the least that I could do, not just for Erin, but for me, too. I needed to do this.

I would rather have been holding on to Erin, but each time I carried her uncle's remains, I couldn't even look at her. I'd allow myself glimpses to know her condition and to assure myself that she was okay, but I couldn't meet her eyes. The once vibrant blue that gazed into mine last night when I held her in my arms were now red and sullen from sadness.

While I was doing my duty, Erin was consoling her sister, Kate, and her mother, Christine.

No one from my unit was here, not that I would expect any of them to show. A sliver of angered disappointment rippled through me. None of the men that screwed up that night and caused these two innocent and greatly loved people to meet an early death were here to say they were sorry.

I'd carry that weight, too.

I wasn't directly responsible. I didn't cause this, but I was part of a series of actions and events that made it happen, and for that, I needed reparation. I had held Erin's hand during the entire church service, seeking my own forgiveness.

As far as I could tell, none of the family knew the full circumstances of the night of the fatal wreck. We had ended our pursuit of the stolen vehicle because of the dangers and rising risk to civilians. Our field supervisor called all units to stand down.

Despite our efforts, our worst fear happened anyway.

As I helped carry the casket to its final resting place at the cemetery, I resolved that the truth would be a secret I'd take to my own grave. Not only could it put my unit in a compromising position legally, it would drive an iron wedge between Erin and me and I couldn't let that happen. Whenever I held her, whenever I felt her lips on mine, I could see her being a part of my future and my inner selfishness coveted that.

The sun had finally broken free from its cloud cover, warming the dismal gray and muddled piles of leftover snow with its golden rays. I'd been raised to believe in God and Heaven and maybe it was just me, but I was taking the shining sun as a sign. We walked in step down a pathway that had been cut through the snow; the remaining ice crunching under our feet the only sounds breaking the solemn silence.

Erin's mother let out a sob when we set the casket on the straps that would lower it into the ground, causing my chest to ache all over again. She was sitting in one of the folding chairs graveside next to Erin's cousins.

I felt their pain.

I put my arms around Erin the first chance I got. She'd been stoic all morning—a rock for her mother, a pillar of strength for her distraught father. I was proud and worried at the same time.

Erin's arms slid around my waist and her face rested on my chest while the priest and the words of his final sermon about Heaven and greener pastures made the entire moment almost unbearable.

I placed a kiss on Erin's head, wishing my growing love for her could ease the turmoil I knew was brewing in her mind and heart. I could sense it, feel it in the way her hands were curling into my clothes.

Her body trembled, her breaths ragged and hitched.

I held her tighter.

I would be *her* rock.

CHAPTER 21
Erin

"His LIVER IS lacerated. You can see it clearly here. Shit." Bile threatened to erupt as I scanned the next picture.

"Ribs four and five are also fractured. A fragment punctured the lung. Blood is pooling in his abdomen," Doctor Ben Parata said, pointing at his screen with the tip of his pen.

"These fractures on his ribs here are already mending. Jesus. I wonder how long he's been going through this?"

We tore our eyes away from evaluating the MRI results and numerous X-rays to stare at each other, both of us at a complete loss of words. There was no restraint to the level of abuse this child had endured. That much was evident.

Ben blew out a deep, forlorned breath, echoing my own sentiments. "This kid is six?"

I nodded.

"He's a baby for Christ's sake. How? This is just... Unbelievable. This is the worst case of child abuse I have ever seen. I hope the person who did this goes to jail for a *very* long time."

I couldn't agree more. "Child Protective services have been notified. How could a parent do something like this?" The plethora of life-threatening injuries peppering this little boy was incomprehensible.

Ben shook his head. "I have no idea."

My God, the unfathomable injustice. Do all women mentally snap after childbirth?

The thought petrified me.

"What do we got?" Doctor Nate Tomic from Pediatrics stood beside me, resting his hands on his hips.

I reviewed the patient's injuries with him, quickly forming a game plan for emergency surgery. "We have him stable but he's on borrowed time. We'll need Orthopedics to handle the clavicle fracture."

"Agreed," Doctor Tomic said, wasting no time to schedule an O.R. "Is the family here?"

"I'll check." I glanced at my pager, but it had been my cell that had vibrated my pocket. Adam's latest text would have to wait.

Ben was fuming. "Whoever did this to this child should suffer the same treatment."

He needed to chill. "I'll speak to them."

Ben shot me a fleeting look, silently laced with encouragement and appreciation. I knew if he stumbled upon the abuser, he just might put them through the waiting room wall. Ben's daughters were close in age to the patient.

I checked in on my patient one more time before addressing the family, assuring myself that he was still stable. His blood pressure was concerning me. So was the discoloration of his fingertips and the bluish tint to his lips. I checked his arms and legs, even down to the bottoms of his feet, looking for something I might have missed. I checked his pupils. "Oh, little man, hang in there. We're going to fix you, sweetheart. I promise."

This wasn't right. No. No. I'd missed something. My gut was telling me that there was something else happening here. I scrolled through his chart on screen.

I snagged the R.N. who assisted when this little boy first arrived. "Kimberly, did we get the tox screen results back?"

"I don't think we ordered it."

My frustration spiked, but that didn't mean I had the right to take it out on her. "I ordered it when we started working on him. Check, please. We need a tox screen on him, stat."

"For?" she asked.

I checked his lips and mouth around the tape holding the intubation tube. "Heroin is my guess right now. A beating like this? He got into something he shouldn't have."

Her face blanched.

I was hoping my hunch was wrong, but instinct was telling me otherwise.

ADAM HAD BEEN texting me all night. He was just what the doctor ordered, cheering me up without even realizing it. How a parent could purposely beat their child to within inches of death was weighing heavily on my mind, like a torrent of unfettered rage waiting to be unleashed. After reviewing the test results, my hunch that the trauma was a result of him getting into somebody's drug stash had been confirmed.

Each of Adam's messages were growing more and more suggestive, and the note I was reading on my phone right now was making me blush in several places.

> If you were here with me I'd make you ride my tongue until you screamed.

I grabbed my dinner out of my backpack and shoved my stuff haphazardly into my locker, grinning for the first time all night. I needed his brand of healing as I typed:

> I miss your face by the way

Ten seconds later:

> Breakfast and then a thorough tongue bath for you.

It was impossible to hide my happiness.

> You're terrible.

> What are you wearing?

The truth of "dirty scrubs" with God-knows-what decorating them seemed too disgusting.

> Nothing but the smile you just gave me.

> Killing me doc. My house after shift? Promise to let you study.

I couldn't type "OK" fast enough.

He'd been working at his headquarters for the last few nights instead of being out on patrol while investigating his case, which, in all honesty, after dealing with a gunshot wound yesterday, made me a bit more relaxed. I could tell he was itching to get out on the streets, as sitting on his ass at a desk was clearly not his thing. Two days ago he informed me that he had to go to Manhattan to sign a new television appearance contract and then had suggested (and then persuasively insisted) I switch schedules so I could go with him.

He promised me that he'd give me some peace so I could study in the car on the ride up, which had been the only thing really concerning me. "I know your fellowship is important to you," he had said after he'd made love to me. We were in his bed, wrapped around each other, enjoying a moment when the outside world wasn't demanding anything of us. Just the simple fact that he was making concessions to assure I was happy was enough to make my heart swell.

Regardless, the constant hounding from the network that produced his television show was adding to his frustration. Unfortunately that was just part of my worries.

Jen was grinning at me while bouncing in her chair in our break room. "You look like you're in love."

I rolled my eyes and shoved my cell in my pocket. After reviewing the child abuse case, my spirit was still withered and broken, but Adam's messages were helping me cope. "Hello to you, too."

"You are," Jen teased, nudging me with her elbow when I sat down next to her. "Finally. I've gotta tell ya, it's nice to see you smile again. I've missed it."

"Thanks." I shoved a spoon into my yogurt. Blueberry was my favorite.

Sherry raised her hand in solidarity. "I agree. You have that rosy, post-orgasm glow in your cheeks, Erin. It's lovely."

It took effort not to crawl under the table from their remarks about my resuscitated sex life.

Sherry clutched at her heart. "I want to give Officer Hottie a hug for giving us our Erin back."

I studied her face. "Officer Hottie?"

She wasn't the least bit remorseful. "I'm serious. You'd better warn him that I'm gonna hug the shit out of him the next time I see him. I don't want him to accidentally shoot me or something. That would suck."

"He won't shoot you," Jen chided. "Just don't call him that to his face or he just might."

Sherry surrendered. "Hey, I didn't make up the name. That's what they call him on Facebook." She took a drink of her water. "I can't believe he's got like forty-seven thousand fans on there. It's crazy."

Forty thousand what???

"I wonder how many likes that other hot cop from San Francisco has," Sherry mused, painting one of her French fries with mustard. "I saw a post on him yesterday. He's cute, too."

My gut sank. Her use of condiments wasn't helping. "Are you serious?"

Sherry nodded. "I thought you knew that. You've been dating him for weeks and you haven't cyber-stalked him yet?"

Dread was pounding my nervous system. "No. I barely have time to study and sleep—"

"And have sex," Sherry added.

I smiled at her while chewing the last bit of granola topping. "And have sex. No, I haven't stalked him—at all."

Jen eyed me over. "Nothing? No Internet searches or anything?"

Their expectations were ridiculous. "No. Why? Is that what all the crazy women are doing these days?"

"Not crazy women, well-informed women." Jen pointed a baby carrot at me. "Knowledge is empowerment. You know that. I thought you'd at least be curious about the television star you're dating. See what you're getting into."

Now I was worried. "Why? What am I getting into?"

Jen shrugged. "Beyond him being a local celebrity? I don't know. You should see some of the comments they make on his fan page. I know you

331

don't do social media much but some of the stuff they say, well it's sort of scary. I guess that means you've never watched his television show either. Did he show you any clips yet?"

"No." I opened my bottle of mineral water and took a sip. "It's not a subject he likes to discuss. Ever."

Jen finished chewing. "Well, you can always watch a few of them on YouTube. There are about twenty of them, right Sherry?"

It bothered me that they knew more about the guy I was dating than I did. "You two watched them?"

Sherry shrugged it off and decorated another French fry.

"Without me?" I added.

"We thought you might be uncomfortable or something so…," Jen said. "I'm sorry. We should have asked."

Sherry reached for her pocket, retrieving her cell phone. "You want to watch one now?"

My head was swimming. *Did I?* "Not right now."

"Maybe some other time then," Jen said. "Does he know he's all over Facebook?"

Images of my last patient—that little boy—unconscious, battered and bruised from head to toe, was dominating, drowning everything else out. "I honestly don't know."

"Is this bothering you? Maybe we shouldn't talk about it. We'll change the subject," Jen said. "Let's change the subject."

Sarah waddled in through the doorway. The second our eyes connected, heavy-hearted sympathy flowed between us.

"Hey," she said to the table. "Oh Erin." She hugged me. "That was awful. Are you okay?"

I rubbed the forearm she had across my chest. "Yeah."

"What's going on?" Jen asked, scanning us for answers.

Sarah released me; the added weight of her pregnant belly giving her some discomfort as she straightened. "We just had a ped trauma. Horrible, horrible abuse case. Poor baby. Made me sick to think of it."

"Abuse?" Sherry questioned. "Is that what was going on? I had heard something but I wasn't sure. I can't believe they cut back on overnight pediatric trauma coverage. As if we don't have enough to do."

"He was my patient," I muttered, wishing we would never see cases like that ever again. "Makes you lose faith in humanity." I studied Sarah's jutting stomach. "Just confirms why I never want kids."

A collective "What?" rose from the table.

Sherry stared at me in utter disbelief. "You don't want kids?"

Sarah appeared wounded. "Why is this the first time I'm hearing this?"

I was beginning to worry I'd sprouted a second head or something. "After seeing the condition that little boy was in, it just proves that... never mind." I held my tongue, knowing I was sitting at a table with three fierce mothers, all of who were ready to pounce.

I held up a hand. "Before you all start on me, it's a personal choice. Some women want them. I don't. I just don't think motherhood is for me, that's all." I scanned their faces, knowing they would fight me tooth and nail on my declaration, but none of them, *none of them* knew the horrors I'd seen or the blackest depths a woman's soul could reach when under such pressure. No, my decisions were final and that was that.

Within a nanosecond, all three of them started to argue their points. "Listen, it's my choice. I don't want children."

"Does Adam know this?" Jen asked.

I shook my head, wanting to find a safe place to hide. Memories of being alone, of being terrified while trying to give a baby CPR, seized me. "It's not something we've discussed yet. We've only known each other a month or so. It's too soon for that."

"No it isn't," Sarah interjected. "You should know where he stands on wanting a family. You have to know if his wants and yours align now before you..."

"Was it even mine?" Adam's words from his confrontation with his ex ghosted through, smothering out their verbal debate. *"I'm glad you went to that butcher,"* he had said.

His voice had been pained, filled with hurt when he'd said it.

My heart sank; the pending loss of losing Adam overwhelmed me like a thousand knives to the heart, draining the last fragments of my soul through its gaping wound.

He'd want children.

Of course he would.

A son to run around the house in a cowboy hat and play gun, trying to be just like his daddy. Or a daughter—a little girl with ringlets in her hair that would light his face in a magical way no woman ever could.

"...feeling that life inside you... baby kicking..."

Skipping pictures, like fragments of a torn movie, showed me in dizzying fast forward exactly how his life should be.

The woman he smiled for, the woman he embraced in his arms and kissed at the end of the day wasn't me.

The smiling children running through the grass to tackle hug their father weren't mine. They wouldn't be. Couldn't be.

The babbling gush of happy laughter erupting around them were sounds I'd never hear. They were meant for someone else to cherish.

Someone else to covet.

He would leave me.

Of course he would.

It may not be today or tomorrow even, but eventually he would.

It would be ugly and brutal and lethal to my heart.

The chest pains were agonizing.

I'd committed myself, my future, to be barren. I wasn't enough. I couldn't be enough for him. How could I ever be enough? Why would any man want that?

"…didn't mean to upset you. Erin? Honey? It's okay. It's your choice."

The streak of black hair came into clearer focus.

Jen.

My pager chimed, vibrating my pocket for good measure. I remembered to breathe.

I smeared away the traitorous tear and focused on the pager. "I have to go."

"Are you okay?"

Jen again.

I nodded. "Yeah. Sorry. It's been…," I took a deep, steadying breath, "it's been an emotional day. I'll see you later?"

I crammed my uneaten sandwich and the rest of my lunch back into my bag, tossing it in the trash.

White walls. Tiled floors. Smells of pungent fluids. I was losing my mind.

I wiped my face again, swapping heartache for self-assuredness.

I didn't need the staff asking me questions or doubting my leadership.

Doctors were made of tougher stuff than that. It didn't take long before I'd be put to the test again.

I PULLED THE curtain behind me, cutting off the prying eyes of other patients. "Start chest compressions."

The patient we had in room nine, a twenty-seven-year-old female who'd been in and out of consciousness with a BP and pulse that had been steadily skyrocketing, had just coded.

Sherry had her knee on the bed, pressing with all her might. This was the moment it all came to a head; my own pulse racing with every passing minute.

We didn't have time to wait for the results from the lab; this girl was slipping through our fingers rapidly and precious seconds counted. I called out all the necessary protocols I knew of to treat her. I was grateful I took the time to question her two friends who were out in the waiting room. They confirmed my initial diagnosis. Still, nothing made you feel as vulnerable as when you were playing God.

Watching her body jolt when we shocked her, giving her the last bits of hope we could offer before surrendering to the hands of fate, made me hold my own breath.

"Check for pulse," I instructed, remembering that I was also responsible to pass the torch of knowledge along to the two residents assisting me. Good, bad, or otherwise, it was not only my job to cheat Death, but to teach others how to do it, too.

Relief washed over me hearing we established a rhythm, becoming almost euphoric in its wake. There was no other high quite like this; it's the kind you want to celebrate with cake and fireworks and a huge-ass banner that announces loudly, "Fuck you, Death."

Sherry gave me a fist pump, followed by a quick celebratory hip-check. "This was a caffeine OD?"

I nodded. "No more Jager-bombs for her. The future bride out in the waiting room almost had to find another bridesmaid."

Twenty minutes later, I was reviewing party-girl's latest ECG when one of our nurses announced we had multiple patients en route. "Three males with multiple gunshot wounds. ETA is ten minutes."

So much for enjoying a victory.

"Doctor Novak?"

I spun, seeing one of our pediatric on-calls hailing me. I wondered if he was looking for my boss Sam since the two of them were best buddies. I'd never played golf, so I couldn't understand their passion. "You need me, Doctor Weinstein?"

He gave me a quick chin nod. "Hang on. I want to talk to you."

I braced, ignoring the wrinkle that creased his receding hairline, preparing to be chewed out for *something*. It was status quo around here; there was always someone your senior lurking behind a curtain to correct you. My mind quickly sifted through my caseload while I waited for his verbal berating on how he isn't happy.

His partial smile was disarming.

"I just wanted to say you did a good job with the ped patient, Micah Brown. Doctor Tomic said your keen eye saved us precious time getting the patient into the O.R."

His verbal pat on the back felt amazing. "Thank you, sir."

"You ever consider taking a shot at pediatric trauma full-time? You're really great with kids."

Me? Kids? Hell no. Had the boy been located another ten miles in the opposite direction, he would have been treated by a dedicated ped trauma team at Children's. "I'm actually going for my tox fellow."

"Tox?" he echoed, surprised. "I heard that. Why? No, wait. Not for me to judge. Explains how you knew about the drug interactions." He checked his pager. "Probably saved his life."

"We did. He coded on arrival."

His smile was thoughtful. "Then you saved his life twice. Would be a shame to lose someone of your caliber to another department. But if the lab is where you would be happier, then I wish you luck. Some doctors just aren't cut out for emergency med."

His underhanded comment stung. "I love working here. I've made the cut for five years now."

Doctor Weinstein shrugged. "Then why leave? This is where you make a difference, not down in the basement in a lab." His name echoed over the central paging system. "I hope you reconsider, Doctor."

He left me holding my future with a pat on the shoulder and a wry grin.

My pager was going crazy. I rushed down the hallway to ready for my next patient.

We all stood in teams, getting briefed, planning our responses to the preliminary assessments given by the ambulance crews. One patient was already non-responsive; the paramedics were conducting CPR en route, although we were probably looking at a DOA.

As soon as my patient arrived, male, nineteen years old, we sprung into action, all of us knowing what role we played in this young man's survival. The EMTs briefed us as we transferred him.

I brushed his shoulder, trying to calm him down so we could do our jobs. "Jamal, can you hear me? My name is Doctor Novak and you're at University Hospital. I need you to hold still, all right? We're going to take good care of you."

My surgical resident, Nate Cooperman, helped roll Jamal to his side. "No exit wound," Nate announced.

I slid my hand up Jamal's back. "It's in the midline. I can feel it. Can we get a chest tube?"

I was doing my job as the team leader, keeping everyone calm and on task when our patient grabbed my shirt, pulling with more strength than I thought he would have considering his present state with two bullet holes in his body.

He started to speak; his words garbled and incoherent at first. Fighting with a hulking teenager was not on my agenda. Hands and arms mixed in, trying to free me. Jamal pulled me right to his face, his eyes wild with primal fight or flight survival instinct.

"Cah, cuh, Carter…," he stuttered in between moans of pain, begging me with his eyes to listen.

"Carter?" I said and Jamal nodded.

"Muh…" He shook his head, wincing in pain. "Man… Mancuso…,"

"Carter Mancuso," I repeated, fighting the arms and hands that were trying to break me free. "Let me go," I ordered over my shoulder.

Jamal's nods were short and quick jerks. His other arm waved weakly in the air. That's when I noticed he had his hand shaped like a gun.

My eyes flew back to Jamal. "Carter Mancuso shot you?"

Jamal nodded and then visibly relaxed, relieved.

"Jamal, we're going to put a tube in your chest because your lung is collapsed, okay? I know it hurts but you have to try and stay still for me. You're going to feel a little pinch and burn, but that's the numbing medicine going in."

Within nine minutes, we had him stabilized, prepped, and ready for surgery.

IT DIDN'T SINK in at first, the name my patient had conveyed to me. We'd been so busy that non-essential details like names didn't register. Vitals, CT scans, central lines, and knowing which came first dominated. It wasn't until I briefed the detective assigned to the case that it dawned on me why that name sounded so familiar. I called Adam right afterward.

"Erin, got a minute?"

No, I didn't, but there was Randy Mason, ex-asshole boyfriend, standing three feet away, shoulders hunched with the expectant look of a ten-year-old boy who wants something.

Shit.

It had been almost two weeks since his girlfriend Mandy messed with my head, telling me I'd lost my opportunity for the fellowship, and in that time I strategically ignored and avoided him. There was nothing Randy could say that would make a difference, and it was easier to hate him than feel defeated.

I stopped in front of him, not even bothering to ask what he wanted. He had six seconds, and that was being generous.

"Look, I know you're pissed at me." He scratched his head and glanced around. A med student brushed my back as he rushed past. Two nurses hurried in the opposite direction. "Can we go somewhere private to talk?"

I held my ground. "Say what you need to say."

Randy scowled at me and snagged my elbow, towing me along reluctantly. We stopped outside of a utility closet tucked beside a large steel rack of starched, white linens. I pulled my arm out of his grasp. "What?"

"Listen for a second, all right? Jees. I'm sorry."

I didn't like being this close to him, nor did I like being cornered. I opted for appeasement to speed this along. "It's fine."

"No, it's not. Mandy had no right to say that stuff to you. We, uh, actually got into a huge fight about it and, well," he tugged his hair, "we split up."

I wanted to feel happy about that but the truth was that I didn't feel anything at all. It was rather liberating, and quite surprising. I actually didn't care one bit. *Huh!* Randy actually looked quite pathetic. "Sorry to hear that."

He leaned one hand up on the wall, creating a barrier with his body. My hand brushed over the cold metal rack pressing into my shoulder. I was trapped.

"I've been doing a lot of thinking, and, well, I miss you."

"Oh, God." I needed to run—fast. Or throw up. Or throw up and then run.

He leaned closer; so close that I could smell that familiar cologne he wore. That scent once made me stupid. Now it just made me sick. I folded my arms across my chest, creating a barrier between us, thankful for the pungent smell of bleached linens behind me. Did he actually think I'd jump back in his arms and be grateful for leftover scraps? "You're kidding, right? You've got some nerve—"

"Am I interrupting something?"

My head snapped up at the deep rumble, seeing a wall of black uniform and Adam glaring like he wanted to tear Randy's head off. A tinge of panic flooded my nerves, hoping Adam wouldn't think he caught me doing something wrong. The second Randy eased up from the wall I made my break for it, shouldering him out of my way.

Adam pulled me into his side, tucked me under his left arm, and faced off with Randy.

That was the moment it all hit me.

Randy meant nothing to me. The feelings of loss that once consumed me were gone. It was as if they never affected me to begin with. There was no gaping hole in my heart. There was no harbored resentment or even a hint of longing. He was nothing more than a stepping stone, a piece of history to be filed and forgotten.

And I was falling in love with Adam.

Adam's body was rigid and tensed, like a panther poised to strike.

He switched between gazing down at me with concern and glaring warnings at Randy. "You okay?"

Correct that. Not falling. I'd already fallen into that scary phase of relationship newness, where being unsure, petrified, and humming with renewed excitement wrapped itself around blind hope.

I nodded, putting an inch of breathing space between us, though Adam didn't let me separate that far. I was at work after all. I needed to keep public displays of affection to a respectable limit, though my body was craving every ounce of his attention.

Adam didn't give a shit. He leaned down, cupped my face, and kissed me anyway. Even though he had never met Randy before, he made sure whoever he was got the message. I felt woozy.

"He's still standing there. You going to introduce me?" Adam muttered privately.

I wished Randy would just disappear into thin air but much to my chagrin, he was still behind me, appearing quite nonplussed, I might add.

Whatever.

I waved a hand between them, trying not to make the side-by-side comparison, although my loyalties and attraction to Adam were unquestionable. "Adam, this is Doctor Randy Mason. Randy, Detective Adam Trent."

Adam reached to shake Randy's hand. His smile turned very predatory. "I ever see you caging my woman in like that again, I won't be this nice. We clear?"

"Your woman?" Randy's forced smile fell into a deep scowl. He yanked his hand back and shook out his fingers. "Relax. We were just talking."

Adam was much more astute than that. "Then please, continue."

Randy cut his eyes to me. "I think we were done. For now."

Adam's fingers flexed on my shoulder and then he let go and captured my hand in his. "That's what I thought. Word of advice? You need to talk to her you can do your talking out there where it doesn't look like you're trying to make a move on her. Erin may be forgiving, but I'm not."

Randy took a step back, stammering. "Yeah, okay. We'll talk later, Erin."

Numerous replies to that swirled around my tongue, none of them being anything that could be delivered without screaming. My teeth locked together. "I don't think that's necessary. There's nothing left to be said." I didn't wait for him to utter another word. I led Adam in the opposite direction.

"Was that the ex?"

"Yes."

Adam tugged my hand. "Do I need to be worried?"

"Not in the slightest."

"Good. Where we headed?"

"Away from him."

Adam's deep rumble was sexy. "So you're positive the vic said 'Carter Mancuso'?"

"Shh." I hoped none of the people rushing around us would overhear. The conference room at the end of the hall was vacant. I flicked the light on. "Yes, I'm positive."

"Where's the vic now?"

"Patient."

Adam rolled his eyes.

I pulled him deeper into the conference room. "Look, I don't want to get into trouble with this. I've already told the other detective what my patient said to me. But I didn't tell him about your case or that I recognized the name."

"Where is your patient now?"

I glanced over Adam's shoulder quickly to assure our conversation was still private. "He's in surgery. The way the two slugs expanded and slowed upon entry, I'm guessing they were nine millimeter hollow points. Neither shot was a through-and-through." I ran a hand over my side. "One bullet deflected off a rib."

His eyebrows rose right before the wolfish grin of pride spread across his face. That was all followed up with a very distinct glimmer of lust.

"Quit looking at me like that." I crossed my arms to let him know I was serious.

Adam stalked closer and seized my upper arms. "I want to do you on this table right now."

"Why? Because I know what a bullet slug looks like?"

He raked his teeth over his bottom lip, nodding at me.

My palms landed on the wall of his chest. "Focus!"

"Oh, I'm *very* focused."

"Adam."

His grip moved to my hips, one hand sliding to cup my ass. "Okay, I'll give you a pass, this time, but you better be pulling into my driveway by eight or I'll put an APB out on your ass."

"On my ass?"

He grinned and squeezed. "For starters. Besides, you don't want to miss breakfast."

"I don't?"

His eyes narrowed on my mouth. "No. You don't. I need you to butter my toast."

He was so freaking cute. And a wiseass. "I'll butter your toast, anytime."

"I *was* having a shitty night," he growled. "Until now."

"Ditto. Shitty?"

Adam downplayed it. "More like frustrating. I haven't been able to get a hold of one of my informants. Oh, and I did a background check on your sister's boyfriend. He had one prior for drunk and disorderly, but that's it."

"That's it?"

He drew back and nodded.

"I thought there'd be more."

Adam moved a lock of my hair. "I'll keep an eye on it. You have enough on your plate dealing with punks with gunshot wounds."

"It's a daily occurrence."

"Well then, when I get home I need to know you'll be naked in my kitchen or I might just lose my mind. You've got to give me something to look forward to."

I felt the conference table press into my legs. "Will you be naked too?"

Adam nodded, his features all set with his determined smolder. "Most definitely."

"Good. Then *I* have something to look forward to."

"Sounds like a plan," he whispered on my lips, and then he pulled away just as quickly, studying me with the keen, discerning eye of a seasoned detective. "Something else is wrong, though. I'll ask one more time. Do I need to be concerned about your ex?"

My want was instantly doused. "No. Oh, God, no. That's... it's been over a long time."

Adam slid his teeth over his bottom lip, measuring my reply. "Good, though it didn't look over for him."

"Well it's over for *me* and that's all that matters."

His eyes settled on my mouth. "You say it's true, then I trust you."

I raised my chin. "It is."

Adam wasted no time closing the distance. Tasting his mouth was both hypnotic and addictive, as though his essence was made of pure sweetness combined with the flavor of recently chewed spearmint gum. His tongue caressed mine, swirling as if the two had known each other their whole lives. For a moment, I completely forgot I was at work or that I broke down earlier over my neurotic fears. A random page over the central communications system was a bitter reminder to simmer down. I released my grip on the back of his neck and pressed his chest, just enough to sober us both before we got too carried away.

"*Fuck me*," he muttered low. "Your mouth drives me crazy." He had the greatest smile; gleaming white teeth with that total affect of a hungry predator masked behind the charm of an innocent boy. "I can't wait to be inside you." His grip tightened on my hair with just enough meaning to kiss me softly once more. "*But,*" he drawled, "back to the shooter."

"Yes, back to um…"

Adam brushed his thumb over my jaw. "If it *was* Carter Mancuso, then your patient was supposed to end up dead. You talk to any other officers, besides the one you told me about?"

I touched my tingling lips and then shoved my hands into my lab coat pockets to keep myself from grabbing him again. "No. Just that Detective Holihan."

"I need to go find him before he fucks up my investigation."

I pulled out the paper in my pocket. "He gave me his contact info."

Adam glanced at it, his brows furrowing. "I don't know this guy."

"So who is Carter Mancuso?"

He leveled his eyes on me, no trace of humor or playfulness left in them. "Salvador Mancuso's son."

"Shit." A shiver ran the length of my spine. "There were three."

Adam retrieved his cell from his pocket. "Three?"

I nodded. "Three victims, er, patients. One expired in transport. We lost the second one soon after he arrived. They were all from the same shooting. Am I allowed to tell you all of this?"

"Call it *purging*." Adam blew out a breath. "This kid—anyone else hear what he told you?"

My mind reeled. For some reason, Randy's pathetic pouty face kept ghosting through, clouding things. "I'm not sure. Maybe? Several of my team tried to free me when the patient grabbed me."

"He grabbed you?"

I nodded, startled by his strong reaction. "Just my scrub top."

He tugged my arm, straightening it. "Fucker hurt you?"

"No." I withdrew my arm from his intense scrutiny. "I'm fine."

Adam frowned. "You're sure?"

"Yes. Completely unharmed. But you'll have to ask that Detective Holihan if anyone else heard what the kid said. I think he questioned the rest of my trauma team. I honestly don't know."

"Okay, I'll ask him." Adam thumbed the card with the detective's name and number on it, frowning when his phone chimed. "What the...?" Confusion rippled his face. "It's my mom."

I could relate to his concern, considering it was almost one thirty in the morning. Within moments he turned white as a sheet.

"What?" he breathed out, trying to keep his voice from faltering. "Oh God." He covered his eyes. His mother was crying so hard, I could hear her echoing out of his cell.

I pulled out a chair, needing him to sit down before he fell. Adam was tall and solid but the bits I was picking out of his side of the conversation were enough to buckle his knees.

Someone had been seriously hurt.

Jason.

Jason? Oh, his youngest brother.

He alive? Yes, he's alive. Oh, thank God.

My heart squeezed so hard, hearing him comfort his mom as best he could. She was nearly hysterical; he kept repeating "Mom" and "slow down," encouraging her to calm and breathe.

I pulled out the chair next to him and put my hands on his knees. Seeing his eyes turn watery, his anguish twisting his normally stoic features, I wanted to cry for him.

"My brother stepped on an I.E.D.," he said after he ended his call, his voice choked on the last word.

"He's alive?"

Adam nodded, rubbing the heel of his hand over his eyes, trying not to show me his tears. "His C.O. just called my parents. He's being air lifted to a hospital in Germany. It's not... they said he's in bad shape."

"Oh my God, Adam." I was in his arms within the next breath, holding him just as tightly. His fingers clenched into my skin. He buried his face into my neck.

I knew his pain intimately.

God, how I knew.

It was crushing and cruel and utterly devastating.

But his heartache was my heartache.

And my heartache was his.

His shoulders shook beneath my hands.

A tear trickled down my neck, and then another.

My own eyes swam in their unshed pain. Knowing this solid, formidable man had been reduced to tears was killing me.

I held him tighter, hoping my arms would be strong enough to hold him together.

Love wasn't about sex. It wasn't skin smacking and orgasms and superficial shit. And maybe it wasn't about fears unfounded either.

It was a private moment in an empty conference room when you were gutted and completely vulnerable, only to find strength willed to you through another beating heart.

ADAM PICKED THE business card up off the conference table after taking a series of steadying breaths. He swiped his face several times, trying to hide the evidence. "I need to find this Holihan guy, talk to him before they blow a tri-state investigation."

"Adam—"

"None of my leads are telling me that there was a hit put out, so *somebody* fucked up. I've got to figure this out. None of the Mancuso family has ever been convicted of murder, but nothing surprises me anymore."

He was numb, wooden, and growing distant quickly.

"Hey." I drifted my fingers over his cheek, combing them from the shadow of his sideburn back through his hair. His face was still damp. "It's okay."

He sniffed and tapped my thigh. "Hop up."

"No."

"Erin—"

"No."

He nudged but I refused.

"I don't have any rope handy, but we do have four-point restraints for combative patients. Don't make me use them." I knew he was suppressing his anger and frustration. His muscles were coiled tightly, straining all the way up to the stretched tendons in his neck. Had he really wanted me off his lap, he could have easily stood and deposited me onto the floor. "Look at me. Just relax a minute."

Adam's lips twisted at my lame threat but he slowly eased beneath me. "My mom's a mess," he finally said on an unsteady breath. "No parent wants to bury their kids."

"Hey, no. Don't think like that. We'll go to Germany. I can book flights right now. You have a current passport? We can use the computer by the lounge."

Adam clamped a hand on my thigh let out a deep exhale. "Hold up. Jason's commander said he'd contact my parents as soon as Jay arrives at the hospital in Germany. Until then, we're supposed to sit tight."

"But—" My mind was already packed and ready to go. I needed to see vitals and CT scans and X-rays.

"Erin." His admonishing gaze through red-rimmed eyes left no room for argument.

"Okay." I rested my head on his while every fiber of my being was screaming to get on a plane and fix this. I knew talented surgeons, leading neuroscientists. I could gather a team, save Adam and his family from having to endure another second of grief. "I'm so sorry. Did they say what kind of injuries?"

A sharp rap on the door startled us both. "Excuse me, Doctor Novak? One of the nurses said I'd find you in here."

I slipped off of Adam's lap; Detective Holihan filled the doorway. I guessed he was in his forties, with wide shoulders and a thick midriff. My guess was that he hadn't been running down the streets of Philly chasing criminals lately.

Adam tensed, slipped his hand around my hip, and drew me back. His hand rested on his own sidearm until he held out his hand and introduced himself, unphased by the questioning gaze from the other cop.

It was then, when Officer Holihan moved from resting on his gun to shaking Adam's hand, that I realized that no matter the situation, Adam's actions were always deliberate. He didn't move me out of the way to discount my presence; he placed his body between me and anything he perceived as a threat, and didn't relax until the threat was neutralized.

He put me first.

Always.

Oh my God. I love him. Is he…? Could he be in love me, too?

I smiled inwardly, slightly baffled, while watching these two intimidating police officers greet each other.

"Have a few additional questions for you, Doctor Novak," the detective said, eyeing me around a wall of Adam. "Can we speak somewhere privately?"

I stepped closer. "Yes, of course."

Adam's quick warning glance stopped me in my tracks, reading his unspoken message as clearly as if he'd said it aloud. "ATTF is conducting a comprehensive investigation into the Mancuso family," he said. "It's my case. Any information you can share here is crucial."

Detective Holihan appeared confused, obviously trying to determine why I was just sitting on Adam's lap a few moments ago.

"Doctor Novak is aware of the case I'm working," Adam said without further explanation.

Holihan's brow rose. "She called you?"

And I was just sitting on his lap a few minutes ago, too.

Adam remained composed and stoic. "As I stated, she is aware. That's it. So where did this shooting occur?"

"On Chestnut, a few blocks from Washington Square Park. Three were hit. So far Doctor Novak's patient is the only survivor and the only lead."

"You got names on the DBs?" Adam questioned.

"Yeah," Detective Holihan said, rubbing a hand over his buzz-cut hair. He flipped open a small spiral bound tablet. "Cody Powell, age twenty-two, died en route, and a Benjamin Deets, age twenty-nine, expired upon arrival."

Adam rested his hands on his hips. "Wait, hold up. Did you say Deets? D. E. E. T. S? Benny Deets?"

Holihan nodded. "Yeah, why? You know him?"

Adam's head dipped and swayed while he strung together a few curse words. "Yeah. He's one of my CIs." He pegged me with his attention. "Was."

I pulled out a chair and sat down; my knees had grown weak.

"FROM NOW ON you do not walk to your car without an escort," Adam declared. He was all business, which had started from the moment that Detective Holihan entered the conference room. Now that we were alone again, Adam was worse. "When you're ready to leave work, you call me. If I can't get here I'll have a unit dispatched or get hospital security to do it. Someone. Just, you're not going out there alone. And from now on I drive you in and pick you up."

"Adam—"

"No arguments, all right? Shit just got real, Erin."

"Don't you think you're being a bit—"

"A bit what?"

"I don't know. Excessive?"

The angered glint in his eyes said otherwise. I instantly regretted my affront.

"I'm not risking anything, *especially* your life. Right now there are only two people who can link a Mancuso to murder and one of them is you. So I don't give a shit if you think it's excessive, and I sure as hell ain't gonna pretend that everything is cool. Shit plays out, you may have to testify, Erin. You know what that means? A target gets painted on your head. And there's an entire city of lowlifes willing to take someone out for a favor or a... or a fucking crack rock."

My mind flashed over the dozens of rap sheets he'd shown me, the crimes all those criminals had committed, the vacant or sometimes smug look on their faces when they were arrested. Gang members came through our ER on a daily basis. Their smack-talk and wannabe gangster attitudes were an everyday occurrence. His anxiety was valid.

"I still don't know if we have leaks within the PD, and I can't shake that Benny was just hitting on you at Al's Tavern a few weeks ago and now he's on a slab in the morgue. You think that might have been just a coincidence?"

No, not really. I didn't want to think about it.

"And now...," he continued. "Now your name is going into a case file on a double homicide. You've got to see why I—"

I halted him. "Okay."

"Okay?"

I studied the hard lines of his face and his heaving chest. He'd run the gamut of emotional overload; he didn't need me adding to it. "I got it, babe. We'll do this your way."

"You sure?"

I nodded again. "Yes, positive."

"No arguments?"

"No arguments."

He blew out a relieving breath and wiped a hand down his face. "Good. Okay. Thank you."

Adam took a step and hugged me tightly. I wrapped my arms around his waist.

"My brother…" His lips pressed against my hair. "I can't lose you, Doc."

I snuggled into his chest, feeling his body relaxing slightly, though his hands were still trembling. "You won't."

"We can't be lax. These people are very dangerous."

"I know."

"I should have never—"

I squeezed tighter, not wanting to hear anything resembling regret. "Stop. It's okay."

His hand scraped across my back, catching on the threads while we pulled ourselves together. "You called me 'babe.'"

My muscles tensed, though his stance didn't warrant it. "I did."

"I like it," he said.

There in the warm, familiar dip in his chest, life was perfect. "Good."

"I need you to do something else for me."

I looked up, waiting to hear his request, enjoying the fine nuances of being needed. "Yeah."

Adam placed a soft kiss on my lips. "You've gotta take these stitches out of my hand. Now."

The lingering tightness in my chest eased. I was in awe of his resilience, mesmerized by his bravery, and completely smitten to the core.

CHAPTER 22

Adam

THE TWO-HOUR DRIVE to Manhattan had helped somewhat to keep my mind from spiraling. So had Erin's presence and her stories of med-school hijinks, although I had to admit I had a newfound respect for pig cadavers. She had censured herself when we touched upon anything that could lead me to thinking about my brother Jason, but despite her best efforts, my injured baby brother dominated my thoughts.

I appreciated her for trying.

I loved her even more for trying to make me laugh, for keeping me grounded, for just being by my side and not giving up on me when my moody shit surfaced.

Yeah, this wasn't just filling the loneliness anymore or hiding my bullshit behind my best behavior. Even the sunrays streaming through her hair knew the truth.

Negotiating the traffic funneling into the Lincoln Tunnel took concentration, giving my mind a chance to ease up, though the nightmares plaguing me were never far away. In the last twenty-four hours, my brother Jason had been transferred to a hospital in Germany and was undergoing yet another surgery. Watching my impenetrable father break down when he updated me on Jay's condition was unbearable.

I couldn't even imagine… I'd had a few things shake me to the core in my thirty-two years but this… it was gutting me like a slow twist of a very sharp blade. I had to keep fighting the haunting images from carrying

Erin's uncle's casket. I didn't even want to think about what her two cousins must still be going through.

The corner of my eye blurred.

Erin squeezed my hand. "We can be on a plane tonight," she said as the darkness inside the tunnel surrounded and swallowed us. Some of it even seeped inside me.

I let go of her hand and shoved my sunglasses up on my head. "I know."

"He was awake, Adam. And talking. That's a great sign."

She was dead serious and shifting effortlessly into doctor mode with her reassuring bedside manner.

I nodded while praying to a god that I sometimes had a hard time believing in. "As soon as he's stateside…"

Her fingers tightened on my thigh. "The second the plane is in the air, we're D.C. bound. I have contacts at Walter Reed."

The bright afternoon sun was warming the end of the tunnel, casting beams through my inner darkness. I fought back the shit that threatened to take me over and tapped my sunglasses back into place. She didn't need to see a grown man cry for God's sake. *Again.*

I cleared my throat. "What about your fellowship?"

I didn't need to look to know her reaction; I could feel it through her hand and the chill that followed when she pulled it away. "I can apply again. It doesn't have to be now. Don't worry about it."

I tugged her hand away from her mouth and put it right back on my thigh. "Erin. No."

"I've met all the prerequisites, Adam. And I did a tox rotation during my residency. I'm—"

"You're what?"

"I'm not sure anymore."

Traffic slowed to a crawl. So did her voice. "What are you saying? You changing your mind?"

"You need to be in that lane." Erin pointed. "Behind the silver truck."

Fuck, I hated traffic jams, especially into Manhattan. "You're not giving up your dreams for me. No fucking way." I hit the gas and maneuvered in front of a small car while some other asshole chucked his finger at me. Screw them. "Let's set that shit straight right now."

Erin braced her hand on the roof. "I'm not."

I was glad we were stopped so I could let her see I wasn't kidding.

"Your brother is going to need a lot of help when he gets home."

That crushing pain I felt yesterday when I sat in my parent's living room and heard that Jason had lost both of his lower legs in the explosion pressed the air out of my chest. Thinking about his hearty laugh, that troublemaking smile, the fact he'd no longer be able to press down on a fucking brake pedal with his foot—it was suffocating.

"We'll deal." My molars were hurting again. I noticed her shift in her seat.

"I know you will," she muttered.

"I didn't mean it like that, Erin. But I won't allow you to put your life on hold for me. For anything."

"I'm not. Believe me."

"Good."

"I just don't want…"

Her words died on a vigorous head shake, as if she was trying to erase them from the air.

"Don't want what?"

"Nah." She fluttered a hand.

"I brought rope *and* cuffs, Doc. Fair warning."

Her head whipped my way. "Is that a threat, Cop?"

"Nope. That's a promise, sweetheart."

I enjoyed seeing her squirm in her seat. The way her thighs sealed up told me that part of her liked my brand of interrogation, too. "You were saying?"

"Two more blocks and you need to make a left."

I nodded, trying not to hit the variety of shit in my lane. People swarmed all four corners of the intersection like ants in a giant maze of insanity. A delivery truck was blocking one side; a black stretch limo was straddling both lanes in front of me. New Yorkers were a special brand of dedicated crazy.

Since we were going nowhere fast, I figured I'd stare at her until she confessed. She needed to know she was out of options with me.

"I'm not sure the fellowship is the way I should go," Erin finally said. "I'm not sure I'm cut out to be stuck in a lab every day. My hours would be different and that's gonna cause…" Her arm straightened. "That lane. Next intersection is your turn and then I think we only have about five blocks."

Instead of finishing her sentence, she fiddled with the map on her cell. I'd questioned craftier criminals with much better diversion skills. "Gonna cause what, Erin?"

She acted surprised and confounded by my question. "What?"

I listed my mental notes while she made this Q&A into a challenge. "Fellowship. Lab. Hours changing. Gonna cause what?"

"Distance," she finally said.

Would she work out of another building or something? It took my mind a minute to catch up. Had I not been negotiating traffic with pedestrians on every side I would have slammed on the brakes and pulled over. "Between us?"

One shoulder lifted. "It's a concern."

"It shouldn't be."

Another shrug followed by some fidgeting. "I've been so singular in my focus for so long that it's become engrained. I'm not sure why I even want it anymore."

I knew she was sidestepping. "I'm not going anywhere, Doc. If you change your mind about what you want to do, then that's on you, but it has to be what you want, not what you think you need to do because of me."

She stared out her window. "Hotel should be on the left."

I glanced over at her quickly, frustrated that she'd even think I'd let distance come between us. "Did you hear me?"

"Yes, I heard you."

The ache in my shoulders subsided. "Good. If you don't want the fellowship, then that's your career decision. It has nothing to do with what's growing between us."

Her attention whipped my way. "What is growing between us?"

I pulled her hand to my mouth, finding it hard not to pull the rest of her into my lap and show her exactly what was growing. "Good things."

MY LATE AFTERNOON meeting with Melissa Werner and the asshole who worked for her went as I had expected—pressure tactics to sign the new contract mixed with a healthy dose of patronizing ass-kissing.

The second she sauntered around her oversized glass-top desk to greet me, wearing a short black skirt and skyscraper heels, I knew I had to get the hell out of there fast. She leaned forward a lot, accentuating several thousand dollars of enhanced breasts, and did the shy smile thing meant to entice.

It was difficult paying attention to the legalese that covered twelve printed pages while sitting in the same room with a woman who looked ready to devour my cock. Knowing that I had left Erin curled up in my hotel bed was enough to snuff out Melissa's obvious advances.

Ms. Werner was less than pleased when I turned down her offer for dinner but there was no way I was going to put myself into that situation. Erin gave me her blessing to go, saying she'd order room service and just study, but only an asshole would leave one woman to go out to dinner with another.

I was already selling a chunk of my soul signing this contract; I'd be damned to lose my integrity dicking over a woman I cared very much about in the process. I don't know why, but Erin's opinion of me mattered, and I didn't want to let her down.

I probably let Nikki down a lot when we were together, but she never gave me a reason to care. Shitty, I know, but the truth.

I tipped the next sheet up to kill the glare. The print on the page was starting to blur. Melissa's sickly-sweet perfume was making it worse, creating a headache on top of my annoyance. Erin favored the simple scent of peaches and honey—flavors I had grown accustomed to and was missing to the point of distraction. I wished she were here with me. She'd probably understand this mumbo-jumbo contract better than I could.

The fancy pen in my hand felt hot and poisonous.

Stabbing Harry in the neck while watching his condescending smile fall into stunned fear also crossed my mind.

Bastard.

I got to the section outlining my responsibility for attorney's fees and all costs incurred from any breach or threatened breach of contract when the sweat started trickling down my back. "I'd like my attorney to take a look at this." I didn't have an attorney, but fuck if I'd sign this shit on the spot.

Melissa's heavy sigh was unnecessary. "We gave you this contract weeks ago, Adam. I presumed you'd already reviewed it with your counsel."

Didn't take much to bring out her inner bitch. Made the desire to get up and walk out that much more enticing.

"Been a little busy." I didn't need to justify my actions to her or anyone else for that matter.

She started rapping the pen in her hand on the tabletop. "Your absence from the show from your injury has cost us a lot already, Adam. I can't keep delaying production because of this."

"Shit happens on the job." Her lecturing tone caused automatic guilt to arise. I was backed into a corner and there was only one way out. "You already have a signed contract for production. I don't see why not signing this would hold up anything."

She stared right at me. "You don't understand—"

My chair rolled back when I stood. "I understand perfectly." I snagged the papers, wrinkling them in my fist. "But I don't recall seeing all this stuff about you having the right to sue me if I don't perform for you for a certain amount of hours per week before."

Melissa huffed. "Adam, please sit."

Harry's gaping pie-hole would have pissed me off had it not been so amusing.

"Actually, Ms. Werner, I think we're done here."

"My head of Production feels we should air the footage from the auto accident."

Anger spiked right through me, welding my feet to the floor. "Is that how you want to play this?"

She didn't seem to care either way.

I wanted to wipe the smug grin off Harry's face. He shrank back in his chair when my desires registered. He cleared his throat. "Melissa, I don't think your father would have wanted—"

Her glare turned arctic. "The company is mine now," she huffed, and then collected herself. "It would be best to not delay this any further. Page two outlines the additional compensation we discussed. I was able to adjust that to fifty thousand for the last twelve episodes with a guaranteed one hundred fifty thousand for a second season. That doesn't even include the variety of endorsement and modeling requests that will most likely arise, though you should probably get an agent to handle that for you. Stipulations are outlined on page seven. That's the beauty of New York. One fantastic opportunity can lead to many."

There were very few women in this world that I envisioned hitting, and this one was moving quickly to the top of the list. I turned my glare on the balding douche-bag. "Thought I said that any salary adjustments would go to the entire team." The contact crinkled in my hand.

Melissa twisted in her chair, setting her long legs back on display. "Listen, Doll, it's you we want on camera, not them. It makes no sense to give them what's rightfully yours. I'm trying to make this a win-win for you. I don't know why you're making this so difficult. You're going to be famous."

My knees unlocked, getting me closer to the door. Screw this. Fame was the last thing I needed or wanted. These people had no clue who I was or what I wanted, beyond a solid exit strategy. And I sure as hell didn't want her misplaced affection. "I need a few days to review all of this. I'll be in touch."

She was calling out my name to stop, but my entire focus was on the elevator doors in front of me.

ERIN SAT UP on the bed when I came through the door to our suite. Melissa Werner went all out reserving this place. I didn't know what a room like this cost but it couldn't have been cheap. I had no doubt that she had an ulterior motive but after that meeting fiasco, I expected to get the bill.

Erin was wrapped head to toe in white towels, relaxing with her computer tablet. She never left home without it, always studying something.

"You're back early. You okay?"

I set the room key card and my wallet on the desk and pulled my coat off. I thought the walk back to the hotel would clear my head, but seeing her all washed and clean made me feel even dirtier. My choices were simple: either I give into their demands and turn my life into a joke or tell them to fuck off while destroying the career of the woman who held my heart.

Fuck.

Erin softly padded across the floor and hugged my waist. "I didn't expect you to be back so soon."

I studied the wood grain in the desk, unable to meet her eyes.

She started to slip away. "I'll go get ready."

I grabbed her wrist and pulled her back, needing her arms around me. I had to find a way to tell her that didn't ruin us both, but for the moment it was easier to ignore it.

"Adam?"

Her cheek was tucked in the curve of my spine, making the strength I was trying to muster up even that more difficult.

"What happened?"

Two words. Two words that would lead to so many others I wasn't ready to say. I didn't want her to worry. The last thing I wanted was for her to feel bad about the decisions I was left to make, because there was no way in hell I was going to ruin her life while I was making a mess out of mine.

"Nothing, babe. It's just a lot to take in."

Her arms tightened. "Liar."

My woman saw right through my bullshit.

"I need a minute." The bathroom seemed like the safest place for me to hide while coming up with a plan. I untangled her and gave her a quick kiss. I knew she was disappointed and probably confused but I didn't want to lie to her.

I hoped spending a few quiet moments locked behind a door would help, but the messages on my cell were nothing more than another irritating distraction. Several texts from the same unknown number littered my screen.

> Please come and see me :'(I dunno what to do

> Why won't you see me? I don't deserve this!

> Sorry

> Are you just gunna ignore me?

> Oh because u have a new gf

I stared at the texts, trying to determine if Nikki sent them, but something didn't fit. I thought about replying—telling the sender to fuck off—but instead, I just deleted them. Knowing my luck, Erin would accidentally see this stupid shit, which would undoubtedly cause unnecessary problems.

I washed my hands, my face; even brushed my damn teeth.

Staring at my reflection just made everything worse.

I switched the bathroom light off. Erin was sitting on the edge of the bed, legs crossed, one foot bobbing while her focus was absorbed by the wrinkled page in her hand. Several papers lay next to her on the bed.

My chest felt heavy.

She was engrossed in whatever she was reading until her eyes met mine. "I think I understand."

Each breath was like dragging dirty air into my lungs.

"Did you sign this?"

She'd found the contract. My head swayed, giving my answer.

"Good. This…," she exhaled, nodding, "this is a lot. Is this what you want?"

I'd rather have a punch in the face. It would be easier. "No."

"I presume you already have a contract with them, or is this it?"

I should have sat down and talked this out but my legs weren't cooperating. "That's a contract amendment."

"Amendment?" Her brow tipped. "Seems heavily in their favor."

"I thought so, too."

"Like here, in paragraph… what is it, fourteen B, they retain the right to withhold compensation for episodes that you fail to appear in due to your negligence. I suppose this is in case you're injured again, but I'd have a contract lawyer look this over because, dayum. That's pretty vague."

My shoulders ached. I must have misread that paragraph. Apparently Melissa Werner was into fucking me any way she could.

"They are not required to compensate you for regular wages lost during public appearances. My God. This is a train wreck. Don't sign this, Adam."

"I have to."

She slapped the papers down on her lap. "Why?"

"I don't have a choice." My admission burned right up my throat because they were words I had no intention to ever say out loud. Self-loathing and regret made my skin feel like it was on fire. I knew I couldn't stop bullets, but that didn't mean I wouldn't take one for her.

I wanted to shred the paper into tiny bits until nothing existed but a pile of dust, because no matter how I tried to protect her I was going to be the source of her hurt.

Erin turned indignant. "Of course you do."

The knock on the door caught both of our attentions. Erin gripped the front of her fluffy robe. I watched her run around the room. "Shoot. Let me get dressed."

I really preferred knowing she was naked under that thing. Whoever was on the other side had bad fucking timing. Or good timing.

No, it was definitely bad.

I peered though the peep hole, taking in the uniformed figure of a hotel staffer. Male, approximately twenty-two to twenty-four years old, didn't look nervous. He seemed mostly bored than anything.

"Did you order room service?" I asked, unlocking the door.

He greeted me with a smile. "Mr. Trent? I have a bottle of wine for you." He pushed the cart right past me, stopping a few feet inside.

Great. Just what a recovering alcoholic needed. "Whoa. Hold up."

Erin was tying her hair back while I shifted into a new level of pissed, already settling on the fact that this would be over right then and there if this is the way she wanted to be around me. "You order this?"

Her eyes narrowed. "What?"

I pointed at the dark bottle sitting in a silver bucket. "Did you order this?"

Erin's mouth popped open. "No. I... I didn't order anything." She scanned the cart. "Where did it come from?"

"Doesn't matter. I don't want it."

"There's no charge," the guy said.

Erin slipped past me, drifting her hand down my back in her wake. "Thank you for the offer but we're fine. Please take it back."

The guy stammered. "But it's paid for."

I wanted to toss him and the bottle out into the hall, but Erin blocked me.

"Then please feel free to enjoy it." She gave the cart a tentative push toward the door. "Just remove it, okay?"

"That's a hundred and forty dollar bottle. Are you sure?"

Erin was watching me out of the corner of her eye. "We're sure."

If he thought he was getting a tip, he had another thing coming.

She shut the door behind him, leaning on it for a second. "Are you okay?"

"This day is testing my patience."

"I can see that. Well, as your doctor, I'm prescribing a hot shower and some dinner."

My mind blanked, stalling all over visions of wet doctor and things my cock could do to her. Hands, too. My hands definitely wanted in on the action. My tongue felt thick, demanding to participate. She was fantastic with diversions. "If you think it would help."

She crossed her arms. "I do."

Her stance was propping her boobs up nicely. The entire package leached the anger from my bones. "Well, you are a professional."

"I didn't order the wine."

I know. I'm an asshole. "I know."

"You thought I did."

She had me there.

"I wouldn't do something like that to you, Adam. Not now; not ever."

I could easily see she was telling the truth.

"It hurts that you'd think that of me."

I'm a very big asshole. Dad always told us to man up when we were wrong. "I'm sorry."

"I would never disrespect you like that. Never." She huffed. "Promise me that this is the last time you'll doubt me on that."

Her knocking my ass in line was sort of a turn on. "I promise."

Erin nodded, still holding her ground. Her focus shifted to the mess of papers she left on the corner of the bed. Just when I was sure she'd want to talk about that fucking contract, she motioned toward the bathroom. "Time for an attitude adjustment. How about a hot shower and then we go find a place to eat?"

I crossed the distance and squared off with her. "Is that your final order, Doc?"

She put up her best front. "Your swagger isn't going to save you on this one."

"My swagger?"

Her chin jutted out, and for a second I could see her taking the same stance reprimanding our children one day. The boy would be a spitting image of me, no doubt earning her starch on a daily basis. A daughter would be just as much of a hard-ass, but she'd have me wrapped around her finger just like her mom.

"I'm not used to people doubting me."

I pulled her in, breaking her feeble wall with effortless ease. "I'm not used to people giving a shit."

Her hands slid up my arms. "Well, I do. Very much."

Her words were like a shock to the heart, but for some reason they didn't scare the hell out of me. The only thing I was concerned about was making that crinkle of pity disappear from her face.

"Very much?" I didn't need to ask, but I did anyway. The way she was staring me down, drilling her meaning into me with just a look, left zero doubt.

"Yes," she said.

"Then let me apologize." One lift up and her feet left the ground, my tongue was much better with words than I was. A few more steps and I had her flat on her back on our hotel bed, showing her instead of talking myself into another corner.

The entire world ceased to exist whenever I was between her legs. She was a safe haven, a place I could weather any storm. After Nikki, I was convinced love was for saps. It was the last thing I wanted and sure as hell didn't need it clogging up my life. I was sorely wrong.

Erin moaned in my mouth. "I like the way you apologize."

My hand squeezed harder, blocking out the ping of another incoming text. I wondered if her hard nipple would taste as good as it felt. "Protect, serve, admit when I'm wrong. All in a day's work."

She giggled when I slid her shirt up.

I was moving her bra out of my way when Erin startled underneath me, peering over my shoulder in the direction of the noise.

Renewed frustration made me borderline homicidal. "Somebody has a death wish."

I glared at the door, willing the interruption to go away. It didn't take long for that second knock to sound.

Erin combed her fingers through my hair, groaning when I lifted off her. "You have my permission to shoot them."

I pulled my shirt down over my aching cock, feeling it deflate after looking through the peephole. *Fuck*. How was I going to explain this one to Erin?

The pain in my ass knocked again.

"You going to answer it?" she murmured, straightening her shirt.

"Do I have to?"

Erin frowned and rolled up off the bed, curious.

I gripped the doorknob, stopping Erin in her tracks.

Melissa Werner's instant sultry smile made my stomach roil. She eyed me up and down as if I were a feast or something. I should have just closed the door.

"You going to invite me in?" she purred.

I blocked the doorway. "I didn't look at the contract yet."

She focused on my hair for some reason, then down to my crotch. "You look a bit frustrated. Anything I can do to help?"

My grip on the doorframe tightened. "No. I'm good."

She wet her lip. "A man of few words. Did you get my gift?"

"Gift?"

She tried to look past me. "I ordered a bottle of wine for us. Thought we could have a drink, discuss things. Whatever concerns you may have. I hate that you left my office so angry."

"I don't respond well to strong-armed tactics. And I sent the bottle back."

"You what?"

I hated having to explain myself. "I'm a little busy right now."

Erin put her hand on my ass. How other guys could juggle more than one woman at a time was beyond me. It'd be more of a pain in the ass than it was worth.

"You're busy," Melissa repeated, as if she didn't believe me. "Too busy to have a drink and go to dinner with me? I know a great place. The food is fantastic."

Erin's hand shifted just enough to be a reminder that she was standing right behind me.

I opened the door wide enough for Melissa to see in. It was time to shut down her unwanted attention.

CHAPTER 23
Erin

EVERY WOMAN WANTS to believe that the man she's with only has eyes for her. That old adage is almost akin to flipping a coin in the air and hoping you guessed correctly. My mom had a saying that she repeated often: "You can find trash on every street corner. Try to find gold instead. You're gold. Never forget that and never settle for anything less."

Not only was Adam handsome, he was extremely cute, too. Killer dimples when he smiled. That boyish charm he exuded without even trying. All of that mixed in with a fantastic body and formidable badass vibe made him very desirable. And so far, though he may have stumbled along the way, he'd treated me like gold.

It was only natural that I wanted to classify him the same.

Apparently the woman on the other side of the door thought so, too. I could hear it in her delivery, the way she drew out each of her words to give them a flirtatious undertone all meant to entice him.

I had no idea what was really waiting on the other side of that door, but I was more than ready to confront it. New York, meet Philly. We hit just as hard and probably with less finesse.

Adam shocked me by opening the door wider, letting me size up what I could only assume was the competition. I felt my inner claws coming out, ready to scratch out the shocked eyes attached to the raven-haired model staring back at me.

"You're kidding," the woman murmured.

I didn't think Adam would bring me with him to New York to humiliate me, though the thought did cross my mind seeing he was right in the middle of being caught unexpectedly. Why else would I be staring down a very attractive woman who knew which door to knock on?

At least Adam didn't seem too worried about this showdown. No, he was definitely unruffled.

"Erin, this is Melissa Werner. She owns the production company that oversees our show."

I saw her switch tactics, donning one of the many masks women wear when we don't want to appear beaten by the game. In an instant I had to decide what kind of woman I wanted to be. I'd allowed women just like this one to defeat me before, to take what was mine right out of my hands and leave me in the dust, feeling victimized, crushed, and lonely.

I'd been hurt before, been tested more times than I cared to admit, but I still had a choice on how I was going to react.

I stuck out my hand, waiting while she decided to return the gesture. I found the action to be just as unappealing but I wasn't going to be rude.

She eyed me shrewdly. "You look familiar. Have we met before?"

I dropped her well-manicured hand, her fingers just as cold as the aura that surrounded her. I stopped trying to have pretty nails my first year of med school. "I don't think so."

"I never forget a face." She stepped inside our room uninvited, scrutinizing our bed.

Her perusal felt like a violation. "I'm sure we've never met."

Her simple "hmm" was annoying. "You returned the wine?"

"I don't drink," Adam simply replied.

This also confounded her until she turned back on me. "I know where I know you from. You're the doctor they pulled over in the stolen car, aren't you? That's how I know you."

No. Wrong. "That was *my* car. It wasn't stolen."

She gaped at Adam. "Wait. You're dating her now? You don't waste time."

Adam glared back. "My personal life is none of your business."

"It is when it turns my show into a media embarrassment with the network," she snapped.

His stare turned lethal, a wordless warning that he was one more snide comment away from tossing her out into the hallway.

"What does that mean? Why would that even be a concern?" I was sure there was something in that contract that I must have missed.

"The footage they filmed of you," Adam muttered over to me, his chest rising and falling rapidly.

"I'm not a criminal." Renewed panic rolled through me. "I didn't do anything wrong. You can't show it, can you? I told them no. I didn't give my consent."

"You said 'no'?" Adam asked.

I nodded. "I thought it was for the local news. They shoved that paper at me so fast and said I had to sign it but I refused."

He set his hands on his hips. "You didn't sign anything?"

"No. Why would I? I shouldn't have even worked on those injured people but I couldn't just stand by and do nothing. I didn't know if the news could show it anyway."

His head snapped over to Melissa. "And you knew this the whole time, didn't you? Didn't you?"

Melissa shrugged as though she didn't have a care in the world.

"Unbelievable," Adam growled.

"We can air any footage we want, with adjustments, of course. Surprisingly most people want their fifteen minutes of fame. But for those who do not consent, we can simply blur out their faces."

I wanted to do worse to hers. "You do that and I'll sue you."

Melissa shifted on her pointy stilettos. "You can try, but it will be after the fact. Well, this conversation is going nowhere fast." She shoved her purse under her armpit. "The deal still stands. The network expects our formal marketing and rebranding by next week. I'll expect to hear from you soon, Adam."

"Deal? You call having the rights to withhold compensation if he gets hurt doing his job a *deal?*"

"Erin," Adam censured.

Reining in my anger was difficult.

"You uphold my demand and I'll consider it," he said, "but I want it in writing."

This entire exchange baffled me. "What demand?"

Adam frowned, quickly dismissing my question.

"You care for her that much?"

"Yes." His reply was instant, without pause or doubt or contemplation.

"Wow." She sighed, nodding at me for some reason. "Wow. Okay. You have my word."

"Wait. What are you agreeing to, Adam?"

His lips smashed into a hard line while his subtle head shake said he wasn't going to answer.

"Adam?" I wanted an answer and I wanted it now.

Melissa glanced at me, tisking as if I were stupid and she was inconvenienced. "He doesn't want your footage aired."

"So you're what? Blackmailing him to get him to do what you want? Capitalizing on the misfortunes of others?" It felt like a blow to the chest. "You're unbelievable. Someone almost died that night."

She glowered at me. "I'm offering to make him a star."

Adam was a police officer. Privately he was as low key as low key could get. No, this didn't add up. "Is that what you want?"

"No," he said emphatically.

"So you're doing this to what, protect me?"

Adam ignored me. "I want it in writing. Then I'll sign."

"No. No, screw that." I stepped in between them. "You are not going to sign anything." I pointed at Melissa. "And you are not going to pressure him into this. I don't care who you are. You even think about airing that footage of me and I will sue you so fucking fast your head will spin. So whatever it is you hope to accomplish here, your methods leave much to be desired."

"I don't believe this," she muttered to herself. "Adam, surely you can see the benefits here. The endorsement deals alone will make you a millionaire. How many years would it take you to earn that amount on your salary? Trust me; you want this opportunity."

I could see the temptation warring with his values.

"You have no clue what I want," he snapped. "None. You don't know me."

She looked indignant. "You really want to be just a cop the rest of your life?"

I grabbed the contract off the edge of the bed, shoving it at her. "That's it. Time for you to go. And take this bullshit with you."

"You can't talk to me like that. Besides, I paid for this room," she countered, unabashed.

"Well then, I'll be sure to fuck his brains out on that bed

before we leave."

Adam snorted.

Her jaw ticked until a hint of a smile played on her lips. "I like you. It's a shame; we could have been friends."

"After you just insulted my boyfriend? Not in a million years."

Melissa righted herself. "Yes, well… boyfriends are temporary." She eyed Adam up and down one last time while I held the door open. "I'll be in touch."

"Thanks for the warning." I shoved the door closed.

Adam rested his hands on his hips and sighed. "Well…"

I leaned on the door, guarding it. "Now I know what the antichrist looks like."

Adam laughed. It was good to see his smile again.

"I hope I didn't make things worse."

Adam shrugged it off. "I don't think things could have gotten any worse than they already were."

"Were you really going to sign that to protect me?"

His refusal to answer was answer enough.

"Adam." The magnitude of that knowledge settled hard on my chest. "Now I know why you were so upset earlier."

"I don't want that shit touching you. Any of it."

"I appreciate that, but I wish you would have told me."

"It was my decision," he said flatly.

"Yeah, but if it affects you, it affects *us*. You know what I mean? This is part of that trust thing. Well, at least it is for me."

He crossed his arms. "Stuff like this… you'll just have to trust that I'll take care of things."

"No, that's not how this works. I want a partnership with someone, Adam, not you thinking you know what's best for both of us."

He combed his fingers back through his hair, tugging while nodding at the floor. "Yeah, you're right."

I liked the feel of winning. It was warm and cozy and empowering. So was wrapping my arms around his thick shoulders, although it all paled in comparison to the overwhelming love I had for him. "Thank you."

"I suppose I should get used to admitting that," he joked.

"What? That I'm right?"

He smirked and rolled his eyes.

"That's not why I said it. I'm just relieved that you *want* to take care of things."

His hands slid from my hips to cupping my ass. "Speaking of which… I believe you mentioned something about fucking my brains out?"

"Oh, you caught that, did you?"

He nodded. "It was well played, too."

"She was a bitch."

I found myself being lifted and relocated across the room. The mattress hit the back of my legs.

"As I said, well played."

The billowy comforter caught me like a soft, cottony cloud. Adam pressed some of his weight down on me, pinning me to the spot.

"I was afraid she might try to take a swing at me."

"I'd never let that happen." He brushed the hair off my cheek. "I didn't want any of this near you, but I see now that I can't prevent it."

Each piece he gave of himself made me fall hopelessly deeper to the point that the actual word hovered in my throat, desperate to be spoken. "You can't hide parts just because you think I'm not strong enough to take it."

"I know you're strong enough; believe me." His fingertip tickled through my hair. "Still doesn't change things." I loved his smile. It was devastatingly beautiful and quickly becoming something I feared I couldn't live without.

He rolled his hips, distracting my constant need for self-preservation, snuffing my internal monologue that continuously reminds me of my fear of abandonment, and fueling my need to tell him I'm madly in love.

His lips sought my neck, working a path up to my jaw. "Getting all defensive and feisty. I like it."

"Good."

His heated stare roamed over my face. "Thank you."

I sifted through his hair. "You're welcome."

He nuzzled into my hand. "My doctor says I need an attitude adjustment."

I grinned at his playfulness. His need for me would have to be enough, for now. It's a role I was capable of filling. I met his gaze, letting him see my raw honesty. "I'll take care of you. I promise." I opened my thighs wider and clutched the muscles under his back pocket, letting him settle in where he belonged.

His kiss was soft at first, then became demanding.

"Good," he said, searing my mouth with another kiss. His fingers curled around mine, letting me see his own vulnerability in his hooded eyes. "I'm counting on it."

"YOUR PHONE PINGS a lot."

I don't know why I stated the obvious out loud; perhaps it was my way of acknowledging Adam's growing annoyance while he drove us through Manhattan and into the northern section of Queens.

He glanced at the screen and then tossed it face down in the cup holder. "Just ignore it."

"Is it important?"

"No." One word, delivered clipped, definitive.

"All righty, then," I drawled.

Adam frowned.

"You know, the moodiness is not a very attractive trait of yours."

He glanced over quickly, partially smiling. "Moodiness?"

"Yep. I've been studying it for a while now and it usually comes on when you're either keeping something from me or you don't know how to deal with me because you're unsure how I might react."

"Huh. Is that so?"

I stared out my window, watching the array of gray and brick buildings and graffiti-coated concrete slowly morph into a more residential area. "You scowl first—like this—and then you do that little thing where you chew on the inside of your mouth. Then your eyes get all squinty, like you're trying to see the answer but it's too far away."

Adam snorted. "I think that's my usual face, actually."

"No. It's not. Usually your face is relaxed, like everything is cool, and when you smile… those dimples come out and you're absolutely adorable. But this, well, whatever it is, combined with short answers makes it pretty obvious something's up." I may not be an expert on relationships, but to hell with dealing with not knowing. "Just so you know, I'd rather hear the painful truth than the false comfort of beautiful lies."

His broad shoulders dipped. "You don't pull any punches."

"Not usually. Medical detective, remember?"

He reached for his phone, holding it for a few seconds. "I've been getting annoying texts from someone. I don't know the number or who's sending them. And before you get all bent out of shape, I'm not seeing anyone but *you*. Just so we're clear on that."

Adam stopped at a red light and then entered his password in. "Here, detective. I got nothing to hide."

I was surprised he handed it over. "You have to turn left at the next street." I put my cell on my thigh and looked at his.

> Was U gunna mention ur
> new gf to me at all or no?

"Was u gunna?" *This person is about as smart as a box of rocks.*
Adam rolled his eyes. I scrolled down his screen.

Today 12:19 PM

> Answer me now

> Please answer me

> Just tell me please

> Answer me damnit

"This is pretty alarming, actually, not to mention their blatant butchering of the English language. Did you text her back?"

Adam was negotiating cross traffic. "No."

"Why not?" My arm squished into the door when he hit the gas.

"I don't have time for stupid shit like that."

"How will you know who they're from then? Did you use your cop superpowers?"

"My superpowers?" His lips wrinkled. "I checked. It's a burner."

"A what?"

"One of those cheap throwaway phones. No way to trace it."

So he did have super-sleuthing powers. "Do you think Tampon Girl would text you this?"

"I don't know," he mumbled.

"Do you want me to text her back?"

"Erin," he groaned.

"I won't say anything weird. I know a few doctors who treat mental disorders. I might even be able to get coupons."

"Ignore it." He leveled his "look" on me before finding me to be somewhat amusing. "I'm serious. If you're done calling me out on my shit maybe you can tell me which road I'm supposed to turn on. I'm blaming you if we're late."

You need help. Stop texting my boyfriend

Delivered

As soon as it delivered, I deleted them, seeing the only texts he had saved were from me, his "Hot Doc."

CHAPTER 24

Adam

OFFICER JOHN TURK was busy showing me surveillance footage they'd filmed of a warehouse that was suspected of being used to modify stolen cars, but I couldn't help stealing a few glances over at Erin while he was talking.

She was sitting at the other end of the long wooden dining table in their kitchen, being sweet and social and engaged in her own conversation with John's wife, Joanne. I should have been paying closer attention to what Turk was explaining but watching Erin lick the lunch off her fingers was more intriguing.

"We think they're changing the VINs, making them virtually untraceable as stolen," Turk said, taking a swig off his bottle of beer.

Beer. Just the smell alone was making my mouth water, causing me to do that internal negotiation that I'd be able to stop after just one. Even one sip would satisfy my taste buds. *Cold, crisp, the bite of hops on the back of my tongue. Just chillin' on a lazy Saturday with new friends.* I'd already turned down his offer of a cold one but I was reconsidering it now. The want was thick in my throat, dry and parched as the craving felt like sand mixed with my failing resilience.

Erin glanced my way, silently telling me that she was enjoying our company but concerned about the frosty bottle with that enticing condensation dripping down its sides being so close to my hand.

I moved my hand away and gave her a nod, letting her know that "just one" and I would not be meeting up, no matter how tempting the idea was. I'd already fucked up too many things in my life because of it; I wouldn't let Erin become a casualty of my weakness. Besides, she'd probably smack the bottle out of my hand before it got anywhere near my lips. She sure as hell wouldn't drink one in front of me while running her mouth around other people either, publicly humiliating me and making me feel less than a man for not being able to control myself like Nikki often did.

Erin came from good stock. Parts of the conversation I had with her dad after the funeral drifted back to my memory, and I was glad that we had such a long talk when I met him. She and I had agreed not to tell her parents the real way we'd met, opting for simple lie of "mutual friends" instead. Her dad was a car guy through and through and letting him think there was a "stolen" issue with his daughter's car was not the way to go about getting on his good side. "We'd have to check VINs coded on the chassis and within the computer systems, but we'll need different diagnostics."

Erin's adorable smile had me thinking I'd need to check her chassis soon too. I'd been inside her no less than five times since we'd arrived in the city yesterday, making good use out of the room Melissa had provided, although after our showdown I was sure I'd be getting a bill for it. I could still taste Erin's flavor on my lips, flashing back to holding her hips above me while she ate me for breakfast. I started counting all the different positions I'd had her in since we started fooling around, categorizing them to see if we'd missed any.

I'd like to see her orgasm face when I have her suspended. Hear her scream when she comes. That would take special knots and the hook in my ceiling. She'd probably give me a hard time at first until I got her up off the ground but then she'd love it—

"...barges and then they'd have to... You even listening to me?"

I felt Turk's nudge. "Huh? Yeah. Barges."

He smiled at me and then flashed his attention down the table. "You got it bad, bro."

I sat up a bit, trying to figure out what I was looking at on his computer screen. "Where did you say this warehouse was again?"

Turk shifted in his chair. "Corner of you're and in love, outside of Hoboken."

Now he was just fucking with me.

Turk waggled his eyebrows, grinning like an ass.

The baby monitor on the counter crackled and the little one who was babbling to himself started huffing, until he broke into an extended wail.

"Excuse me," Joanne said, standing. "I'd hoped he'd sleep longer but Colton is nosy, just like his dad."

"Hey," Turk snipped. "We're inquisitive. Nothing wrong with that."

I studied the information on his computer screen; what Erin's father had told me made sense. "Canada."

Turk pulled the laptop closer, squinting. "What?"

"This ring… they have a spotter collecting VINs, they replace US registration for Canadian, and then the car is clean."

"You shitting me?" Turk asked.

"Border patrol doesn't check registrations. They only ID occupants. No barges, no bill of ladings or any cargo paperwork. It's clean. Car disappears and reappears on a foreign lot to an unsuspected buyer."

"They'd have to reprogram the on-board computer," Erin added. "You'd have to add in someone who has access to the make and manufacturer software to override it."

God, I loved her. This bit of info wasn't news to me but hearing the words come out of her mouth was surprising. "And how do you know this?"

She shrugged nonchalantly. "My dad owns two dealerships? There was a problem with the system in my SHO when it arrived. It kept giving false tire pressure readings. One of the guys in my dad's shop showed me how he could plug in and reset stuff. It seemed pretty simple, but you'd need the right authorized dealer software to do it."

"Did your woman just blow a huge hole in our case?" Turk asked, gaping at me in disbelief.

Proud was an understatement. "Or added a major component that we need to pursue. Either way, I don't think these cars are going overseas."

"Hey little man," Turk crooned at his child.

"Here's everybody, nosy boy," Joanne said, bouncing a wide awake baby just a few months old in her arms. "Now you can see what's going on." She stood next to where Erin sat. "You want to hold him?"

"We've got several hours of surveillance video," Turk continued.

"What? Um, no. That's okay," Erin said, edging away.

"Just for a minute?" Joanne prodded "You can feed him if you want."

Erin backed up as if a bomb had just been set on the table instead of a baby bottle. "No. I can't. Fingerprints. Er, I mean my dirty hands."

Her hands looked clean to me.

"I don't want to get any germs on the bottle. I should wash them. It's cold and flu season and…" She stood and stumbled aside, her wooden chair scraping across the floor. "May I please use your bathroom?"

I held my hands out. "Pass him over. I'll hold him."

Joanne placed the little guy in my arms. "Got him?"

I settled him in, watching his little features scrunch up at me. "Hey little dude. What's up?" He didn't know who the hell I was, so I tried to set him at ease with some guy babble.

Erin stood stock-still, slightly gaping at me. Maybe I should have washed my hands, too? I didn't touch anything and I sure as hell had no plans of sticking my fingers in his mouth.

Turk was talking, but it was hard to be in two conversations at one time. Something was wrong… the way she ran off like that.

Turk and I scanned through weeks of video surveillance, stopping only when there was activity. And then it happened. "Rewind it."

Erin sucked in a breath behind me. "Is that…?"

The two men on the screen were unmistakable.

And one of them was already dead.

The other was wanted for his murder.

OVER THE NEXT few weeks, Erin and I started falling into a comfortable rhythm. Whenever possible, I was in her bed or she was in mine, except the Friday night before Ramirez's wedding.

Erin wanted nothing to do with intruding on my poker night, which was a shocker. Nikki always gave me a hard time, saying that she didn't do shit like that so I shouldn't either. Erin made her own plans with her friends, keeping her life instead of stopping it. I had invited her along, figuring she'd hang with Cherise, but she didn't seemed phased with doing her own thing—even though she strongly advised I "put my ass in bed and rest" since I'd been fighting a bit of a cold all week while spending extra hours looking over all the evidence from the Martins and Wyndmoor dealership robberies. I'd let her baby me for a few days but I was really feeling much better.

Come to think of it, all that care she gave me, I felt great.

All of this was swirling in my mind while sitting in God's house mid Saturday afternoon. I'd be lying if I didn't admit I spent most of the time sitting in that church pew imagining Erin standing up there in white. I'd considered marriage before but there was always that big chunk of doubt that made me realize something just wasn't right with the relationship to take it that far.

My parents had been married for almost forty years, and though they fought with the best of them, they never called it quits. Dad had said to us once that we needed to find the girl that would make us want to be a better man.

I held Erin's hand while we sat and watched fellow ATTF officer Jesse Ramirez's wedding. I didn't fully understand what my dad had meant by that, until now. It's not a comfortable feeling for me to do the self-analysis to acknowledge how I react to things. Now that we'd been officially dating for almost three months, little things were becoming crystal.

Hearing Erin tell the server she couldn't have the champagne when the woman tried to pour the toast at our table brought on a swell of guilt mixed with appreciation. Marcus was sitting across from us, giving his subtle nod of approval. He knew all my shit and now he knew that Erin knew my shit, too.

"You don't drink either?" Cherise asked.

What a leading question.

Erin shook her head. "No, not really, and oddly I'm not a big fan of champagne."

That was a lie.

A little lie she made up and tossed out effortlessly for me.

"You can have some," I whispered near her ear.

I watched her lick her bottom lip, leaning just as close. "If you don't, I don't. It's that simple."

I guided her chin, needing to kiss my woman.

There was a level of comfort there I'd never felt before. It was effortlessly easy. I pulled my cell out of my pocket, feeling the need to capture the moment. I leaned closer to Erin, snapping a few new pictures of us together to add to my growing collection.

Out of the corner of my eye I caught the blur of bright red interrupting my moment.

Then I heard *her* voice, trying to be sweet to Cherise. I watched Nikki work it, knowing she and Cherise were never tight. Cherise only tolerated Nikki for my benefit and that was not without effort.

Cherise, being the sassy mocha woman she was, was two seconds away from telling Nikki where to get off, and would deliver it without batting an eyelash.

"How are you, Adam?" Nikki asked, sizing up Erin more than anything. She had a date with her—some meathead looking dude that was busy eyeing the bar or the closest exit—probably in that order. That was until he noticed Erin.

My girl was looking especially gorgeous tonight. Flawless hair and makeup topping a killer dress that made me wish I had a private escape of my own. I could appreciate the package, but Nikki's date had three seconds to stop staring at Erin's tits before he'd meet my fist.

I leaned into his line of sight. *That's right, fucker. Eyes on me.*

"Aren't you going to introduce me?" Nikki said.

Cherise scoffed. "Does he have to?"

God, I loved that woman, too. She was the sister I wished I had.

Nikki shot her a dirty look.

I focused on Erin instead. She gave me a small eye-roll, making me check my manners. When it came to Nikki, I had none left.

"Nice to meet you, Nikki."

Yeah, Erin had much better manners than I did, but she still didn't reach to shake Nikki's hand. Ten points for our team.

"So how did you two meet?" Nikki asked, eyeing us both to see which one would answer.

This was getting old, fast. She wasn't asking just to make small talk.

I was just about to end this bullshit when Erin said, "I'm pretty sure you already know the answer to that, just like you know my name, where I work, and how long Adam and I have been seeing each other. Oh, let's not forget what kind of car I drive, too."

My partner Marcus choked on the other side of the table. It was fun to watch Nikki's smugness wither away. I'd shown him a few of the crazy texts I'd been getting the other night; the disgust rolling over Cherise's face confirmed that he'd shared that information with her.

Cherise turned in her chair and faced off with Nikki, letting the flair of her hands punctuate her message. "You satisfied now? You get all the information you were fishing for? I think it's best you move on now before you spoil my dinner. Go on. Get gettin'."

Right after Nikki stormed off, Marcus relaxed back in his chair, eyeing both of our women as though he was seeing them anew. "Daayum, I don't know which is hotter—white woman sass or black woman sass—'cuz you both are off the charts hot right now."

Erin's laughter lightened me right up.

Cherise leaned over toward Erin, doing the girl version of a fist bump. "I'm totally *all* over white woman sass myself. Damn, girl. I like you. Adam, I totally approve. You keep this one. That one over there, she's nothing but trouble. But this one, she's a keeper."

Good, then you'll all get along. "Glad to hear it."

It was hard to keep my hands off of Erin throughout dinner while she charmed the pants off my friends. I skimmed my hand over the top of her thigh, keeping low enough to let her feel my desires without being a perverted ass. Just watching her squirm while she tried to form sentences was providing me with unlimited entertainment. Even Nate Westwood and his wife Katie were hanging on Erin's words.

After dinner, the lights dimmed and the DJ's music filled the room. All eyes were pointed at the dance floor.

Jesse's groomsmen were tanked, making the first dance into a joke. Chucking the finger at each other and cursing with little kids watching? *Assholes.* My wedding would be classier than this, although Erin wouldn't want to put on pretenses. She'd opt for elegance.

Erin would dance with her father.

He'd twirl her in a circle, adding his love and suave footsteps to her joyous smile and laughter. Her dad was a class act. Her mom was gracious and warm and had me envisioning how beautiful Erin would become later in life.

My mom would be beyond ecstatic. While we slow danced, she'd tell me how proud she was of me while her eyes welled with tears of happiness. I'd make sure to have tissues on hand.

Marcus would be my best man.

I squeezed Erin's hand in mine, feeling drunk those possibilities when she lovingly brushed the edge of my jaw with her fingertips and smiled.

Picturing Erin as future wife material was effortless, although the fact that I was picturing her like that at all was a bit unsettling.

Didn't matter. As soon as I had my first opportunity, I seized it. I pushed my chair back and stood. "Come with me. I want to introduce you to someone."

Erin placed her hand in mine, giving me her trust. I weaved us through the maze of tables and bodies, finding a corner of the wooden floor I could call my own.

I spun Erin to face me and pulled her to my chest. The cling of her gorgeous dress, the fresh citrus smell of her hair—I was lost in it all.

"I thought you were going to introduce me to someone?" She gave me that sultry look I'd come to know and enjoy so well.

I pressed her body up against mine and swayed us to the slow beat. "I am. I hope you like him."

Her hand snaked over my shoulder, resting on the back of my neck, lightly caressing the hair under her fingers. It was ownership, which I willingly surrendered to. It also, though I know she didn't intend for it to be that way, sent a clear message to Nikki, who was trying not to watch us from the opposite side of the dance floor. "He's a good dancer."

I focused on Erin's lips. "I've got moves you haven't seen yet."

"Oh really?" Erin kissed the edge of my mouth. "I look forward to you showing me each and every one."

The want was too much; my restraint crumbled to pieces. Her mouth tasted so damn delicious, teasing her tongue with mine was all I could think about.

"People are staring," she whispered.

"I don't care." I didn't know if it was the music, the atmosphere, or the mood of the day, but it was overpowering. "Let them."

"Nikki is—"

"Don't. Don't even mention her name." I pressed Erin closer, swaying her hips with mine. She had to know being here in my arms—there was no other woman I would rather be holding. Even my fingertips pressing into her bare back felt desperate to get that through to her. Erin tucked her face into my neck; my eyes slipped closed, enjoying the feeling her lips softly whispering out each of the words in the song.

So this is what feeling completely happy felt like.

This is what breathing easy was all about.

Those three words were there on the edge of my tongue.

I placed a soft, lingering kiss on Erin's skin instead.

I'd have to tell her soon. It needed to be said that all of me loved all of her. Her curves, her edges, her perfect imperfections—just like the song. She needed to know that's what was inside me, pressing on my heart.

Our bodies naturally moved together with each passing beat, separate but whole somehow, as though I was holding on to the other half of me.

The song ended, breaking into a thumping tempo, which quickly killed the mood. That was until Erin started grinding her ass into my cock. I held her hips, imagining her repeating each of her moves while I was buried deep inside her.

I didn't need an alcohol buzz to push the rush through my veins. Erin was twice as heady and lethally potent, swirling me into a stupor. *That's it, baby. Let go.*

She grabbed my ass and owned me, making me a slave to whatever she needed. The power shift flowing between us heated my blood. Her back pressed to my chest, I slid my hand up the column of her throat, taking the power back. We were surrounded by a packed dance floor and sweaty bodies, but Erin smiling shyly over her shoulder at me commanded my complete attention.

She was getting tied up tonight.

I'd pound into her so fucking hard she'd lose consciousness. Sometime before that I'd tell her I'd fallen in love with her.

That's it, baby. Slide on me again. Who knew all it took was a bit of Usher and that Timberlake dude pumping in the air to light my girl up.

We needed to get out of here.

I needed her naked and to be doing this dance inside her—as soon as possible.

The next song started but I towed her off the dance floor.

"They're cutting the cake," she said.

"Fuck the cake." I needed the door.

"Don't you want any dessert?"

I weaved through the tables, focused on getting my suit jacket over the back of my chair. My keys where in the pocket. "I'm having you for dessert."

"Oh really?" She laughed.

Cherise passed us with two plates mounded with desserts and slid back into her seat at the table. She knew how to turn Marcus on. All it took was a pile of sugar and a fork.

One of the servers placed cut cake at our seats. Much to my displeasure, Erin sat down. *Okay, sips of water, the taste of sweet icing flavoring that mouth of yours for me, and then we're out of here.*

I swiped a nip of icing off her slice, smeared it on her bottom lip, and licked it off while kissing her. Icing was my new favorite thing. I'd take my slice to go. "I'm hitting the men's room. Then we're out of here."

I ignored Cherise's questioning eyes. She should know a man on a mission when she saw one.

CHAPTER 25

Erin

A TRICKLE OF sweat dribbled down between my breasts from dancing. My chest heaved after Adam left me breathless.

Icing. Mmm.

My tongue searched for any remaining sugar.

Cherise had me pegged in her sights from the other side of the table. "Mmhmm," she murmured, taking another bite of something that was coated in chocolate.

A tinge of embarrassment rushed over me, wondering how others perceived our little public display. The way she was nodding at me, it could have been one of several perceptions.

"Told ya," Marcus drawled, clearly speaking to his wife.

"I've seen it with my own eyes now," she added.

My cheeks were warm.

"So Erin…," Cherise leaned up on the table, "you falling for our boy Adam? Because I got to tell ya, he's a good man."

"Cher," Marcus groaned.

She shut him down with a glare. "I was just going to say that he's been through a lot and I'd hate to see his heart get broken."

Marcus rolled his eyes, clearly not supporting his wife's intervention. It was quite the dynamic, seeing as Cherise was a tiny thing compared to the linebacker of a man she was married to.

I'd hoped Adam would come back soon before they accused me of something. I couldn't see him anywhere through the crowd. "I think if anyone's going to get hurt here, it will probably be me."

Cherise's eyebrows rolled up on her forehead. "How you figure?"

I'd think that was obvious. "Ex-girlfriends, enamored fan girls… He has *a lot* more options for variety than I do." I took another bite of my cake, savoring a renewed taste of the memory of vanilla icing before the other thoughts took me down. "I see winos and crackheads with gunshot wounds. It's not like my dance card has a waiting line."

Her long fingernails twirled in my direction. I was thirty years old and I'd never treated myself to a professional manicure. "See now, that's the thing. He isn't like that."

I met her head on, knowing her scrutiny was coming from her love for Adam. It was respectable. "I know." Nikki was still watching me from the other side of the room. "I don't think his ex got that memo though."

"Psht. That girl needs to get a clue. That trip's been over for a *long* time. She needs to move the fuck along."

"Cher," Marcus warned low again.

She just ignored him, cutting into her cake with the side of her fork. "He's different with you. I ain't ever seen him like this. I gotta say, I'm liking it. 'Bout time he found his slice of happy."

"Word," Marcus agreed.

"I'm telling ya," she answered.

Part of me had wondered how this evening was going to play out. Adam had forewarned me about Nikki being here but his partner's wife was a bit unexpected. At least his friends looked out for him. That said a lot, actually.

"Adam tell you about Sadie's birthday party?"

I tried to read her since it was appearing as though I should know what she was talking about. "Sadie?"

She dabbed her mouth with her napkin. "Our daughter. She's turning two and we're having a birthday party. You should come. Adam's a great godfather, so he'll be there."

"He's her godfather?" My mind flashed to a church scene, picturing him smiling fondly.

She nodded. "He didn't tell you?"

"Mmn, no."

"Well, it's not this Sunday but next Sunday. Two o'clock. Make sure he brings you. We'd love to have you there."

Mmm. Okay.

"I'll tell him," she added. "Those two have something special. Sadie lights up like he's Santa or something when he's around her. Adam's great with kids. Who knows... you keep this good vibe going with him, you'll be having your own babies before ya know it."

Babies? Oh fuck. My bite of cake hit like a bowling ball in my gut when I swallowed.

"Cher, getting ahead of yourself," Marcus droned low.

"I don't think so. He's your partner; you going to deny that boy's in love? You seeing what I'm seeing?"

"Yeah, but... not sure that's any of our business."

"Psht. Adam is my business. He's your business, too. Someone's got to make sure he stays the course. And look at her. Sweet and gorgeous and smart. The two of them will make beautiful babies."

Babies???

I don't want to have babies.

Babies made women insane.

Damning fingerprints.

Broken collarbones.

Perforated kidneys.

Buying ethylene glycol by the gallons. Why?

No.

No, no. no.

I won't be a statistic.

It was hard to breathe.

Cherise going on and on about it; her insanity was shining through bright and clear.

Adam would want children. Wouldn't he? "I don't even know if that's what he wants."

I started sweating again without even moving. I needed air. Cold, refreshing air, preferably at sixty miles per hour while holding my head out of the window as I sped in the opposite direction of this table.

"Here he is. Ask him," she said.

Adam slid into his chair next to me. "Ask me what?"

"You want kids, right?" she asked bluntly.

He was totally caught off guard. "I don't know. I guess."

Her eyes were like laser beams. "What do you mean, you guess? I know you do."

He was uncomfortable, being put on the spot like that.

"Well, yeah, I guess. Eventually." He stared at me as if I was the one who'd lost her mind. "Where did this all come from?"

I gestured across the table, wishing I could shrink down and hide under the tablecloth. I needed to escape. "Where were the bathrooms?"

Adam pointed. "Down the hallway on the right."

"Excuse me please." The doorway was promising all sorts of air on the other side. My high heels had me leaning forward, quickening my steps.

I didn't really need to pee, but hiding in a stall for the rest of the evening was starting to sound promising.

I made it three steps inside the ladies' room before I almost ran over the bride.

I pulled up quickly before falling over a pool of white taffeta.

She was standing in front of the bank of sinks, cursing and crying, using wads of paper towels to wipe the mess of cake and icing off her face. Cake was everywhere: her hair, her nose, and down the front of a very poufy gown.

The tradition of smashing cake in each other's faces was disgusting. It was so disrespectful, like saying "here, bitch, fuck you" and defiling hours of beautification with no mutual consideration.

The way she was privately distressed, I'd say she agreed with me.

"Do you need help?"

Her bottom lip wobbled. "Would you?"

I yanked a wad of paper towels from the container, not really knowing where to start. I picked a spot near her neck. "He got you good."

"Bastard," Ellie groaned. "Shoved the whole piece at me. I told him not to, but..." She sighed. "My dress is ruined."

I had no idea how to remove red icing from white either.

Ellie gave me a weak smile. "Thanks. You're Erin, right? Adam's new girlfriend?"

I tossed a chunk of cake into the garbage. "Yes. Sorry we're meeting like this. I hadn't had an opportunity to meet you before."

"It's okay. I'm just glad for the help. My maid of honor is drunk off her ass. My mom is gonna be so pissed when she sees these stains. Two grand in the mutha-effin toilet."

"Maybe if we get some club soda some of this will come out."

Ellie swiped at the black smear that had now turned gray. "It's no use."

I pulled a chunk of icing from her dark hair. "Do you have another outfit you can put on?"

"No. I thought the whole point was to have my husband take me out of this dress later." She smacked the garbage can lid as she disposed of the last of her wet paper towels. "Fucking A. I am so mad. How could he do this to me? Take note, being married to a cop isn't all it's cracked up to be. Ask Nikki. She learned that the hard way."

My brain almost imploded. "They were married?"

"No, well, almost," Ellie said, squinting at me. "He didn't...? They had a date set but... I probably shouldn't be telling you this."

"No, please. Go on."

"Apparently Adam was having fun on the side with some fan or something. I'm not sure of the details, just what Nikki told me." More cake hit the sink. "Woman to woman, just be careful, okay?"

Oh my God. My stomach churned, burning acidic torment up into my throat.

"But that doesn't... Oh, I'm sorry. I shouldn't have said anything. You know what I mean. You must have been shitting yourself that night they pulled you over."

I didn't know how to answer. I feared anything I'd try to say would come out as a scream. Washing the icing stains from my hands was a good diversion, though hiding in the bathroom had turned into a huge mistake.

"You know all the guys in the unit are sorry about what happened to your relatives. Weird. Jesse said they almost had that car pulled over, too." She tisked. "If Adam and Marcus hadn't tried to pull them over—"

The bathroom lighting seemed to dim. "Wait, what?"

"Jesse said they were told to pull back but I guess Adam knew the driver or something and kept going after them. Once a car gets out onto the Schuylkill it's just a matter of time."

A pain shot through my forehead. "Adam knew the guys that killed my aunt and uncle?"

"Yeah." She nodded. "You didn't know that?"

Her words disappeared behind me.

This new information twisted in my gut, driving my feet to move. I hit the hallway and stopped, unsure of which way to go. I had my purse under my arm and enough cash for a taxi. Adam was in the other direction, scorching my mind as the source of this increasing misery.

Left or right—either choice left me hurt in the end.

I don't want to do this anymore.

The secrets. The lies. Settling for a piece of a man's heart instead of the whole. What he'd already given away to another would never be mine.

I should have prepared for this. I knew it was coming, but I tricked myself. Told myself that if I ignored it, it would just simply disappear.

The irrational hopelessness doubled me over.

Inviting someone in always left me broken and doomed to making concessions with what I wanted out of life.

My mother was seeing a grief counselor now just to cope—cope with the tragedy that he'd somehow had caused.

He knew.

Son of a bitch! He knew!

He knew that night he ran out of my living room!

What was this? Was this relationship appeasing his guilt?

Anguish flamed over me.

Watching him from afar as he smiled and laughed, so carefree and unaffected, while I crumbled inside. I couldn't face him. Not yet. Not when I wanted to scream and cry and throw up. I needed to gather my thoughts.

I found a settee at the end of the hallway. Seeing Nikki's smug face when she came out of the ladies' room was the final straw. My hands shook as I searched for a taxi service. Cell reception inside the building was poor. The little icon on my screen swirling in a circle mirrored my emotions. My eyes stung.

"Erin?" Adam's voice echoed.

I knew if I looked up he'd see the unshed tears in my eyes.

"Babe, are you okay?"

I held my breath, afraid to let any sound escape.

Adam crouched down in front of me. "Erin, what's wrong?"

EVERYTHING!

The word rattled around inside me; a fury of sound punishing my sanity. "Nothing. I'm, um… I'm just not feeling well."

"You sick?"

I'm dying.

"Can you?" *Breathe. Just breathe.* "I'm going to go home. You stay. Have fun. I'll call a cab."

"If you're sick, I'll take you home."

I thought you were my home.

I knew he was concerned but inner rage was warring with my rationale. "I'll be fine."

"I'll get our coats." He was already taking a step away.

"No, really. You stay. I can find my own way home."

That instantly displeased him. "Stay put. I'll be right back. You're not leaving here without me."

God, why did he have to be nice? Why couldn't he be a typical jerk and leave me to my own devices so I could hate him even more? Maybe he should take me directly to the hospital, because the pain consuming me was excruciating.

My pulse was elevated, galloping instead of beating.

My skin felt like it was on fire. My chest was tight. My inner practitioner started listing symptoms and treatments.

He. Knew.

He stayed away from me for an entire week, sneaking around my house, making repairs to my shit. Why? To make himself feel better? He'd said he tried to stay away from me. I distinctly remembered those words coming out of his mouth.

And now I'd put my heart out there. Given it to him.

I needed to make an appointment with a Cardiologist as soon as possible. Maybe some crack whore died tonight and I could receive her hardened, uncaring heart. I'd give her mine willingly. Wouldn't take long to gather a transplant team together; *anything* to take the pain away.

Agony.

Adam held my long wool coat out for me. "Stay inside. It's raining. I'll get the truck."

My eyes slid closed while the rest of me crumbled.

It was a silent twenty-five minute drive; my only words being that I wanted him to take me home to my house when it appeared that he was headed to his. "You don't want to stay at my place?"

He sounded wounded; his expectations were not my own.

If I'd only waited another ten minutes instead of running to the restroom. Why did Ellie feel the need to ruin me so effectively? Did she have an ulterior motive? Didn't matter. The fact still remained that he knew and didn't tell me. I could understand, in a way, why he chose to keep it secret. We'd be right here where we were now, well, me at least, but it would have happened weeks ago.

Too many thoughts were slamming into each other, flashing like the lightning that rippled through the sky. I couldn't form a solid resolution on anything. Feelings too numerous to identify bombarded the spaces in between, leaving me dizzy and disoriented within my own head.

"I'm just gonna go to sleep."

"You feeling that bad? Do you think it was something you ate?"

The only answer I was capable of was in the form of a non-committal shrug.

Adam pulled into my miniscule driveway and shut off the lights.

My mind told me not to, but the swell of emotions pushed the words out in a whisper. "Were you ever going to tell me?"

He turned toward me. "Tell you what?"

"About the accident. About the chase before it."

"Jesus," Adam groaned, cupping his head in his hand.

"You knew. For weeks you've known."

"Erin. What do you want me to say?"

Nothing. There was nothing to be said, just a final admission.

"Do you want children?"

"What?" Shadows from the streetlights broke through the rivulets of rain, casting gray streaks over his questioning face. "Kids? Yeah, I guess. Eventually. Why are you—"

A dry ache formed in the hollow of my throat. "I don't want children."

His confusion turned to shocked surprise. "You don't?"

My decision was absolute. "No. Never."

I'd stymied him. "Ah…" He blew out an exasperated breath. "Is that with me or—"

"I don't want kids with anyone. This is a problem." I pulled on the door handle, flicking the interior lights on in the process. I'd had a few panic attacks before, but this one was full on. "You should have them. You'll be a great dad. I have to go."

"Wait. I'm coming in. We need to talk about this."

Everything inside me was fragmented. Part of me already knew that this was going to end one day. Another part knew I was behaving totally irrationally but I couldn't stop the avalanche. I was powerless against the anger and disappointment. "Please just go home." I shut the door and ran through the rain.

"Erin. Come on."

The keys shook in my hand. "Please, Adam. Just go home."

"Erin, for fuck's sake."

I shoved my thick door open and closed it just as quickly, feeling Adam's fist pounding on the other side. "Erin. Open the fucking door. What the fuck?"

He was mad. The pounding became more vicious.

He didn't have the right to be mad.

I didn't cause my aunt and uncle to be sliced and compressed under thousands of pounds of tumbling steel. My family had been permanently scarred that night too. Me included. And he knew all along.

It was all too much; I was drowning in information overload.

"Just go home. Please." I knew he didn't hear me.

"It wasn't my fault!" he shouted. "Damn it! Would you just talk to me?"

I could barely hear myself over the gasping sobs that finally broke free.

Children made women into homicidal maniacs capable of unspeakable things.

My cell rang while the random pounding continued. He was inventing curse words now, stringing many together. I swiped my face, smearing mascara and eye shadow, which instantly burned. I left everything at the door: my coat, my cell, the remains of my dignity.

A short while later I heard his tires squeal as he backed out of my driveway.

The unexpected surgery had been excruciating.

IT TOOK EXACTLY one hour for the onslaught of regret to hit. It was worse than the previous sixty minutes of uncontrollable sobbing. My cell eventually stopped ringing around two in the morning. It was close to three-thirty when the Valium kicked in.

It was quarter after nine when the need to pee woke me up. It was nine twenty when I took another Valium.

I moved to the couch at one thirty with a roll of toilet paper and an empty box of tissues.

I ate stale crackers around four.

I ate a tablespoon of peanut butter off my finger around five.

I cleaned up the remains of the antique candy dish that had somehow slipped off the table by the dining room window and shattered onto the floor. I didn't recall bumping into it.

I called Jen at seven twenty. She listened to me cry for an hour then made me question my reactions.

There was one missed call from Adam—just one.

The damage I'd caused was irreparable.

A loud pop woke me up at ten thirty. My legs jerked, sending the sofa pillows that were between my ankles to the floor.

I turned the television off and went up to bed.

ALL DAY MONDAY I tried to keep busy, keep my head in the game, but the special meeting to review changes to hospital policy left me too much idle time to wander in my head while staring blandly at a slideshow presentation.

This was worse than when Randy told me he was seeing someone else. That had been an explosion of anger, followed by an attempted cleansing by piling his shit next to the door. My current state was akin to having a soul excision without anesthesia. I had zero energy and even less enthusiasm for breathing. I wanted to tell every whiny patient to fuck off. Couldn't they see I was broken too?

I hid in the quiet of Jamal Clement's ICU room for a while, watching him sleep, thinking about how vastly different his problems were from mine. While I sat nursing a broken heart, he'd survived several gunshot wounds, had gone through major surgery, and was finally breathing on his own. His road to recovery was littered with hurdles, and I wondered how long after he'd be discharged until his life would be in mortal peril again. My mortality seemed to be contingent upon my own stupidity. At least I wouldn't have to testify about who he'd said had shot him. Thank God that responsibility didn't fall on me.

I spent the remainder of Monday night flipping through a sad array of Netflix movies, settling on watching Niecy Nash tell family after family that they lived in pigsties. I felt just as cluttered and disorganized inside.

Maybe I needed a trio of well-meaning designers to come clean me out, drag my shit out into the yard, and put my shame on public display.

Maybe the shit inside my head was my version of their hoarding saltshaker collections? It was all stupid stuff that we clung to, useless crap we'd collected over the years that we gave power and meaningless value to.

I had too much crap.

I wanted to call Adam, tell him about my self-discovery, but it was too late. The pillow beneath my head scratched my face. Something was poking my cheek. I smoothed the fabric beneath, finding the frayed edge of a tiny hole with my fingertip. Great. Now my belongings were starting to decay along with me.

A chill shook my body; the cold, drafty desolation in my living room was too much. I wrapped my fleece blanket over my shoulders and turned up the heat. I'd allow myself to wallow for one more night and then tomorrow I'd get back into focus, get back into studying, and put my original plan in the forefront.

I never even asked him if he'd be okay with not having children. I totally overreacted. No, I didn't. I wasn't what he would end up wanting.

And he knew the bastards that killed my aunt and uncle and didn't tell me. But what good would it have done it if he had? He held my mother when she cried, for God's sake.

Most guys didn't want to even think about knocking a girl up either. Adam had been inside me quite a few times without a condom. He'd never finish inside me that way but we were still relying on my IUD to keep us from procreating.

I flipped to the other side of the couch. Sleeping was out of the question; my mind was heavily laden with thought after thought. I had drifted into a numbing zone when my cell pinged, showing I'd received a text from Adam.

There were no words surrounding the photo he'd sent, as the image of the two of us together said it all. I don't know when he'd taken the picture, but we were in his bed. I was apparently asleep in his arms, though my mouth was curled with a serene and quite content smile. Adam's eyes were heavy, as though he'd just awoke and taken the picture. We were blissfully happy.

Were.

My cell rang in my hand, showing Adam's name where our picture just was. It was almost midnight, so he had to be out in the city somewhere. The relief that he hadn't given up on us hit me hard. "Hi."

"You gonna talk to me now?" He was on guard and short with me, and rightly so.

"Yes."

"Ritchie, you point that camera at me one more fucking time, I'll shove it so far up your ass you'll choke on it," he warned. "I can't even move anymore," he mumbled to me. "She's got every camera crew on me."

I listened to him stress out. He was pacing in some parking lot, no doubt.

"You still there?" he finally asked.

"Yeah, I'm here."

"You going to give me a chance to explain?"

"Yes."

"I didn't cause the accident, Erin. I swear to God I didn't."

A tear formed, followed by another, prefacing the thickening in my throat.

"Baby, you have to believe me. I'm so sorry. I tried... I tried to stop them but they just... I swear I tried."

I wiped my eyes. "I believe you."

"I'd never hurt you. I didn't know how to tell you. You'd been through enough. You. Your family." Adam drew in a breath. "And now that you know, I don't know how to fix it."

"You knew them."

He sighed. "I'd arrested them both once before. I didn't know they were the ones in the vehicle until afterward. Our field supervisor called off the pursuit after they almost hit a pedestrian. We had no choice, sweetheart."

He was following orders.

"Tell me how to fix this, Erin. Please"

"I... I want you to be happy, Adam. That's all."

"You make me happy, baby. You."

I recognized the desperate truth in his voice, but eventually he'd come to resent me. I knew I couldn't give him the future he deserved but the greedy, selfish part of me didn't care to concede.

"So who filled your head? Was it Nikki?"

I swirled a few passes of toilet paper around my fingers. "The bride, actually."

"You fucking serious?"

"She told me you were engaged, too."

Heavy breathing mixed with silence. "I never gave her a ring, Erin. Never. We never got to that point."

Some of the pressure left my chest. "Ellie said you had a date set but you were cheating on Nikki with someone else."

"Jesus Christ. No. It was actually the other way around." Adam was getting creative again with his curse words. Weird, but I could actually hear him rubbing his face. "Please tell me you didn't believe her."

"You're not a cheater, Adam. I know that."

His wordless answers were filled with relief.

"You know she and Nikki are friends, right? I wonder how she would feel if she found out everything Nikki's told her were lies."

"Adam…"

"I never asked her to marry me, Erin. We talked about it, won't deny that, but… Christ. I don't want to be talking about this over the phone with you."

"I know. Maybe we can—"

A loud bang went off outside, followed by another. And another. Glass shattered. The pillow next to me moved on its own. I hunched and then screamed when the lamp next to the couch exploded, sending the room into darkness.

Adam yelled in my ear.

I hit the floor, cutting my knee on something sharp.

Another bang. The mirror above my sofa cracked and then smashed to the floor.

"Stay on the phone with me!" Adam ordered. He was shouting so many things but I lost him when my phone skidded across the floor.

I scurried down the hall, tripping over my own feet as another shot went off. Pain blistered into my forehead when I smacked into the wall at the mouth of the hallway. Forward momentum knocked me down. My arm gave out under my weight but I had to keep moving.

Absolute terror folded me effortlessly.

There was no place for me to go. Nowhere to hide.

I ended up in the downstairs bathroom, huddling between the toilet and sink cabinet.

Something warm trickled down over my eye while I shook uncontrollably in the dark.

CHAPTER 26

Adam

MARCUS COULDN'T DRIVE fast enough.

Other units were dispatched; their lights and sirens lit up the night sky behind us. But it didn't matter. I didn't want to think about what I might find when I finally reached her.

He drove our rig right onto her front lawn. Gun drawn, I was up at her door, shouldering it in easily. Marcus was at my back.

"Erin!" I shouted, hoping and praying with every fiber of my soul she'd answer me back.

Shit was scattered on the floor: broken glass, pillows, a lampshade.

Marcus shoved me up against the wall; the whites of his eyes drilled reminders into me of years of training, of protocol, of keeping the team safe. Several other uniformed officers entered behind us.

"We clear first," Marcus growled low through his teeth.

All I could see was blinding rage and a terrifying fear that I wouldn't get to her in time. I pushed back but he shoved me harder, knocking some sense into me.

Flashlights lit up the rooms, the stairs, announcing police presence with every step.

"Adam!"

I heard her shaky voice before my flashlight scanned over her petrified face. Her arms were around my neck in the next step. I had her pinned to the wall two seconds after, shielding her body with mine until all threats were neutralized. She was barely dressed; I at least had a vest on, able to protect her.

"I'm here, baby. I'm here. You're safe."

The familiar smell of her hair, the feel of her warm skin against my cheek as she shook in my arms—it was the best and worst feeling in the world, making it harder to breathe.

I caged her in, unwilling to holster my weapon in case I needed to kill the fucker who did this. I'd think about revenge and retribution later.

"Are you hit?" My words came out choked with everything I'd been feeling, knowing I'd seen blood on her face.

She was trembling. "N… no."

I wiped her hair back, scanning her from head to toe, moving clothes to see her skin, assuring myself that she was okay.

My heart clenched. "You're bleeding."

She touched her forehead. "I tripped in the hallway."

"Did they come inside?"

"No." Her head shook. "I don't think so. I… I didn't hear anything. Adam…"

I hugged her, taking her tears as my own threatened to follow. I kissed her hair, trembling with her. "I know, sweetheart. I know. I got you."

All throughout the house officers were calling out "clear," announcing that each room was free from perpetrators. Lights in every room were turned on.

Marcus holstered his weapon. "You all right?"

Erin swiped her hair back, nodding.

He shined his flashlight on her forehead, minding her eyes. "She need an ambulance?"

I wanted him to quit looking. "She's okay. Just shaken."

Marcus glanced around while more officers paraded through. "Any ideas who'd do this?"

I didn't want to state it out loud, but whoever did this was trying to kill her to hurt me, and that made the list of possible suspects quite long.

I DROVE PAST my house slowly before circling the block and pulling into my garage. Erin had been quiet for the last few hours, withdrawing pretty hard while local PD processed the scene. She answered questions as best as she could but beyond describing hearing the gunshots and seeing things break, she had no valuable information to share.

My captain had shown up shortly after we cleared the house, providing a great buffer between the leading questions posed by the investigator assigned and me. As if I'd want any harm to come to the woman I was in love with.

I knew he was just doing his job but I didn't like him implying that I was directly involved. I wanted to question her neighbors myself, but there was no way I could leave her side. I had to take the other officer's word for it that they'd do a thorough job.

"What makes you think we'll be safe here?" she murmured. I let her doubt slide as I knew she'd been through the wringer and her voice was still shaky.

"I have an alarm system and plenty of weapons. This is safer than a hotel."

She nodded; the life had been sucked out of her.

"Erin, look at me."

She was on the verge of tears again. It killed me.

"I won't let anything happen to you. I promise. You trust me?"

I didn't like her pause before she nodded.

I grabbed her suitcase and her duffle bags and set them outside the kitchen door. I punched in my alarm code and then reset it, moving Erin into the corner of my kitchen, away from windows.

I had a Sig Saur loaded in the cabinet above the microwave. I made sure a round was chambered and handed it to her. "Don't shoot me. Safety on, safety off. Red is dead. Remember?"

I knew she was confused. I pulled my service weapon. "You stay here. I'm clearing the house to make sure you feel safe, and then we're going to bed. Okay?"

The fear was back in her eyes.

"That's just like the weapon you fired at the range. You know how to handle it. We've got this." I touched her face. "You with me?"

Erin nodded.

"Words, Doc. You with me?"

"I'm with you."

"Good. I'm going upstairs first. Try not to accidentally shoot me."

She frowned at me, but it had to be said.

I checked doors and windows and then went room by room. She was mostly a zombie, reeling in shock when I got back to her. I relieved her of the weapon and grabbed her bags. "Come on. Let's get some rest."

We moved around my bedroom in silence; gone was the comfortable familiarity and effortless ease. In its place was separation and mistrust. She took a shower by herself and then crawled under the covers, putting her back to me, spanning that distance even farther.

I rested up on my hand and stared at the back of her wet head, aching to fix this.

"Erin."

She made no effort to move so I moved her.

I held her cheek so she wouldn't be able to turn away and ignore me. I searched her eyes, praying I'd see some remaining love staring back at me. Her brow furrowed.

"I love you."

Her frown deepened.

"I've been in love with you for a very long time. I can't even think about not having you in my life." The images plaguing my mind were too vivid, too real. I couldn't bear being without her; the thought was too painful, beyond anything I'd ever felt for another person. I'd almost lost her. Almost. Part of me felt dead just acknowledging that. "I can't lose you."

My vision of her face blurred as the pain crushed into my chest. She'd become as necessary as breathing to me and losing that would take me out with it.

Her thumb caught one of my tears.

Her eyes were just as watery, making me say a silent prayer that she wasn't going to tell me goodbye.

"I love you too," she broke. "So much, it hurts."

I leaned down to kiss her, feeling her cry into my mouth, crushing me inside. Our fears turned into need—need to feel alive, to reconnect, to drown out the internal agony that consumed us both. She let me make love to her, allowing me to show her how much I couldn't live without her. Soft whimpers left her throat every time I told her I loved her, as though it physically hurt her to hear those words. I didn't care; I'd tell her a thousand times a day just so she'd know.

I wrapped her into my chest when we'd finished, forming a protective cocoon around her so she'd feel safe enough to sleep.

I woke up several hours later to an empty bed.

An empty house.

Erin and her bags were gone.

MY CALLS WENT unanswered.

My texts to her—ignored.

I drove by her house; her car was gone. The bullet holes through her large front window were easy to see in the light of day.

I cruised through the hospital's parking lot but there was no sign of her car there either.

Over the next few days I rolled through every emotion: from anger and aggravating betrayal to remorse and resentment. I managed to accomplish the very thing I had tried to prevent. I'd fucked up her life. Her house getting shot up had made the news. Pictures of her and her house were broadcasted on all of the television news channels, in the local section of the newspaper, and spread throughout every crevice on the Internet.

Erin had obviously shut her phone off; her voice greeting picked up immediately. Call it resourceful—I put my detective skills to work and eventually found her car at her parents'. I just needed to know she was somewhere safe with people looking out for her—not that she was incapable of doing that on her own, but it gave me some peace of mind to know she wasn't alone.

Local investigators managed to pull fifteen slugs out of Erin's walls and retrieved most of the spent shell casings outside, but without a weapon and a suspect, the case was cold. None of her neighbors had seen anything either, only reporting that they'd heard the gunshots. No one had even seen a suspicious car driving through the neighborhood. The elderly woman who lived directly across the street told me she'd heard loud cracks quite a few times over the last few weeks but never saw where they came from. The shots reportedly happened in the cloak of night, which led me to this new level of desperate insanity.

Someone had been firing a nine-millimeter at Erin and I needed to know who.

My hand squeezed harder on his throat, choking the dirtbag I'd snatched from the street. "I'm losing my patience, Felix."

"Get the fuck off me, pig," Felix groaned.

I crammed his face into the chain-link fence, pressing my advantage. The sun had already come up, revealing our position. DEA had recently seized this property, locking it down from local gang radar. There was nothing around us but an empty lot and abandoned buildings. "Yell all you want. Ain't no one gonna hear you."

Marcus was on point, being my backup, looking the other way while I bent the law. I tried to keep him out of this but he insisted he had my back. We were off duty when I snagged Felix; if anything happened now, we'd both be in trouble.

"I don't know nothing," Felix spat, trying to wiggle his scrawny body loose.

"They executed your brother, Felix." I put my next words right into his ear. "Two bullets to the head, not just one. Apparently one wasn't enough. Your cousin was on the slab next to Benny. Who's next, Felix? You? Your mom? Your sister? My woman?"

Felix rolled his face on the chain-link.

I was tired of him stalling. "Who put the hit out on my woman?"

"Man, I don't know nothing about a hit."

I shook him hard. "Do not fucking lie to me!"

"I'm not! No one is talking about taking out a cop or anything. I swear."

I twisted his arm higher, adding to his misery. "Who the fuck unloaded a magazine on my girlfriend?"

"I don't know," he snapped. "No crew even give a flying fuck about pig pussy."

I wanted to snap his neck. "You know they're coming after you next. If I found you, you think Mancuso's crew can't fish you out?" I could feel the small pipe in his front pocket. "You end up in gen-pop, you'll be shived before lunch."

"Man, fuck you."

"Sorry, not into skinny white dudes."

Marcus cleared his throat, telling me to speed this up.

"Why did they take your brother out, Felix? I already know who did it; help me understand why."

His resolve was wavering.

"Give me something. Help me get them off the streets. Your

mom, your sister, all safe."

"I talk to you, I end up like them."

"Not if I get to them first."

Felix scoffed. "Like mofos are worried about ATTF, 'n sure as hell ain't worried about Mister Hollywood. Boys have been playin' you for months. Ain't even breakin' a sweat over it."

I gave him another hard jostle as a reminder that time was ticking and I wasn't above beating his ass for answers. "Enjoy jail. Fuck if I care you become someone's bitch."

"All right. All right," he groaned. "You gonna let me walk?"

"Up to you. It's all just paperwork for us."

"Shew." He glared over his shoulder. "I'm a dead man."

"Then do your brother a solid."

Felix bowed his head, slowly rolling it. "All I know was Benny was talking to this dude."

"Who?"

"Name's Akim."

"Akim?"

"I don't know what went down. Benny didn't share."

"Where do I find this Akim?"

Felix sneered. "Man, what do I look like? The muther-fucking phone book?"

Marcus reached back, palmed Felix's head, and shoved hard, bouncing his face off the fencing. That got the punk to change his answer.

He spit blood onto the ground. "Try Savage Lexus, you fuckin' fucks."

"I DON'T KNOW, brother," Marcus drawled.

I caught the sight of Felix walking in my side mirror as the tires kicked up stones and dust behind me.

"If they wanted her dead, she'd be dead." That realization had hit me soon after I had dragged Felix by the hair from the back of the truck. Criminals didn't send "messages" —they made statements and drove them home painfully.

Marcus nodded. "Harsh but true. And we sure as hell have been getting played at our own game."

I glanced at him quickly.

"Yeah," he said, reading me, "I thought about that too. Don't want to think about one of our own but nothing surprises me anymore."

"Don't know how else they could know our moves."

Marcus scoffed. "Shit. We've been broadcasting our deal every fucking Sunday. Even my eight-year-old nephew can call it."

I peeled out of the lot, heading north back into the city, retribution the only thing on my mind.

"Adam, want you to know that I get ya. Someone tore up my house putting my family in danger, I'd be losing my fucking mind. Just got to play this smart, you follow? Can't fire off half-cocked; that shit will get you hurt."

Hurt? I already felt dead inside; the rest was still blistering out, leaving a path of char and agony in its wake. "I lost her, Marcus. Wasn't bad enough that Ramirez's wife filled Erin's head with shit. There were bullet holes in the pillow where she'd been resting on the couch. As much as I don't want to admit it, someone tried to take me out, I'd probably leave, too."

Marcus nodded. "She back to work?"

"Yeah. Last two nights. One of the security guards there has been giving me updates. He knows the deal and is keeping watch."

"Good. You ever think…?" He looked out the window. "Nah."

I hated open-ended comments. "Think what?"

Marcus glanced over. "Shit like this makes for exciting TV."

I ground my teeth together. "Thought of that, too. But there's no connection between someone firing up Erin's place and the show, beyond Melissa, and as much as she's another one to be leery of, she ain't crazy enough to attempt murder."

"Dumb and Dumber were with us when we got that call, though. I don't remember if they filmed the scene, do you?"

My mind was a swirling vortex of rage. I'd been focused on one thing and one thing only that night—making sure Erin was alive. "Can't say if they did or not."

"I hate to say it, bro, but this ain't over."

Something inside my chest twisted.

I knew it wasn't my heart.

Erin had taken that with her when she'd left.

HOURS HAD TURNED into days, and days into another week.

I trudged through each one, knowing that Erin would never come back to me while the threat to her life still existed.

Ballistics came back empty on the slugs removed from Erin's house, so matching bullets to a gun was another dead end.

Yesterday I received a certified letter from a law firm representing Werner Communications, threatening to pursue damages since I'd been pulled off normal patrol duty while leading this investigation in Philly. Just one more thing I had to fucking worry about although Cap said lawyers for the department would handle it on my end.

Melissa Werner could go fuck herself.

Ritchie and Scott could go fuck themselves, too.

I ended yet another call from Scott asking me when we'd be getting back on regular patrol. His constant calls were getting annoying. It was a relief not to have cameras in my face.

"Surveillance is boring," Marcus grumbled, making a racket while emptying a small bag of potato chips into his mouth.

I scanned back and forth again with my binoculars, waiting for movement outside Savage Lexus. We'd codenamed the case "Operation Trident" as we were working with units out of New York and New Jersey as part of a massive tri-state investigation.

Another Lexus and two new Ford trucks had been stolen out of a suburb of Newark and two Lincolns disappeared out of the upper east side of Manhattan.

Between the three teams working this case, we had amassed a list of twenty-nine suspects, including the possible "key master" working under the guise of an auto mechanic at this dealership.

Either the end buyers were getting anxious or the ring was getting sloppy. It was just a matter of time before we pulled up nets and snagged them all.

It was also time to get "Operation Recoup" underway as well.

HOSPITAL EMERGENCY WAITING rooms had to be one of the worst places on Earth, especially going on ten-thirty at night. Marcus and I had been working odd hours depending on what we had going on, but there were a few people still holding strong on the night shift.

And here I sat amid crying children and people who didn't look all that sick, waiting patiently for a person I'd never met to come save me. I'd give her props though; she made me suffer just a bit, leaving me waiting out here for almost an hour.

Finally a slender woman with wild hair came into the waiting area and stopped in front of me, none too happy, I might add.

I looked up, taking in her no-bullshit stance. "You must be Sherry."

Yeah, obviously.

She rested her hands on her hips. "She'd kill me if she knew I was out here talking to you."

Part of me didn't feel guilty about that. "I know. I appreciate it."

One of Sherry's eyebrows rose, waiting.

"She doing okay?"

"No. She's completely miserable, actually. We're blaming you, just so you know."

I guess I deserved that. "She's not the only one who's miserable."

Sherry didn't need to say the word "good." It was written all over her face. "I have to get back to work."

"Look, I know you don't know me, and all her friends probably hate me, but I love her and I miss her and this, this messed-up bullshit—"

Her arms crossed, taking a new stance. "Did you tell her this? That you love her?"

I nodded. "Yes. But she won't take any of my calls; she won't talk to me. I honestly don't know what to do."

"One question." She held up her index finger. "This love that you speak of, does it come with a future? I mean, none of this 'I love you' crap now until something else comes along, wasting everyone's time, because that would be a total dick move on your part and would hurt her even more than she's hurting now."

I squinted at her. "Something else?"

Sherry huffed. "You know what I mean. She deserves someone who is in it for the long haul, not some guy whose ego has been bruised and needs to prove something to himself."

"I've got nothing to prove." Actually, I felt quite defeated. "She's already made up her mind. Told me she didn't want kids with me." I started to question why I was even trying. I needed to quit this pity-party and accept the facts. I stood. "Sorry I wasted your time. Thanks for seeing me."

"Wait."

My legs stopped on a glimmer of hope.

"You love her that much?"

I nodded. "Long haul."

Sherry exhaled and then pulled her phone out of her pocket. "Give me your number. I'm not making any promises but we can try."

I didn't know what came over me, but right there in the crowded waiting room, I gave this woman a hug.

I'VE BEEN IN hand-to-hand combat with drugged-out criminals wielding weapons, been through countless court appearances and testimonies, and even endured thirty-two years of my mother's disapproving gaze, but none of that really prepared me for the interrogation that was happening at this table.

Erin's two best friends, Sherry and Jen, sat across from me. I had convinced Cherise to be in my corner, but still… she had ovaries and an opinion, which made her loyalties questionable. And then just when I thought the team had been formed, in waddled a third for Erin's side—the pregnant nurse, Sarah, who was looking ready to drop at any second.

Maybe I'd have to add "delivery of a baby in a restaurant" to my resume before this day was fucking over.

Sherry was all business. Jen had been somewhat starry-eyed until she eased into the real purpose for this meeting.

Jen glanced at her watch. "We have to speed this up as she's meeting us here soon."

Just hearing that Erin was on her way made a strange ache develop in my chest.

"We're going to look at a few apartments with her after lunch," Jen continued.

"She's moving?" I don't know why this detail surprised me, and hurt.

Jen became somewhat indignant. "Someone shot up her house. She won't even go back to pack up her stuff."

Cherise raised a hand. "Now hold up. Before everybody goes blaming

Adam again, I've been a cop's wife for years and this situation is very unique."

Sarah leaned in. "Erin hired a moving company to do it."

My guilt was crushing. I rested my head in my hands; it was hard to face all of their reproachful stares. "I'm glad she has all of you looking out for her," I muttered. "I can't fix it so why bother trying."

"Unh ah." Cherise cracked me in the back of my head—hard. "You love her, you fight for her. None of this 'I'm giving up' crap. You hear me?"

I rolled my gaze over. "Entire city heard you."

She scowled and then smacked my shoulder for good measure. "You want her back?"

"Isn't that why we're all here?"

Cherise turned meaner. "I said, do *you* want her back?"

My head was close to exploding. "Yes, of course I do."

"Well then." Her face softened. "Here's what I suggest we do."

CHERISE'S PLAN PRETTY much involved random forms of kidnapping, which didn't sit well with me at all. Forcing Erin's hand was never going to work, and each second that ticked by made this latest play seem like an equally bad idea. My mouth was dry, like I'd been sucking on cotton balls for the last hour.

I never wanted a drink so bad in my fucking life. My nerves were shot, sending tiny shakes down into my fingers. My hands were sweating, making me question the differences between love and losing my fucking mind.

The second she slipped through the door, the sunlight at her back, the air seized up in my lungs.

With perfect precision, the three from Erin's team surrounded her, leading her like a sacrificial lamb to the waiting lion.

The bloody bandage was ripped off when Erin's smile crashed down into irritation.

"Nope." Sherry body-blocked her from retreating. The pain in my chest turned into agony, knowing with absolute clarity that Erin didn't want to be here, facing me.

"You're going to talk. You're going to listen," Sherry said, laying down the law to both of us.

"You two love each other," Sarah said with a knowing smile.

"And as your best friends," Jen added, "we all agree that this has gone on long enough. You're miserable without each other, and any man who has the guts to ask us for our help deserves a second chance."

I don't know why I stood. Part of me was ready to chase after her should she decide to turn and run. And I was acutely aware of my shoulders and ribs and the muscles and bones in between.

"You going to sit?" Sherry asked her.

Erin's magnificent blue eyes were locked on mine, wavering in her resolve. I could see that a part of her wanted this, which gave me hope. Her friends were poised to argue, which left her without much of a choice.

"I have an appointment at two," Erin muttered over to Jen, but her stare was pointed at me.

"Hear him out," Jen said. "We took a vote and decided unanimously that Adam's offer is better."

"Adam's offer?" Erin questioned, confused.

Sherry grabbed a chair, steering her by the shoulder. "Just sit and hear him out. FYI—the pregnant one is prepared to take you down if you bolt."

I stifled my grin. Erin's friends were fucking awesome.

Erin sat roughly. "You have an offer?"

"Move in with me." I held my breath.

Erin twisted in her seat, ready to stand, until Sherry smacked her in the head. This intervention was turning into a no-nonsense smack-down.

"Ow!" Erin squealed.

"Cherise cracked Adam in the head earlier and figured it worked so," Sherry shrugged. "looks effective."

Erin rubbed her scalp. "You met Cherise?"

"Yep," Jen answered. "Woman is fierce. We've adopted her. Oh and we're all going to her house tonight. You should wear those new boots you got. With the lacy dress and blue sweater? You looked so cute in that. Josh is taking our boy to his grandmas."

"Jen—" Erin frowned.

"What? It's Saturday night and she's making margaritas… and you looked adorable in that outfit. Now you have a reason to wear it."

Erin's questioning gaze flashed back to me.

"It's poker night," I said with a shrug, wishing her hands were near the tabletop so I could hold them.

"Doesn't seem like I have much of a choice," Erin growled reluctantly through her teeth.

We'd effectively cornered her, but that's not how I wanted us to come back together. "Ladies?"

"Yeah, let's give them some privacy," Jen said, ushering the other two away. "We won't go far," she muttered to Erin.

They sat at a table a few feet away.

It felt so good to be seeing Erin's face with my eyes instead of my memories. "You always have a choice, Doc. If you really want this to be dead and history, just say so and I'll walk out that door and never bother you again. It's that simple. This was my last ditch effort to show you how much I miss you and how much I am still madly in love with you, but I'm not going to force you to feel it back."

My legs wanted to stand, to get up and put distance between me and the pending rejection. "You don't want a future with me, it will hurt like hell but I'll accept it. Can't hurt much worse than these last three weeks have been without you."

I studied her, waiting, praying, hoping… Thirty seconds and still… nothing. I tapped the table with my knuckles and stood, taking the silence as her final word. I'd lied… this hurt so much worse than I thought possible, but I'd be damned to let her see how completely gutted I was.

"Adam, wait."

I had to remember to breathe.

"Why do you love me?" she asked.

So many words crossed my mind. Between that and the hurt watering my eyes, I was blinded by it all. But one thought out of them all rung true. It was all I had left. "You make me want to be a better man, Erin."

She stood.

Two steps and I had her in my arms. The feel of her body finally pressed up to mine, chest to chest, maybe there was hope to come out of this alive after all. "I've missed you, so much."

Erin's hand tensed into the back of my head. "I've missed you, too," she cried softly into my neck.

I had to see the feelings in her eyes, make sure they were there, that this was true. Air mixed with every emotion, stuttering out of my lungs.

Her kiss was the only medicine that could heal me.

I clung to her, to my lifeline.

There was no way I'd ever let her go again.

It was till death do us part now for me.

CHAPTER 27
Erin

"THE GIRLS SEEMED like they had fun tonight. Everyone get along?"

Adam turned left onto Fourth Avenue, definitely not taking me back to my parents' house. Jen and Josh had picked me up, giving me some space to think about Adam's presence back in my life, but they had left me at Cherise and Marcus's house after seeing how happy Adam was with me being there.

God, I'd missed him, but I'd made the conscious decision that I had to draw the line between love and having someone shooting at me and unfortunately, self-preservation had won that round.

The familiar scent of Adam's truck, his commanding presence behind the wheel, feeling his attention and affection throughout the entire night, all brought about a sense of contentment I hadn't felt in weeks. "It was a great time. I think your poker circle has expanded now though."

Adam's smile was marvelous. "Josh is a cool dude. Pretty much fit right in. And Sherry's husband is funny as shit. We don't mind losing Booger at the table, that's for sure."

I got the willies just thinking about someone touching their nose and then touching the food plates. "That's good, because Cherise is expecting girl company from now on. She's already planning on making some sort of Jell-O shots for next time."

"You can drink with them, Erin. Just because I don't doesn't mean you can't." He rubbed his scalp, muttering about me resenting him.

I was stone-cold sober. The rest of girls, not so much. "It's not a sacrifice, Adam."

"But it is."

"No, and we can argue this forever. It's hard enough to fight an addiction and beat it without the people who care about you making it more difficult."

"Does that mean you care about me?" His smirk was playful and yet he was truly worried asking.

"I've never stopped."

He nodded, chewing his bottom lip. "Good. That's good to know."

"I was scared."

His grip on the steering wheel tightened. "I know."

"I still am."

"I don't want you to be scared. You need to know I'll do everything in my power to make sure you never feel that way again."

I knew he meant every word but there were so many things out of his control. It wasn't worth arguing about or pointing out how he'd failed in the past. Wounding him that way would solve nothing. "I'll need time."

He pulled into his driveway; watching his garage door rise up made me nervous, as if the mouth of his lair was welcoming me to a point of no return.

"I'm not sure jumping back into things so quickly is the best decision."

"Christ." He parked and left me sitting in his truck, which was something he never did.

I followed him into his kitchen, carrying a handful of guilt in with me.

He tossed his keys onto the counter.

I slipped my coat off. "Adam, I—"

"No." His glare was daunting. "We do this, we go all in. I'm not going to spend the next year taking shit slow and seeing if we can make things work. Either we get along or we don't. No more skirtin' issues and making assumptions. You want this with me? Here I am, offering. You want it? It's a simple yes or no, Erin."

"I want to try."

"No. Fuck trying. It's a yes or no."

"Yes, but—"

"Then strip."

"What?"

"You heard me. All in. I won't settle for less and frankly, neither should you."

I hesitated. "I think we need to—"

"Put your coat back on." He sighed. "I'll take you home. I can't forget about you with you standing in front of me."

"Adam…" Pushing him away was easier to do when it was on my terms, not his. "That's not fair."

"Fuck what's fair. If you want me, you will take all of me and you will give me all of you—NOW. Not later, not after a month of tryin' or waiting and seeing. *Now*."

My nerves skittered at his demand. His brow rose, waiting, daring me to say no to his ultimatum.

"Okay."

He tossed his jacket and grabbed my hand, leading me down the steps. When we hit the lower level, his silent demand was in full form.

I sat and pulled my boot off, worried that if I didn't I might regret it later.

"All of it," he ordered, fetching his bag of tricks. "Jeans, sweater, everything."

Weeks of bitterness and anger welled. If he wanted to solve our problems with a fuck, then so be it. I'd lock what was left of my shattered heart away in its protective box.

Watching him peel his black T-shirt up over his head, exposing those solid pecs, rippled abs, and that light trail of hair that disappeared into his jeans, made my anger wrestle with my uncontrollable desires.

His chest rose and fell hard while he gazed at me, tucking things away in his back pockets.

I stopped at my bra and underwear. Adam folded his shirt lengthwise and then twisted it. "You don't look all in, Doc."

I straightened. "You want to solve things with a fuck, you can work for that."

His nostrils flared, making his partial grin quite sinister. I locked my bones in place when he stepped up to me. I hated feeling this vulnerable, being on display while he circled me. Fingernails lightly grazed down the hollow of my spine, stopping to unhook my bra.

"I've never just *fucked* you, Erin." With the softest of touches, he slipped the straps down, tossing my bra to the side before it fell to the ground. He guided my arms behind my back, dusting my shoulders with his mouth.

He folded my arms so each of my hands cupped my elbows. I felt the bite of hard plastic when he zip tied my forearms together.

"Adam…" I tugged at the second cinching, my pulse racing from the implications.

"Shh…" He stilled my arms; his soft lips trailed over my shoulder to the nape of my neck. "We're working out our problems." He covered my eyes with his T-shirt, tying it in place. "Blind trust, Erin. Time we get back to basics. You and me." He shifted my hair; his fingertips' gentle caress sending tingles throughout my body. "I've told you so many times, I will always take care of you. No fear between us."

I actually feared being plunged into darkness, where everything heightened. Each touch magnified. The smell of warm masculinity amplified. Each breath becoming music to the ears. Sensations normally taken for granted transformed into my sole purpose for existing, just to relish in the joy of experiencing them. Pleasure came from nips of pain.

"I love you," he whispered on my neck. "And I know you've missed me, too. You wouldn't be standing here if you didn't. But I know you think they are just empty words. I know you've been hurt, let down, disappointed. It all scares you, right?"

How did he know?

"Going forward, I want there to be no doubts, no mistrust." My underwear slipped over my hips. "I want us to be absolute."

Fingers scored down the sides of my legs, eliciting a gasp to roll out of my mouth.

"Do you want that?" His teeth bit gently into the space where thigh turned into ass, making me step out of my underwear.

"Yes." I wanted that more than anything.

I felt his smile on my skin.

The waiting, anticipating, was nerve-wracking.

I heard the sharp sound of a long metal zipper separating, the rustling sound of weighted nylon. A pass of cording went around my waist, over my hips, wrapping around the tops of my thighs. Endless looping, fingers wiggling between my flesh and the bindings, Adam's deep concentration audible in his breathing—the spider was weaving me into his web.

Oddly the experience was quite soothing, even though I knew in the end the spider would devour me, leaving nothing but an empty shell where the last of my vitality once existed. But I knew, somehow instinctively, that his mastery of human macramé was executed with the sole purpose of taking us to another level of understanding.

I still wanted him to stop this, to allow me adequate time to analyze and to draw educated conclusions. Normal love didn't include these perversions and yet my body was tingling.

Adam worked quickly but precisely. He bathed me in tenderness, preparing each area with soft kisses before his ropes made their next pass. Above my breasts, below. Around my ribs, across my back, and over my shoulders. The zip ties were cut, allowing me to straighten while each arm, each wrist was wrapped. The ropes pulled my arms up straight above my head and bit into my skin, driving me to stand on the tips of my toes.

Then he moved on to wrapping my lower half.

"You look so beautiful," he whispered below my ear, and, without any control of my own body, my feet left the ground. He kissed my left ankle and then wrapped and tugged, tethering me to the sun or the moon or whatever center of the sky he commanded.

He wasn't the spider. He was the puppet master.

I was the marionette, awaiting his bidding.

He tugged on one of the ropes, sending my body gently swinging.

My every thought, every stress, every insecurity and responsibility fled, solely focused on swaying in the air. I was free.

Adam cradled my head against his bare chest and kissed me. I'd been starving but until I felt his tongue caress mine, I didn't realize how close to expiring I'd been. His kisses were infused with so much intensity, they were silent words and meanings and messages meant only for me. He slipped the covering off my eyes, connecting us even deeper.

"Do you love me?" he asked.

"Yes." I'd been broken down into the rawest of truths.

"Tell me why," he whispered, stroking my hair.

"I don't know. So many reasons." Each one was like trying to catch a leaf in the swirling wind. "I see you in everything. I hear you in every song. I feel you in places I didn't know existed."

His smile was gentle and kind; a panther momentarily friendly before it sank its teeth.

"Do you remember when you put those stitches in my hand?"

I nodded.

"You said to me, 'my first priority is you'. Do you remember that?"

It was hard to think through the hazy fog his kisses had left me in.

"I remember," he went on. "It shocked the hell out of me. That's what love is all about, right? Putting each other first?"

My heart felt even more impossibly heavy. Could dreams actually come true?

"Why don't you want children?" he asked, still caressing me.

"Adam…" This was not a conversation to have and yet there it was—tossed out front and center.

His tenderness ended when he pinched and rolled my nipple between his fingers, sending a zing of pleasure-filled pain right into my bottom. It was a punishment—instant retribution for my apparent insolence.

"It's an important question."

When he stepped away, my head hung back, weighted by gravity. Ropes tugged and my thighs parted, and not on their own volition. My arms were bound to the ropes running to the metal circle in the ceiling, but after a few adjustments, he left me with some range of movement. I could hold on or relax back, cradled within his webbing. Right now, I was holding on for dear life, trying to pull myself up to watch him, but it was nearly impossible.

His hands squeezed my inner thighs. "I can't tell you how many times I'd envisioned you like this."

"What? Bound and helpless?"

He added another length of rope, cradling my calves. "Sweetheart, you are far from helpless. And your body is in a sling, so you shouldn't be in any pain. Well, maybe just in here." His finger tapped on my forehead. "But bound and helpless has worked for us before."

I hated when he was right. I felt like I was lying in a loosely-woven hammock. Another pull and tug and my thighs split wide open.

"And I think you're going to enjoy the hell out of this." His hands took ownership, his warm breath heated my anticipation, and then his tongue struck out. My body arched, all needy and wanting more. I hated my body for betraying me so quickly. A finger worked inside me, then two—in and out—scissoring and curling with master precision.

Every thought, every synapse, tied to the rising sensations. My focus—singular. Only one direction—up—reaching for the ultimate release. Oh so close. So close.

Abruptly, his fingers withdrew, his warm mouth left my skin, and he shoved the ropes, spinning me.

"Let's see how much you want my body," he drawled, opening up his pants. Silky flesh rolled over my lips, firm and ready. His musky scent bloomed across my nose, adding depravity to my surmounting want. My mouth opened, tasting him with my tongue. He grabbed the ropes above me and hissed, groaning as I took him deeper.

His woven web was quite convenient, allowing all sorts of rocking movements that were left unexplored on the static ground. His strong abs, the swell of his chest, all looked different at this angle. I wished I had the use of my hands, just to feel his hot skin, merge us together in different ways.

He pulled out of my mouth and released the ropes, letting me swing freely again. Being suspended like this, he was upside down taking his jeans off his legs. Watching him stroke his length had to be one of the most erotic things I loved about him.

Love.

There it was again.

Love wasn't an emotion—it was a misdiagnosed mental condition with physical symptoms and no medical cure. I'd spent days, weeks, lamenting over the word and its meaning. And here I was, exacerbating the situation by putting stipulations on what we'd built together. What we *could* build together.

Adam stepped in between my legs, rubbing himself up and over me repeatedly, driving me slowly insane. He grabbed my hips, finding grip on the bindings, and pressed in.

Air stuttered out of both of us.

He eased in and out, setting a beautiful pace, before pounding into me. Skin smacked violently into skin, breaching the surrounding silence. His face twisted with his determination; it was challenge and anger and other emotions I'd recognized. I was getting close to coming, relishing the clenching rush inside me.

"So tell me, Erin…" His fingertips bit into my skin. "What happens if I get you pregnant?" His eyebrows rose. "No condom between us…" He rolled his hips over and over again, bouncing me hard and rough over his bare skin. "Pretty sure if I dig in there I can find the strings to remove that thing."

Fear caused new pressure to build. I was drawn and quartered and completely unable to stop him from doing anything he wanted.

"So what happens, huh? You gonna cut our baby out of your body? Toss it in the garbage like Nikki did?"

I felt the bottom drop out, knowing with absolute certainty what angry fucking felt like. He stunned me and broke my heart, railing into me so hard it took my breath away.

"She did that, you know. Told me she miscarried and I believed it... 'til I got the fucking bill."

I didn't know. I gripped the ropes in both hands, wishing to get free, wishing I could take his pain away, wishing he wasn't inside me while losing his mind. My head shook back and forth, trying to deny that I'd be like that. I knew the value of life and how precious it was and how quickly and violently it ended. We weren't humans—we were biological marvels. *If Adam got me pregnant—*

Sweat dripped down his chest. His teeth were clenched. "Would you do that, Erin? Would you? Answer me!"

"No!" I'd never hurt him that way.

"No? I saw the way you shied away from Turk's kid, so I know you're fucking lying to me. You know what I think?"

I didn't even want to venture a guess.

"I think you'd rip that miracle right out of your belly and lie to my face like she did."

Tears stung my eyes. I'd never felt so hopeless in all of my life, powerless to convince him beyond what he believed. His lack of faith in me tore open new gaping wounds. I was nothing like his ex. "I wouldn't."

He squeezed my legs together, pressing my thighs to his body within his muscular arm and fucked me harder, ebbing the pleasure toward pain. "Why don't I believe you? It's okay, I'll give you want you want. After all, my cock is good enough for you."

"I wouldn't," I cried out, needing him to believe me. "I swear."

He released my legs as if they'd burned him. They flopped apart with a twitchy jerk, back to their bent positions. Muscles within my thighs quivered and quaked. Adam reached forward, grabbing me by the back of my neck, pulling me up to meet the ferocity in his eyes.

"Lie to my face, Doc."

He impaled me again.

He was just as torn, equally as broken.

"I'm not lying."

He slammed into me, holding our gaze with each thrust. "Then fucking tell me the truth. You want a future or a memory?"

I wanted the moon and stars, wrapped in his unyielding promises. "I want you."

My hair tangled in his clawed fingers. "Would you want what we created too? Would you?"

"Please don't." He was asking too much—asking me to become a danger to myself and others. "Please."

"Answer me!"

"You'll hate me," I cried, my chest cracking into a million pieces of pain. "I'm not a murderer. Don't... Oh God, please. When I turn, you'll hate me."

His scowl turned cruel. I tried to hide my face in my shoulder; my self-loathing burned the edges of my eyes. I choked on my tears, sputtering through the rising sobs that shook me while I dangled in the air. He'd turned our love to hate and me into my darkest fear, where the ugliness consumed me. The desolation and despair pulled me under. "You'll hate me." I barely whispered the words, drowning in their validity.

Adam's arm cinched around my waist, my legs circled his hips. With one hand, he pulled one of the ropes, releasing some of the tension holding me aloft. He bent sideways, fetching something long and silver. With a few passes, the sharp blade sliced through the tangle of rope above me.

His knife hit the ground, using both arms to hold me to him as my legs failed to support my weight. A few steps and he sat with me sprawled over top of him.

"Shh... sweetheart." He brushed my hair back over and over again. "What is it that has you so scared? Please, please tell me. I want to understand."

"I didn't do it. I could never... I save lives." Memories slammed into each other with such violence, it was hard to stop shaking. "I didn't do it. I'm not like that. I could never... hurt... but so many women do. So many women... She made me carry the jugs, putting my fingerprints over everything. And when the police came she just pointed and said that I did it. I didn't. But they didn't believe me. They didn't even care or question her."

Adam just watched me intently as I fell apart. The silence was deadly.

"That's why I need to finish. So that never happens to another child. But what happens when *I* break? Will I turn into a monster, too?"

I knew he didn't understand.

I had nothing left. Irrationality had taken control. "I don't want to turn into a monster."

"That won't happen, Erin. You're an angel. You're a savior, not a monster."

We were both in denial, except mine was wrapped in a thick layer of hysterics. "You don't know that. Women change. The hormones or something." I shook my head. "They do unspeakable things."

He held my face in his hands, imploring me. "What happened to you?"

It was a simple question, one of which I'd been avoiding answering for years, masking it under a façade of righteous purpose. But one look in his eyes and I unraveled, the agony from hidden shame bubbled up out of me. "She had me feed the baby poison, but I swear I didn't know. I didn't know."

He tried to hold me still. "Who, sweetheart?"

Desperation was making me wild. "You have to believe me. I swear I didn't know."

"I do."

I covered his hands with my own, thankful that his grip was holding me together.

"Tabitha." The memory of her name tasted like bitter acid on my tongue. "Morton." It was the first time I'd spoken her name out loud in fourteen years, though the burning animosity didn't feel as fresh. I, my parents—we'd boxed that dirty secret away, adding ignorance and well-crafted lies to our family memories. But I couldn't hide them anymore. I can't protect and pretend and go about as though it didn't happen. Detachment was what was separating us. "She was a friend of my mother's."

Just admitting that eased the constricting panic in my lungs somewhat. "I was young, Adam. I didn't know about such things. I was a self-absorbed teenager, not a mother. I would never…"

He wiped my face, taking special care in my fragile state. He was built so much larger than me and yet he tended to me as if I were made of glass. He listened while I slowly explained about Mrs. Morton's divorce and her odd behavior, which now made a whole hell of a lot more sense and should have been glaring signs of looming danger. At the time, I was clueless.

I had expected his revulsion, but instead he just gazed at me impassively while untangling me from the ropes. "What happened? It's okay. Just tell me."

"What did you do?" Tabitha Morton shrieked. "You killed her! You killed my baby!"

My head swayed as I stepped back in time.

"She was jealous, officer. She tried to punish me for hiring her little boy-crush to do yard work at my house. That has to be it. I left for two hours and she murdered my baby!"

"She bought four gallons of antifreeze that day. Four. Made me carry each one from the car." My breath hitched after each admission. "Hannah was only... she was only a year old."

Adam's hands massaged over each spot he'd exposed, rubbing and soothing my skin. It was starting to feel wonderful, relaxing, but I didn't deserve it. I'd never atone for my transgressions.

"I didn't know the signs of ethylene glycol poisoning. I thought... I babysat her all the time. I just thought the baby was sick."

He unwrapped the ropes around my ribs. "You didn't know, Erin. How could you?"

A chill ran through me; I was cold and exposed and completely naked.

"So many children come in... neglected, beaten, sexually..." My throat constricted. "Sexually abused, malnourished." It was hard to swallow. "Left in hot cars... poi... poisoned."

Adam tossed the length of rope aside and then brushed my hair over my shoulder. "You're not like that, Erin. You could never be. Is that what scares you?"

Oh God, yes.

He must have sensed my discomfort because he grabbed the thin blanket from behind his head and pulled it around my shoulders.

"Look at me. Tell me the truth. Let's lay it all out. Did your mom ever hit you?"

He was dead serious asking. *Do I look as though I've been physically abused? Maybe he thinks...*

"No. Never."

He nodded once. "Your dad? He ever hurt you, or your sister?"

"No. My parents never hit me or Kate. They yelled plenty but never smacked us or anything."

He pulled the front of the blanket together, covering my exposed chest. "Sweetheart, that's my point. You didn't come from an abusive home and neither did I. What makes you think that you'd ever be capable of doing that to yours?"

He didn't understand. "Why does it happen then? So many women just snap. They lose their minds. I'm sure not all of them came from abusive homes or whatever, but they do it anyway."

"You have a fear. I get that. But you've also dedicated your entire life to taking care of sick people. You honestly think you'd turn into the exact opposite of who you are now? I can't see that happening, Doc."

"She poisoned her baby, Adam. Medical exam said it had been going on for a little while. She kept on adding it little by little to her formula and then every time I babysat she'd have *me* feed it to Hannah so it looked like I was the one trying to kill her. Mrs. Morton didn't seem psychotic, but she was. Her new boyfriend didn't even know she had a kid at home."

Adam rested his hands on my upper arms. "You'll never be like that, Erin."

"How can you be so sure?"

His mouth smashed into a hard line. "You remember a few weeks ago when I had that head cold? One sign of a sniffle and you were all up over here with vitamins and saline shit for my nose, making soup and hot tea for me. Remember?"

He'd really had an upper respiratory infection which I was worried might turn into Bronchitis when he started coughing. Then he'd need corticosteroids and...

"Erin, remember?"

"Yeah. So?"

"My own mother never made a steam tent with a towel for me, Doc. You think someone who would do all of that for a grown man would be capable of doing any less for an infant she grew in her own body?"

His brow tipped up.

My mouth poised to argue but I had nothing. "But…" *Oh hell. Was I really this pathetic?*

The reality of my fears felt heavy, making my shoulders slump. Defeat was exhausting. And there he was, completely naked underneath me, still giving a shit. His compassion for my mental breakdown was written all over his face.

I rubbed the bands of rope still around my calf between my fingers. "What are these ropes made out of anyway?"

Adam dropped his gaze.

"You put truth serum on them or something?"

He chuckled softly, tracing the braid under his hand. "Something like that."

I took a few regrouping breaths, relieved to see the severity that marred his face earlier had subsided. That's when it dawned on me. Not only did the truth spill out of me while bound in his magical rope, so did his.

I traced my finger around the curve of his pectoral, delving into the area of his heart, circling the spot. "You really want children, don't you?"

He met my eyes. "Yes. Eventually." He covered my hand with his, pressing it flush to his warm skin. His other hand reached up, his thumb softly brushing the edge of my jaw. "But I want to have them with you."

"Even after all of that?"

"Yes. We may have to live with our guilt, Erin, but together we won't let it define us."

I didn't know what I'd done to deserve this man but I now knew I'd kill to keep it. Both of us, damaged and flawed, and yet together we were more than the sum of our fears.

Words he'd spoken to me rang true and snapped all the pieces together—he made me want to be a better woman.

This is what love was truly all about.

CHAPTER 28

Adam

TABITHA MORTON HAD been indicted by a grand jury on charges of first degree murder, aggravated child abuse, aggravated manslaughter of a child, and four counts of providing false information to police.

I scrolled down the screen, seeing justice had been served when she'd been sentenced to life behind bars. Erin had been named as a witness for the prosecution but all other information and original charges had been expunged from record.

Good. That's good.

I rubbed my forehead, imagining her at sixteen, scared shitless, facing murder charges. And now she was dating a cop who loved seeing her wearing his handcuffs. That was something I'd have to curb going forward. I probably forced her to relive some dark moments while testing her limits.

"Erin all moved out?"

Marcus leaned on the cubical wall divider behind me, coffee mug in hand.

I closed the link to the judicial system web portal. "Yeah. Got everything out yesterday."

"Sorry I couldn't help ya." He took a sip of his coffee. "Now that they extended the hours at the bank, Cherise has been working every other Saturday."

"No worries, man. We had enough help. She didn't have that much shit actually."

"You sure about moving her into your place?"

"I moved her into my house; her furniture and stuff is all in storage."

Marcus tossed his eyes. "That's not what I mean."

"I know what you mean." I wasn't stupid. "Let me ask you a question—were you sure about marrying Cherise when you did?"

His eyes widened a smidgen. "You at that point already?"

I leaned back in my chair. "No. Just trying to make a point."

Marcus bobbed his head. "When you know, you just know."

"There you have it."

"You ready for marriage? That takes shit to a whole new level."

The rickety chair protested when I leaned back farther. "Slow down and let me enjoy living in sin for a while. We got time. For now, going to sleep and waking up just got a whole lot nicer."

"Yeah, well. Enjoy that shit while it's *nice*. We'll have this conversation again when your balls are blue from too much hallway sex."

"Hallway sex?" He stumped me with that one. I hadn't fucked Erin at the top of the steps yet, but I could move that location up on the to-do list if it was recommended.

"Listen, there are three different types of sex in a marriage. There's exciting sex, necessary sex, and hallway sex. Exciting sex is the kind of sex you're having right now, when you first hook up and can't wait to get at each other. Necessary sex comes along after you've been married a few years and your woman sees it as more of chore than anything. And hallway sex is after you've been married so damn long, you pass each other in the hallway and say 'fuck you!'"

I cracked up laughing.

"There's actually a fourth kind of sex," he continued, "but we don't like to talk about it. That's courtroom sex—where your wife and her lawyer fuck you in public. Ain't no man want to get anywhere near that kind of sex."

My gut started to hurt. "You're too much."

"That's what she said." He grinned broadly at me.

I hopped up and gave him a pat on the arm. "Any lawyer tries to fuck me, I'm capping his ass."

"Damn straight. Trick is not letting it get there by picking the right one."

I stopped. "You don't think she's the right one?"

"Didn't say that. She's as right for you as they come. Shit between you and Nikki was toxic. I think Erin keeps you balanced. Just don't let yourself get off course."

I adjusted my utility belt, forcing myself to focus. Someone out there was threatening to ruin everything I held sacred.

Someone had fired twelve shots into Erin's house.

She didn't know about the two rounds I'd found embedded in her bedroom wall yesterday, but thankfully she didn't argue when I said I was driving her to work tonight.

Somebody had been watching her house, watching her, and there was no telling how long it had been going on.

The anger seethed inside me, begging for an outlet; someone was stalking the woman I love.

Worry also compounded on top of that, knowing the fucker was still at large.

I climbed into the passenger seat of our rig, fighting the remorse. Nikki was psychotic to a certain degree and extremely vindictive, but I'd never thought she'd go this far.

IT WAS ALMOST two in the morning when dispatch relayed the call that alarms were going off at another dealership.

When Marcus heard the name and location, one look between us made him punch the gas pedal. Control gave me the callback number as I'd been requested by name by the caller.

We were about a mile away from Novak Ford when I turned on the two jackasses in our back seat. "You cannot film any of this. I see you even touch your equipment and I will arrest you both for obstruction of justice."

Ritchie held up his hands. Scott was too busy fucking with his phone to acknowledge me.

"Scott, you copy?"

Fucker twitched when I yelled. "Yeah, yeah."

I didn't have time to figure out what his problem was. Other units were already on scene when we rolled up. After checking in with them I assumed tactical command. This was my show now. Erin's dad, Steve, was standing near his car with an officer while others cleared the scene.

"Steve." I shook his hand and gave him a manly hug though it was clear he was stressed. I'd seen him just yesterday when he moved his daughter into my house, and was getting familiar with seeing his scowl.

At least he was cool about it, though Erin's house getting shot at was not making me his favorite person at the moment.

"Thanks for coming, Adam. Guess it was just a matter of time, huh?"

I pat his shoulder, hating we were meeting like this, and completely pissed this bullshit was now touching those I'd consider family. This shit had to stop, like yesterday. "Hang tight a sec."

As I'd suspected, the maintenance area of the dealership had been breached. The door locks had been snapped with what looked like a crowbar wedge.

It was going to be a long night.

ERIN'S FATHER RUBBED his forehead. "Well, it looks like they just got the five new deliveries that were in for premaintenance inspection."

It was eating me alive that I hadn't been able to stop them before they struck again. Saying I was sorry didn't alleviate my guilt.

"This isn't your fault, Adam," Steve said.

Yeah, it kinda was. "I'll check in with you later. I have to go pick up Erin."

I could sense Marcus was ready to roll. He'd taken Dumb and Dumber back to Headquarters hours ago, dumping them off of our watch. Both of them had been squirrely—Scott especially. Guess if they weren't busy making my life fucking miserable, they were bored.

Steve glanced at Marcus and then back at me. "Adam? A word?"

"I'll be waiting outside," Marcus mumbled, eyeing me.

Steven closed his office door. I knew what was coming next.

"I love her," I preempted.

"I know you do. But one day you'll be a father too, then you'll know where I'm coming from. Cars, inventory—that can be replaced. My girls...," he drilled me with his most serious look, "can't. I need to know what happened here, what happened at her house, that it's going to stop."

"I can't make any guarantees, but I'm trying my best."

He put his hands on his hips. "She came home to her mother and me in tears, didn't hear from you for weeks, and then overnight she's moving in with you? I know she's a grown woman, but I'm still her father."

I raised a hand. "I called her—every day. I left messages—*every* day. Apologized every time. I never quit trying."

"I can see how you are with her." He looked me up and down. "I haven't seen anything yet to make me think you aren't a good man."

"Thank you, sir."

"I just need to know she's safe."

I rested my hand on my weapon, knowing I would not hesitate using it to protect her. "No offense, but she's safer with me than she is with you and your wife."

His gaze fell to my gun. "I don't like that she's in danger in the first place."

And you think I do? I held my tongue. "Believe me; I'm using all my resources to find out who did it. And this here, tonight, is second to keeping Erin safe and breathing easy. I have security at the hospital keeping extra eyes on things. I'm going to escort her to and from work as much as possible. Beyond sleeping with a loaded gun, I'm doing my best. We have a lot of good people working on both cases."

Steve sighed and nodded at me.

"And one day, once all of this is settled, I plan on asking you and Christine for your blessing. Until then, I'm going to guard your daughter with my life and find out who the hell stole from you. You good with that?"

It was relieving to see him smile. He reached out and shook my hand. "I'm good with that."

"Good. Now maybe you can tell me how to break all of this to your daughter."

Steven laughed. "You're on your own there."

"Leaving my ass hanging in the wind already?"

His grin widened. "Yep. And if you don't get going soon, you'll have more than this to contend with. At least I won't make you deal with her mother on top of it."

Now was as good of a time as any. "While we're being real, I want you to know that I know what happened to her when she was sixteen."

Steven paled. "She… she told you?"

"Reluctantly, but yeah. I got it out of her."

Steven glanced around his office, muttering. "She had no knowledge of what that woman was doing, Adam. No one did."

I nodded. "I know. I read the court transcripts and reviewed the case file. There are no records of her being detained as a suspect."

"Good. That's good. Then you know she was alone with that little girl when she died." He sat behind his desk. "I guess I don't need to tell you how traumatized she was. She, well, she withdrew on us, hiding in her room, refused to see her friends—what ones she had left. We had to put her in counseling. We changed her school." He choked up, trying to hold back his tears. "She had nightmares for years. Would wake up in the middle of the night crying. Her mother and I felt helpless."

I knew she'd left some details out—things she'd feel embarrassed about. "She thinks she's going to turn into the same if she gets pregnant."

Steven let out a small scoff. "That's ridiculous. Erin's always been the caretaker in the family. Even after it happened, she didn't want her mother or me to worry. She would downplay it, make up excuses."

"I pointed that out to her, but it's going to take some work convincing her. I could use your support here, knowing that I know what went down. Need to know you and I are on the same team."

"Yeah, of course." Stephen stood, joining me near his office door. He reached out, wanting to shake my hand. He pulled me into a hug and gave me a few firm pats on the back. "When that time comes and you're ready, there's no need to ask."

There were no other words necessary.

I was still smiling when I climbed back into our rig and texted Erin to tell her I was running late. Fortunately for me, Marcus liked to drive fast.

I WAITED UNTIL Erin and I were home to break the news to her about the robbery at her dad's business. I had thought about dropping her off and going to the gym for a few hours to burn off the hostility, but that seemed like a move a coward would make.

Having her hear about it from someone else while I evaded and avoided would only create another disaster and prove her point that we shouldn't have jumped into this so quickly.

After all, it was my doing that she was here, living with me now. Most of her stuff was boxed up and locked in a storage unit; her clothes and personal items were stacked in boxes and garbage bags in the spare room upstairs. And from the looks of it, she was walking around on eggshells, trying not to disrupt my life or my routine.

I knew for a fact she was reading my mood, asking where she could stow her dirty clothes as though it was a precursory step to defusing a bomb.

It wasn't lost on me that I was the one ticking.

"Are you going to tell me what has you tangled in knots or do I have to go and get your bag of rope?" She opened one of my drawers and pulled out a T-shirt. "And yes, I'm wearing your clothes. It's a girl thing. Helps me feel like I belong to you and that you actually want me here."

"I don't care if you wear my clothes." Seeing her in nothing but a pair of cute panties, pulling one of my shirts over her head did stuff to my chest. "It's hot, actually."

Her chin rose. "Good. If there's nothing else, I'll be down in the kitchen looking for something to eat. I used my dinner break to work on a man who lost a battle with a jammed nail gun and I'm starving. I'll try not to eat too much of your stuff. I'll grocery shop later so I have my own food."

"Erin…"

"This was your idea, Adam, not mine. I do not want a relationship with someone who forces me to spill my demons and then clams up conveniently because he's in charge of making the rules. You asked me to live with you but here we are, day two and you're already avoiding me."

"I'm not avoiding you."

"Yeah. Okay."

"I'm not."

"You barely said ten words to me the whole way here. And now…" The hurt in her eyes was killing me. "Did you change your mind? Just tell me. Do you want me to go?"

Why was she even thinking that? "No. I don't want you to go."

"If you don't want to live with me or whatever please just say so." She pulled a pair of jeans out of a suitcase and started to put them on. Her stuff was here but she was far from settled in. I didn't even want to think about how easy it would be for her to just carry her belongings back out of my house.

"I want you here, Erin. I'll make some room for your clothes. Is that what you want?"

"Don't go out of your way. I'll manage."

Damn it! "Why are you being like this?"

She glared at me. "Why haven't I met your parents or anyone in your family?"

She wants to meet my parents? "I don't know."

"Are you ashamed of me?"

"What? No."

"Maybe this was all too fast. We shouldn't have... Trying to live together like this."

"Erin, listen." I hooked her arm, halting her mumbling retreat. I had no other choice. I held her, firm but gentle, needing her to understand. "Babe, your dad's dealership was hit last night."

Her mouth fell open. "What?"

"Thieves made off with five cars." She could see I wasn't messing around. "I've been trying to figure out how to tell you, 'cause I don't want you upset and worried."

"Is he okay?" She tried to tear out of my hold. "I have to call him."

I held her fast. "Your dad is fine. Pissed off, but fine. No one was hurt."

"Oh, thank God."

I pulled her closer, ignoring everything including the new text message chimes going off in my pocket. "I told him I'd talk to you. But first, I want you to quit thinking I don't want you here. No more of that, Doc. I love you. You're my girlfriend. We're living together. What's mine is yours, okay? *Okay?*"

"Okay. I copy."

That's my girl.

"I'm meeting him in a little while to continue my investigation. While I'm doing that, rearrange the closet. Put your shit in there. Unpack and settle in. I'm going to find out who did this, I promise you, but you've got to give me time."

She nodded at me but her body was still rigid.

"I can't risk you feeling unsafe with me, Erin. And yeah, I'm worried this will just be another wedge between us."

She attempted to step back. Tried, but failed.

"Sweetheart, you've got to give me that chance." I put her hand on my heart, holding it there. "That's yours. This house is your home. I will

431

protect you with my life. But you've got to let me try."

"Someone tried to kill me, Adam. And now my dad…" The fear choked off her words.

"I have not stopped trying to figure out who attempted to hurt you. Do you for one second think I've forgotten or that I know the danger still exists out there? Your dad… well I can't say for certain if it was personal as we've had numerous dealerships hit. Not just here but all over Jersey. But I can't do my job, I can't *stop* this while worrying that the woman I love is going to leave me."

I searched her eyes, her face, hoping to see her fear and distrust diminish. "I lost you once, Erin, and it nearly killed me. I'd rather take a bullet than watch you slip away."

"I just want to be normal. To be happily oblivious."

"I swear I'll do everything in my power to give you that. Give me your trust and understanding and let me bury these fuckers. I'm working with the feds to get Jamal Clemons moved into protective custody until Carter Mancuso gets indicted. I don't want you testifying unless there are no other options. We have units processing the scene at your dad's lot. I have surveillance tapes and forensics to review. But I'm going to put them all away."

"Then what?"

She'd lost me.

"You put them away and they come after you for retribution. Where does it end?"

"It doesn't work that way. I'm not the only investigator on this. And a District Attorney will put them away, not me."

The worry plaguing her was tangible. "Then you're safe?"

"Then *we're* safe. I can't change that you worked on Jamal when he came through your emergency room. This shit touched you too, babe. But I promise, I swear it will be over soon."

Erin nodded, filling me with relief when she rested her head on my chest. "I need puppies and rainbows, Cop."

I kissed her head. "I'll get you a puppy, Doc. Rainbows only come after the rain."

She tilted her chin up and reached to kiss me. I needed that more than she knew.

"I'll call my mom, make arrangements," I said on her mouth. "They know I'm seeing you. My mom is over the damn moon and will probably drive you nuts. It's just been hard to get over there with our schedules."

I needed to stop thinking about my parents while Erin was tucking her fingertips underneath the elastic band of my underwear.

"We still have one more problem."

She sagged in my arms and groaned.

"I got the hospital bill for my stitches. Seems my emergency physician charged me six hundred bucks."

Erin snorted. "Told you I was expensive. Wait until you see the ER bill."

"I'm not sure I got six hundred dollars worth of service out of you."

Erin's lips wrinkled. "Feed me, let me call my dad, and we'll see if we can work out a payment plan."

MARCUS PULLED UP a chair next to me, eyeing my monitor. "What's this now?"

"Surveillance video from Novak Ford. One guy breached the door, and then watch as five more come out of the shadows."

Marcus leaned closer. "They were aware of the cameras. None of them looked up. Didn't even bother to take 'em out."

"Yeah. Can't see any of their faces. Looks like all were wearing ski masks."

Marcus sighed. "Five new cars in, five drivers and one muscle to get them out."

"Yep." I pushed all the background checks on the dealership employees over to him. "Just like the other thefts. I checked the delivery schedules. Only five new cars were delivered to Novak, so somebody knew what inventory was coming in."

Marcus glanced over the printout. "They could easily put a crew together in an hour."

"And figure out when they'd go through pre-inspection service. Haven't ID'd anyone, but one guy has a bit of a limp." I played the recording again. "See, this one here. He's dragging his left leg. We got any suspects that fit?"

Marcus sighed. "Could be a recent injury or could just be a brother with a strut."

This case was starting to pile up mounds of details. I had papers spread out all over the desk, in boxes on the floor, until something from the Johnson Ford heist caught my eye. I tore through the other file boxes, looking for one thing. "You're not going to believe this."

Marcus spun in his chair.

I held the two papers up to him. "Notice anything?"

His eyes widened. "No shit. Same carrier company."

"Same fucking carrier company." I pinned the crucial detail to the wall where I had all the known players, dealerships, and possible drivers laid out in one huge visual map. The noose was tightening.

"SEEING ANYTHING GOOD on there?" Erin leaned up on my shoulders while I sat at the kitchen island with my laptop. She was cooking dinner for us, which I had to say smelled fucking fantastic.

"Not yet." I held her arm to keep her in place, needing her closeness to wash away my lingering frustration until I realized the recording was still playing.

She rested her chin on me. "What footage is that?"

I paused the video. "Uh, sweetheart, no offense, but I can't really discuss that with you."

Erin tried to pull away; I felt like a huge asshole.

"Doc, it's part of an ongoing investigation. I can't…" She slipped out of my hand and walked away, shutting me out.

"It's okay. I shouldn't be discussing any of my patient cases with you either." She set a dirty pan in the sink. "No matter what we do… I guess we have no choice but to live in secrets anyway."

FUCK. I was able to hurt without even trying. Her shoulders fell—instant defeat.

"I don't want that."

"Neither do I," she said to our dirty dishes.

"Erin… please come here."

She ignored me for a few beats, pretending to be busy washing a plate.

"Baby. Please."

I tucked her between my legs, rested her on my thigh, and clicked the arrow to play. "This is the surveillance video from outside Benando Auto Salvage in Newark. Their ATTF has two cameras on this place. They asked me to give it a scan."

"Auto salvage? Guess it's a good place to hide car parts."

I rewound the last thirty seconds. "Yep. They seem to do a hell of a business, especially after hours."

She leaned against me. "Was that your stomach?"

"Yeah. I'm starving. When's the pasta ready?"

"I just put the garlic bread in the oven. Few minutes."

"Garlic? You gonna kiss me later?"

She put her arm over my shoulder, doing that soft scratching thing in my hair that I loved. I gazed back at her. God, she made me happy. "I'm sorry. No secrets, babe. Agreed?"

Erin nodded. "Yes."

I brushed her hair back from her face. "We're partners."

"Partners." Her smile was breathtaking. "I like that." Her fingers drifted over my cheek. "I just want to be there for you. No matter what you need. Every part of me is yours."

I twisted the tips of her long hair around my fingers, needing her mouth on mine. "I love you." I adored that twinkle in her eyes.

"I love you, too. And I promise," she uttered on my lips, "our conversations will stay completely confidential. I know you can tell when I'm lying, so you know I'm being truthful."

"I know." I was just about to turn the oven off and take her upstairs when I lost her lips and her attention to my computer. Guess I'd take a rain check, though scanning hours of video had completely lost its appeal.

She leaned, brushing a bit of unintentional attention against my partial erection. "Isn't Pantera that heavy metal band that wears those freaky masks?"

"What?" *How did she go from my tongue in her mouth to death metal?* "Where did that come from?"

"On your screen. Go back. No, stop. Too far."

I let it play, since I was quite distracted a moment ago and missed a bunch.

"See? There next to the dude with the gimp." She pointed. "Pause it."

"Gimp?" I was squinting at the stilled image. *Could it be the same dude?*

"Yeah, he's dragging his leg when he walks. Here, babe. Let me." Erin commandeered my computer. "I'm just surprised so many people listen to that band. Aren't they like scary metal or something?"

Women.

"They aren't scary metal. They're…" The warm rush of shock flowed through when the recognition hit. "No. It can't be." I must have rewound and played it over twenty times to be sure. "You've got to be fucking kidding me. That son of a bitch. You know who that is, right?"

Erin moved my screen closer. "Oh my God. He was wearing that coat the night your hand was cut."

We stared at each other while the betrayal twisted my gut into knots.

"SO YOU UNDERSTAND you're not under arrest or anything like that? We just want to ask you some questions." I moved our tabletop microphone closer to him, fumbling with it on purpose.

We'd called all six of the camera crew in and sat them in one big room together, letting them speculate that they were in some sort of trouble. Now it was time to put my primary suspect in the hot seat.

I closed the door behind me. "Thanks for waiting, Scott."

"Yeah, no problem, Adam."

"Have a seat, buddy."

"What's going on?" he asked.

"I'm hoping you can tell me," I joked, needing him to relax for me. "Hey, do you want a can of soda or water or something before we start? I'm pretty sure we have your favorite Pepsi in the fridge if you're thirsty."

Scott sat down in the chair. "Nah, I'm good. So what's up?"

Pressing for info already? All in due time.

"Let me just get this working. We don't have the sweet technology like you guys have. We'll be recording our time today both on audio and video." I pointed out the camera system. "You ever been interviewed before?"

He bobbed his head. "Yeah, for my job with Werner, but I wasn't videoed."

"It's a formality for my protection and yours so that there's an official record, ya know? Today's date is May first, 2014. The time is five twenty-nine p.m. Detective Adam Trent interviewing Scott Kirschner." I filled out the standard interview log sheet we had for all suspects. "So how've you been? I haven't seen you in a couple of days."

"Yeah, I know. You've been busy, I guess. Our boss has *not* been happy at all. No one is telling us where you've been or what's going on."

I shrugged, keeping it casual. "Police work comes first." I wasn't going to let him know that Melissa Werner was on her way from Manhattan after bitching out everyone she could reach by telephone. I ignored her calls.

"So before we get started, I want to review your rights with you. You've probably seen them on TV before but we'll go over each. We're doing this with everyone on the crew so don't think this is only being done with you." I reviewed each of his Miranda rights, getting his documented initials and sign off on our form.

"Scott, just to avoid any confusion... you're obviously not under arrest here today. The door isn't locked so if at any time you want to leave or feel you want to speak to counsel, a uniformed officer is out in the hallway and will walk you back to the lobby. If anything comes up during our interview that you feel you want to speak with a lawyer about, you just let me know."

"Yeah, okay." His right leg was bouncing.

"Cool. So how's that new Charger of yours running? I've been meaning to ask you and every time I think of it, something always comes up."

Instantly, he relaxed a bit. Just like with every interrogation, I started with nonspecific chitchat, needing to get his emotional baseline. Everyone had "tells;" it was time to get familiar with his.

"Yeah man. Runs like a champ."

"So no problems?" I also needed ammo to counter any of his potential denials.

Scott shook his head. "No."

"Wow. You're lucky. A friend of mine had one but he got so sick and tired having to fix it, he just traded it." That was a lie but he had no clue. "I remember he had to replace the alternator, then the exhaust had a leak and he replaced the whole system. Hell, even the rear tires didn't wear evenly."

"Wow. No, mine runs great. Haven't had to replace anything on it."

Direct eye contact. No fidgeting or signs of deception. Truth.

"You'd try to fix it yourself if you had to? You know your way under the hood?"

Scott rolled his eyes. "Yeah, I can hold my own. Been known to fix up my rides."

"Yeah? That's good. I got a buddy selling a sweet Mustang convertible. Shit, he's practically giving it away. It needs a lot of work though. Interested in a project car?"

"Nah. I don't have much time. Between school and this, I'm pretty jammed."

"I hear ya. I remember those college days." I lived on Raman noodles and drove a piece of shit—not a forty-thousand-dollar new car. "How about any of your friends?"

Scott pushed his hat back and scratched his head. "Nah. Parts for that would be expensive."

That's it... relax and talk to me. I'm going to lead you right where I want you to go.

"Dude, I think you live in that hat. I take it Pantera is your favorite band?"

Scott smiled and adjusted his cap. "Seen 'em in concert probably like ten times. What? You don't like them?"

"I didn't say that. I'm just wondering if you ever take that hat off your head."

He chuckled. "Not usually."

"Hey, I got to step out for a minute." I gathered up my files. "You want anything? Bottle of water or something?"

"Yeah, water would be cool."

"Okay. Hang tight. Hey, before I go, how tall are you?"

I watched his reaction, visually marking his fact recall and truth indicators. "Five ten."

Marcus and a few others were in the surveillance room next door, watching the video feed. I didn't need to get anything. I needed my suspect to stew for a minute, observing his behavior when isolated. Oddly, he used the sleeve of his hoodie to wipe the table where his fingers just touched.

After another ten minutes of questioning him, hearing his denial that he hasn't been to Newark lately and watching him blatantly lie to me, I pulled out the video stills. "We have some problems, Scott. I will continue to treat you with respect, but I'm not happy that you've been lying to me. I have video evidence that disputes your statements."

I laid out each photo one by one.

"We've been working with a video expert who does facial recognition and all sorts of identification on recordings, and these are the images they captured from video surveillance at Benando Salvage."

"Here's a close-up of your hat. Here's a clear one of you wearing the same jacket you've got on now. Here's another that they digitally enhanced to see your face. They can even calculate height." I showed him the report that stated the suspect was five foot ten inches.

Scott's fingers trembled over each photo.

"Scott, look at me." I needed to restore our connection. "I'm going to give you the opportunity to tell me what's going on as I'm sure you haven't been truthful with me. You said you hadn't been to any places in New Jersey and yet these photos put you at an auto scrap yard with solid ties to our case over ninety miles away."

He leaned back, distancing himself, knowing he'd been busted.

"I'm not asking you to confirm you were there because I already know you were. I don't even need to prove that. I have the video evidence that places you there. That's enough to hold up in court. Even without it, your eyes tell me you were there."

"My eyes?" He sounded skeptical.

"Yeah. So what I want to know is why you were there. You know, we all make mistakes. It's okay. It's in the past. But here and now, it's time to be honest with yourself, Scott. It's okay to say 'hey I messed up,' and be man enough to make amends and do what's right."

I was wearing him down.

"I thought we were friends. Are you hoping that harm comes to me? To Marcus?"

"No, it's not like that," he muttered.

"Why don't you tell me how it is then? How did it start? Did they contact you?"

His head nodded ever so slightly.

"Who contacted you? It's okay. It's just you and me here. I know you're a good guy, Scott. You're going to film school. Working a full-time job. That's all very respectable stuff, man. I know how tough it is. That's how I know you don't want this burden. Just lay it out. Let me help you."

Scott's resolve was wavering.

"I've got to tell you—the evidence doesn't look good. I'm being straight up with you. Conspiracy, aiding and abetting, all make you an accessory to robbery, Scott. Doesn't matter if you didn't commit the actual theft; you can still be charged with the crime. These are all felony charges you're facing. It's just going to get worse if you don't start explaining things."

I gave him dead silence—just a stare. Waiting. First one to speak loses.

"I didn't go looking for trouble, Adam. All right? They came after me."
Scott dropped his head into his hand.

"It's okay, dude. I get that you're scared. I'm right here. Talk to me.
Just you or did they go after any of the other crew that you know of? You
can tell me. They try to get Ritchie, too?"

He pegged me with an obvious glare. "Ritchie's uncle is a state cop.
They knew that."

"Who are *they*, Scott?"

He started wringing his hands together.

"They said they'd make me disappear if I didn't give them what they
wanted," he whispered. "No one would ever find my body."

"Why do you think they chose you?"

Scott shrugged. "They know we're filming you. Wherever you are,
pretty safe to say the rest of the ATTF are too."

I tamped back my rising anger. "What were your orders?"

He started to withdraw, shutting me out.

"Scott."

His head shook more adamantly.

I rolled my chair closer to him.

Eyes filled with fear met mine. "They are going to kill me. You get
that? I'm dead."

"I won't let that happen."

He scoffed. "They put a fucking gun to my head." His emotional
control was unraveling. Tears fell down his face. "And now, now when I
go to prison for helping them, someone in there is going to kill me. That's
what they said. Nowhere is safe."

"Help me understand and I swear I'll do whatever I can. Is my team
compromised?"

Scott appeared confused. "Compromised? What do you mean?"

"Are we in danger?"

He shrugged and receded. "I don't know."

I leaned in closer. "Anyone else on the team involved in this? I need to
know if we have any others on the camera crew, production, a cop
perhaps, working for them. You need to tell me what you know."

Scott kept shaking his head. "I never saw anyone else."

"You know all of the ATTF officers," I said. "You ever see or hear any
mention of their names being involved?"

I was sort of relieved to see the shock register on his face. "No."

"Okay. What were your orders?"

He drew in a breath. "They gave me a number to text. I sent updates with our location. But it's just been recently. That's it. I swear."

It was hard to mask how I felt about being betrayed. One thing was certain. Our television careers just came to an abrupt end.

Thank fuck for that.

"You went to Newark to get paid, didn't you?" It wasn't a question. Scott's shame was obvious.

"Who contacted you, Scott? I want to help you. I do. But you have to tell me."

Scott nodded at the picture on the desk, pointing to the one with the noticeable limp to his walk that we were unable to identify. "That guy. I don't know his full name. They call him Switch. I think he's the one who coordinates everything. He's a driver too."

"If I showed you some photos, you think you could pick him out?"

He reluctantly said, "Yeah."

"Do they have eyes on you?"

Scott shook his head. "I don't know."

I didn't want to use Scott as bait, but it was time to play the players at their own game.

FINDING MILTON CRAWFORD—also known as Switch—wasn't easy. He moved about a lot, but once we located him, everything fell into place. Still, something gnawed at me. That little niggle of doubt I'd harbored kept worming its way around everything, at the start of every shift.

I had no solid proof, but I couldn't ignore the facts—no matter how coincidental. This investigation was mine. The blowback from the team could get ugly, but it was a risk I had to take to being thorough.

Ultimately, it was my captain's decision, and when faced with the knowledge that we'd already been compromised by the film crew, it was easily justifiable.

All of us—every one of us who wore a badge—had taken an oath to protect and serve. Even thinking about the possibility that we had a traitor in our midst made my stomach twist into hateful knots.

I watched the closed-circuit television from an adjoining room as

Officer Brian Sidel was questioned by an interrogator from Internal Affairs. They'd connected him to the polygraph machine after he agreed to subject himself to a lie detector test.

I needed irrefutable proof. Did he or did he not have any ties to Vincent and Salvador Mancuso?

CHAPTER 29
Erin

SARAH WAS SITTING at the nurses' station, pale and exhausted. "You look so happy. I'm glad." Her observation was genuine, though she was breathing hard through her mouth. Her knees were parted while she and her enormous belly molded to the desk chair.

I was. Well, beyond my dad's dealership getting robbed, being under Adam Trent's mandated "I'll drive you to work" orders, and occasionally being home alone, living with him these last few weeks had been beyond blissful. My sister, though, had been sort of avoiding me, making lame excuses for not being able to converse every time I called. Kate had been upset about the robbery, but it was quite obvious that there were other issues affecting her, which I presumed were caused by her current boyfriend.

"You look like you're in pain."

"Braxton Hicks," she muttered, rubbing her lower back.

I leaned onto the counter. "Why are you even here?"

Her pained smile faltered and scrunched. "I have two weeks yet and then…" Another scrunch. "Oh shit, that hurt."

I'd just worked on a twenty-four-year-old male who'd been on the losing end of a bar fight and yet seeing my friend in distress was making me all sorts of nervous. "I think we should call Obstetrics, get someone to take a look at you."

Sarah groaned. "I'm not in labor."

"Then maybe you should go home and rest."

"Can't." She was puffing her words now. "Brett's in Utah at that seminar. I'd be alone. I'm better off here." She tried to sit up. "What better place to be than a hospital, right?"

I looped my arm under hers, helping to keep her steady. "Kimberly, help me?"

Kimberly set some things down and rushed over. "What's going on, preggo?"

Sarah hunched over in pain. Her tight grip was starting to hurt my arm. "Let's get her over into an exam room."

"I'm not in labor," Sarah insisted, that was until another contraction seized her.

"Humor me. Can we get someone from L&D down here?"

We shuffled Sarah closer to one of the empty bays, but she stopped in the middle of the hall. "Oh shit."

"Oh shit?" Oh shits were not good sounds.

"I think I just peed myself," Sarah panted.

After seeing every which way people could lose their dignity and having no threshold for being grossed out anymore, we all looked down her legs.

That was quite a bit of pee. "I think your water just broke."

Sarah squeezed my arm harder. "No. My water can't break until Sunday."

We moved the last twelve feet, getting Sarah situated on a bed.

"Brett's going to be so pissed." She groaned while we propped her up, hissing when another contraction hit. "And I peed myself."

I pulled the privacy curtain over the window and grabbed some exam gloves. "Well, apparently Brett Junior doesn't care if dad's home or not. He wants his birthday." I tried to keep her calm and in good spirits while Kimberly got her vitals.

"You have to stay with me, Erin," she pleaded. "If I have to deal with Brett's mom by myself, I'll go crazy."

We covered her legs with a fresh sheet and I grabbed shears. No sense trying to save amniotic fluid-soaked scrubs. I sliced up one pant leg, trying to ignore her "crazy" comment while in labor. My fears were unfounded. "I will. I promise."

Sarah calmed her breathing, thank goodness. She was actually making me nervous. "Officer Hottie won't mind?"

"Nah, he's busy catching bad guys." I purposely left out the details, as I wasn't even supposed to be aware of them, but Adam and I had made a pact that there would be no more secrets.

I knew every name, every suspect, which made me privy to information I had no business knowing, but how else could we support each other without knowing the full extent of the stress?

We needed full disclosure. It was the only way we'd make it as keeping things bottled up was a recipe for disaster.

Adam also made sure I knew exactly where he was too, most of the time. Over the last few weeks, he and several teams from different units had conducted simultaneous raids, taking out locations in Pennsylvania, New Jersey, and two places in New York City, seizing almost a million dollars' worth of stolen cars. Today he was going after the leader. My nerves were shot.

He told me not to worry and that he'd be fine but it didn't make me worry any less. I knew loving a police officer came with a certain set of understood rules that I had to abide by. He willingly placed himself in danger every time he left the house.

They were rules I was quickly coming to terms with, because loving Adam was no longer an option—it was a fundamental need and vital to the survival of my heart.

This case had him working different hours of night and day. Our paths crossed here and there, and we made the most of our time together: bonding, connecting, wrapped up in each other's arms, falling deeper in love.

And now, while he was hunting down the mastermind of the operation, I needed to tend to my dear friend who was well on her way in labor.

I DIDN'T KNOW how Sarah was holding up this long. She'd been in labor for almost ten hours and now her OB was telling her to push. I'd managed to catch a two-hour nap while she continued to dilate, but now that she was in active labor, I was exhausted just standing here, gripping her hand in mine.

Her husband Brett was on his way after managing to get an emergency flight back to Philly, but his indirect stop in Dallas was still two hours out.

There was no way he'd make it in time.

This wasn't my first live childbirth as I'd done a month-long rotation through obstetrics my first year, but it had been something I'd avoided ever since. Seeing my friend experience it though was an eye-opener, especially as she tore through the emotions from her husband so selfishly leaving her here alone to go to that seminar.

At least I was able to use some of my Psych 101, talking her down from everything from castration to murder. I imagined Adam wouldn't miss his child being born for anything. He was on his way here and it wasn't even his child.

Sarah breathed through the contractions and when the baby's head was out, I was close to sharing Sarah's tears. Our bodies were fucking marvels, capable of mysterious and astonishing things. I felt like an interloper while all the activity flourished about, but I wasn't here as a doctor; I was here as her friend—a friend who stuck with her through the entire process.

"DO YOU WANT to hold him?" Sarah asked after all was said and done, cooing at her newborn. Gone was the strained face of a woman birthing a child; in its place, complete serenity and adoration. The nurse had wrapped her son like a little baby burrito, down to the little blue cap.

Part of me wanted to put as much distance between her child and myself as humanly possible, but another part, a much larger part, was surprisingly curious. *My fears are irrational*, I told myself. After all, I knew my touch didn't cause death. I didn't put that antifreeze into that innocent child's formula. I knew that. Still, just the mere thought of being accused of doing something so atrocious, of even putting myself in the position of being suspected or accused, was paralyzing.

My friends didn't know. None of them knew of the horrid crime I'd once been accused of. If they did, I was sure they wouldn't be so willing to hand over their newborns.

"Erin." Sarah smiled, encouraging me. "Take him for a second. I want to sit up."

She left me no choice. I swallowed hard and fought the rising panic.

Okay, I can do this.

Oh my God. What if I break him?

Stop shaking before you drop him.

Okay, I can do this.

Holy shit.

I tucked him close to my chest, cradling him as best I could in my arms. The little bundle was warm and cozy and so fragile—a tiny human in a cotton cocoon. Little button nose. Such tiny little pink lips.

Oh, he yawned! How cute!

His face scrunched and puckered.

No, No. Don't cry. You're safe. I got you.

His cheek was feathery soft.

"Hey little one," I crooned, gently patting him to keep him soothed. "Happy birthday. It's nice to meet you." I didn't even realize it at first, but I found myself swaying from foot to foot, a rocking motion that seemed so natural.

Could I do this?

I never thought I'd regain those maternal instincts, but here they were, coming out without me even trying. A strange tingle rolled all throughout my body, easing the worry.

Could I really do this one day? Be holding my child like this? Adam's child—a son or daughter that he and I created together? A tiny human with the same soft cheeks and perfect eyelashes?

His tiny mouth formed into an "O" and then he scrunched up again, poking the little tip of his tongue out.

Amazing.

There was a small knock and then the answering smile of my badass police officer, clad head to toe in his badass black uniform. His strides ate up the distance separating us.

Adam beamed at me with such awe, I felt electrically charged and giddy. It was hard to hide my excitement—Sarah had created life and I wasn't afraid. That alone was mind-blowing.

He graced me with a cherished kiss and a grin filled with wonderment. "Who's this little guy?"

I loved Adam's soft, sweet voice—overflowing with pure tenderness. I felt my heart clench. Would I ever stop falling in love with this man?

"Meet Aiden."

"Hey, Aiden. Welcome to the world, little man," Adam whispered. I knew exactly what Sarah was thinking without her saying a word. Her broad smile said it all, duplicating my thoughts exactly.

Maybe motherhood wasn't so bad after all?

I exhaled and let the fear, anxiety, apprehension, and paranoia I'd held tightly within for years flow out.

ADAM AND I barely made it into the kitchen before stripping each other out of our clothing.

He showed me a new way to utilize the dining room table, making a meal out of me. Fingers, tongue, his expert touch. I unraveled.

I straddled him on the dining room chair while he rocked his hips up into me. His mouth on mine, sharing each breath, scoring my cheeks with his stubble. His strong hands held me, lifted me, branding my heart forever with his fingerprints.

My back hit the cold wood, feeling him drive into me with purpose. This was lust and carnal desire mixed with the feeling only invoked by merging with the other half of your soul.

His thumb circled vigorously, rending all the air from my lungs when my second orgasm hit.

"That's it," he whispered out. "Come for me. Fuck, baby."

The cool air brushed my back when my body bowed into the sensation. Adam shifted my thigh and slammed up into me, groaning as he came. My legs were like jelly, feeling the last stutters of him pressing inside me.

"That was incredible," he panted, resting his face on my chest.

I succumbed to the after-orgasm happy giggles and the powerful aftershocks that quaked through my muscles.

Adam scraped his stubbly chin between my breasts, playing with me. "I think we should break in all the furniture this way. Sound good?" He pressed his hips again. Another shudder rippled across me.

I wiped a lock of hair off his damp brow. He made me laugh. "Is it too early to worry about serving Thanksgiving dinner on this table?"

Adam chuckled, making those adorable dimples appear. "No, it is not. I'm afraid you're stuck with me, Doc."

"I love you." My smile was so wide, my face started to ache.

"Just remember who said it first." He kissed my bare chest and then moved up to recapture my mouth. "Thanks for helping me celebrate."

"Celebrate?" I clutched his neck. "You got them?"

"Yep." He grinned proudly. He pushed his hips up into me one last time and then slowly withdrew, leaving me feeling sticky and chilled from the loss of his warmth.

"Mancuso, his brother, the crew that hit your dad's dealership—*all* of them."

"All of them?"

"*All* of them. The name that Scott gave up to us? Switch? He was shocked as hell to see us at five a.m., I tell you *that*."

"I bet." Elated didn't seem like an accurate description to define how I felt. "I'm so proud of you!"

He hid his face on my chest, smiling while I ran my fingers through his hair. His shy grin rolled up to greet me. "I'm proud of you, too."

"For?"

Adam kissed me softly. "In the hospital earlier."

I could see he was more than proud—he was gloating. The smirk he wore was filled with it.

Adam helped me off the table and strolled into the kitchen, giving me one hell of a delicious view. Those muscles in his lower back… the way they blended into those sculpted ass cheeks and down into those muscular thighs. He exuded power and authority without even trying.

"Babe, we seized four laptops, a pile of key fobs, forged shipping manifests… all sorts of electronic equipment and software. He's fucked. That combined with the sting op Newark ATTF conducted last week, we netted all seven drivers. We met with the DA right before I met you at the hospital. He told us we have enough solid evidence to prosecute them."

He washed his hands and then grabbed a few paper towels. "Man, I wish I would have been the one to apprehend the Mancusos, but NYPD took care of them." He shrugged. "I'm sure Turk will tell me all about it." Adam's head swayed. "This is going to get messy with all three jurisdictions involved."

I picked our clothes up off the floor. "What about the one who shot your informant? Carter Mancuso?"

Adam's jubilation crumbled down quickly. "He's still a fugitive. We haven't been able to form any solid leads." His eyes were somber, though he tried to be comforting. "Don't worry. We'll catch him. Let's get cleaned up. I'm exhausted. I'm sure you are too." He pulled the pile of clothing out of my arms and set everything on top of the table. "Just leave it. We'll get it later." He took my hand. "Come on, Doc. Let's get some sleep and then afterwards I'm taking you out to dinner."

Watching his incredible naked body and that luscious ass lead me up the stairs to his bedroom, I felt like the luckiest woman in the world.

I DIDN'T LIKE answering Adam's door, especially while I was home alone. My stomach was full from the delicious breakfast he'd cooked for us and my lips still tingled from the amazing kiss he planted on me before he'd left a half hour ago, clad in his badass cop duds.

I'd rearranged my schedule when Sarah went into labor, so I was off today while Adam was working. The doorbell sounded again. So much for staying in bed enjoying my post-breakfast orgasm.

Even though I was living here it wasn't my house, and the likelihood the person on the other side was actually here to see me was very slim. I made a mental note to tell Adam that the bush in his landscaping blocked my view of the front door. There wasn't a peephole either.

I cracked the door open, instantly regretting answering. "Can I help you?"

Melissa Werner's surprised sneer was annoying. "Is he here?"

"What do you want?"

She clenched her teeth. "Is he here? I need to speak to him."

I held the door firmly. "I suggest you try calling him first."

Melissa held up her cell phone, scowling at me. "Tried that. He's not answering. I went to the station twice; they won't tell me where he is."

I fought my smile. "Then I would take that as a sign that he doesn't want to speak to you. And you showing up at his house like this? How the hell did you even know where he lives?"

"It's listed on his contract." She pressed her hand to the door. "Where is he, Erin?"

I was shocked she even remembered my first name. "His whereabouts are none of your business and if he isn't returning your calls then he has nothing to say to you."

"Adam!" she yelled over my head.

There was no way she was getting invited in. "Save it. He's not here."

"You tell him to get his ass out here right now."

"Excuse me?"

"His bullshit is costing me millions," she shrieked. "We need to start filming again. Everyone cleared their lie detector tests."

"*His* bullshit? Unbelievable. It was *your* sound tech that put their lives in danger, not him. Now move."

"I fired Scott."

"Convenient, seeing as he's in jail."

"There's no reason why they can't keep filming. Adam needs to tell them that."

"You need to get off my porch." I pushed the door, but she pushed back.

"You don't understand," she insisted. "My reputation will be ruined. I can't let that happen. I have shareholders… He needs to fix this—*right now*—or else—"

"Or else what?" I snapped back.

She sneered at me. "You have no clue who you're messing with."

"Oh, I think I have a good idea."

Melissa scowled, pushing the last of her weight against the door. "I will sue him, understand? Him, his entire unit, everyone."

Her aggressive behavior was alarming. "Go for it. Leave or I'm calling the police."

"He needs to *fix this*. You tell him to call me immediately."

I gave the door a final shove, which made her stumble back on her high heels.

The deadbolt snapped in place, assuring it was locked.

She smacked the door and called me a few nasty names.

Screw her. I didn't have time for her nonsense. I had laundry to do—that's about as important as she was to me. Adam needed to deal with her because as far as I was concerned, her showing up at his *home* crossed the line. I took the laundry out of the dryer, stewing as I folded. She had some nerve! And she called me a bitch on top of it. Wait until I tell him what she called me. He'll want to rip her head off.

The doorbell rang again, making my anger blister into fury. She just wasn't going to quit.

I flung the front door open, completely incensed. "What do you *want?*"

Instead of seeing Melissa Werner, I was staring at the barrel of a gun.

I should have tried to close the door; I should have tried to do a lot of things. Scream. Run. A flash of clarity told me that any of those choices would get me shot. My first instinct after the flood of panic was to back up—put distance between it and me.

The girl pointing the gun at my face followed me inside, shoving the door closed behind her.

My mind raced trying to recall if I knew her. She looked familiar but my panicked mind could not place her. *A past patient?*

"Please don't shoot." My hands rose in front of me. I kept backing up. I knew if I tried to run, I wouldn't be fast enough.

"Shut up," the girl ordered.

She was rail thin and petite. Straight brown hair fell past her shoulders. I bumped into the leather chair in the living room. "What do you want?"

Vacant eyes that held no remorse stared back at me. She looked strung out, possibly on drugs.

She shook the gun at me. "You couldn't just go away, could you? You just kept at him and at him and at him and at him. He's mine! Understand? MINE!"

"Okay, calm down."

"Don't tell me to calm down. You stole my boyfriend, you fucking bitch, and now he doesn't even come to see me. He wasn't yours! He was mine!" She rubbed her head, pulling on her own hair. "Why would you do that?"

Her mouth continued to tremble as though she were having a conversation with herself.

"Easy. Let's talk about this." I'd dealt with enough mentally ill people over the years to recognize the signs. "You're talking about Adam, right?"

She shook the gun again, scowling. "Do not say his name. Do not. You have no right. No right to say his fucking name."

"Okay, sorry." I kept my hands up, scrambling for my own sense of clarity. One wrong step and I knew I'd be dead. "I didn't know he was yours. You have to believe me."

Her head tilted, regarding me anew.

"He's not here."

She rolled her eyes. "I know that. And I know you know who I am."

I took another step back. "He, um, never said anything to me about you. I swear."

"Liar!" She scoffed. "You knew. He paraded you right in front of me at the diner so do not stand there and lie to me."

"Diner?" My mind reeled. "The Parkway Diner?"

The gun rattled in her hand. "He used to come in every morning to see me. Every. Morning. For months we saw each other. He was falling in love *with me*. And then you come along and suddenly what? I don't exist? I don't matter? I'm supposed to just take that?"

I found myself shaking my head, agreeing with the psychopath. "I'm sorry he hurt you."

"You're sorry?" She charged forward, forcing me deeper into the living room.

I shielded myself, fearing she'd strike or shoot. "Yes. Stop. Please."

"You're fucking around with my man and you're sorry. Did you know that I'm pregnant?" Her face twisted, landing somewhere between pride and righteous rage.

I glanced over her flat, shapeless body. "You're pregnant?"

She nodded at me as if I were stupid. "That's right. We're having a baby, me and Adam, so you need to quit interfering and leave him alone. Get out of our lives."

Impossible.

Adam had stated their "one time" had happened months before we'd started dating. I cautioned her to stay where she was. "Does Adam know?"

"Of course he knows. I text him every day."

"You text him?"

"You think you're special? He's mine." She growled at me. "We want to be together but *you* just won't go away. He told me over and over again how he was going to leave you but he's too afraid of how you'd react to do it himself."

She was beyond delusional.

"So I'm doing this for him. He doesn't love you, got it? He loves me. He. Loves. Me."

I shrank back, fearing that her gun would discharge. "Okay. I got it. Let me get my keys and I'll go. I'll leave here and you'll never see me again. I promise."

She wiped her cheek with the heel of her hand, panting hard while muttering to herself. I'd hoped she was considering letting me go.

My cell rang in my back pocket, startling her. She shook the gun at me. I didn't know if she'd shoot if I tried to reach for it. I decided to slip it out of my pocket anyway. "It's him." I showed her the screen, taking another risk. "Let me just answer it, tell him I'm leaving and you two can be together. Okay?"

I thought she was going to pull the trigger. "You try anything, I swear I will fucking shoot you."

I hit the button, hesitantly lifting it to my ear.

She stepped closer, sending ripples of terror through my nerves.

"Hi." My voice cracked.

"Hey, Doc. What are you wearing?" Adam joked. "Listen. Cherise and Marcus want us to come over for dinner on Saturday. We got anything going on?"

My hands were trembling, knowing I'd never see his smile again.

"*End it*," she mouthed. "*Now.*"

Would this be the last conversation we would ever have before I died? I wasn't ready to say goodbye to him. To anyone. He was my sunshine. My lover. My heart. And yet I knew, one false move, one wrong word from my lips, and this crazy person waving a gun at me would pull the trigger. "I can't do this."

"Why? You scheduled to work?"

Work was the last thing on my mind when faced with having to say goodbye forever to the man I loved. "I can't do this…"

He drew in an exasperated breath, probably growing tired of my indecisions. "Sweetheart, what's wrong?"

The tear felt cold against my cheek. "Everything."

"Are you okay?"

I bit my thumbnail, at a complete loss for how to answer. "No," quaked out of me.

Psycho girl slammed her hand against the wall.

"Babe, what's wrong?"

I flinched while thousands of answers barraged my brain all at once, adding mayhem to my terror-addled confusion. *How do I tell him goodbye?*

"I can't…"

I love you so much.

Life is so unfair.

"You can't what, Erin? I'm not following."

She stepped closer, jabbing the gun in my direction, making me jump.

I can't… meet you in ten or in fifteen."

"Sweetheart, what are you talking about? Was I supposed to be someplace? Are you crying?"

I wiped my face and sniffed. "I *said* I can't meet you in *ten* or in *fifteen*. You'll just have to go without me."

"Okay, Marcus and I are leaving the courthouse now. I'm confused. Where am I supposed to be going?"

I cleared my throat of fear and doom, needing him to understand. "Do you remember the story you told me about that kid, Casper?"

My captor's eyes scrunched.

"Casper? Yeah but—"

"I'm in the same situation."

"Situation?"

"You're a smart detective. I would have thought you'd see that by now. You belong to someone else."

"*Excuse me?* Baby, what the fuck—"

"Stop!" I interrupted, panicking. "Just listen. Don't come home because I won't be here. Just like Casper the ghost."

"Wait. Casper put a gun to my head," Adam said roughly. "Baby, please tell me you're joking."

"I wish I was. I can't meet you in fifteen."

"Ten fifteen?"

"Yes."

"Are you…?"

I tried to mask my relief. "Yes."

"Oh fuck. Okay, stay calm. Is someone there now?"

"Yes."

She shook the gun harder, getting impatient, but I couldn't see any other way out of this.

"But… but I can't stay with you anymore. You belong to someone else." It killed me to say that. The words physically pained me beyond all reason.

Adam was frantic. I could hear the rustle of fabric, the sound of doors opening and closing. "I'm on my way. Where are you?" Adam spoke to someone around him, mentioning hostage situation.

"I can't live with a liar," I bit out, trying to sell it for all it was worth.

"House? You're in the house? Where? Where in the house?"

I glanced around quickly, feeling pressured and terrified. A rustic picture dominated his wall. "Don't call me 'deer.' I'm not a furry animal."

"Don't call you dear. Deer. Living room. You're in the living room?"

"Yes."

"There's a gun in the kitchen above the microwave. Can you get it?"

"Absolutely not."

"Stay on the line with me. I am on my way. I swear to Christ." I heard a car door slam, the crackle of his radio, calls to dispatch. Orders for Marcus to fucking drive. "How many in the house?"

I stared at my captor, trying to understand the mania that drove her to this point. Desperation, mental psychosis, all without control, or fear of the repercussions of her actions. To allow your psyche to snap to the point of drawing a gun on someone and considering cold-blooded murder…

"I thought I was your only woman. You want more than that? Isn't *one woman* enough?"

"One armed," Adam repeated aloud. "Armed. Female. Yes, armed and dangerous. Has my girlfriend at gunpoint."

The stress was getting to this girl, making her pace and ramble to herself, as though several people inside her mind were having arguments.

"It is Nikki?"

"No."

"Stay calm, baby. You're doing great. You said female. Do you know her?"

The female in question was leaning and snarling at me, ready to lunge.

"Sort of? I'm sorry I didn't make time for you. I can't be *texting* you all the time like your other women."

"Texting?" he questioned.

I heard their siren echo through my cell. So did my captor. Her gun lifted to pointblank range. I flattened the phone as close to my ear as possible.

"Hang up," she ordered low, jabbing me with the barrel of the gun.

I tried to back away, refusing to end my only connection to Adam. She grabbed for my phone; playing keep-away wasn't the smartest idea, but fuck her, I wouldn't go down without some sort of fight. I aimed for her face, shoving her back a step.

"Hang up!" she ordered louder, swinging violently at me. She smacked the phone out of my hand; it flew through the air, sliding after it hit the kitchen floor.

I thought about diving for it.

I thought about hitting her.

I thought about wrestling her for the weapon.

But all of those thoughts ended when she pulled the trigger.

CHAPTER 30
Adam

"TEXTING?"

It had to be another clue of some sort but it didn't make sense. Erin and I texted all the time, every day, every time we were apart. My mind was so consumed with getting to her that deciphering the details was becoming muddled.

"Hang up!" I heard a crazed female voice order in the background between Erin's petrified breathing. I tried to concentrate on the voice above our sirens, but it was so brief that I couldn't identify it.

"Baby, I'm on the way. I'm coming. Stay on the line with me." I was praying, clinging to each one of Erin's sounds with a level of desperation I'd never felt before. Each passing second that it took to reach her was sheer agony.

"Hang up!" the female ordered again. This time I could tell she was much closer and yet I still could not place the voice.

Agony turned into utter helplessness, hearing a tousle, hearing Erin's grunts and groans as she struggled.

A loud thud cracked in my ear. "No! Erin!"

Everything accelerated—time, space, the forward momentum.

I gripped the handle bolted to the ceiling as Marcus drove faster. The scenery outside the windshield blurred into streaks of random shades of light and dark, pulling me under the confusion of adrenaline overload. If I could have beamed myself through the phone, I would have.

"Erin!"

My world shattered when I heard the gunshot.

"Erin!" I screamed. "No, baby, NO! ERIN!"

Marcus took us sideways through an intersection, slamming my side into the door.

"Erin? ERIN! Oh God, baby. Please no." I squeezed my cell so hard the plastic creaked. The sharp pain in my chest took my breath away. My partner shook me. When I met his glance, one word trembled out. "Gunshot." There was a final rustle and then nothing.

Marcus growled and used his mic. "Romeo Seven to control. Shots fired. I repeat. Shots fired inside the residence." His hand landed on my shoulder, grabbing and shaking the strap of my Kevlar. "Stay with me, brother. Get your shit together and focus. Other units are just about there. You keep positive and strong now. You do that for your woman. You hear me?"

I couldn't hear anything beyond the dead silence. We'd been disconnected. My calls went unanswered.

Several units surrounded my house, turning my nightmare into a sickening reality.

A uniform stopped me halfway up my driveway. I shoved him back. "Get out of my way!"

Marcus's arm came across my chest, putting me into a restrained chokehold. "Calm down." I struggled but he lifted and spun me like a ragdoll when I tried to escape. "Calm the fuck down! You can't just barge in there, dude. Settle." He plastered me against a squad car.

"Erin is in there! That's my woman!"

"I know, man. I know." Marcus grabbed my coat in both hands and shook, showing me his seriousness. "You need to pull your shit together, right now. You hear me? Pull, your, shit, *together.*"

I'd never been this terrified.

Marcus gave me a final shove and released me. "Now think. You see a familiar car out here? Recognize the suspect's voice? Anything that can help."

I glanced around the street, momentarily blinded by all of the red and blue flashes. Random cars dotted the street, but nothing looked familiar.

Another officer trotted over to me and introduced himself. "We have a perimeter set. This your residence?"

"Yeah." I nodded, refocusing. "My girlfriend is in there. Don't know if she's wounded. I heard a single shot before we were disconnected. I don't know who has her at gunpoint. Only way into the first floor is either through the rear door to the garage and in through the kitchen door or the front door. My woman is about five foot six, a hundred thirty pounds. Long blonde hair."

My cell rang in my hand, showing a number that I'd become quite familiar with. *Texting... that's what she'd meant.*

I tried not to lose my patience when I accepted the call. "Hello?"

"Adam?"

My grip tightened, hearing a female voice that wasn't Erin's. "Who is this?"

"Make all the cops go away."

She was lucky I wasn't busting my front door down at that very second. "Can't do that. Not until you tell me your name." I waved Marcus over, letting him know I had the suspect on the line.

"It's me," she said. "Make them leave or I'll kill her."

"Do you know who—?" Marcus mouthed.

I had no fucking clue. "Is Erin okay? Let me talk to her."

"Make. Them. Go. Away," the girl ordered.

I could hear the cornered desperation in her voice.

"Easy. All right? Just tell me if Erin is okay and I'll tell them to back off. Work with me and we'll settle this peacefully."

"I didn't want this. I didn't. Things just... make them *leave*."

"Tell me your name first. Can you do that?" I turned my radio down so I could hear her.

"It's Kara, Adam." She sniffed. "It's Kara."

Reality slammed me in the chest. "Kara? Kara Simmons?"

"Yeah."

Regret the size of a mountain crashed atop of me. My moment of weakness, of selfish need and empty loneliness, led me to one meaningless encounter with this girl, and now she had Erin.

"Kara, listen to me. I'm coming in."

"No," she screamed. "You just want to come in so you can shoot me."

Several officers surrounded me, monitoring my every word. I held them off. "Kara, that's not what I want. I just want to talk. That's all. Just let's talk, okay? You want to talk to me? You're in my house. Put down the gun, let me come in, and we'll figure this out together."

All I could hear was her breathing. A shadow crossed back and forth behind my front window. I saw the curtain move.

"Kara, is Erin okay? Is she hurt?"

"I just wanted us to be together," she cried. "You wanted me. I know you did. That's why. But I wasn't good enough for you, was I? I was *never* good enough."

I shook my head at Marcus and held up three fingers to ready our assault. Things were deteriorating. If Erin had been shot, her time was running out.

"Why, Adam?" Kara whined. "I never cheated on you. And you brought that whore to where I work?"

Another patrol unit rolled up; men hustled about.

"Flash bang and breach," Marcus said low, coordinating our entrance.

I held the phone away. "They don't go in without me." I glanced at all the faces standing by making sure they all got the message, then started scribbling a physical description of the assailant. "Kara, no one wants this. I want you to put the gun down and come out. I promise no one will hurt you."

"No," she mumbled adamantly. "I'm going to hurt you like you hurt me. This is all your fucking fault!" Kara screamed. "All your fault, you fucking slut!" Several dull thuds accompanied her grunts. It sounded as though she was kicking something. Muffled groans and a pained moan assaulted my brain, which I could only presume were coming from Erin. Another crash resounded inside, which was clearly heard outside my house.

I drew my weapon. Fuck waiting another second.

We had our assault team organized within moments; I headed up my walkway. We had speed, surprise, and violence of action on our side—none of which our suspect would be expecting.

As soon as I heard my dining room window shatter and the flash bang discharge, we came in through the front door.

"Police! Lower your weapon," the officers flanking me ordered.

Everything happened all at once—the ringing in my ears from the concussion of the flash bang grenade, the rising white smoke billowing out from my dining room, a blur of bodies and angered shouts. Years of training took over, moving me through the melee, though my singular focus of taking the suspect out of the equation warred with the underlying burn of getting to Erin.

The high-pitched scream broke through the air, followed by the trail of the tip of her weapon rising through the air.

"Lower your weapon!" I shouted, praying that she'd listen but instinctively knowing it was all too late. There's only one outcome when you point a loaded gun at the police.

Long brown hair swirled in the air and then an officer was upon her, taking her down into the wall behind them. The distinct crack of gunfire pierced through all other sounds, sending a blaze of white-hot fire through my lower leg.

The register of pain was instant, and blistered around immediate anger and regret as I fell down to my knee. My gun hit the ground, still wrapped in my fingers.

Kara struggled while several officers rushed her, pinning her face first to the floor. That's when I noticed a pair of bare feet and toes that appeared a shade of red too dark to be normal.

Erin.

Her body was hidden from my view, blocked by the wall dividing the living and dining rooms, and partially covered by an overturned end table and broken lamp. Blood was splattered and streaked on the white paint above her.

I holstered my weapon and held my breath through the blast of pain that throbbed up into my knee and through my thigh.

She wasn't moving.

Kara was writhing, her teeth gnashing at the officers subduing her.

I threw my broken lamp aside, trying to get to my feet and move the table that covered her, but my leg refused to hold my weight.

Erin was so still.

I fought through the agony and crawled over to her side, only to have it become insurmountable. Erin's face was pale and lax. Blood dripped out of her nose and down her cheek. It soaked into her shirt and pooled on the floor around her.

Oh, baby. Please, God. No.

"Aw, no. Baby… no."

Erin.

I couldn't breathe.

Couldn't breathe.

A sob choked off the last of my air.

My love.

My heart.

I cradled her limp body in my arms.

"Erin! Baby, please. Oh, God. Please. Please don't leave me. No, baby. Wake up. Please, baby. Wake up."

I'd done this.

I'd caused this.

This was all my fault.

"Sweetheart. Please—"

I'd give my life for hers in a heartbeat.

I moved the hair stuck to her cheek, lost in the agony.

She was so still; so pale.

I knew I'd never see her beautiful smile again.

The realization was too much.

Without her, I was dead inside.

Dead.

Right then and there my heart shattered into a million pieces.

EVERY TIME I tried to surface, the *nothing* pulled me back under. It was black and heavy and settled deep within my bones. I tried to swim to the top a few times, to break the surrounding darkness enveloping me, but whenever my fingertips breached the edge, the *nothing* swallowed me back down.

My first thoughts were murky, as though I'd just woken up from my worst night of drinking, making even the simplest realizations difficult to wade through.

Something was stuck to my nose.

The air was cool.

I couldn't feel my body.

The *nothing* pulled me back into the dark.

"Adam, can you wake up for me?"

Hmm?

My head felt as though it weighed eighty pounds. I wanted to sit up, but sleep was so much better.

A steady beep, beep, beep echoed about.

So sleepy.

Paper crumbled. Women spoke.

Something loud scraped across the floor.

A male voice spoke to a female voice.

They were talking about me. I wanted them to shut up and let me sleep.

Something kept brushing over my scalp.

"Honey, can you hear me? Open your eyes."

It was hard to focus.

The light hurt my eyes.

Bright.

"Hi, Son."

Mom?

My mother smiled at me. "Doctor said everything went well."

"I just…" The ceiling was too bright.

Where am I? What?

She kept petting my head. "You just want what?"

I wanted to go back to the *nothing*. I didn't hurt in the *nothing*. "…just wanna sleep."

My father's face invaded my view. His hair was whiter than I'd remembered. Things were different in this dream. "You're old."

His eyes crinkled. "You boys made me this way."

I tried to move but the pain stopped me. "Ow. What? What happened?"

My mom rested her hand on my arm. "Try to keep still. Doctors had to put a pin in your leg, but they said that everything went well and you'll be good as new in no time."

Something was wrong with her smile. *Pins in my what?* A warm, throbbing burn began to pulse in my leg. I hated feeling this doped.

The light was still too bright.

I'd been shot.

I remembered now.

Memories brought pain.

Erin.

Realizations started slamming into each other, followed by the crushing weight of dread.

So much blood.

I needed to get up, but I had zero muscle control.

"Where's Erin?"

My mother's indulging smile all but vanished.

"Where is she?"

"Calm down, sweetheart. You need to relax."

"Mom, don't fuckin'... Where is she?"

My dad gave me a stern look. "Hey. There's no need to curse at your mother."

I knew better, I did, but I just didn't give a shit. There was no way to control the avalanche of panic.

"Mom, please... Tell me where she is. Please, Mom."

"I don't know, Adam." She glanced over at my dad—the two of them communicating in some secret silence.

I knew the answer, but I didn't want to face it.

Her face gave her away.

No.

NOOOOOO!

I remembered now. The gun. The shot. The blood.

I'd caused this.

The pain in my leg paled in comparison to the devastating burn crushing my chest.

It was all my fault.

Erin's pulse had been so weak when the ambulance finally arrived—everyone in the room knew we'd failed her. I wanted them to quit tending to me. They needed to fix her before it was too late.

My mother's lips were drawn together.

That only meant one thing.

They'd been too late.

I'd been too late.

My vision swam in streaks of fractured light.

She stood over me. "Oh sweetheart. Shh. Don't cry."

I can't live without her. I don't want to.

I couldn't stop myself. The sobs were too powerful. The pain in my heart was too much.

My Erin was gone.

Oh, sweetheart... no. I'm so sorry, baby.

I'm so sorry.

Why couldn't it have been me instead? Why, God? Why?

Everyone leave.

Just get out.

Oh, God.

Please just let me die.

"How's it going in here?" a woman asked.

My mom tugged the sheet covering me and started wiping my face. I tried to push her hand away but I had no coordination or strength.

I wanted the *nothing* to come back for me.

I didn't deserve to be the survivor.

"Hey, Officer Hottie. How you feeling?"

A familiar face framed with wild hair bounced into view. She was smiling at me. "Wow. Anesthesia sucks, doesn't it? Your doctor just ordered some pain meds for you. That will take the edge off." She turned to my mom. "Hi. I'm Sherry. Erin's friend. We work in the ER together."

My parents greeted her while I seethed. Rage overtook my emotions, making me wish I'd regain some muscle control so I could shake some sense into this woman. Erin was dead and she was all fucking chipper. I wanted to punch her.

Sherry glanced at her wristwatch. "As soon as they release you from Recovery, we'll wheel you up to your room. I told Erin I'd come down here and check to see how you're doing."

Wait. What?

"I don't know which one of you is in worse shape." Sherry tisked. "This is what happens when you play with guns."

My mind was playing tricks. "What?"

"Guns," she repeated.

"I heard you."

"Okay, good. Then your hearing isn't as messed up as hers is. Apparently that grenade thing your guys tossed into the house landed right next to her."

Hope surged into my chest, radiating urgency throughout my muscles. "She's alive?"

Sherry seemed stumped. "Last time I checked she was. She's already out of surgery."

I needed to get up. *Fuck, why can't I move? Oh shit.* "I need to see her."

"Whoa." Sherry braced my shoulder and nudged me back. "Hang on. Just relax for a bit. You'll get to see her soon."

Screw that. "I need to see her now!"

Another nurse came into view, this one older, gray-haired, and chunky. "What's going on here?"

"He's a bit excited, that's all," Sherry informed.

Excited?

The other nurse seemed just as pissed off as I was. "You shouldn't be upsetting him."

Exactly.

"He's doing that all on his own," Sherry countered.

Fuck this. "I want to see her. Take me to see her. NOW." Someone had to realize how important this was before I crawled out of this damn bed *on my own.*

Several dirty looks made me add, "Please."

Big old lady boobs drifted awfully close to my face, adjusting my pillow. Then she fussed with the clip on the end of my finger. "You need to relax."

Could I get away with murder?

I'm a cop. I probably could. Your name has way too many a's and c's in it. R a b a c c a a a c. Fuck, that tag thing is blurry. Hold still.

"Who does he want to see?" Nurse Ratchet asked.

My mom crowded her; now both of them were fussing over me.

My entire body felt fuzzy, disconnected. I needed… "Erin."

Sherry crossed her arms over her chest. "This is Doctor Erin Novak's boyfriend. He's anxious to see her."

Nurse Ratchet lit up. "Oh, so this is the one." She played with my IV and then stuck a needle filled with clear fluid into my line. "I thought so but I wasn't sure. We'll get you moved to your room in a little bit. That's to manage your pain. Do you want some water?"

I wanted a beer, a shotgun, and for everyone to get the fuck out of my way. Or… maybe just a quiet nap. *Yes, a nap would be good. No. Great.*

On a floaty cloud.

Fulloaty. What a weird word.

I woke to being jostled. Lights and ceiling tiles passed over me while murmurs and other random noises invaded my brain. I didn't like this ride. My bones felt like they were weighted down by sandbags.

"I wanna… see Erin. Mom?"

She smiled at me. I'd seen that face a million times—it was the same expression that was always followed by "no."

Smile. "No, you can't have two peanut butter sandwiches before dinner."

Smile. "No, you can't spend your birthday money on a used motorcycle."

They were going to stuff me in a room. I grabbed the door frame and held on. "Where's Erin? I wanna see her—*now*. Doesn't anyone hear me?"

"Adam…?"

It was weak and groggy and sounded from behind my head, but the angelic voice was unmistakable. My heart skipped a beat and choked up into my throat. I let go of the metal frame.

I tried to turn my head to see her. "Erin?"

The nurses wheeling my bed around couldn't move fast enough. Desperation clawed at me. I needed to see her. There were bodies between us, blocking my view, driving my need into frenzy.

Someone needed to move that fucking curtain out of the way, too.

They stopped moving me forward, maneuvering me in the opposite direction. "I want to see her. Erin! Let me see her." Fire shot down my leg when I twisted, making anger and agony my unwanted companions.

I grabbed Sherry's wrist. My vision was slightly blurred but I could still make out her familiar face. "Please."

Sherry nodded at me. "Okay." She pulled out of my grip and shoved the top of my gurney. "Let's wheel him over." One of the nurses bitched but Sherry was my voice of reason. My dad moved a chair out of the way.

A nurse pulled at the curtain, revealing another bed. Erin's father gave me a lukewarm nod. Her mom, Christine, was standing near the dark window.

None of it mattered.

My tears broke again seeing Erin's sleepy face curl into a smile.

"Doc." I reached for her.

Erin's left arm was bandaged up into a sling. A purple bruise shadowed her jaw.

"Hey, Cop," she whispered.

My heart wanted to leap out of my chest. "Oh God, Erin. I love you, baby. Move me closer. Please. I want to touch her." I stretched, catching her fingertips. The pain in my body would have to wait. "I'm so sorry, Erin. So sorry. Are you okay?"

She nodded. Tears of her own cascaded down her tender cheeks. "Yeah. I'm okay."

"Oh, thank God." My hands were trembling, but we managed to touch. Her fingers were warm. "I thought I'd lost you. I'm so sorry."

She let go and wiped her eyes. "I was so scared."

Guilt the size of a mountain smashed into me. "I know, sweetheart. I'm so sorry."

"Okay, let's get you into bed," some nurse said, rudely reminding me that there were others around.

I grasped onto Erin's bedrail. "No. Leave me here."

My cot was jostled, breaking my connection with the only thing I cared about. A new ache formed in my chest when they moved me away from Erin. Just when I thought they were going to wheel me out of the room, the nurse parked me next to the empty bed in Erin's room.

Confusion struck me for a moment. "I'm staying here?"

"Yep," some nurse said, smiling.

Okay. Good. Staying here. Fuck, my ass is cold.

My parents introduced themselves to Erin's, and everyone seemed to be happy and in a good mood while the staff settled me in. I couldn't help but keep a watchful eye on Erin's reactions. It helped me to be strong and to fight through the sheer agony of being jostled and propped up.

Oh, thank God. More blankets.

Erin was bundled up, too. *Good.*

I almost lost her.

I'd never lose her again.

I just pray she'll forgive me.

"I love her." My IV line snagged when I pointed. It was tangled up underneath me.

My mom gaped at me, apparently in shock, and then her face lit up. Erin and her mother appeared equally as stunned. Even some skinny nurse who obviously needed to eat more was smiling at me. Why they found this a surprise, I'll never know.

Everyone seemed to be happy and getting along, talking and laughing as if they'd been friends for years. Well, that was before I stunned them into silence.

Their continued stares were becoming unnerving.

"I'm gonna marry her, you know. So start planning."

Several mouths hung open, including Erin's.

What?

I tried to shift but my balls pinched; the skin was stuck to my leg. That's when I realized I was completely naked, covered only by a thin hospital gown thing with the snaps. A string hung down over my shoulder. This shit wasn't even tied on. And where was my gun? *Someone better have secured my weapon. It was loaded and chambered.*

I don't know why I looked under the blankets. "Where's my gun?"

Erin was still staring at me; her sleepy eyes beautifully crinkled.

I couldn't decipher her scrutiny. "What?"

Her beautiful face scrunched up even more. "Did you just propose to me?"

Wait, what? Did I?

Erin held up her hand. "Forget it. You're high." She turned away. Addressing her mom, my mom, and Sherry, she said, "He's confused and babbling."

I wasn't confused; I'd just feel better knowing where my damn Glock was. "No I'm not. Who has my weapon?" I was hoping my dad would know. I didn't see my stuff anywhere. "It was loaded, Dad. Please find it."

My dad nodded at me and walked out into the hall. At least someone was on it.

I rolled my head on my pillow, catching Erin's watchful gaze on me. *God, I love her, and now she's hurt. Again.*

"I'm sorry this happened. Please don't hate me."

Her head shook slightly. "It's not your fault."

"Yes, it is."

"No." She firmly disagreed. "That girl was very unstable."

"I should have seen it."

Erin scratched her chin. "Sweetie, no. Don't think like that."

I studied her face, which was coated with determination *and* forgiveness. Could I have prevented this? Were there signs that I'd missed? Kara had shown signs of being obsessive/compulsive, but I never, ever imagined her being capable of—

"Adam."

I focused back on her piercing eyes. *She called me sweetie. That's got to be good, right?*

"Do not blame yourself," Erin ordered. "Don't."

I wanted to argue but she shook a finger at me.

And that was it.

That moment right then and there was *it*.

...each time she let me sleep peacefully all curled up around her.

...each time she made sure I was taken care of: fed, warm, loved.

...when she took each stitch out of my hand, making sure I was healed and pain-free.

And now she was making sure my heart was free of guilt, too.

There was only one thought left.

"Marr—"

"Is this it? Nurse said Room Twelve-A." Marcus's profile appeared in the doorway. "Yep." He smiled at me when we made eye contact. "He's in here. Yo, Cap," he motioned, pointing, "he's in here."

It was good to see the big bastard.

Marcus dipped his head and eyed everyone cautiously, taking in the roomful of people already crowded around us as though he was walking into an unknown shit-storm.

"Looks like you two are popular," the skinny nurse with the weird black glasses said, smiling. She was messing with the machine that controlled my IV, hitting buttons and making shit beep.

Our captain skidded to a halt outside the door and then followed Marcus inside—both of them still in their ATTF uniforms.

"All right. You're all set," the nurse said to me. She flipped the bed control thing around the metal rail, locked me in, and shimmied past a blockade of cops. My leg was throbbing, my body felt like hammered shit, but I was glad to see so many people surrounding Erin and me with their love.

Officer Brian Sidel wrapped his knuckles on the door, checking to see if it was okay to enter. He had a bouquet wrapped up in cellophane in his hand. He gave me a quick nod and headed over to Erin, presenting her with the flowers.

Good.

It may take a while for Brian and me to patch the rift between us, but I was glad to see he was making an effort.

"How you feeling?" Marcus asked. He gave me a once-over, pausing on my bandaged leg.

My toes had a pulse of their own. "Like a million bucks."

"Yeah? You look like shit, bro," he tossed back, grinning.

"Thanks, man."

Cap gave me a pat on the shoulder. "Glad to see you're in one piece."

Yeah, me too.

My eyes flicked over to Erin, watching her being sweet and social while probably suffering in private—just like I was.

She was alive and smiling. That's all that mattered.

"Local PD needs to see you then," Cap said. "You'll have to give them a statement of what went down."

"Yeah." I scratched my head, finding the motion tricky with the IV line taped to my hand.

"So you dated this girl?" Cap asked.

I knew he was waiting for an explanation and was pissed that I got shot. "Barely."

Marcus muffled his mouth with his hand, keeping his words private between us. "If you call getting a blowjob datin', that is."

Cap's brow rose. "Yeah?"

There was no denying that. It was what it was.

I tried to sit up more, manning up to my mistakes. "Won't be making *that* mistake again."

Cap's eyes flashed across the room, nodding in Erin's direction. "Yeah. Hopefully she'll make an honest man out of ya."

The meaningful look Cap, Marcus, and I shared put us in agreement on that one.

"Your suspect is in custody, so I'd say that shit is over and done with," Marcus added. "Same with our television careers."

Cap nodded. "Miss Warner ain't too happy with that but there's nothing she can do about it now. Top of the food chain is involved now. She was in my office earlier. I told her that the safety of our officers comes first and I will not allow our team to be put in jeopardy."

It didn't take much effort to imagine Cap chewing out Melissa Warner. Shame I didn't get to witness that. "Yeah? How'd she take that bit of news?"

"Not very well," Cap said, "but I think she understood, not that I give a fuck either way."

It felt good to laugh.

Cap's cell rang. He checked the screen. "Excuse me. I've got to take this." He slipped past Marcus, almost knocking him into my bed.

I watched Sidel shake my dad's hand. I hoped his gesture was sincere.

"Hey," Sidel said to me, "how you feeling?"

"In one piece."

He chuckled. "I'm glad to see it." He offered his hand.

I shook it.

No words were necessary. Shit between us would get put behind us—in time. Felt good to take that first step.

"That was the crime lab," Cap said, pocketing his cell. "They're still running the recovered weapon and casings through Ballistics, but their preliminary findings indicate that the gun the suspect fired was the same weapon used in the shootings at Erin's house."

My gut sank. "You serious?"

Cap nodded.

Marcus drew in an incensed breath.

"Kara was the one…?" I wanted to puke. It was hard to fucking breathe.

Cap crossed his arms across his chest and glanced over at Erin quickly, minding his volume. "Looks that way. We won't know for sure until we see the final report but the score marks on the casings are identical."

I rolled away from my woman and pegged them both with my gaze. "This shit stays between us for now. I don't want her hearing that from Cherise. You get me?"

Marcus nodded.

"I need her to heal up. I got enough shit on my plate."

Marcus gave me a reassuring pat. "No worries, bro."

As if Erin didn't already have enough reasons to leave me.

VISITING HOURS ENDED at nine, which meant it was closer to eleven when our parents finally left. It was hard to stay awake; the pain meds they pumped into me made sleep so very desirable.

Erin was at least able to get out of bed and use the bathroom. I was bedridden and pissing in a fucking plastic bottle.

"Here, let me help," Erin said, shuffling across the floor to take my latest piss away.

"Guess the honeymoon is over," I muttered.

She rolled her eyes at me and held the clear plastic up toward the light. Even as a patient she was in doctor mode, fucking monitoring my fluids.

I heard the toilet flush and running water in the sink.

Erin set the emptied bottle on the small table next to my bed. "You need anything, babe?"

I snagged her free wrist. "Yeah. You."

Her head tilted and she smiled, finding a space on the edge of my bed to sit.

I nodded at her wrapped arm. "What happened?"

She sighed. "It was a through and through, but it nicked my subclavian artery."

I pulled her good hand to my mouth, needing to worship the fact that she was alive. Memories painted with red pain forced their way past my weak hold, pressing onto my heart with the weight of a million regrets. My eyes turned watery; the sob I fought to restrain too powerful to be contained. Just the mere thought of what could have happened was too much to bear. "I thought I'd lost you."

"Oh, baby. Shh," Erin whispered. She rested her uninjured side onto my chest, leaning up to give me a kiss. "I'm here, Adam. Shh."

I didn't care if she saw me as weak. I was already crying like a baby. She wiped my face and kissed me again. I wrapped my fingers into her hair, holding on for dear life. "I'm so sorry, baby. So sorry."

"Shh, it's okay."

I sniffed, feeling utterly helpless and desperate. "Please don't leave me. Don't leave me over this. I swear. I promise. I love you so much, Erin. So much."

"I love you too. Don't worry. I'm not going anywhere. I promise."

"I didn't... I swear I didn't know she was—"

Her fingers drifted over my lips. "Please stop blaming yourself. This wasn't your fault."

I wished I could believe that.

"Look at me," she ordered.

It was almost a relief to see the absolution in her piercing gaze. My hands were shaking.

"It *wasn't* your fault. That girl was sick. Understand? She was sick, Adam."

Yeah, but that, too, was my doing.

474

"I promised you I'd never hurt you and—"

"Stop," she said sternly. "I love you. *You*, Adam. We've been through so much together. So much. But we're still standing."

The irony wasn't lost on either of us.

She gave me a weak nudge. "You know what I mean."

Erin smiled *that* smile—the one laced with so much love I wasn't sure I deserved.

My mind wandered, picturing exactly what our daughter's smile might look like. It was so damn adorable. She tilted her head and gazed at me, conveying a thousand messages without saying a word.

I imagined our daughter would do that too, just like that… one day.

God, I love you.

I took her hand in mine. "Marry me."

Her breath hitched ever so slightly.

"Okay," she whispered.

I had to be sure. "Yes?"

Erin nodded, gracing me with a smile I knew I'd never be without.

"Yes," she said.

I gently tugged her to me, sealing my question with the amazing feel of her answering lips on mine.

Mine.

I vowed to love her for the rest of my life.

CHAPTER 31

JASON

DECISIONS.

So many thoughts clouded my head; it was difficult to find focus through the clutter.

Decisions.

I stared at the television screen bolted to the wall, pondering the notion that our lives are built around an infinite amount of decisions, moment by moment, day by day.

Decisions. Decisions. Decisions.

They are born from an equally infinite amount of questions, aren't they? Those invisible forks in the road that present themselves every twelve seconds and force us to come to a conclusion of some sort.

Should I?

Shouldn't I?

Will it hurt me?

Will it taste good?

Will a fucking I.E.D. be hiding under rocks strategically placed where they hit the Humvee and blow my fucking legs off, forcing me into this state of pointlessness?

As Tyler had said in physical therapy this morning, "Crying ain't going to make things grow back." I hated that he had seen me so weak. He'd pushed me too far. I wasn't ready for it.

The memorial card on my bedside table was a harsh reminder of the pointlessness. A two-by-three inch shot of Luke in his dress uniform. The American flag waved across the card's surface, bleeding red and blue into the white background. His birth date in bold font followed by the date of his death.

Fucking waste. He *should be alive.*

Some decisions are just out of our control. They happen and we are fucking powerless to do anything about it.

Like missing Lance Corporal Luke Dawson's funeral.

I'd said goodbye to him over there while he took his last breath; I hope to hell he heard me.

Christ, do I have the strength to go on?

I don't want to think about it anymore.

I wish I could just stop the noise.

Stop, please.

Some days I just wanted to feel sorry for myself and wallow in my misery. It had become as natural as breathing.

Some days I was just so fucking angry, wishing everyone and everything would just fuck the fuck off.

Some days I was so drugged up and high, disappearing into the black void was a godsend.

But most days lately, like today, my level of apathy was off the charts.

From the moment I woke up in that first hospital in Germany until now, my days had been measured by watching the doorway to my room. Wondering sometimes with anticipation as to who would be the next to walk across its threshold.

A decent-looking nurse?

Well, one could dream…

A sour-faced doctor coming to give me his version of "good news"?

Sometimes in my narcotic-fueled haze I'd wish for a machete to magically appear, so good ol' doc and I could *really* be on the same page of life. I often wondered how they'd *really* feel to be missing both of *their* fucking legs.

It was a shitty outlook, but fuck if I was able to shake it.

Some days—well, most days—I wondered why I just didn't die out there in the field.

Would I have been better off?

I didn't have a death wish, but damn, would dying have meant not having to relive the horrendous memories?

…the daily agony?

…hearing the screams echo through my skull?

I hate the color beige.

Hate the fucking color.

It's the constant reminder of dust and endless blistering heat of a Hell on Earth that will never see rest.

The vibrant green hues outside my hospital window do nothing to expel the crusted beige dirt that's encased my soul. It's as if it has seeped below my skin and resides with me daily. I hate the shit.

I wanted a cigarette. I knew my mom hated that I'd picked up the habit, but her constant lecturing me was a waste of air. Hell, could it be any worse than inhaling the acrid smoke of a burning Humvee that charred my lungs?

Being forced to quit cold turkey was just cruel.

I rolled away, buried deeper into my pillow, and ignored the chatter of my parents talking.

I should be social.

I know I should. Adam and Erin drove them down this weekend, and I know they're here to help me, but I'm so lost I don't know if it's even possible anymore.

I used to be invincible.

Unbreakable.

Now, every time I close my fucking eyes I recall with painful clarity the images of other soldiers' mangled, bloodied bodies.

The stench of burnt flesh and blood and melted plastic are forever seared into my sinuses. Agonizing moans and groans from the mouths of good men haunt me with every breath I take.

I can remember the deafening sounds and the weightlessness of flying through the air. Residual horrors like strikes of lightning ripple behind my eyelids. I can see flashes in the night sky and feel the searing pain before having my memories fade into the darkness.

I wanted to believe God and Country had a purpose for all of this.

I truly did.

But now, everything just seemed pointless.

I tried to concentrate on the cartoon playing on the screen, but nothing seemed capable of drowning out the noise inside my head.

Adam's hand clamped down on my forearm, breaking my internal chatter.

I gave his hand a pat while we exchanged pathetic smiles. I knew he didn't know what to say to me anymore. Pep talks usually just pissed one of us off.

I glanced over at his woman; she was focused on the screen of her cell. The big diamond Adam had given her recently cast a rainbow of spectral light onto the wall.

"Good to see you, bro. You doing all right?" Adam asked.

Fuck no.

"Yeah. I'm good." Staring at Erin's bare legs and great tits was easier than lying to his face. "Congratulations, dude. You look happy."

Adam nodded. "I am. I hope you get there too one day."

Yeah, right.

Not unless double amputees have suddenly become all the rage amongst twenty-somethings.

"How's your leg doing?" I asked, feebly trying to shift the focus.

Adam nodded, hiding most of his smile behind his casualness. "Healing up. Setting off metal detectors."

"Well, at least one of us doesn't need crutches anymore."

He frowned at me. "You'll get there. I swear. It sucks but you keep going forward. How are the new legs coming along?"

The muscle in my left thigh cramped, causing phantom pain to zing all the way down into toes that no longer existed.

"Didn't get them yet. Maybe by the end of next week they said."

We both watched Erin stash her phone in the pocket of her shorts and walk to the end of my bed, helping herself—as usual—to my medical chart.

And then came her narrowed focus—that intense scrutiny—followed by a few disapproving sighs. I'd been an EMT for six years, and I'd never seen a female doctor on any part of the planet as hot as her.

I glared at my brother for being so fucking lucky. *Bastard.*

"Looks like I have to have another talk with your doctor," she muttered.

Adam turned in his chair and gazed up at her, waiting just like I was for the cause of her latest medical disapproval.

She flipped back and forth over the top two papers. "Jason, have you been having tremors in your muscles?"

Christ, here we go again.

I pegged Adam with a questioning glare. "Does she ever quit working?"

"Not usually." He shrugged it off.

Erin gave me a teasing scowl and rambled off the names of the shit they'd been pumping into me lately. "And they have you on *two* very addictive narcotics for pain. Don't they know they shouldn't mix…"

I tuned her out. SpongeBob and Patrick were lifting weights on TV, which was more entertaining than watching her get spun up. Erin would *strongly advise* the nurse on duty and they would continue to give me pills every six hours. It was an endless cycle.

Either this morning's drug cocktail was perfectly formulated or a Victoria's Secret model just walked into my room carrying a fucking multi-colored puppy in her arms. One thing was for certain: this hallucination was *much* better than the others before it.

Holy fuck.

Long blonde hair framing a heart-shaped face. A thick braid hanging down over her shoulder, resting softly on a soft mound of—

Oh my God. Look at those tits!

Must touch those. Please.

For the love of all that's holy, lift up your shirt and let me see them. Just a quick flash. Really. That's all I'll need.

Bouncy, luscious tits.

My mouth started to water.

My dick instantly hardened.

Thank God THAT didn't get shot off by shrapnel.

I tugged the edge of my blanket across my waist, hiding my arousal. This chick didn't need to see my junk reacting like we were hormonal teenagers.

I'd been forewarned that Erin's sister was coming here today and bringing some sort of a surprise for me but damn, I was not prepared for this. *Her.*

She kissed and hugged Erin with one arm, holding onto a tiny lump of fur and dangling legs with the other.

My mind glazed over with a million dirty thoughts, all centered around this smiling creature in my midst. And I sure as hell wasn't referring to the puppy.

Erin introduced her to my parents and she hugged them both. *Good. I like huggers. Shows she's not standoffish.*

I wanted a hug, too.

Self-doubt and a shitload of insecurity bounded right in to douse that wish with a huge dose of reality when she shifted the pup and offered her hand.

"Hi. I'm Kate."

She had a great smile.

Hi, I'm Horny. Why don't you put the dog down and suck me off quick?

"Hi. Yeah. Jay." I cleared my throat and reached for her. "Jason." Her fingers were tiny in my hand. I tried not to squeeze too tightly. *Nice fingernails with a fresh manicure. High maintenance kind of girl or just one that takes care of herself?*

Her shorts were puckered up around her crotch and the dirty bastard in me enjoyed imagining what things might look like if I spread her open. She had great legs.

Erin was obviously thrilled to see her sister and viewing them side by side, I could see the resemblance. Two adorable blondes with big blue eyes, pouty mouths, and asses meant to be grabbed.

I wondered if Adam was having the same thoughts as I was. I'm sure he'd never share with Erin, but one side glance and an eyebrow raise between us, and I was positive he was having the same dirty thoughts I was.

He may be hooked deep into one, but he was still my brother.

"I brought someone to meet you." Kate set the tiny puppy down on my bed, letting it stretch.

It started to sniff around my blankets, hesitant to move too far. Don't know what it was but the damn thing was so cute, I tried to get its attention. "Come here, boy."

I quickly glanced up and noticed Kate was gazing at me with what looked like worry. What'd she think I'd do? Toss the little furball off my bed?

"She's a girl," Kate corrected.

Girl. Boy. Didn't matter. The paw pressing on my semi hard-on was what I was most concerned about. I snagged her behind her arms and lifted her before a puppy claw pierced my dick.

Round little eyes gazed up at me, and then she made herself comfortable on my chest, staring back.

"Aren't you the cutest little thing?" Weird urges were coming over me, like wanting to kiss her black little nose and hug her.

"Her name is Victory. Tory for short," Kate said. "She and her two siblings had been abandoned." She shook off her thought and ran a caring hand down the pup's back. "Long story. Anyway, we've been taking care of them at the clinic."

The pup and I were locked in a stare-down. "Hey, Tory."

The puppy yawned. Apparently I wasn't a threat. She was so soft and warm and had tiny white teeth.

The pup stretched, sniffed at my chin, crawled a few steps, and then climbed up my face. When she was done sniffing at my eyes and making me smile, the pup settled herself under my chin, sharing my pillow with me.

I took a deep breath and relaxed.

The soft flutter of puppy resting peacefully was the only sound I heard, apart from the relieving sigh from one very sexy future sister-in-law.

READ JASON TRENT'S STORY
IN THE UPCOMING NOVEL

AMPED

ACKNOWLEDGEMENTS

It takes a village to create a novel. Seriously. I have many people to thank, not only for moral support but for my endless technical questions while writing.

So many questions arose while weaving the details into the storyline. For instance, did you know that the police "10-Codes" are not universal? Each jurisdiction has their own set of codes, which makes communications between neighboring counties almost impossible. While some codes are basic—like 10-4 for acknowledging/understanding—most are not, and since the tragedy of 9-11 in NYC many police departments have abandoned using 10-codes altogether.

Each department has their own protocols for handling when an officer is injured on scene as well. Should I have an ambulance come for Adam when he sliced his hand open or would one of his fellow officers simply drive him to the hospital? This is just an example of the bazillion questions that I required answers to.

So many questions.

So many details.

While the rules change from city to city, state to state, and country to country, I tried to be as close to accurate as possible for situations occurring in Philadelphia and may have used "creative license" in some places, as this is a work of FICTION at the core. Some street names, places, etc. are fictitious.

So here goes: my list of awesome people who so graciously gave me their time, patience, and expertise:

To my two collaborators and BFFs, Dr. Jennifer Johnson and Sherry Durst. Your friendship, love, patience, and utter devotion mean the world to me. Jacked would not be what it is without either of you—you know that, right?

My talented muse, Mr. Erick Baker, for crooning your songs into my ears for months and for helping me write the emotion between the words. Your music is what feelings sound like. It is an honor and privilege to call you friend.

Detective Nathan Woods and his wonderful wife, Chrystle, for fielding my police questions.

David Tretter, EMT with Cumberland Goodwill Emergency Medical Services. I know our conversations stretched the boundaries, touched upon the stress and pressure on our First Responders, and I am eternally grateful for you answering ALL of my texts.

Ms. Kimberly West and her hospital staff friends for assisting with my laundry list of questions.

Seriously—I texted these people to death.

Sarah Hansen, Okay Creations, for the awesome cover. It's beautiful.

My sexy cover model, who wishes to remain a beautiful shadow. I love you with all my heart.

My editor, Marion Archer of Marion Making Manuscripts, for the hours of love you gave me to help this novel all that it is. Thank you for knowing the difference between rigid and ridged ;-) I'm glad you knew what I meant.

My interior formatter, Angela McLaurin of Fictional Formats. You amaze me! I can't thank you enough for all you've done to make this novel special.

The officers of the Newark Auto Theft Task Force for countless inspiration.

My Beta Readers: Melissa, Katie, Jolene, Michele, Morgan, Kimberly, and Joanne for your valuable input.

My readers from around the globe for believing in me and showering me with your love and support.

To all the wonderful women in my Tribe who give me their unending encouragement daily. I hope you smile when you see some of your names inside. I adore you all.

To all of the wonderful book bloggers out there. No author would be what they are today without you and I owe you a huge debt of gratitude.

To the wonderful women of FP—I am honored to know you and feel your love daily.

A special thank you to my dynamo agent, Jane Dystel, and her equally fabulous cohort, Miriam Goderich, at Dystel and Goderich Literary Management. Thank you for taking me under your beautiful wings.

For more information, visit the author at www.tinareber.com

Find her on Facebook:
www.facebook.com/authortinareber

On Twitter:
www.twiter.com/TinaReber

On Instagram:
TinaReber